IN THIS

LAND

OF

PLENTY

IN THIS
LAND
OF
PLENTY

A Novel

MARY SMATHERS

mks publishing

Carmel by the Sea, California

Book Design by *the*BookDesigners
Cover Image © Shutterstock.com

Library of Congress Control Number: 2020910724

ISBN # 978-0-9978557-2-2 (paperback)
ISBN # 978-0-9978557-3-9 (e-book)

mks publishing

Carmel by the Sea, California
www.marysmathers.com

First Edition
Printed in the United States
10 9 8 7 6 5 4 3 2 1

*In memory of the Native Californians who flourished
in this land of plenty for thousands of years,
with hope that we current residents can find
harmony with each other, and the land,
in order to thrive for another thousand years.*

For the truly outstanding history, literature and writing teachers and professors who ignite their students' curiosity to learn more about the past and motivate them to love the written word.

And especially for those who did exactly that for me:
Leonard Helton (in memoriam)
Claire Pelton
Peter Dale Scott
Peter Collier (in memoriam)
Stephen Greenblatt
Mike Kirst
Larry Cuban
Pam Wilson
Constance Hale
Susanne Lakin

CONTENTS

IN THIS
LAND
OF
PLENTY

CASTRO/BRENNAN

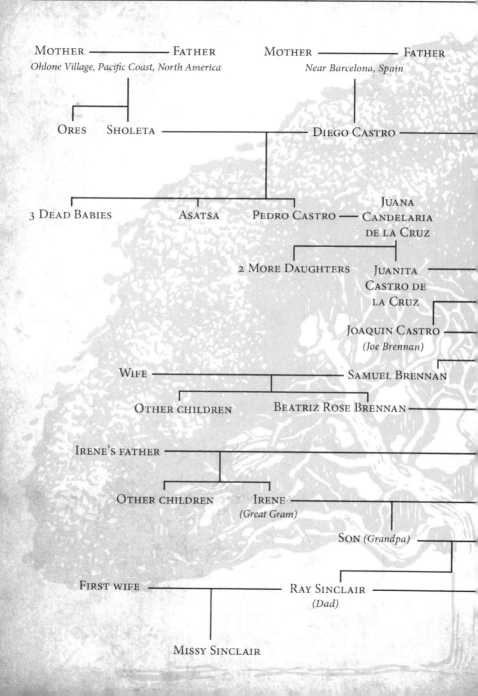

MOTHER ——————— FATHER
Ohlone Village, Pacific Coast, North America

MOTHER ——————— FATHER
Near Barcelona, Spain

ORES   SHOLETA ——————— DIEGO CASTRO

3 DEAD BABIES   ASATSA   PEDRO CASTRO —— JUANA
CANDELARIA
DE LA CRUZ

2 MORE DAUGHTERS   JUANITA
CASTRO DE
LA CRUZ

JOAQUIN CASTRO
(Joe Brennan)

WIFE ——————— SAMUEL BRENNAN

OTHER CHILDREN   BEATRIZ ROSE BRENNAN

IRENE'S FATHER

OTHER CHILDREN   IRENE
(Great Gram)

SON *(Grandpa)*

FIRST WIFE ——————— RAY SINCLAIR
(Dad)

MISSY SINCLAIR

FAMILY TREE

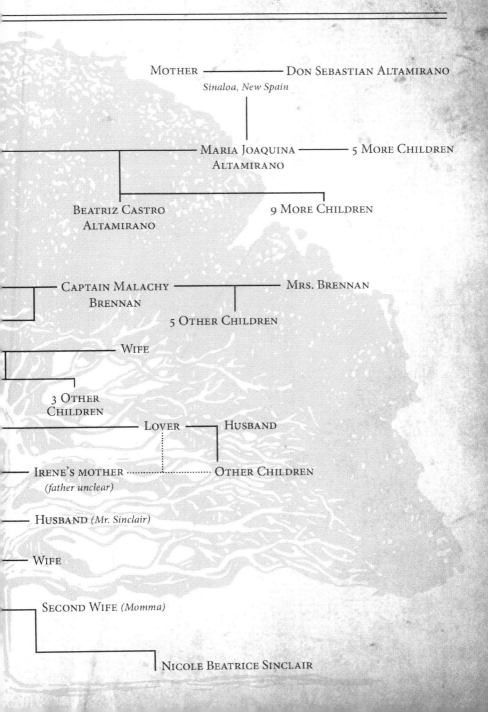

MOTHER ———————— DON SEBASTIAN ALTAMIRANO
Sinaloa, New Spain

MARIA JOAQUINA ———— 5 MORE CHILDREN
ALTAMIRANO

BEATRIZ CASTRO   9 MORE CHILDREN
ALTAMIRANO

CAPTAIN MALACHY ———————— MRS. BRENNAN
BRENNAN
              5 OTHER CHILDREN

WIFE

3 OTHER
CHILDREN

LOVER ———— HUSBAND

IRENE'S MOTHER ·············· OTHER CHILDREN
(father unclear)

HUSBAND *(Mr. Sinclair)*

WIFE

SECOND WIFE *(Momma)*

NICOLE BEATRICE SINCLAIR

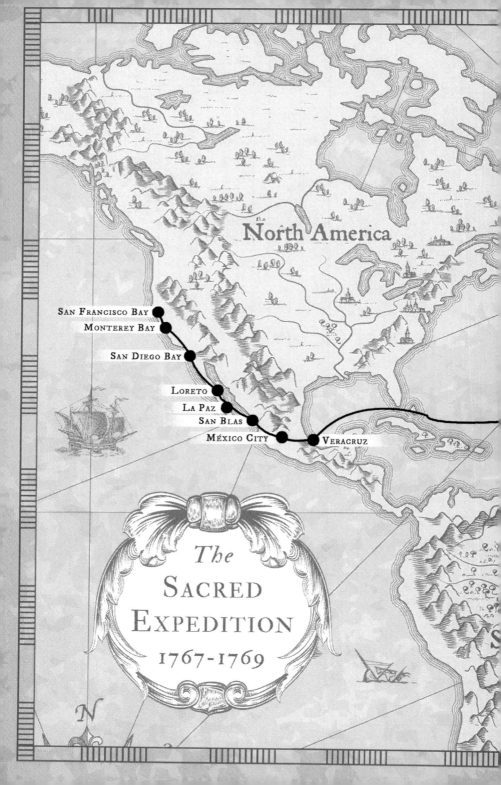

North America

SAN FRANCISCO BAY
MONTEREY BAY
SAN DIEGO BAY
LORETO
LA PAZ
SAN BLAS
MÉXICO CITY
VERACRUZ

The
SACRED
EXPEDITION
1767-1769

N

Europe

Barcelona

Cádiz

Canary Islands

Atlantic Ocean

Africa

America

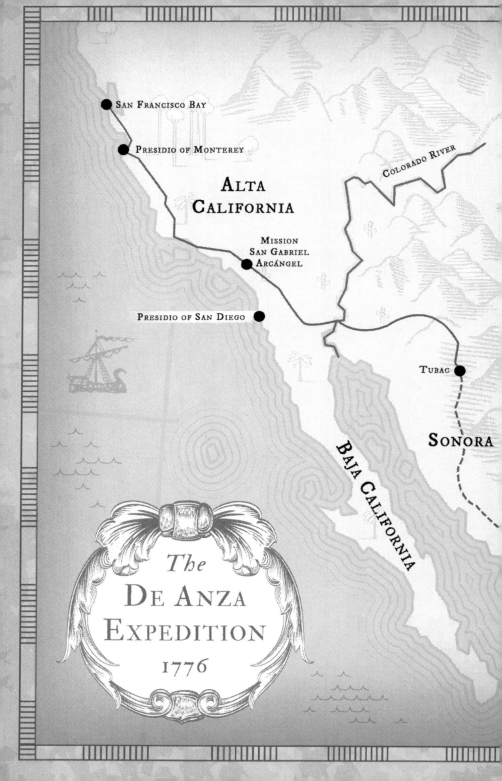

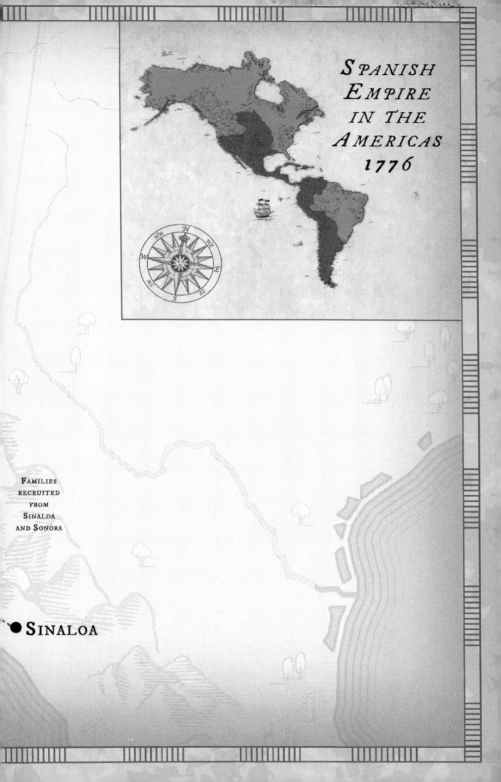

SPANISH
EMPIRE
IN THE
AMERICAS
1776

FAMILIES
RECRUITED
FROM
SINALOA
AND SONORA

● SINALOA

San Francisco Solano de Sonoma (1823)

San Rafael Arcángel (1817)

Presidio of San Francisco (1776)

San Francisco de Asís (1776)

San José de Guadalupe (1797)

Santa Clara (1777)

Santa Cruz (1791)

San Juan Bautista (1797)

Presidio of Monterey (1770)

San Carlos Borroméo de río Carmelo (1770)

Nuestra Señora de Soledad (1791)

San Antonio de Padua (1771)

San Miguel Arcángel (1797)

San Luis Obispo (1772)

La Purísima Concepción (1787)

Santa Inés (1804)

Santa Barbara (1786)

Presidio of Santa Barbara (1782)

San Buenaventura (1782)

San Fernando Rey de España (1797)

San Gabriel Arcángel (1771)

California Missions and Presidios on the El Camino Real

San Juan Capistrano (1775)

San Luís Rey de Francia (1798)

San Diego de Alcalá (1769)

Presidio of San Diego (1769)

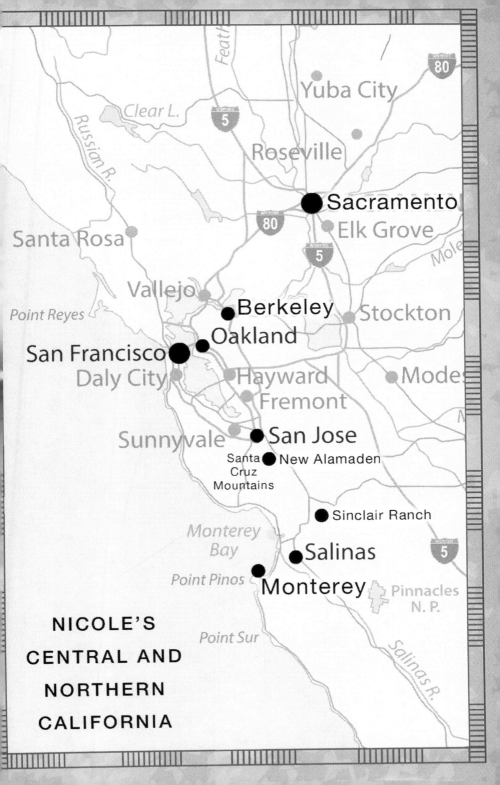

NICOLE'S
CENTRAL AND
NORTHERN
CALIFORNIA

FAMILY MYSTERIES

SINCLAIR RANCH, CENTRAL COAST, CALIFORNIA

2018

Your genetic-test results are in! read the subject line of an e-mail alert that popped up, then vanished, at the top right of Nicole's computer screen. Even though she was on deadline and could usually ignore pop-ups, this one froze her rapidly moving fingers. Her hands covered her mouth. She sat up straight and let out a groan. A queasiness percolated in her gut.

"Oh God, here it is," she whispered. Her coding project forgotten, she closed the laptop harder than usual and tipped her head back. Now what? Nicole inhaled deeply, then pushed the air out through pursed lips. No reason to delay. Gotta keep looking for answers. Why had Momma died so suddenly, and from lupus, just days before Nicole's college graduation? Was it genetic? Was there some other underlying disease that ran in the family?

She was jobless and distraught, feeling like an orphan even though she was living with Dad in their Central Coast farmhouse. She had so many questions. Her mother was so young and seemed healthy. Maybe she actually had been sick for some time and no one knew.

She scooped her hair back into a long, auburn ponytail and pulled tight. She took another deep breath, then slowly opened the laptop and found the email from *Genetix4You*. She scanned through the cover letter, filled with disclaimers and legalese, and clicked on the link to access their secure server for *Genetic Test Reports—Health Data, Traits, Ethnic Ancestry, Migrations, Connections—Sinclair, Nicole Beatrice.*

Nicole spent the next few hours poring over medical reports, graphs and percentages. There had to be a reason why this happened. Not lactose intolerant. Well wouldn't she have known if she was? Not likely to get Early Onset Alzheimer's. Thank God for that. Pre-disposed for coffee addiction. No kidding. No predisposition for Cystic Fibrosis. Well, that's good. Nor for Mediterranean Fever, whatever that was.

It was amazing how much information could be gleaned from your saliva. But her search seemed to be in vain. There was nothing new. No smoking gun. No clear medical results in her genes indicating if she too would get the disease. If other relatives could have had it. If it was a family trait. She kept digging.

She took a sip of tea and decided to click around the rest of the *Genetix4You* site to reports beyond the medical ones. *Migrations.* What was that? She opened the file to *Find Your Migrations* showing maps covered with red lines arcing toward California. Long thick arrows came from the Iberian Peninsula, Mexico, Ireland, England. A short one over California was labeled North American Native. A thinner one originated in the South labeled African American. It was all surprising. What did these arrows mean?

She clicked on *Ancestry* and a pie chart popped open: 20% Iberian Peninsula; 25% Mexican; 6% Native American from the Western U.S.; 5% African; 15% Irish; 4% French; 10% English; 10% Germanic; 5% Other.

Dad had always said they were English, maybe some German,

maybe a tiny bit Irish but all Protestant. She'd never heard anything about Spanish or Mexican ancestors. And those would be Catholic most likely, Nicole reasoned. And Native American? African-American? This was confusing. Was there some family history she knew nothing about? Were there relatives out there she'd never met, like on those TV shows?

She could have used a few more relatives growing up. Momma had been her everything. No siblings, her father barely involved, no cousins close by. Only one grandpa that she knew at all and he was always sickly. No real family events or get-togethers. It had not been a family-oriented childhood—more one focused on hard work. She would have to ask Dad about this, which was not likely to go well.

A few nights before, she'd finally coaxed him to leave the apartment over the barn, where he'd been hiding out since the funeral, to join her for dinner. Over the chicken with potatoes and carrots she'd baked, she told him that she'd done the saliva test with one of the DNA companies.

"Genetics test? What the hell?" A spray of spit and orange carrot bits flew out his mouth. A weathered ranching man, he now just looked craggy and old to Nicole. His grief had zapped the handsomeness right out of him. "Why'd you go and do that? Not gonna bring her back, you know. Let's get that straight right now. Plus, so you got it in your blood? Whatcha gonna do? Kill yourself? Change out all your blood? Don't be ridiculous. She's gone and we gotta accept it."

"But don't you want to know everything possible? I mean..." She hesitated. "Maybe, we could have prevented this."

He slammed down his fork and swiveled to look straight in her eyes. The dark, hollow she saw in his expression told her he would not forgive her for a long time. The pouch below his left eye twitched and the flush in his cheeks transformed to fully red. He stood up, shook his head back and forth, stalked out the door and slammed it behind him, stomping across the gravel and up the stairs to the barn apartment. She hadn't seen him since.

Nicole knew she'd crossed a line. Did Dad think she blamed him? Well, didn't she, in some way? Even though she knew they'd both lost their moorings, awash in grief, she was still mad at him. Why hadn't he told her earlier about her mother's illness? Maybe they'd been trying to protect her but she and Momma were so close. She should have known the truth from the beginning. She should have seen her before that shocking call that still had her reeling. She felt like a raw, open wound now. And so alone. Protecting her had failed miserably.

How could Momma have deteriorated so quickly? He had repeated they thought she had the flu, then maybe a viral infection when the flu seemed to hang on too long. By the time they went to a doctor, the disease had progressed so far there was little they could do. The doctors had put her on strong drugs but those just made her weaker. And then she had the heart attack. Dad said he wasn't sure if the disease or the drugs killed her. He was as angry and shocked as she was. Didn't she see that he had said with impatience.

This self-imposed exile was ridiculous. She left her computer and the genetics website to go search for him. It was good to get outside. Sergio, one of the ranch hands who specialized in the squash and pepper crops, was out at the toolshed.

"You seen Dad lately, Sergio?" she asked, holding up her hand to shield her eyes from the sun. After what seemed like a month of rain, today's sky was solid blue. A chill hung in the spring air. She zipped up her down vest and stuffed her hands in the pockets.

"Yeah, he's out at the corral. They just moved the cows in from the far hillside."

She nodded her thanks and walked quickly toward where he'd pointed. She had to ask Dad now while the shock of the ancestry reports still gave her courage. She found him walking from the corral toward the barn, his gait slower and more uneven than she remembered, as if a limp were slowing him down.

"Dad, can I talk to you? It's important."

"The way I see it, we don't got much to say to each other that's civil right now, you know. So let's just leave it at that." He kept on walking, picking up the pace as if he needed to get somewhere quickly. She stumbled after him. "But I gotta ask you something." He didn't stop. She grabbed his arm. She felt him flinch and then go stiff.

"Dad, I'm not a rabid dog. I get it. You don't want to talk. We're both a mess is how I see it. But I have questions about the family. I got the results from the saliva test. You know I did it to see if I could find anything about Momma's sickness. Why'd it happen? Could it be in our family?"

He looked up from studying his dirty work boots and stared at her. "I already told you my opinion on that," he said.

Nicole jumped in. This was her chance as he was standing still for the moment. Maybe some long lost relatives would fill in just a bit of the hollow she felt. Maybe discovering her roots could help return a sense of belonging she'd been robbed of by Momma's sudden death. Maybe she was desperate but she didn't seem to be able to focus on anything else.

"Yeah, I remember," she said. "I didn't find any medical information anyways. But I also got results on our ancestry. They do all that stuff together now. And it says some things that are way different than I've ever heard. Like we might have come from Spain and

Mexico and have Native American blood, and Irish, and even some black blood, like from the South. And some English and German too like you said but not that much. I mean it's weird. Do you know anything about where we came from? Do you think Grandpa or Great Gram would? Maybe we have some relatives around that we don't know about."

She stopped talking when she saw the familiar blush creeping up his neck to his chin and cheeks until his whole face looked as bright as a fresh strawberry on the vine.

"What the hell you talking about? What kinda shit you think you found on our family? That company could've just made it up. How you know they can really get your true history? Let it go, damn it. Stick to those computer programming contracts you got and make some money, why don't you? Shouldn't you be looking for a real job anyway, not searching ancient history?"

"But I wanna know the truth. Why'd Momma get sick? And maybe where we came from has something to do with it. I don't know but I gotta keep looking. Don't you want to know your past? Momma's past?"

"No, Nicole. I don't." He sighed, running his hand through his short, graying hair. "She's gone and none of this digging up the past bullshit is gonna bring her back." He stared at the ground and kicked at a dirt clod with the toe of his boot. Then he looked at her once again, face still red, eyes bulging in anger. "And you know what? You know what the worst thing is? It's that you're disrespecting your mother. Going behind my back to do some crazy tests. Digging into things that don't matter. You're sullying her memory and all the good she did in the world. All the good she did for us. We knew who we were, Nicole. Why you gotta mess with that? Now leave me alone. I don't wanna hear any more of this shit."

He marched toward the barn stairs and climbed toward his little apartment, slamming the door behind him. Nicole was pretty sure she heard a sob coming through all the swearing and grumbling. Defeated, she let out her own sigh and kicked the ground with her boot, just like he had.

This distance between them was nothing new. Throughout high school, Nicole, inspired by her mother's endless community service at church, had argued with her father on political topics, calling him closed-minded and anti-immigrant. Their relationship completely deteriorated when she left home for college hours north in Berkeley. Before freshman year, he'd sent her off with Momma to move into the dorms, leaning in through the car window to give her a warning.

"Now don't go dating anyone too different from you up in that goddamned communist Berkeley. Relationships are hard enough. But you got cultural differences, that's mostly impossible. Look at us, your mother and I. European background. Both Protestant, hardworking ranching folks, you know. Easier that way." Nothing about their ten-year age difference or how they'd gotten married when Momma was just nineteen. Or how he'd had another wife and kid before but had no relationship with them now. At least he hadn't gotten her pregnant first, he'd always chuckle to anyone who'd listen. And Nicole would just roll her eyes.

Once she was taking college courses and discussing politics late into the night over pizza in dorm hallways, their disagreements during her occasional weekends at home escalated.

"California's getting ruined by outsiders, foreigners, gang bangers coming from El Salvador and that goddamned little Honduras. What a troublemaker that place is," he'd rant. When she debated his logic, giving her view that Central American wars caused refugees to flee to the US, where some joined gangs, then years later without opportunities had transported those gangs back to El Salvador and Honduras. He just shook his head.

"Oh, blame the US. Is that what you're doing? That's ridiculous. These people need to find their own work in their own goddamned countries and not send their drugs here. What are we? The employment agency for the world? It's mostly Mexicans in Soledad prison, you know. Proves my point, exactly." The conversation was over.

There was nothing they could discuss without getting into a heated argument in which each of them left angry and alienated. Somehow Dad ignored the irony of his views and Momma's work on the refugee support committee or collecting backpacks for farmworker kids' first day of school. Momma got a pass on most everything. Despite his rigid beliefs, Nicole also knew he could be generous when he thought it necessary. He believed in personal commitment to the community, not in government handouts. If a tragedy befell one of his ranch hands or a neighbor, Dad would be the first to offer assistance. He had his own moral code. It just wasn't an inclusive one.

The sudden death of the one person they both loved had pushed them to grief-induced paralysis. After the shocking call that her mother had suffered a heart attack and died without warning, Nicole immediately drove home, missing graduation. In a fog of numbness, she headed south. Past San Jose, on down 101, past the freeway stop towns, on farther south into the hills still spring green but hinting at brown dryness coming after the season's last rains. On into the next valley. The gravel crunched beneath her tires as she turned onto the dirt road leading to the farmhouse and drove between the shiny peppers and the fallow zucchini field lining the drive. She stopped the car abruptly and raced for the house.

She threw open the screen door and burst in, looking for Dad, hoping it was all a mistake and Momma would be at her usual place at the kitchen table. The room looked faded and worn in a way she hadn't remembered. No sign of the usual brightness her mother put into making the old house cheery. No fresh flowers in mason jars on the side tables. No bowl on the kitchen counter overflowing with fruit. It looked dreary and unkempt, with bedroom pillows on the couches and blankets looped across their backs. No Momma. Exhausted, in shock, she collapsed on the sofa and listened to the house, for the quiet noises of her mother's daily routine, for the familiar back and forth of her parents discussing ranch business. Silence. Emptiness. She was so alone.

When she asked Dad why he'd moved out of the house into the tiny apartment above the barn he'd said, "Can't live there. Don't wanna be in that room." His voice had lost its strength and every word came out in mumbles. He was as depressed as she was.

"House's a mess, Dad. Stuff's broken. Looks like no one's been livin' here," she told him. Good thing he had the ranch guys who knew what to do to keep the place functioning. He was so skinny. She wasn't sure he was bathing regularly.

They got through the logistical cruelty of death barely pulling together a funeral and obituary and managing the well-meaning, but overwhelming, glass dishes of quiche and lasagna from the church ladies. She tried to clean up the house. She took a few online coding gigs to bring in some money. She and Dad avoided each other. But every time she was on the Internet she ended up in medical websites trying to figure out what had happened to her mother. That's why she'd spit in the test tube. For answers.

Now what? she asked herself the morning after Dad told her she was disrespecting her mother's memory. She felt paralyzed. She couldn't stomach a job search to start her engineering career right now. But she couldn't just feel sorry for herself either. She didn't want to go off on some crazy grief-fueled adventure like hiking the Pacific Crest Trail or driving across the country alone. She could work the ranch with Dad but then she might have to talk to him. Plus she'd studied engineering on purpose to avoid working the ranch. But she couldn't just abandon him either. She had to find her solid footing right here. That's what Momma would've advised. She was quite sure about that.

Maybe Dad was right. You couldn't bring back the dead even with knowledge of what had happened to them. Maybe she should give up on finding a medical reason for Momma's untimely death. She knew that bad things happened to good people. She just refused to grasp that life's capriciousness had alighted on her family so negatively. But why did Dad react so strongly about genetic testing? Was he hiding something? She had to find out the truth, and so returned to the DNA company's website.

She clicked through her medical reports and read them from top to bottom again. Nothing new. She hadn't missed anything. Then she switched screens to sift through the ancestry data as well. A section called *Connections* showed a list of people who might be some level of cousin. There was a photo of her half-sister, Missy, looking about the same age that Nicole was now, twenty-two. Missy was at least thirty-two, she reasoned. She thought maybe she'd met her once when she was really little. She knew nothing about her except that she and Dad didn't have a good relationship. Hmmm, not surprising.

She clicked on Missy's picture and limited information popped up, but she could see their ethnicity percentages were similar. That was weird. The Spanish and Native American and Mexican were from Dad's side? Nicole had no way to get Momma's DNA in the system to find her roots so she'd explore what was here. She stared at the *Migrations* map with the red arrows. Was her blood really from all those different countries? Was she really almost half Hispanic? What about the family stories of that guy leaving Ohio to come to California for the Gold Rush? Wasn't he English or Irish or something? She needed to know. Momma gone. She and Dad estranged more than ever. Her friends far away and focused on their own lives. She was so alone. She needed a family. Could there be one out there for her?

Did Dad really know his family background or was he just repeating stories he'd heard as a kid or picking out the ones he liked? Grandpa or Great Gram must know more. She would call them soon to ask some questions. Maybe go visit. Grandpa was in a nursing home after multiple heart attacks. She figured he could use some company. At the moment, with so little to go on, online seemed the best place to start a more in-depth search. She clicked through the *Genetix4You* site and made a decision. She set up a profile and started assembling a family tree, beginning with Dad's side. How could these ethnic breakdowns and migration maps be so different from the family narrative? Oh God, maybe she was actually adopted? No, of course not. Missy's percentages were very close to hers and they only shared a father.

So Nicole ignored her coding gigs for days, which turned into a week, and filled in the online trees as far back as she knew. The ancestry questions replaced the medical ones and she grew determined to unearth her origin story. She used the site's tools to search for old county records. Since her great grandmother lived in San Francisco in a really old house she looked through anything based in the city.

Census records. Birth records and death certificates. Social security and military files. Old newspapers. Whatever she could find. That guy who came out to California from Ohio for the Gold Rush. Maybe she could find him.

She wondered how her family had gotten into ranching. Ever since she was a tiny girl forced to do grueling chores at dawn she had hated the ranch. She remembered being just six or seven struggling to milk a cow in the dark. Her hands raw and blistered from squeezing hard and soft at the same time. Just the right touch so that the hot milk would hiss into the pail. Just the right angle and crouch so she wouldn't fall off the stool into the hay under the cow. She'd been terrified of being kicked. Every ranch hand had scars and stories. She knew that from her first years. But Dad had no sympathy.

"That's life on a ranch," he'd repeat. "Everyone helps out. It's an honest living, Nicole. Don't forget that."

In those years, before she grew so adept and accustomed to milking that she was almost sad when Dad announced he'd finally purchased a milking machine, she'd always thought that her half-sister Missy, whoever she was wherever she lived, was the lucky one. At least she didn't have to do barn chores in the freezing dark before sunrise. She didn't have to shovel horse manure from the stalls and wheelbarrow it out to the far side of the pasture. She didn't have to throw kitchen scraps out to the pigs or chase stray goats out of Momma's garden. Missy never had to milk a cow.

Where did the land come from? Grandpa was a rancher and then passed it on to Dad when he retired early with heart problems. But how had Grandpa ended up in agriculture and not law or engineering or real estate development? Grandpa went to Berkeley too. He could have been a lawyer or doctor or something. Why did he move to the countryside and work so hard it seemed like he'd made himself sick? And Dad had tried something else for a while before marrying her mother and moving to the ranch to help Grandpa, but it hadn't gone well. She didn't really know much at all.

With an endless list of questions, she grew increasingly frustrated at the dead ends. A lonely childhood with no cousins left her with few personal resources to tap. Grandpa was too sick to talk. She called Great Gram a few times at her San Francisco number but no one ever answered the phone. Maybe she should message Missy on *Genetix4You,* but that might not be a good idea. Probably just make Dad madder, if that was even possible. The public online trees she could see looked so robust, so inviting, like there were families out there who wanted to interact, to get to know each other and their pasts better. She longed for such connection. For a welcoming embrace from people who actually wanted new family members.

She didn't find anyone from Ohio back in the 1850s or much of anyone else in online databases beyond her great grandmother. Maybe there was something here at the ranch? Nicole snuck into her parents' folders in the filing cabinet at the back of their bedroom closet. She found tax returns, birth certificates, social security cards. She found files and files of her mother's projects. Church minutes on the service committee, on the social committee, on the refugee support committee. She found a drawer full of her father's ranch records. Bills, orders of seeds and tools. Lists of their horses and documents on their backgrounds. Ironic, isn't it, she thought to herself as she sifted through folder after folder. There was more information about the lineage of the horses than on the family.

In a moldy accordion file at the back of the closet she found the deed to her great grandmother's house in San Francisco. At last, something. But even that discovery revealed little. It was built in 1891 by a Samuel Brennan. It was unclear who all the owners were before Great Gram. There was a hand-written document attached showing a loan for $4,000 from the Bank of Italy to rebuild a portion of the house that had burned. It was dated 1907. The earthquake was in 1906. Nicole's hand trembled as she looked over every word. The earthquake had almost destroyed Great Gram's Victorian? She had to know more.

The next night after dinner, Nicole took the deed up the stairs to Dad's apartment and knocked on the door. "Dad, you in there? I need to talk to you."

He opened the door but just nodded at her, no verbal greeting. "I gotta talk to you too," he said as he gestured to a chair at the battered kitchen table.

She put the deed down next to his plate of spaghetti. "Look what I found in your files. The deed to the San Francisco house from the 1890s. Oh, sorry I went in without asking, but I didn't think you'd say yes and I really need to find out about our past. I can't seem to concentrate on anything else right now." She looked at him directly then and saw his cheekbones were protruding more than usual and the sockets around his eyes were sunken, purplish.

"Are you eating?" she asked. "You've lost weight. Why don't you come to the house tomorrow night and I'll cook you dinner?" Maybe it was Momma's spirit guiding her but she just knew her mother would be saddened by their estrangement.

"I'm not interested in old records," he said. "You gotta move out. We're gonna drive each other crazy. I know you hate ranching so you can't freeload here anymore. You gotta get a job, but I have one to start you off, for right now. Something I need you to do for me."

Nicole looked up from the old deed she'd wanted to show him and forced herself to listen. What was he talking about? Move out?

How cold could he be? Momma's just died and he's kicking me out? She felt a tingling in her chest. She swallowed hard, determined not to cry in front of him. She said nothing but looked at him for an explanation.

"I need you to go up to the city and take care of your great grandmother," he said. "Go in every day, like a babysitter, and help her with meals and medical appointments. That big house is too much for her. It's old, like your paper says," he pointed to the deed on the table. "We gotta sell it. Grandpa's too sick to help out. I'm…well, I'm busy here. I'm getting calls from her renters and I can't go up there. I can't handle that right now. So manage the inspectors and get the house ready. There's no one else to do it. We'll pay you a fair wage so you can get an apartment while you look after her and take care of the renters. Maybe you can even find a buyer too. One of your college friends have rich parents who'd like an investment?"

Nicole shifted her weight and sighed, trying to understand what he was saying. This was so sudden. She was just getting used to living at home again but being there didn't seem to improve her relationship with Dad. That was true. Was he just trying to get rid of her? She felt like a throwaway. "But why me? I've never even met her. Is she really sick or something?" she asked.

"Look, she's in her nineties and there's a bunch of apartments she rents out. The house needs work before it goes on the market. Just take care of her and manage the house sale preparation while your Grandpa and I find a senior facility for her. You don't have a full-time job. Seems like a deal to me. Go back to that goddamned Berkeley if you want. I don't care. But we sell within the year. Then get a real job with that degree I paid for. You got a week to find a place near her." He stood up and waved his arm toward the door. She was dismissed.

In a daze, deed clutched in her hand, she lumbered down the creaky barn stairs and across to the main house and slumped into a chair at the kitchen table. Dad was kicking her out. Her family had just dwindled even further. The farmhouse suddenly felt colder and lonelier. Maybe some space away from Dad while they each made sense of their new reality without Momma would be helpful. Goddamn him for not even trying. She didn't know Great Gram but she'd really been wanting to ask her family history questions. Maybe she could improve things with Dad if she did what he wanted.

Getting out of this frosty environment he'd created had to be better for her mental health. The ranch, for all its thousands of acres and wide-open spaces, felt claustrophobic now. Did she even have a choice? He'd made it pretty clear she didn't. She pulled herself up and went to her room feeling as if she were swimming in sadness. Focus. Maybe getting out of here would be good. A fresh start? But I don't want a fresh start. I want it the way it was before.

Nicole shook her head and stomped her feet. Get some blood moving and deal with reality. She'd go meet Great Gram and check out this job. Maybe this was an opportunity. She must know more than Dad about their true ancestors. She was really old. Nicole pulled clothes out of the drawers and started packing, then went back to her computer in the kitchen. Better look on Craig's List for an apartment in Oakland or Berkeley. Too expensive in San Francisco. What did you have to do to sell a big, hundred-year-old Victorian?

GREAT GRAM AND
THE HISTORIC HOUSE

SAN FRANCISCO, CALIFORNIA
2018

◦∞◦

icole knocked on the door of the top flat of the Victorian-Edwardian clinging to a steep hill rising up from the Mission District.

"Great Gram, it's me, Nicole," she said loudly. She guessed a ninety-something-year-old might not hear very well. She shuffled her feet while she waited. She knocked again. Harder this time. It was uncomfortable to be presenting herself as a babysitter to an unknown relative. Oh, and by the way, do you know any family history? What if she threw her out too? Then what? She had to get in to make things better with Dad. Feeling like an orphan was devastating.

The door opened and Nicole looked down into the watery, piercing blue eyes of a small woman who looked as if she'd shrunk with age. She was perfectly put together but almost in miniature. Her gray hair was styled around her ears, dotted with pearls, with a poof in back and bangs swept over to one side. She wore a sweater over a white blouse, a plaid wool skirt, panty hose and black shoes with a low heel.

"Nicole, come in, come in. I've been looking forward to this visit all day."

"Are you going somewhere? Did my dad call you? He and Grandpa want me to check in on you and help out. You know, with your errands and stuff."

"Oh no dear, you're the only thing on my agenda today. Come in and we'll have some tea."

Nicole realized Great Gram had dressed up for this meeting. She took off her puffy jacket and brushed her untucked shirt with her hands, as if she could iron the wrinkled fabric right there. Embarrassed she hadn't thought to dress a level above ranch hand, Nicole followed her great grandmother into the kitchen and offered to finish the tea preparation. At least she hadn't worn her work boots and had clean city shoes on under her jeans. She'd have to improve her wardrobe if she was going to work here.

Great Gram directed her to bring the tea and cookies into the living room where she had a table set for two at the window. The view was impressive. She could see the green of the park below, bordered by Victorians, giving way to downtown high-rises, cranes swaying above the shoreline, the bridge and East Bay beyond.

"You like my view? It is lovely isn't it? It's changed a lot over the years. I'm so happy to have you visit. Your father should have brought you here long ago," she said, her tone sharp. "Oh, I'm sorry," she said with a gentler voice. "Forgive my rudeness. How are you doing? I was so sad at your mother's untimely death. What a tragedy, a shock. I'm sorry I couldn't make the service but I don't really leave my neighborhood anymore. This must be difficult. Didn't you just graduate from Cal? And how is your father?"

Nicole was taken aback by the tiny lady's forthright comments but also touched by her concern. She agreed. She would have liked to have met this relative earlier and seen her beautiful old home. Maybe learned some family history as she grew up. Isn't that what gave kids foundations, grounding of who they were? She'd sure never had that from Dad, or to be fair, from Momma either. It'd been an insular childhood focused on the ranch and Momma's pet projects. Well, time to take charge of the family story for herself.

"Thanks for seeing me on such short notice," Nicole said. "Yeah, it's been difficult. I should be looking for a job but I got kind of obsessed with figuring out how Momma could've died so young. Without anyone knowing she was sick. I was living back at the ranch for a while. I just moved back to Berkeley. Dad and I are both pretty lost in our grief and on how to move forward…" She stopped. What was she saying? Why had she blurted all this out?

Great Gram reached over and patted her hand. Her gaze softened over Nicole's auburn hair, her hazel eyes, her soft round cheeks, her thick dark eyebrows. "Oh, dear, you are so young," she said softly. After a moment she continued. "The deep pain will persist. It will become part of who you are. But I promise, it will lessen and become more of an ache than the piercing you feel now. I'm so sorry you lost your mother so young. A good mother with whom you can have a long relationship is a treasure. Not everyone is given that gift."

Nicole choked up and couldn't say anything for some time. She looked out the window at the expanse of San Francisco. She gazed around the room at the old photos on the walls, the lace doilies, the velvety furniture, the antique desk and worn side tables. She felt a warmth flow into her veins. A strength from Great Gram's historic home, from her wisdom, her caring. She had not had such a conversation with anyone since her mother's death. No one had expressed as much concern or even given advice. No one seemed to know what to say.

Nicole nodded, swallowing hard. Maybe helping Great Gram could actually be a nice respite. Buy some time to get beyond that piercing pain she'd so accurately identified.

"I see this is a huge house. Dad and I thought you could use some help with your appointments, the renters and cooking. I'll come by every day to see what you need." As she spoke, Nicole decided to present her alignment with her father as stronger than it was. No need for Great Gram to worry about their conflicts. Plus she was anxious to discuss other topics. "I have questions for you about family history. What you know, if you have any documents? While I was searching for information on Momma's health problems, I did a DNA test and got some weird results. They don't match what I've been told. I really need to find out about my family right now. It's the only thing I seem to be able to focus on. Could you help me?"

"And what about an engineering job? Eventually you'll need to use that degree. Would be a shame not to."

"Yes, ma'am. I'm planning on it. Dad and I were thinking maybe I could help you out for say, six months or a year, while I get my head straight. Plus I gotta research different companies. I don't like the ones that just help you get your take-out dinner faster. I want something that contributes to society. Something real."

"Well, that is good to hear, young lady. I like a girl with a plan. Your father did call. Sure surprised me. I haven't heard from him in years. Not much of a family man, is he?" She didn't wait for Nicole to respond, muttering as if only to herself, "Seems to be in my business now." She poured them both more tea and gestured for Nicole to have another cookie.

Then Great Gram continued. "He said it might help you if you worked as my personal assistant. I don't need a nurse or anything, you know that, right? Now let's hear what your questions are. We can talk about the assistant job later."

They talked through the afternoon about the accepted narrative of the family's history and the many gaps. Nicole showed her the

Genetix4You reports on ethnicity, migrations and cousin connections. She explained she'd built a preliminary family tree on the site but was missing a lot of relatives and was mystified by the company's reports. What did it all mean? "What about that Gold Rush guy who came west? That's how our family got here, right? I thought maybe he'd be a good place to start," she said.

Great Gram seemed interested and explained that the Gold Rush ancestor had accumulated a lot of land and preserved a portion of it for family members to use. There was a committee of the land trust to oversee use and protect it forever. She was a lifetime member of the management oversight board. "You can go out there and go camping, have family events, picnics, go hiking. Two hundred acres. It's a beautiful piece with both hills and flatland in it. There's a creek. Your parents never took you there? It's not too far from your place. Maybe a forty-five-minute drive."

She'd never heard of it but she was impressed. "Well then you must know about the guy who bought it and set it up," Nicole said.

"Well, yes a little. Joe Brennan was his name," she said. "He had something to do with the Almaden Quicksilver mine during the gold rush. That's where they mined mercury needed in the gold fields to get the ore out of the rock. He bought land in those years and then had lawyers set up a trust to protect it from development or from any descendants ever selling it. Kind of like a mini national park for the family. Clever, huh? Especially in the 1870s. I believe that's when he established it."

"I had no idea," Nicole said, suddenly even sadder for all she didn't know, had never heard. Why hadn't she grown up with this delightful, tiny but strong, great grandmother? She should have known Great Gram all those years. She should have gone to that land. Her anger at her father deepened, hardened. Any determination to keep

Great Gram out of her problems dissolved.

"He won't talk to me. He's really mad that I'm digging into family history. He thinks I'm betraying Momma's memory. He's a mess. Thank God, I mean, thank goodness, Sergio and the other guys know what to do to take care of the ranch. Dad's disappeared into the barn apartment. And he won't let me feed him anymore. I don't even know if he's really eating. It's bad. I'm so sorry to burden you with this," she blubbered through tears.

Great Gram put her napkin on her plate and pushed her chair back to stand up. "Let's go look up in my attic and see what papers I've got on this house, maybe on the land trust. It's a mess of old boxes up there, but we can look around. You can help me get up those stairs."

Nicole nodded, took the plates and teacups into the kitchen and blew her nose with a napkin. She needed to get it together. What was her problem? Unraveling in front of someone she'd just met. Then a thought struck her. She pushed through the kitchen door and rushed back into the living room.

"Wait. Great Gram. Did you say Brennan? The gold rush guy?" Her eyes were brighter now. Tears dried. "I found the deed to this house in my parents' files. It says it was built by a Samuel Brennan in 1891. And he got a loan after the earthquake to fix some of it that burned. So are all those people relatives? Has this house been in the family all that time?"

A tiny thread of connection tugged, as if a ligament she'd never known was there suddenly twisted to assert its presence, its role, in the family chain. The pain of missing her mother was overwhelming but maybe there was something tying her to this little old lady, to this big, historic house, to her family's history. Something that could relieve the ache just a bit.

Great Gram smiled at Nicole's enthusiasm and renewed vigor. She took her hand to lead her down the hallway to the back bedroom. "Yes, Nicole, you're right. Samuel Brennan was my great grandfather and he built this house. I don't know much more than that. I might have a picture. That was good forward thinking too, just like Joe Brennan, who was some generations before him. Not too sure the connection. I like those people who plan ahead and take the long view. Your father's a fool, pardon my saying so."

Nicole looked at her in surprise but just found the statement comforting. She felt the same way. She cleared her throat and breathed deep. Might as well ask now.

"Would you be willing to do the DNA test? All you have to do is spit into a test tube. I think if we had your DNA in the family tree system, we might be able to find out more. Make more connections to distant cousins. What do you think?"

"Hmmm. I think it's great you've found your family history worth exploring. Usually young people are just not interested. But understanding your background gives you a foundation. Solid ground on which to build roots, then grow from, like a tree. A thread connecting past to present. Well, yes, I guess I should practice what I preach. I'll do the test to help you out."

Nicole smiled. She might finally find out more to fill in her family's profile. Great Gram seemed up for the project. Maybe this old lady babysitting job wouldn't be so bad.

"But I also think knowing your past can help you take responsibility for what comes next," Great Gram said. "We all need to be stewards of the future for our descendants and make some long-term plans. Now pull down that ladder and let's see if we can find anything on Joe or Samuel Brennan."

Nicole attacked the personal assistant job with gusto and quickly discovered that her great grandmother, Irene Sinclair, did not lead a sedentary life. She escorted her to her favorite salon and navigated Medicare appointments. They walked to the pharmacy and bakery, cooing at the strapped-in babies on every corner, ogling the fashionistas patrolling the vintage clothing stores and giggling at the marijuana smell wafting from the park. Nicole discovered joy in cooking and experimented with new recipes. They went to a symphony. On Thursday afternoons, Nicole joined her great grandmother in tutoring local teens at the writing center a few blocks away. She escorted her to pool aerobics and listened to the eighty-plus-year-old ladies gossip about neighborhood changes. There wasn't time for any more attic exploration as Great Gram needed long afternoon naps to keep up the pace. Disappointed they had not found anything besides moldy boxes of old photos from Great Gram's youth, Nicole accepted she needed to learn the routine and figure out her BART commute before they'd get a moment to dig through attic relics again.

Nicole met many of the building's tenants, tagging along to a baby shower and an anniversary dinner. Great Gram, always called Mrs. Sinclair, was like a benevolent queen in her castle home, treated gingerly with respectful distance and begrudging appreciation. She had not raised the rent in years. The plumbing worked. She had put in a new elevator when Mrs. Sanchez was pregnant with twins. Nicole could sense they were afraid to make waves for fear of losing one of the best deals in the neighborhood. Friends and relatives were moving to Oakland and even farther east to dull places like Fairfield and Stockton, forced out by rising rents and sales of the historic buildings. Below Great Gram's top floor suite, the building felt as if it were holding its breath, as if it were hoping no one noticed it in a bustling game of hide and seek, hiding in plain sight.

In those first weeks, Nicole was so busy navigating her great grandmother's daily activities that the house sale plan never came up. Great Gram hadn't mentioned a word about it. There were no inspections on her packed calendar. Everything seemed to be in working order. The tenants seemed happy to have Nicole respond a little more quickly to their needs; calling the garbage company when pickup was missed or getting the locksmith out when eighty-five-year-old Mr. Borden locked himself out of his apartment while his wife was visiting a new great grand baby.

Maybe, Nicole surmised, Dad didn't realize that Great Gram was completely lucid and living successfully on her own. A caregiver checking in on her was all she seemed to need to maintain her regular routine and manage the apartments. Remembering she was getting paid, this was a job after all, Nicole did do some research on potential buyers and realtors who specialized in San Francisco's historic houses.

Then, just a few weeks after she'd arrived, she overheard Great Gram talking to her lawyer.

"I am not selling. You can tell that rich young man over and over again I'm not selling. The house isn't even on the market. Why does he think it's for sale?" Great Gram's voice rattled lightly but the emphasis was clear. Nicole, listening from the kitchen, was shocked. It hadn't occurred to her that Great Gram didn't want to sell and was unaware of her father's directive. Oh man, she'd have to tell Dad. She'd enjoyed a few weeks away from him, distracted by Great Gram's activities, yet also grateful for the deposit in her bank account every two weeks. She was loath to call him about anything right now.

"Just have your boss call me back. No assistants. I need my lawyer to help me protect my house and myself. I can't have my son and grandson declaring me incompetent." Nicole heard her slam down the black receiver of the old dial phone.

"Great Gram, you all right?" Nicole glided in from the kitchen through a swinging door. She found her crossing the wooden floor with the Persian carpet, slowly, with a slight lean to the right and an up and down rise in her step, to sit in her favorite armchair. She picked up the delicately painted china cup on the side table covered with a lace doily to sip tea and gazed out at the view.

"What was that about?" Nicole asked. "You sounded mad. How about some lunch? And then you can lie down for your nap."

"I'm fine, dear. Just peeved. Some hotshot young Internet billionaire wants to buy the house but it's not for sale."

"Well, that might be perfect," Nicole said with an enthusiastic smile. She gently touched Great Gram's shoulder to make sure she was solidly in her regular spot, while presenting a plate with a ham and cheese on rye, no crusts, mustard only. Nicole's movements were graceful as if she were a ballerina twirling to calm nerves and serve sandwiches. "You could buy a smaller place and not worry about all the tenants, the bills, the old wiring. And you'd have plenty to pay someone to come help you at a new apartment. I bet you could get a lot for it. The neighborhood's hot now. I can't even afford rent here."

"That's not the point, dear. I just care about my home and my renters." She almost snorted in disgust. "Do you really think some rich, single guy needs all this space? I want this house to stay in the family. It's disgusting how your dad, and my son, who's barely holding on with his heart problems, have green dancing in their eyes over home prices."

Nicole, starting to realize that Dad's family conflicts were more complex than she'd known, asked quietly about its history. "Was it your father who divided it into apartments?"

"That's right. The Bordens have been here ever since," she said. "They're almost as old as me. Where would they go? And what about the Sanchezes with their little twins? They live on his garbage man salary while she works at Mission-Valencia Grocers down the block. How would they afford anything around here if I sell and they have to leave?" Great Gram raised her faint eyebrows, now colored in with brownish pencil. Nicole shrugged.

"Hector, my favorite hair stylist," she went on, "told me he lives in fear of a rent increase or getting evicted because he can't afford to move. He doesn't want to leave the neighborhood. He's lived here his entire life. I'm not budging. Your dad and grandpa can carry me out of here when they're pallbearers!"

The phone rang. A tinny bell from a forgotten era. Great Gram got up slowly, inching toward her double-layered desk. "And, by the way, it's not right that you can't afford rent here. The Mission used to be the affordable neighborhood. If any of my renters were to move out, I'd offer you the apartment at a fair rate. That's what a family property should be for."

She picked up the receiver. "Oh, finally," Great Gram said into the heavy phone. Her voice warbled a bit at first. She cleared her throat, once, and again. "Look, I know you're busy up there in Sacramento being Senate President or whatever it is you do. But you're still my lawyer. Okay, look, I don't care how important this kid thinks he is or how much money he has, the house is not for sale. I refuse to kick my tenants out. They're just working people trying to make ends meet. And I am not leaving my home of sixty years to move to some awful old people's home. Those places are completely depressing. They make you sick so you want to die. I have plenty to live for still."

She paused, coughed and sat roughly at the wooden desk chair. Nicole came over with a concerned look. Great Gram waved a hand

and gave her a don't hover, don't over protect, I know what I'm doing glare. Nicole returned to the kitchen.

Great Gram's clear, determined tone to the lawyer was confusing. Dad had made it sound so matter of fact. Like everyone was in agreement on selling the house. What an idiot she'd been. So absorbed in her own mess. She hadn't even asked her yet about getting the house ready to sell. Was Dad trying to put one over on Great Gram? And her for that matter, not being honest that Great Gram had conflicting views over a house sale. Or, maybe she needed to give Dad the benefit of the doubt. Maybe he didn't realize that Great Gram wanted to stay and was completely lucid. Yes, she got tired and moved slowly but she was still spry and opinionated and could live independently with help. Nicole listened through the door.

"I want you to make sure my son and grandson don't try to declare me incompetent. I am completely with it," she said into the phone. "And I want you to help me protect my tenants for as long as possible. Didn't you keep the California coastline away from developers or something? Well, you ought to be able to protect a historic Victorian that survived the 1906 quake. This house is going to last way longer than this current bubble we're in. I've seen it before. Soon these millionaires, billionaires, whatever, will be drowning in bank payments."

She paused, listening to the lawyer, then said. "He'll pay cash? And how much? Oh my," she said loudly. "My great grandfather paid less than five thousand dollars to have this house built in the 1890s."

Nicole returned to the room at her great-grandmother's raised voice. Great Gram looked at her, questioning, pushing the mouthpiece aside. "He wants to meet me. Should I do it even though I'm not selling?"

Nicole raised her eyebrows and cocked her head to one side. Who is it? Why not? she mouthed as she shrugged. "Could be interesting, Great Gram. You're always saying you like young peo-ple," she whispered.

"Okay, that's fine," Great Gram said back into the phone. She told the lawyer to devise a plan to make the house a historic landmark or something creative to allow her tenants to stay as long as they wanted. She just knew her son and grandson would sell immedi-ately upon inheriting the house. Could she prevent that?

"You know how that relative of mine preserved that land for the family? That was brilliant. Can't we do that with a house? Figure something out." Grasping the desk with bony, freckled hands, she steadied herself to stand up. Nicole slipped a hand under her great grandmother's elbow and guided her to the armchair.

She'd have to ask Dad about this unexpected wrinkle. But maybe Dad had a point. It was an awful lot of apartments for an old lady to manage. He was right about that. And it would make Dad happy, get her back into his good graces if she could manage a sale. But would Great Gram thrive anywhere but in her familiar neighborhood? The uncertainty and confusion made her stomach hurt but she had to hide her indecision from Great Gram. She was starting to feel more and more at home every day she came to the flat.

A week later Great Gram asked Nicole to look through some boxes in the attic. Her lawyer had sent an application for the highest level of historic landmark status from the federal government. In order to apply they would need to find all the original documents and house records. Nicole was pleased to be back in the attic again looking for a past beyond her mother. And if the house was officially historic then maybe Dad wouldn't be in such a hurry to sell. A landmark would be awesome to have in the family estate, right?

She realized she'd have to go back to the ranch soon to really talk with him. She had hoped doing one thing Dad wanted would repair their relationship but Great Gram seemed determined not to sell the house. And he'd been insistent on a sale within a year. She had to tell him. How would that go?

Nicole turned her attention back to Great Gram who sat at a card table they'd set up. Together, they began opening disintegrating cardboard boxes, taking out accordion folders and sorting through paper after paper.

"Oh look," Nicole said. "Here's a file on the house." Great Gram put on her glasses and they sorted through copies of the house deed and the loan documents that Nicole had found at the ranch. There was another loan her father had secured to do the remodel breaking the large house into five apartments. The Bordens' lease agreement was there. Nothing more on Samuel Brennan or why he built the house in that neighborhood or what else he was doing in San Francisco. They moved on looking through file after file, box after box.

After a few hours, Nicole could see Great Gram was tiring but she insisted on continuing. "One more box each and then we'll call it a day and go have some tea," she announced. "Oh, look, here's a set of files on the land trust. Somebody gave me this box when I started on the board, I think."

Suddenly, Irene gasped and raised her hand to her open mouth. Nicole looked up. "What is it?"

"Oh my. Here it is. The original trust agreement establishing the Brennan Land Trust. Look, it was signed in 1878. Oh, my goodness. This is wonderful to see."

Nicole picked herself up off the floor where she'd been sorting through an old box of file folders and stood next to Great Gram. She looked down at the faded scrawl on the browned paper. Silently, they read through the legalese on the land ownership and what was to happen to it in the future. The loops and jags of the handwriting more than a century old were tough to decipher. It took patience to make sure they understood each longhand word correctly.

Two hundred acres of Joe Brennan's land, they read, was to be preserved in a land trust such that it could not be sold or developed outside of the family. It was to be passed down to family members for their use only. After Brennan's grandchildren were adults at the turn of the century, the trust would be required to form a board that would oversee land use going forward. The trust included details of the board's composition and operating instructions from 1900 on, into perpetuity. A San Francisco law firm was assigned to guide the board as it was established and began its duties.

As Nicole and her great grandmother read through the legal agreement, Nicole put a hand on Irene's shoulder and squeezed. Filtered light peeked through the dirty skylight illuminating the box and the document Irene held. Finally, a thread trailing into the past, into their shared history.

"Oh my God, this is amazing, Great Gram. I just knew there'd be some good stuff up here. Could this help? Maybe show the family's long history here before even building the house? Look, here's the law firm that did it for Mr. Brennan."

"Well, I'll be. Oh my, look here, dear. Looks like Mr. Brennan was not really that. Look at the final lines and the signature." Nicole squinted at where she pointed and read,

The Brennan Castro de la Cruz Land Trust is officially initiated by Joe Brennan (Joaquín Castro de la Cruz). Mr. Brennan is establishing this land trust to protect 200 acres of his 300 acres to remain forever in the hands of his descendants. He is doing this in honor of his mother, Juanita Castro de la Cruz and his grandparents, Pedro

Castro and Juana Candelaria De La Cruz. True Californios. Mr. Brennan is taking this action at the birth of his first grandchild, Beatriz Rose Brennan, in recognition of his family continuing to thrive as California grows and prospers.

"Oh my. You know, dear, Rose Brennan was my grandmother. They were really Mexican. Look at his name and his mother's name and his grandparents' names. They're all Spanish names and surnames. I've only ever heard it called The Brennan Land Trust. Well, well, well, Miss Nicole." She stopped and caught her breath. "I think we just found out why you have Mexican, and that Spanish blood too, in your ethnicity chart of the DNA report. My grandmother was always called Rose, as far as I know. I never knew her first name was Beatriz. And look at the spelling. You're a Beatrice too, right? But with a C? I wonder if Grandmother Rose, or someone else, changed the spelling?"

Nicole took the trust agreement and set it on the table, peering at it closely. "Wow. This is crazy. *Californios?* What's that?"

THE GHOST

CATALONIA, ESPAÑA TO VERACRUZ, NUEVA ESPAÑA

1767

"*Diego, wake up. Why ya* sleeping on the beach?" A bare toe nudged into his ribs. Groggy from a restless night on hard ground and with a throbbing head, he grunted in pain and rolled over onto his back, sand sticking to his face and shoulder. Before he could open his one good eye, he heard her gasp. It must look as bad as it felt.

"What happened? Your papá again? There's such a big lump. What he'd do this time?"

"The skillet," was all he could say, finally opening his eye and looking right onto those pillowy pink lips set in translucent skin as she leaned over him. She wiped the sand off the swollen eye and raised bruise at his temple. She reached down and tore a piece from the hem of her threadbare skirt and proceeded to clean the wound with the frayed fabric. Her touch was gentle, her voice soft. She lowered her head to meet his gaze so that he now looked into her warm, brown eyes.

Yes, she was only twelve and he just fifteen, but he was convinced he'd loved her since they were toddlers together on the Barcelona shore. Clearly, Isabela, of the pouty pink lips and fair countenance, would grow into a strong and beautiful woman. He had to tell her. He pushed himself up on his elbows, then gestured for her to sit, wishing that he could remain there, suspended in her tender care. But no.

"Mamá's dead. Three nights ago. She coughed up blood 'til there was nothing left of her. Papá got even drunker than usual after that and came at me with the frying pan. I didn't see it comin'. Said I'd messed up at the blacksmith's. But I don't think I did. He's lyin'. Or just crazy."

Isabela's smooth face scrunched up with anguish and she tried to say something. But he stopped her. Before he lost the courage to tell her the truth. "I stood up to him this time. I pushed him into the wall after that and smacked him. I couldn't take it anymore. I've been sleeping on the beach since. I can't ever go back. And I gotta get the little ones out of there." She moved closer to him and leaned in to his side. He put his arm around her for a moment, then turned her and gripping both her shoulders, looked straight into the sympathetic eyes.

"I enlisted. For the dragoons."

"But how..." she started to ask.

"I lied. Told 'em I was sixteen. I told 'em of my work at the blacksmith's. I'm sailing with Governor Portola to New Spain to expand the Spanish empire and spread the word of God," he said, with a little swagger. "I'll learn to be a man and come back rich. I'll marry you and build you a beautiful house by the sea. I promise to return for you, Isabela. Now go on home, don't say a word. I've got to get my brothers and sisters out of there."

He brushed a tear from her cheek and at the same moment she touched his bruise, so gently. He wanted to kiss those rosy, plump lips desperately but realized he didn't really know how and he wasn't sure the response he'd get. Best to just get on with it. He pushed himself up off the sand and walked down the beach toward the shack he called home, leaving her standing there with sad astonishment on her face.

Diego found his siblings still crying over their mother's premature death. Papá gone, at work presumably. He stuffed them into every scrap of clothing they owned, then herded them down the beach to his aunt's hovel. "They've got to stay with you, Tia," he said. "Now that Mamá's gone, he'll kill us all if we stay. I ride out tomorrow for Cadíz with Governor Portola of the Californias. We sail for New Spain from there. I'm going in service of the King, as a soldier of the empire. I'll be protecting Spanish territory from English pirates and the Russians," he added, exaggerating the importance of his role. "You must raise the little ones now, as your sister would have wanted. I'll come back for them a man. A rich man. I'll take care of you all when I return."

He handed her a small pouch with the few coins he had collected from his apprenticeship. He gave her no chance to reject the children and marched off with barely a farewell, the children crying harder and calling his name. Diego tried to push the image of Isabela's lone tear and the cries of his siblings out of his mind as he returned to the family shack for his belongings.

He shuffled through the rough wooden bureaus and scoured the barren kitchen to assemble supplies. A proper sea trunk beyond his means, he stuffed clothes into a coarse wool duffel, stealing his father's second pair of boots as an extra for the voyage. A man always needs to have solid boots, on sea and land, he reasoned. In a kitchen cupboard he found a small sack of dried lemons and oranges, which he tossed into the top of his bag.

At the very back of his mother's drawer, his fingers touched a pocket-sized bible she had inscribed with his baptismal date. Perhaps she had forgotten about it later when the other babies arrived, as only his name was listed. Diego opened it to the red silk placeholder to read the passage on Moses leading the Israelites out of Egypt.

And Moses stretched out his hand over the seas; and the Lord caused the sea to go back by a strong east wind all that night, and made the sea dry land, and the waters were divided. And the children of Israel went into the midst of the sea upon the dry ground; and the waters were a wall unto them on their right hand, and on their left.

Had Mamá been reading this hoping to escape her fate? Diego said a silent prayer of farewell to his mother's spirit still lingering in the emptiness. He promised her that he'd do his duty to her memory and become an important man, perhaps an exalted *capitán* like the great Portola himself. Perhaps, as Moses had brought the sea down on the Egyptian slave holders, his departure would punish his father's cruelty and free his siblings from destitution and fear. Diego was convinced his glorious return would prove that seeking his fortune in the New World was the right thing to do.

He slipped the bible into the sack, threw it over his shoulder and strode out of the family home, imagining the day when he'd walk back into the dilapidated house respectable and wealthy. He pictured a glorious homecoming, one in which he would be the opposite of his father in every way.

The moment he stepped on the leaky galleon's gangplank for the journey to Veracruz, Nueva España, Diego's body swayed with each slosh of the sea, every roll of the hull causing nausea in his gut, raising bile up into his throat. The swell seemed to vaporize his bones, forging his ligaments into jiggling springs. He couldn't get his balance. He was mortified that he had to cling to stray lines and gunnel rails to stay upright. What a fool he was to have volunteered without hesitation. How would he survive the voyage? How could he ever board a ship again and return to Spain?

Once the Canary Islands had melted into a dark line, then evaporated from the horizon as the ship turned its stern to Africa and faced the open Atlantic, Diego's desperation forced him to consider his limited options. Dizzy, he fell to his knees and vomited, then spat, gripping the bulwark so as not to slide off into the sea. He tried to pull himself to standing, grabbing at the rigging and sail. Wind whipped the lines. The sails cracked overhead. Sea spray washed up onto the deck, drenching him. A spasm twinged in his gut and he dropped once again to spew his stomach contents into the blue froth. He contemplated throwing himself overboard to end the agony. But the fear of drowning in a cauldron of sea monsters prevented him from acting on that impulse. From his knees, he gazed into the whitecaps below and swore an oath to God. His only other option.

"Dear Lord, hear my prayer. Why can't I get my balance like the other dragoons who've never been aboard ship? Are you punishing me, God, for abandoning the little ones? For running off as soon as Mamá's body was cold? For lying to Isabela? Because how can I ever return?"

Saliva pooled on his tongue. He spat, lifting his gaze to peer through tangled hair matted to his forehead, searching for solid land. There was nothing as far as he could see but endless blue. The ship tossed and groaned. A sail flapped and Diego heard the coarse yells of the first mate ordering the crew to adjust the jib. He forced himself to kneel properly, as if in Santa Maria's wooden pews back home, and returned to his prayer.

"If I can get off this ship alive, Lord, I vow to serve you fearlessly, selflessly, for a glorious future. I'm your servant now, God. I'll devote my entire life to your service, and for Spain, in the New World."

He felt reckless talking directly to God without the intervention of a priest—this wasn't just a prayer, after all, but a contract. But Diego was desperate. He figured the Lord wouldn't mind under the circumstances. He promised to fulfill his agreement with Governor Portola and his obligation to King Carlos by moving New Spain farther north into Las Californias, preventing the Russians and English from encroaching on the empire. He'd serve God by protecting the Franciscan missionaries as they explored north to deliver Christianity and civilize the heathens. He would give his life for the cause. "Just get me to shore, God, and I'm yours forever," he promised.

Staring at the water, Josue Maximiliano Diego Castro Cardona finally accepted that his destiny lay in the New World. He could never board another ship, never return to Catalonia, never see his siblings or true love again. To serve his captain and King, and God, his feet would remain firmly on the ground.

A master with horses as an apprentice in the forge where his father worked, Diego's self-confidence had led him to volunteer for the Portola expedition without question. His blacksmith skills had already earned him praise from the *patron*. Diego was proud of his reputation along the southern Barcelona coastline for his ability to coax horses to do his bidding. He'd been riding since he was four years old. He was so comfortable and connected to the beast that when he sat atop a horse's swayed back he and the animal appeared to become one, like a centaur. He had yet to meet a horse he could not tame or ride.

It never occurred to him that mastering the tasks of a sailing ship would be different, but the sea confounded him. Despite having grown up alongside the ocean, the key ingredient for his success around water seemed to be the solid ground underfoot. For years he'd confidently fought the tide's pull to catch carp, wriggled his toes to dig for clams, trudged up streams for brown trout. Sailing above the water was another matter.

Once on board, the seasickness brought feverish nightmares. His mind began to collapse under the weight of his misery. He dreamed of sea creatures below. Of Isabela's haunting, betrayed eyes. Diego could barely stand long enough to check on the horses below deck. Even the four-legged beasts seemed to have found an equilibrium and bobbed in concert with the rolling sea rather than fighting its every tug and pull.

There were times during that long Atlantic crossing that his promise to God felt like the only nourishment sustaining him. Many of the crew lost weight from their diet of stale water, hard tack beef and moldy bread. Some got the bleeding gums of scurvy. Diego was even more malnourished than the rest, surviving on his own tea recipe. The sack of dried oranges and lemons turned out to be a lifesaver. He sliced off tiny pieces with his knife and secretly spiked his tea with the shriveled yellow and orange peels. The hot black concoction with the dried citrus was the only drink that would calm his stomach.

He was so thin and so often absent from regular duties that the sailors couldn't remember his name. They began calling him *el flaco*, the skinny one, or the sick one, the absent one, or finally, the name that stuck, *el fantasma*, the ghost.

Once finally on solid ground months later, while many faltered in the oppressive heat and harsh landscape of Central *Nueva España*, Diego recovered. The sea had reduced him to a bony shell but the land revived him. As soon as he could keep down more than just watery *atole*, he stood taller. The hollows in his cheeks and shoulders began to fill in. He was so relieved to be able to stand up straight and recover his strength he just knew he'd endure the upcoming walk across central New Spain better than his crew mates. But the journey was grueling.

Diego and his fellow soldiers trudged behind Portola almost a thousand miles across Mexican deserts and below snow-capped mountains. A few of the leaders had horses but many walked. They wound through jungle swamps filled with hissing insects, over forest covered peaks and through hot, barren hills. They passed miners scratching through the hard soil searching for silver and Spanish missionaries converting natives to Catholicism. There was little fresh water, hardly any food. Men caught terrible fevers and perished in the night. On a slippery trail crossing a mountain pass, two horses slipped and crashed into each other, sending horses and men tumbling down the cliff to their deaths. Each day brought a new disaster or danger. But Portola kept on moving.

Diego, desperate to make himself useful to his superiors, pushed himself to walk on, to find anything to prove his worth and keep himself alive. He mended worn saddles and the long chaps soldiers used against the spines of barrel cactus and agave. He tended horses injured by the cacti and weakened by thirst. He soothed frightened animals on narrow mountain ridges as their hooves slipped and created mini rockslides to the rivers below. Even Portola noticed his ability with the livestock telling his lieutenants, "Keep that skinny one with the horses," before a river crossing or set of treacherous cliffs.

After the months-long slog, the soldiers stumbled into San Blas and spied New Spain's Pacific coast, at last. They waded into the gentle swell of the Sea of Cortez and splashed with glee, behaving like their boyhood selves. As his companions frolicked and shouted, Diego was horrified, mystified at the same time. Hadn't they finally arrived at their destination? He hadn't understood the geography. More water to cross to get to Las Californias? Couldn't they ride and walk to the meeting point at Mission Loreto for the Sacred Expedition? Apparently not, he learned from his companions. What now? He couldn't survive another ship. And he'd promised God he'd stay on this mission. What had he done? Why had he volunteered so quickly and abandoned Isabela and his family?

Dismayed at his ignorance, lonely for the familiar, he desperately missed his Spanish coastal home, lush with fruit trees, filled with those he loved. Diego realized he could stay in the port town of San Blas but the dusty frontier of New Spain was uninviting. Poverty stricken. And to abandon Governor Portola now seemed foolish. He must press on.

"I've got no choice but once in the Californias I'm never stepping off land again," he swore to himself, speaking to the sea as he waded into the surf. Diego managed to survive the short, much calmer, trip across the Sea of Cortez and was delighted to be assigned horse care duty at Baja California's Loreto Mission. He had no intention of walking up a gangway onto a galleon ever again.

THE SACRED EXPEDITION

Misión Loreto, Baja California to Bahía San Diego,
Alta California

1768—1769

"*El fantasma? How'd you get* such an unusual nickname?"
the sergeant asked. "Can you disappear? That could be
useful," he laughed. Diego shrugged.

"No, maybe 'cause I'm thin," he said, mumbling, not wanting
Sergeant Ortega to know the truth of his weakness aboard ship.
Diego had been working in the stables for a few weeks as the leaders
prepared for the Sacred Expedition north to conquer Alta California.
He was anxious to get going, to leave the desolate outpost on Baja's
eastern shore. He distracted the recently arrived sergeant with talk
of the journey ahead.

"Sergeant Ortega, let me show you our horses here in Loreto.
Many are worn out after crossing the mountains from Veracruz
to San Blas, then the trip here to the mission. But I'm working to
get them stronger. And with yours we should have sufficient numbers for the Sacred Expedition. How many land groups is Governor
Portola planning, sir?" Diego would do anything to avoid being
posted aboard a ship. Here might be an officer who could use his
skills with the horses. On solid ground.

Sergeant Ortega nodded but never answered. He gestured to his assistant to bring their horses then followed Diego behind the Loreto mission's dilapidated buildings baking in the Baja California heat. Once in the cool dark of the stable, Ortega took off his hat and wiped the sweat from his brow and thick black hair with a handkerchief. He was every bit a horseman as Diego, confidently examining the legs, teeth and flanks of each animal. "Looking a bit skinny," he said. "What happened here? This big cut on her leg?"

"Oh, she's gonna be fine. Just got caught in some cactus," Diego said. "I've been cleaning it every day with hot water and tallow soap. The natives here use some plants for wounds and I've been using those too. Heals 'em up real fast."

The sergeant finished examining the animals. He had Diego water his own horses and settle them in the feeding stalls. "Look each one over for wounds, sickness. Don't let them drink too much at once. What's your name again? Fantasma was it?"

Diego nodded quickly, resisting the urge to ask him to use his proper name. He could never correct an officer. He was just a lowly dragoon assigned to muck the stalls and water the horses.

"Okay, I see you know horses. Take good care of mine and maybe you can join me going north. Portola just made me his lead scout. Can't imagine you'd want to stay in this God forsaken place, eh, *Fantasma*? Where you from again? Barcelona? Little bigger than Loreto here, eh?"

He laughed. He grabbed Diego's elbow and gave him a solid pat. He walked toward the stable door, spurs clinking with each step, then turned back. "Show us what you can do with these beasts, then we'll decide where to put you. Expedition should be heading out next month or so. Padres are coming in any day now."

Diego grunted instructions to the two native stable boys, the only ones lower in the military hierarchy than himself, to hurry and get to work with the new horses. He could barely contain his excitement. He grinned and did a little jump with a kick. Then stopped himself, said a prayer of thanks and got back to work.

Not only anxious to be included in one of the land groups riding north, rather than on a supply ship, he was determined to avoid being assigned to protect the padres based at the wind-blown mission. There was nothing at the outpost but craggy mountains rising steeply to the west and hard brown dirt. Thank goodness for the breezes coming off the Sea of Cortez. Diego did feel at home in any place with a beach but the Baja missions colonized by the Jesuits for a century, now being taken over by the Franciscans, were almost destitute.

The missionaries had managed to trade cloth, beads, colorful sashes and dried figs for the loyalty and religious devotion of some of the population, who they called *gentiles*. Those who succumbed fully to Catholicism were baptized and given a superior status to their brothers and renamed *neophytes*. The priests moved the converts to the mission grounds and forced them to construct and repair the feeble buildings and till the hard, cracked soil with the limited vegetables, corn and beans that would grow there. If left to their own devices, Diego had seen that the natives wore almost no clothes. Even in the few short weeks since he arrived, he'd noted that they were skilled at fishing, catching birds and rodents, and fabricating medicines and dishes out of roots, cactus and shellfish. There were many distinct language groups among the converted natives and the unbaptized outside the mission gates. The priests taught a few *Castellano* and used them as translators to interact with other potential recruits. It was a hard life and he had no intention of staying in Loreto.

A week later, Diego squeezed into the rough-hewn pew next to his fellow soldiers. There was an anxious tension in the air. Today's Mass would differ from the previous Sundays'. The famous Padre Junipero Serra had arrived in Loreto days earlier to take his post as the religious leader of the Sacred Expedition. The priest was well regarded among the devout for bringing the Inquisition to New Spain, for committing himself to eradicating witchcraft and sacrilegious beliefs of the *Pame* natives in the mountains of *Querétaro*. Father Serra was famous for not only converting the heathens but also developing his missions into thriving ranches. He had a reputation for strict asceticism and severe practices and for clashing with his military protectors. The soldiers were curious to see the man for themselves.

Diego had not been in church for many months and hoped the service could assuage some of his guilt for abandoning his siblings and Isabela with false promises to return. And return rich he'd said. He pictured them in their dirt-floored shacks tending smoky fires and felt ashamed, squirming on the hard bench when he remembered his foolish talk of riches.

The chapel quieted as Serra limped out from behind the simple altar to take his place at the platform installed for sermons. He was a slight man with soft brown hair trimmed in the rounded style of monks. His fifty-five-year-old face was worn with lines. He wore the gray robe of the Franciscans, a thick rope knotted at his waist with a wooden cross attached. A set of rosary beads looped through the belt clicked at his hip.

Diego held his breath and a few soldiers gasped as Father Serra stumbled but caught himself as he ascended the steps to the dais. Everyone knew the venerated religious leader had a badly infected leg from an injury back in the central mountains. It caused him to limp and wince in pain. Yet still, he had walked across México's

45

treacherous landscape multiple times, dragging the leg behind, never complaining. The father clutched something in his hand beside the bible. Diego couldn't see what it was.

"Let us pray, my fellow explorers, members of the Sacred Expedition." His voice boomed, surprising Diego with its power. "God has selected us, each one of you, to venture forth into the great unexplored vastness north of here." He pointed a finger at the crowd.

"God has selected you to tame the wild heathens, to bring God's word to all who inhabit the earth. To bring the glory of Spanish rule to our feeble brothers and sisters in the north. To those who need our enlightenment. Who need our beliefs. Who must come to God and be saved. It is a glorious mission." Diego winced as if Father Serra's pointing finger was a knife stabbing at him. He felt like he was the heathen for abandoning his Catalonian home.

Father Serra's voice rose louder and higher as he preached about their duty. About how they would extend missions further into the wilderness converting thousands more natives. How they must be devout and faithful themselves as they pursued this noble goal. His voice rose into a frenzy. As he preached, he raised a large stone above his head. Suddenly, he crashed his arm down to his chest, striking himself with the rock. Diego jumped in his seat. He and his fellow soldiers glanced quickly at each other. What was the father doing?

"All men are sinners. I too am a sinner and must atone for my sins. I must purify my thoughts and actions to achieve God's plan. You too must repent. You too must confess to those sins that all men commit," wailed the priest. Diego flinched in his seat each time Father Serra struck himself with the stone. Gasps echoed throughout the church. Native converts, the neophytes of Loreto, whispered among themselves at the back of the sanctuary. But the padre did not stop until he had completed the sermon and was ready to administer communion. He reminded them to come to confession before the next Mass.

As he kneeled and bowed his head to take communion, Diego snuck a look up at the battered father before receiving the chalice.

"Take this the blood of Christ, the body of Christ," Serra repeated in Latin as each soldier and native convert approached. Diego was struck by the tenderness in his tone then, the warmth with which he delivered communion, particularly to the neophytes.

"Bless you my child," he added in Spanish to each native and a slight smile crossed his chapped lips. Diego let the wafer melt on his tongue and looked down. Drops of blood dotted the stone next to Father Serra's *huaraches*.

How could one be so ferocious in his preaching and yet change so quickly to calm as he gave blessings to each individual? The devotion and commitment were striking. Not at all like the priests he'd known at home. On the rather lazy shore bordering Barcelona where Diego grew up, priests were barely respected, mostly out of cultural tradition. In his sleepy parish, local fathers were content to say Mass and take confessions each week, helping themselves to the tithe basket and communion cup. That was about it. They were often born the first son and expected to go into the priesthood, whether it suited them spiritually or otherwise. Many were known to have secret alliances and bastard children. As a boy he'd seen a priest, a guest at his mother's table, guzzle the dinner wine and sneakily stuff extra tortillas and rolls into his pockets. Since then Diego had been suspicious. Perhaps the monastery life was more barren than he'd realized but a priest wasn't supposed to steal, was he?

Diego could not imagine any of the village priests he knew willingly taking on conversion of a native people who spoke a strange tongue and walked about naked. It would be too much work for them to try to civilize a group that hunted desert rodents with bows and arrows, gathered edible cactus fruits and painted their bodies with plant dyes. This breed of priest devoted to religious mission and chaste, barren living was impressive, if not odd and surprising. Yet it caused an ache in his gut to watch the father beat himself. Was self flagellation required to be absolved of sin? He didn't think so but he wasn't really sure. He sure hoped not. It was confusing and Mass had not made him feel any calmer.

The soldiers gathered after the service, gossiping about the passionate *cura* and his strange ways. One claimed to have heard rumors that he whipped himself at night. Another said to watch for a vest with metal spikes he wore under his vestments. What could possibly inspire such passion?

"Yeah, he's a bit of a strange one, that priest," Diego agreed with his fellow soldiers that night around the fire. "But you gotta admire his commitment. I mean, are any of you that devoted to anything? Well, maybe you, Luis, at finding some mezcal for the night's fire, or you, Chepe, looking for a girl!" They all collapsed into laughter, passed the bottle and told more stories of the crazy Franciscan priests arriving for the mission north. "But I sure wasn't sleepy in Mass today when Father Serra preached," Diego said. Several soldiers nodded in agreement. He joked with his comrades but inside he was unsure about the father's message.

Later that night he tossed on his straw mat, sleep evading him. He pulled on his jacket and went out to the stable to check on the horses, see if he could get his thinking straight. He was conflicted. Yes, we are all sinners, that's true. But Serra's claim that every man encapsulated sin and needed to purge himself of it through physical self-torture was just going too far. How could a just God desire self-torture from his servants? He admired Serra's passionate commitment to the Church and recognized its kinship with his determination to be a good soldier for the Crown. But was his own devotion to the mission just from a lack of opportunity? Had he abandoned his siblings and Isabela out of loss and desperation? Should he have tried harder there at home?

His anguish growing rather than subsiding, he pulled his favorite stallion out of its stall. He jumped on without even saddling him up. He clicked quietly, dug in his spurless boots and rode the horse down to the beach. A half moon shone brightly over the dark water, creating a white band of light shimmering across the swell. Tiny waves lapped at the shore and the *shoosh, shoosh* calmed his nerves. He rode on, steering the horse to trot on the hard sand bordering the water line.

Wasn't Mass supposed to help you feel better, remind you to follow the commandments and serve the Lord as you went forth? Father Serra's Mass had just stirred up his guilt and raised questions. Maybe he should go to confession. Maybe it would help relieve the tightness in his chest whenever he thought of Spain and the life he'd fled. He longed for the cool breezes off the Mediterranean, the streams filled with trout that easily slithered right into his hands. The markets and the bustle in the streets. His blacksmith colleagues and even Sundays in church with his family. His father was the only thing he now was happy to have escaped. New Spain so far was filled with nothing but harsh landscapes and then yet more wilderness. No family. No Isabela. Maybe if he hadn't been so selfish, so focused on his own loss, so fearful of the future, he wouldn't have volunteered so rashly for the dragoons and fled his home. Now he was stuck here, worlds away from anything familiar.

He stopped the stallion to just sit and stare at the moon and its shining ray beaming across the dark water. The opposite of a shadow he thought. No, forget confession. I've got to survive here. I'm in their service. As a child, Diego had always despised confession, cynically listening for the padre to slur his words or call him the wrong name. Never expecting any redemption from being assigned Hail Marys. Father Serra's preaching was compelling, sure, but in the end Diego wasn't convinced he was a sinner. Or one bad enough to beat himself. Yes, he'd made mistakes but looking back now was not going to be productive. He was just determined to survive on this sacred mission. He'd made a vow to God after all. He did take that seriously.

"I've dedicated this life to God and the King and the glory of Spain. I've nothing to confess," he said right out loud to the horse and the soft breakers turning neon white in the moonlight. He patted the horse's neck, punched his heels into its flanks and rode down the sand toward the mission, his thick dark hair bouncing in sync with the gallop.

Armed with the one-hundred-and-sixty-year-old journal from Sebastián Vizcaíno's expedition and stories of Juan Cabrillo's earlier discoveries, Governor Portola followed the history, and the more contemporary written instructions from King Carlos, to lead the Sacred Expedition northward. Into unknown territory. To colonize Alta California. He divided the group into land and sea parties. Their first goal was a bay Vizcaino had named San Diego. The explorers would meet up there. Diego was ecstatic to be assigned to Lead Scout Ortega's land group

It took weeks to ride up parched Baja California. The desert sun beat down, sucking all moisture out of the parched soil. Native translators escaped. Dehydrated horses perished. They often had to ride longer than was ideal to find a stopping place with a spring. Sometimes they were able to trade dried figs, corn and tobacco with local natives for fish, roasted agave stalks and mussels. Sometimes not. Baja's indigenous were exceedingly poor. Many seemed barely above starvation themselves. They mostly wanted food. Some followed the expedition in quiet, furtive groups. Others ventured bravely out and wanted to trade immediately. Others were fearful at first but then, smelling food or seeing their colorful clothes, could be convinced to emerge. Many of the natives liked the beads and handkerchiefs. One tried to trade for Father Serra's sole pair of glasses.

They pressed on, Serra limping along, often refusing to ride any of the mules. As they approached the San Diego Bay meeting spot, the landscape mellowed, appearing more fertile and lush. A cool breeze came off the ocean and they passed several streams, green hillsides visible in the distance. Exhausted but hopeful for a more agreeable climate, the weary land platoon straggled in to the bay with renewed optimism. Diego and his comrades quickly discovered they had made the trip relatively unscathed compared to the others.

Near the harbor, the supply ship's sails were being used as a large hospital tent where surviving sailors were suffering from scurvy. Most everyone assigned to the sailing parties was dead or sick. Even the doctor was ailing. There was little the healthier soldiers and padres could do for the infirm. It was a gruesome scene. Seeing their bodies with no teeth, hair falling out, bleeding right out of their skin with no apparent injury, in agonizing pain, Diego was even more relieved he'd been on the land expedition. He and his exhausted but healthier comrades hastily built a fence of brush and beams around the hospital tent.

That night, and every night thereafter, natives attacked the make-shift buildings, shooting arrows into the encampment and sick bay. In one attack Father Serra's personal servant was shot with arrows and killed. Serra demanded Portola's troops build a substantial stockade around the priest's scrappy settlement and the infirmary. This would be the Alta California's first mission, Serra proclaimed. It had to be protected.

Diego doubted there were any natives compliant enough to recruit here but he did as ordered and helped build a stronger wall around the Spanish huts. Except for the tiny groups in the Baja desert, most of the natives he'd encountered on the journey so far had been in missions toiling under the priests' control. Father Serra seemed perturbed at the attacks but Diego's leaders seemed less surprised. They were going into new territory after all. Military men were trained to expect there might be local resistance.

Of the three hundred who had started the journey back in Loreto, only half made it the nine hundred miles north to San Diego. Over the next few weeks, Serra's infection grew worse, his spirits diminished at the lack of native conversion, at the loss of so many. Portola insisted they continue the mission. Serra agreed to let the military leader take a much smaller group north, following Vizcaino's description toward la *Bahia de Monte del Rey*.

Diego was determined to continue north with the military leaders and worked hard to win Sergeant Ortega's favor. He could not stay in this God forsaken San Diego and with the mono-focused Father Serra. He decided he'd walk north on his own if he had to. Fortunately, Ortega did select him for the land expedition. Portola dispatched a supply ship to depart at the same time. They would meet up at the bahía.

Diego admitted to no one he was thrilled to bid farewell to San

Diego. To say goodbye to the scurvy ridden. To walk north from the makeshift fort and nights filled with barrages of arrows. And he was desperate to leave the sickly and obsessively devout Father Serra behind. While he admired the priest's sense of purpose, Diego's survival instinct, his sense of duty to his sergeant and a lack of anything to lose kept him going. For him, the mission to bring God to the natives was secondary. They didn't seem particularly interested anyway.

THE GREAT BAY

Ortega woke his platoon of scouts early that morning. "Let's get going. Got a long day ahead. Get moving, you lazy soldiers. You drank too much of that spoiling beer last night. I heard you 'round the fire. You'll pay today." He laughed as he kicked the dragoons and *soldados de cuera* awake.

Diego rolled off his bed of pine needles, straightened his filthy clothes and pulled on his boots. There was not enough fresh water for cleaning, just for drinking. That's why they'd drunk the overly fermented beer. Everyone was tired and thirsty. He took a swig from his goatskin bag, preserving his small stash for the day ahead.

"I want to get up the ridge this morning," Ortega growled. "We've got to see what's up there and then head back to Portola's camp to report. We leave soon."

Diego walked over to the scouting group's cook who doled out the food supplies, then gnawed on his small piece of dried tack meat. He took tiny bites, chewing it very slowly in order to extend its reach to cut his hunger and give him energy. He tried not to picture venison roasts or the spiced beans he craved. He'd survived the ship so most anything seemed luxurious in comparison, but he knew they were all hungry, growing weak. Yet none complained. Soldiers always, the men cleaned up camp, climbed onto their saddles and followed Ortega up the slope.

The sagebrush and manzanita were so thick they had to dismount to lead the horses over felled buckeyes and laurel. They machete-chopped through tightly packed madrone so hard its red, peeling trunks felt like iron. Finally, the soldiers reached a moraine then proceeded north to yet one more ridge sweeping above. Once at the top, Diego let his horse gallop across the expanse. He inhaled deeply, taking in the fresh, cool air and scents of rye grass below the horse's hooves and the redwoods standing sentry past the meadow. He approached the final crest of the hill to join his commander.

Suddenly, up ahead, Ortega stopped his horse and gasped. He did not move. Ortega was a seasoned soldier who did not shock easily. What could have gotten his attention? Diego and his colleagues almost ran into each other behind him. The horses shied and bucked, whinnying loudly at the sudden halt. Diego and the soldiers crowded around the frozen sergeant to look at the view.

An enormous bay, winding south through the hillside below and far up to the northeast, stretched out before them. Another mountain top obscured some of the view but they could see a gap where likely the bay met the sea. Large and small islands rose near its mouth and tributary rivers poured into its meandering shores. Thin pillars of smoke spiraled upward alongside the water. Clearly many native villages found the shoreline a fruitful home. Giant squalls of birds circled and squawked in the sky. A V of pelicans surfed the thermals rising along a hill bordering the bay, aligned in a calm float, not one bird flapping.

Diego's eyes gaped wide. He echoed Ortega's astonished gasp and dug his knees into the horse's flanks to quiet him. For just a moment, the scouting party was completely still, the quiet interrupted only by the swish of a horse tail, the thud of hooves as the animals shifted their weight.

Even though he was a poor, barely literate boy with little education beyond the blacksmith's shop and the Bible, Diego knew that no such bay existed anywhere in Spain. He suspected that no such magnificent port existed anywhere in Nueva España either, even all the way south to Peru and Chile. What a sight. What a discovery for their King.

At that moment, high above the great bay, Diego's anguished guilt at abandoning his brothers and sisters and Isabela, his despair at his mother's untimely death, his fears of ocean journeys, scurvy, and native attacks tumbled beneath his promise to God. He felt as if the Lord, who until this moment he very much doubted had any interest in Diego Castro Cardona, had reached down and alighted a hand on his shoulder. This powerful force coalesced his many pains, his guarded hopes, his loneliness and melded it into one purpose. An ambition. A reason for living beyond survival.

Suddenly, it was crystal clear to him why he was on this earth, why he'd been drawn to the dragoons and the New World. Why he had to sacrifice his Spanish home. The magnificence below him, this great bay of all bays would become a central port for Spain and he would be a part of the new civilization that would develop here. He would be the conqueror and builder of a great port city for the King and God's glory. He doubted even the English had a place quite as grand.

As the horses stirred, restless under their subdued masters, Diego pictured the wharves of Barcelona on the shores of this bay below. He imagined the ships of Veracruz, San Blas and Acapulco sailing into these new waters, bringing Spanish culture, language, gold and silver and the Church to the teeming land. And more than anything he'd ever wanted in his life, he wanted to be a part of it.

"Oh, Sergeant Ortega, it's magnificent, isn't it?" he couldn't help himself uttering to his commander. "What a great bay you've found for Spain. Let's go explore it. We must alert the viceroy and the King of this important discovery. This will be a great port for the Crown, for our ships in Manila and Acapulco. We must let them know of a Spanish claim before any English or Russians find it."

He stopped, embarrassed. But Father Crespi echoed his sentiment whispering, "All of Europe could take shelter in this enormous bay."

A new energy flowed into Diego as if the bay itself had nourished him. Of course, he'd bragged about coming back to Spain a rich man, but in reality, he'd had no idea how he'd accomplish anything to match his bravado. Diego had always been, simply, a survivor. In his father's barren home, on board ship, as a dragoon on the dangerous Sacred Expedition. Now, he felt transformed. He was a missionary, a pioneer. A man with purpose. This land, this bay, they were his destiny. Here he could become a man of importance. Here he could thrive.

Ortega regained his composure, nodded to the padre and had his senior dragoon plant a flag. They dismounted and Father Crespi led a short ceremony declaring the bay below the property of Spain, and to be used for the glory of their Catholic God represented by the pope. And they prayed.

After the ceremony, Ortega turned to Diego, "No, Fantasma, unfortunately, we don't have time to explore this place. Look at its size. That will have to be an entire new expedition. We must return to Portola, tell him what we've found. I expect he'll want to get quickly to San Diego for supplies. For Father Serra and the others. But we'll come back."

Diego was disappointed. But he was not in command. He trusted Ortega's instincts. Duty forced him to obey.

⌒

"Don Jose Francisco, sir, sergeant, sir...we need to slaughter a mule. We're starving, sir. Pardon my impudence, but we're going to die. We're not going to make it back to San Diego and the others." Diego whispered to his commander, pretending to bring him a goatskin full of water at the evening's fire. He was careful to not let anyone else hear him, a lowly dragoon, making suggestions.

Ortega took a sip of water and nodded. Red lines covered the whites of his eyes and his sallow cheeks appeared to be sinking as if under the weight of his mustache. Diego crawled back to the soldiers' sleeping area startled at how weak the sergeant looked. Ortega was a giant to him, even more important than Portola or Captain Rivera. He had demonstrated confidence in Diego's riding and horse care skills and had singled him out to join his expeditionary force, to travel with the land party. Just for that, Diego was forever in his debt.

His new ambitions told him that Ortega could continue to move up in the ranks and that if he stuck by his side, as if a seamstress had sewn them together, he just might survive and even prosper in this new land. Someday. Right now, they just needed something to eat. The return journey had been even more arduous than coming north. It was colder and rained almost constantly. A northerly wind kept up at their backs. The basic foodstuffs—hardtack beef, corn *masa* for tortillas and beans—were gone. They'd found no friendly natives with whom to trade or plentiful rivers to fish. Several soldiers had died. More were weakening. Yesterday, a soldier Diego had sailed out of Cadiz with so long ago had not woken up for the morning's weak coffee. Their last two remaining native translators had disappeared in the night, just days after their trail left the coastal cliffs to wind inland through more passable land.

Now, so close to San Diego but the survivors too weak to walk further, Governor Portola did as many had been thinking and ordered the soldiers to butcher a mule. Diego had been nervous about saying anything to his sergeant the night before but was relieved at their leader's order. Had Ortega listened to him? Maybe even suggested it to Portola? The sickly-sweet smell of the blood drifted off the campfire and the horses stirred and whinnied, as if protesting the sacrifice of one of their own.

Diego patted his own steed as the cook began to roast pieces of meat over the coals. His horse nudged him for a treat but his pockets were empty. "We all have to sacrifice, *amigo*. This is the only way. Or we'll all die out here," he whispered in the stallion's ear.

When Diego and the diminished scouting party stumbled in to the San Diego encampment they found Father Serra in no better shape. The simple fort buildings had been attacked by the natives repeatedly. Not one native had been converted and baptized. Many soldiers and priests had sickened. More had died. No supply ships had arrived from central New Spain. The *San Jose* supply ship sent north toward Monte del Rey never showed up during their exploration north but had not returned to the bay either. They suspected it had been lost at sea.

As the scouting party leaders recounted their northern adventures to Serra and his few survivors, Diego eavesdropped. The entire force was so small now he could sit around the leadership's fire and listen in on most any conversation

"Hey, Fantasma. Maybe that's the wrong nickname, kid. It should be *Sombra*, Shadow. You're always right next to me. Maybe that's good. Could be useful," Ortega told him as they settled in for yet another meeting between the leaders. Diego was determined to stay until they chased him away. He knew that to them he was just a young, uneducated dragoon who'd volunteered to escape poverty.

"We must return to Loreto," Father Serra told the survivors. "No supply ships, no mission. We can't survive here." He scolded them for not finding their goal, the bay of Monte del Rey.

Portola countered, arguing that there was opportunity in the north. "Padre, the natives north of here are friendly. We can trade with them. There are elk grazing everywhere. The sea is teaming with shellfish and the streams are plentiful, loaded with fish. Padre, we still needed to find this Bahia de Monte del Rey. We cannot abandon the King's mission after coming so far, getting so close."

Portola launched into a full report of their scouting expedition. Villages dotted the coastline, some tiny with fifty people and some large with up to eight hundred who lived in huts made of branches and reeds. They hunted small animals and lived off fish, seals, whale meat, shellfish. Farther north, the temperature grew milder, a lushness in the land increased, as if an artist had splashed green and blue paint before they'd arrived. Colorful flowers coated the hillsides. At almost every bay the explorers saw whales spouting and heard seals barking from the rocky shore. Portola and his commanders painted a rosy picture.

In some sections of the journey, the coast was too rugged to cross they explained. They had to move inland to find fresh water and a clear pathway. At one larger bay, they had stopped and debated if it was Vizcaino's Bahia de Monte del Rey. They noted the point with pine trees he had mentioned but it seemed less impressive than the description of a large bay shaped like an O. Fog hugged the coastline and it was difficult to tell where the bay might begin and end. Portola explained he'd decided it was not the coveted Monte del Rey and ordered them farther north. Then the scouts had found the enormous bay, which they'd claimed for Spain.

As Diego overheard Portola, Rivera and Ortega recount their adventures to the San Diego contingent, his mind had returned, as it did so often now, to the great bay he envisioned filled with the galleons of Barcelona and Acapulco. He imagined long wharves filled with men hawking fish, exotic wares from Manila, sugar from the islands, elegant furniture and cloth from Spain. He pictured cattle hides from this new frontier in exchange. The northern lands were so fertile, he was quite sure that horses and cows would flourish there.

Father Serra was skeptical. "What are you saying? Look at the losses. You didn't find Monte del Rey—the whole reason for going after all. Governor, let's be honest, your few men who survived did it by eating the mules. How can you say it's a fertile land in the north?"

"Now we know where to go, Father," Portola said. "We know where to avoid the coast with the mountains and how to traverse up the inland valleys. Let's get our soldiers and padres back into good health, strengthen everyone up. Then go north again. I think we found the bahía. We know where it is now. Plus we must secure the enormous bay for Spain. We must establish outposts there before the Russians find it." Diego completely agreed with his commanders. He would not go back to that destitute mission in Loreto.

Serra relented but said the surviving soldiers must first improve the fledgling fort around their tiny mission. "We can't convert natives until we are safe here and then can venture out to trade and bring them in," Serra said. "And Don Gaspar, we can only hold out for so long. If the supply ship doesn't show up, we return to La Paz and Loreto. We can make it for three months, but no longer."

"Agreed," Portola said and shook the padre's hand and clapped him on the shoulder. "They'll be here, don't worry, Padre. North is our future."

Three months later there was still no supply ship from San Blas and Diego was desperately disappointed that his leaders were packing up, preparing to leave the fledgling fort. He couldn't imagine returning to barren southern Baja and its impoverished missions. And what of the great bay? Spain must have it. What if it fell into Russian hands? They were rumored to be up farther north where it was cold and frozen. And the English? What if they captured that bay? That would be even worse. Hadn't Father Crespi told Father Serra what they'd seen from the hillside that day? He was eager to whisper these questions into the fervent Padre Serra's ear. But he was too unimportant to intervene. No one would listen to him. He followed orders and spent his days cutting down trees to build a strong barricade around the missionaries.

On the last morning before departure there was a loud cry from the beach and everyone looked up to see masts and sails heading their way. The *San Antonio* had arrived. Diego and his fellow soldiers rushed to the beach with Father Serra limping along, up and down, behind them. They splashed into the waves and called out to their sailor colleagues. Diego was ecstatic. Maybe now the expedition could continue on.

To their horror, instead of a celebratory cheer from the decks, they heard silence. Moaning. Two sailors managed to drop a dinghy and row to shore. The others, who hadn't already died and been thrown overboard, were sick with scurvy. Again. Even the captain had bleeding gums, wobbly teeth falling out as he ate, strange patches of missing hair on his head, blood oozing out of his legs and open bleeding on his arms and torso. Diego shuddered at the horrific sight as he loaded dead bodies and the barely living out of the same rowboat onto the shore.

They buried the victims in the dunes along the bay. They brought the remaining sick into the fort's makeshift hospital. Then Diego and the soldiers raided the ship for much needed supplies.

"It is a sign from God," Father Serra pronounced after the Mass for the dead. "We'll continue north, Governor Portola, once everyone is healthy."

Finally, north again, Diego thought as he packed his saddlebags and prepared Ortega's horses. This time they knew the better routes, the length of the journey, good locations to set up camp along the way. Portola thought they could find the Monte del Rey Bay. Master horseman Ortega always was assigned the land party. Diego was now so familiar to the sergeant that he was included in his platoon without question.

As they rode out of the San Diego presidio encampment, leaving two priests to proselytize to the local natives and a small contingent of soldiers to protect them, Diego's focus was on the future, the northern lands. He hoped the spectacular great bay would be their final destination. Maybe they could finally stop in what he was convinced was a land of plenty. He thought Governor Portola and Captain Rivera and Sergeant Ortega must see the opportunity there. If he were the commander, he mused as he jounced in the saddle since he'd now been assigned a horse, no longer a mule or ordered to walk, that would be the final destination. But he was not in charge.

A SOLDIER FOR THE
CALIFORNIAS

BAHÍA DE MONTERREY, ALTA CALIFORNIA

1770–1773

*I*t was years since Diego had been in a confessional, so even a makeshift one of rough-cut pine trunks, bark slabs, adobe bricks, and muddy clay mortar intimidated him. He'd almost forgotten that you were supposed to pretend you didn't know who was on the other side of the confessional. In this one, the priest and confessor were separated by a torn piece of canvas from a ship's sail. The fabric flapped in the breeze and the father held it stable with his hand, skinny fingers visible to the confessor.

Diego's guilt over his broken promise to return to Spain continued to haunt him. But that was not what had prompted him to finally attend confession. Once again, he feared all the pioneers might die and could no longer keep quiet. After several years surviving the dangerous expedition as an order-following soldier, Diego had agonized over criticizing his superiors. But Father Serra was their spiritual leader, he rationalized. And if they all died, it sure wouldn't help the father reach his goals of establishing a mission here.

"Father, I promised a girl I would return to Spain and marry her. I promised my brothers and sisters I would return rich to care for them after my mother died. But I can never go back, Father. My destiny is here in the Americas. I lied to them all," he confessed.

"My son, I hear your anguish. You are paying for your sins of pride and falsehoods with your guilt. But you must also pray and say your Hail Marys regularly. You soldiers are now serving God's purpose. He will protect your siblings. Your work is here now, soldier.".

Diego lowered his voice to a whisper. "Thank you, Father, but there's more. I fear Governor Fages will kill us soldiers. We've no supplies left. He orders us to cut trees, mix mud bricks and build the church and fort walls from sunup to sunset. Even on Sundays after we come to your Mass." Diego particularly wanted to emphasize that point. "The food is dwindling. It's too hilly and rocky to grow anything. The estuary's fresh water is often salty from the sea. He saves the best supplies for you and the padres. We're starving, sir."

The father cleared his throat. He said rather loudly, "Bless you my son. Pray daily and be sure to attend Mass and confession. Ten Hail Marys on your rosary." Then he dropped his voice to a whisper. "My son, I've seen and heard of these problems. I'm already looking for a better place to grow corn and beans, and for the horses to graze. Drink as much milk as you can," he said. Diego squirmed in the hard chair, surprised that the priest was so responsive.

Then the father continued, "And my son, when I move the mission, you must be a leader. You must tell the soldiers there will be better food after we move. Because they will see it as more work to build yet another chapel and barracks. God has shown me that I must move the mission but I will count on your assistance in this holy campaign. There's a future here, soldier. There are many natives and we can baptize them if we build a mission away from the presidio. Go with God, my son."

"Bless you, Father. Thank you," Diego mumbled and pushed aside the brush door to leave. A line of several soldiers waiting their turn stretched before him. He nodded to the next in line and strode off toward the makeshift cook's camp and asked for a ladle of the heavy milk that was often their only nourishment. Be a leader? Was he cut out for that? He wasn't sure his fellow soldiers respected him very much. But if they were to survive here, he'd have to do what the priest had asked.

As soon as Father Serra announced he was moving the mission over the hill beside a river's outlet to the sea, Diego praised the decision to his colleagues who'd been selected to build the new mission—*San Carlos Borromeo del río Carmelo*. The soldiers carried the mission bell to the new site, then sawed down large trees and swung the iron bell between two posts in front of the new outpost. The bell looked more formidable, more permanent, than any structure Diego had seen since Veracruz's port buildings or City of Mexico's cathedral and government palaces years before.

He'd been disgruntled that his leaders had decided to settle and build their second presidio above the bay they now called *Monterrey*. The Spanish viceroy and King declared Monterrey the capitol of Alta California. What about the enormous bay farther north? That would have been a much more dramatic location. But he was also relieved to stop moving after almost three years on The Sacred Expedition. So he took seriously Father Serra's charge to influence his fellow soldiers to build a new mission compound at the río Carmelo. The land was pretty and lush, animals and fish were plentiful throughout the watershed. Maybe they were right that this was a promising spot.

Serra quickly enticed natives from up the river to visit, trade and live at the mission, promising an afterlife in paradise. He covered them up with clothes and put them to work building a *rancheria* of native huts close by. Then he set them to making adobe bricks and stacking them atop each other to aid the soldiers in building the mission's church, dormitories, kitchens and stables. Over time, he taught the baptized natives who he compelled to live at the mission to plant crops and care for the horses, sew their heavy woolen clothes and repair leather saddles and reins.

The religious leader was relentless in this campaign to establish missions and set right out to launch the next one. At each verdant spot near a river or spring, Father Serra would stake out the land, construct preliminary huts and then leave two priests to convert the local natives with nothing but a few sacks of beans, corn, and if there was one to spare, a mule. The fledgling mission also was assigned an *escolta*, a contingent of just four or five soldiers to protect the priests and livestock.

Desperate to not be left at one of these bleak, isolated outposts, Diego decided to make himself indispensable to his military leaders, to do anything to remain in Ortega's battalion for each new exploration. Not all natives or village leaders accepted Father Serra's conversion plans. Some fled the mission after agreeing to be baptized. Some staged revolts, burning mission buildings, attacking with arrows and stealing horses. Many refused to participate altogether. While on the trail and stationed at the Monterrey presidio, Diego observed this new reality and decided his best option was to forge himself into a superior fighter.

He perfected his native suppression skills in those early years. He observed the baptized natives, and those who stayed in their villages, as they hunted quietly. He watched how they used the moon's light and dark to their advantage when tracking an enemy or stealing horses. He imitated their footwear and created shoes that kept his steps soft, sewing a pair of deer hide boots like he'd seen on an elder and the best hunters at a ranchería adjacent to the San Luis Obispo mission. He rubbed his body with herbs to hide his Spanish smell. Adopting many native practices, he became known for quick, quiet, surprise attacks and just as rapid disappearances, earning his "Ghost" nickname but on land this time and for a very different reason. When necessary, he was a ferocious fighter.

From the most agreeable converts, he learned to negotiate with sign language and adopted native terms likely to bring leaders into the mission, often prompting villagers to follow. He learned how to strap up the company's food supply in camp so as not to attract grizzlies at night. And he learned how to hunt the bear if it did get the food. Diego made himself into the consummate soldier. That was the only way to survive in this wilderness as the colonizers wore the *El Camino Real* path into a road, establishing mission after mission along the coast and in its nearby, abundant valleys.

Diego stirred on the ground next to the fire's embers, then fully awoke as he sensed the moonlight dipping below the black silhouette of the steep hillside above them. At twenty, he already had years of trail experience and had perfected his Fantasma persona to earn respect among his fellow soldiers. Most of them were content to let him lead the mini-campaigns when no higher officer was included. This particular night, the dragoons around him still slept, one snoring loudly. He kicked the snorer's leg to quiet him. Diego removed his riding boots and slipped on the deerskin ones he saved for just such escapades.

Now he was up in the mountains near San Antonio de Padua. The villagers nearby had stolen the fledgling mission's horses and he'd been assigned the recovery effort. There weren't many missing. El fantasma could handle this alone. No need to wake the others. Before leaving the camp, he alerted the two night guards that he was off to recoup the stolen horses. "You stay here while I round up the horses but be sure to open up the barley sack for them to smell. Get some water buckets out and have your *reatas* ready to rope them if any run astray. I'm pretty sure they'll head this way." The soldiers pulled out their long rawhide ropes used for lassoing cattle and horses.

He padded out of the camp and headed toward the village huts sniffing for any campfire, ears pricked for bears or native lookouts hiding in the brush. He dropped clumps of barley and hay in a few spots along the route. He felt the presence of something up ahead and stopped under a large sycamore tree to wait and watch, his ears straining for the familiar sounds of horses restless in an unfamiliar setting at night. He barely moved, his breath shallow and quiet, his eyes scouring the dark landscape. Ah, there it was. The smell of manure and horse hair.

He turned in the direction and followed the scent to a scrappy corral the native hunters must have built to keep the stolen horses from running off. He crept closer, slowly, so as not to spook them and lose the advantage of silence. Finally, he could just see the full ring of the corral, its gate, and counted six horses held there. Any wrong move and a horse could wake up, smell him and alert the others and ruin the whole effort. There were likely guards with bows and arrows on post but he didn't see any. He moved in slowly, as if he were a mountain lion stalking his prey, one tiny step at a time. Patience, he told himself, as always.

Finally, he reached the wooden gate. Diego slowly pulled up the pine latch, swung open the gate, then retreated to a nearby oak tree, clicking his tongue and waving the barley to get the horses' attention. Climbing the tree, he wrapped the grain tight in the end of his sash to hide its smell then watched as the horses awoke, caught the scent of barley and hay he'd left on the trail to the soldiers' encampment and ran out the fencing.

Once all were out, he jumped down from the tree, moved over to latch the pine gate, just to drive the thieves even more crazy, then ran back toward the camp, roping a straggler mare along the way. He climbed up on and rode toward where the guards should be roping and hobbling the recovered horses. He was pretty sure no one had seen him or noticed the escape. They'd awake to an empty corral and a mystery of where the horses had gone. El fantasma had struck again.

Suddenly, he felt a piercing pain in his back, like a fire red knife digging into his shoulder. A guard must have woken and seen him latch the corral or catch the last horse. He picked up his speed. Arrows flew all around him as he jammed his heels into the horse's flanks. Damn, of course, no spurs.

He felt another hot flash of pain in the opposite hip. He'd been hit again. He moved the reins to his left hand, pulled his pistol from his breeches with his right while searching for a protected spot. Diego jerked the horse abruptly in behind a cluster of tangled manzanita brush and turned to peer through the branches. He swung himself off the horse and bent down in the bushes searching for his foe while swinging the reins around a branch and offering the horse a handful of barley. The pain in his shoulder and hip burned hot and sharp.

He'd been pierced by poisoned arrows before and quickly grazed the wounds with his fingers to assess the damage. While his shoulder just bled, an obsidian point was lodged in his hip. Not good. He'd have to get back to Monterrey for a doctor to remove it. Or a vet; there wasn't always a doctor around these barren outposts. He cursed himself for leaving his leather armor at the campsite. He had wanted to maintain his stealth and ability to move quickly.

He saw movement now in the clearing beyond the hiding spot. Two natives on horseback galloped his way. They must have hitched these stolen horses close to their sleeping huts. Clever. The riders pushed the horses hard toward him and he quickly assessed he had no option but to shoot; his horse wasn't shielded by the hiding spot and would be visible to them soon. Diego knew the range of his pistols and waited until they rode closer. Then he fired and shot one rider, who collapsed quickly, flopping down the side of his horse. The horse slowed to a stop. He shot at the other and appeared to have hit him in the chest. The rider swung backward while pulling on the reins to stay mounted. He lay back on the horse and moaned.

Diego waited a few beats to be sure no others were on their way. Then he stepped out from the brush and walked over to the man on the ground, grabbing the frightened horse on the way. They were just kids. A young native boy, maybe ten or eleven, lay on the ground, a hole through his chest.

Diego cursed out loud, "God damn gentiles sending their kids to steal horses and attack soldiers. What're they thinking?" At least this one never knew what hit him.

He hobbled the horse and went to grab the other one, spooked, turning in circles as his rider bounced and moaned on his back. Diego calmed the horse, untangled his attacker and rolled him on the ground. Blood poured out of his chest. There was no exit wound at his back. The ball of lead must have lodged in his sternum. The kid would never make it and was suffering.

Diego reached into his holster and pulled out his second pistol and shot the boy in the head. The only Christian thing to do. He grabbed the horses and went to recover the third, then mounted and rode back to the soldiers' camp. The natives would come for their boys in the morning, he was quite sure. They had their own burial rituals he knew, so he felt no remorse at leaving the bodies out in the dust. He'd had to recoup the Spanish horses. Mission accomplished. Why were the natives stealing them all the time and getting their own killed? God damn them, why the hell were they letting kids stand guard?

THE VILLAGE

Coastal Alta California

1773

While Ma and the aunts worked around the fire, Tar darted like a hummingbird between the tule huts, then blended into the manzanita and disappeared into the mist of whispery fog. No one seemed to notice her disappear. The wiry girl slipped downhill toward the ocean, grateful for the squawking gulls overhead that would distract the women. She reached into her favorite hiding place in the crevice of a granite boulder, her fingers finding the stones she had shaped into tools. Armed with her supplies, she scampered over the sand to the algae-coated tide pools and used her arms to steady herself as she balanced across the rocks on calloused feet.

Sighing with satisfaction at today's larger than usual pools, she crouched down on her haunches and set to work searching for mussels and abalone to pry off the rocks. Her long straight hair fell and swayed in the wind. Her hands moved quickly and her strong legs held her firmly above the quiet pools. The angry sea sloshed and sprayed just beyond her perch. Tar hummed a tune she'd heard her mother and aunts singing lately, telling of the spring flowers coming to the hills. Soon it would be time to leave the shore and head inland to the budding grasses and plentiful elk the lyrics promised.

A pelican peeled away from his clan surfing the thermals and soared high, then slowed overhead. Pushing out his feet for landing, he hit the ground next to her. She waved her arms and screamed at him to protect her haul, but it was too late. His companions had noticed her catch and began swirling above, crying out to each other. She knew from experience that a group of pelicans would not leave her alone. They'd peck her head and thwack her with their wings to get any opened shellfish if she didn't finish up quickly. She scraped a last mussel off the rock, wrapped her collection in a deer skin pouch and stepped over the tide pool borders, past the splashing waves, to head for home.

Once on the shore, she broke into a run. She had to get back before anyone noticed her absence. She was in trouble with *Atsia*, Ma, so often lately. Tar, named after the moon, with obsidian eyes and hair black as night, was not supposed to go to the shore alone for shellfish. After thirteen winters she was determined to explore farther than the prescribed routes around the village huts.

Every chance she got, she snuck off to the sea or scrub brush. In the bushes, she'd try to catch hummingbirds with her bare hands or sneak up behind deer unnoticed like her brothers could do. At the shoreline, Tar loved the roiling breakers, the lazy seals and precocious otters. Her sharp eyes followed their paths through the green water to troves of shellfish. Then she'd skip over to the treasure and move in with her nimble fingers and tools. She was great at finding the saltiest mussels and most tender abalone.

Lost in thought about how she would explain her absence this time, Tar scrambled up the soft dunes, under cover of the pines that adorned the coastline. The fog's heaviness filled the gaps between the conifers and deposited a wetness on the branches and dampened the needle-covered forest floor.

Steps from the village, just below the crest of the hill, Tar felt a vibration under her feet. The earth seemed to move. At first she thought it was an earthquake, a movement to pay attention to but not to fear. Then she heard screaming and loud voices yelling in an unfamiliar language. She stopped, almost losing the shells. She scrambled behind a pine, dropped to all fours and crawled slowly toward the hilltop, listening intently, knees scraping the dirt and pine needles. Tar darted behind another tree trunk to see what was going on. Tule and willow smoke hit her nose first before she saw flames. The village was burning.

Tar tried to make sense of it from her hiding place. The wet air smelled acrid. She heard men yelling strange words. Footsteps and a shrill clanking. More shaking ground. Then she heard cries she could recognize. More screams and pounding. She had to get to her parents and brothers and sisters.

She crawled closer, still clutching her bag of shells, trying to stay hidden between the trees. Suddenly, she felt her hair pulled up like a tule rope, almost lifting her off the ground. She screamed as a pair of strong arms grabbed around her waist and neck. The man with heavy deerskin covering his chest yelled to his companions. He stank. She struggled to get free.

He dragged her up the hill to the village where the flames were licking higher and higher. They jumped to the manzanita and then raced up the pine trunks, thirsting for the needles above, spitting as they consumed each drop of mist. She tried to break away to run toward her father and siblings on the far side of the huts but the soldier grabbed her hair again, slapped her across the face, sending her to the ground, kicked her and growled something she didn't understand. He poked her with a strange kind of stick, heavy and solid, pushing her into a cluster of captive villagers.

Past the soldiers, she could see her father and mother, older brothers and younger sisters, several cousins and the village chief all crouched on the ground, terror on their faces. How could she get to them? Even though her eye swelled immediately, closing around the blood pouring down her cheek, she noticed that her eldest brother and his new wife were not among the captives.

A soldier placed a large rope around each man's leg and attached them one to another at the ankle. The rope clinked strangely and looked more solid than any tule rope or elk sinew she had ever seen. They were pushed to walk together, dragging the leg weighted down with the heavy rope and jerking each other with different paces. Many collapsed, pulling others down with them until they determined a rhythm. Babies strapped to their mothers' backs cried. Women yelled at the strange soldiers. The men of her tribe pounded at the guards and heavy rope with only their hands. All weapons were back in their storage sheds now engulfed in flames. No arrows to shoot, no poison to lace obsidian arrowheads. No one had expected a raid.

Tar remembered she'd heard the mothers, as they ground and cooked acorns, discussing the strange new men who had come in to the land in the last few seasons. They were moving closer to the village. Sometimes she crept out at night to the sweat lodge and listened to her father and the elders. They too talked of this new creature who'd appeared with thick, curling hair and hairy bodies, gray skin and terrible smells, foul sounding language. These new men appeared disconnected from any of the other nearby tribelets.

Tar had relatives that had married and moved away to a different village where their language was funny sounding. But they did not look or act very different from her own people. They too lived in tule huts, gathered acorns, hunted elk, feared the grizzly and delighted in shooting quail in the meadows and gathering shellfish from the rocks. Sometimes, they visited each other's' villages to share stories of their neighbors and check in with family members, often learning a few words of each other's languages.

These pale men were different. She had heard they rode on large animals. Now, her eyes widened at seeing the frightening beasts for the first time. The new tribesmen were rumored to slaughter other animals with long horns in bloody enclosures away from their own buildings, attracting bears. The men were harsh in appearance and action. They built strange huts from dirt and sand and grass that were dark and airless. Their words were unintelligible. They wore heavy clothing even when it was hot. "They have brutal weapons. These new people in our land are dangerous," her father had warned.

Rumors started floating among the Rumsen and other Ohlone groups along the coast. The word spread among the Esselen and Salinan. Stories emerged of some people moving to these strange men's villages. They heard of imprisoned natives forced to build the clay huts. A few native men were learning to ride the invaders' large animals. Others were converting to their strange religion. And then within the past year, Tar's own tribe had shrunk.

Several young men not accepted into the leadership inner circle and sweat lodge had left and moved into the strangers' village. A widow joined them and a few families also disappeared. The elders scoffed that they were tempted by pretty beads, meat from the new animals, cloth that the strangers seemed to wear in great abundance, and a powerful alcohol they used in ceremonies. She was old enough now to sense that her father was wary about this disruption of their usual patterns. Of the outsiders' possible impact on the ways of the coast people. Of the peace they kept in honor of *ewshai*, their ancestors. His usually cheery countenance disappeared, lines deepening across his face had created a crevice between his brows.

Tar adored *Aha'ya*, her father. Since he'd secretly begun to teach her to hunt, against her mother's wishes, she'd tried to show him an extra kindness whenever possible. She'd sneak a mussel or two and slide it on to his pile. She poured more seal blubber than usual into his acorn porridge if her mother was looking the other way. Tar knew these small gestures could not really ease her father's troubles, but it gave her a sense of participating in the community drama. She would not just leach acorns all day.

The chief and the elders of her village, including Tar's father, had announced their refusal to trade with these new invaders, as many of the other villages were doing, and she agreed with their decision. It was just like the grizzly bear. She had been taught since infancy that if you have to fight when attacked, of course you should be prepared and fight your hardest. But it was best to stay away from Grizzly in the first place. He was a formidable enemy.

Suddenly, while Tar watched from her hillside position as soldiers ransacked the huts not yet inflamed, a man grabbed his wife, she with their newborn baby bouncing in its swaddling on her back and ran down the hill toward the ocean. A crack hit the air, so sharp and loud and strange that it shook Tar to her core. Again, she heard the cracking noise and searched for its source. The villagers' cries grew increasingly frantic and angry. She followed their gaze to see the young couple sprawled on the ground in a pool of blood. The baby screamed a harsh newborn cry until another pop pierced the air and it, too, was silent. Blood bloomed on the swaddling.

Tar was aghast and mystified. Separated from her parents, she couldn't ask them what was going on. She now regretted she'd disobeyed her mother and gone searching for shellfish. She saw one of the soldiers waving the strange, heavy stick. The villagers instantly quieted and began to march together. It was not just a stick or an arrow she now realized. Its piercing noise had the power to drop a native and make him bleed. To kill him.

The grizzly had finally attacked. Now they were in the fight.

CAPTIVES

Tar and her fellow villagers walked for miles to a wooden building, black bars lining its few windows. The soldiers separated men and boys from the women, crowding them into dark rooms with straw covering the mud floor. A guard sat out front and the heavy pine door was locked. There was no way to escape.

Tar finally found her mother and sisters among the other female captives. They hugged and clung to each other, her little sisters crying, faces streaked with dirt. Her mother's forehead was bleeding. "Atsia, what's going on?" she asked, trying to hold back her sobs, relieved at finding her mother. "Why did these horrible men put us here? We've got to get out and go save what we can of the village. I was at the shore scraping mussels and abalone off the rocks. I'm so sorry, Atsia. If I'd seen them coming, I could've run to find Ores."

She grabbed her mother's shoulder and one of her sisters' hands and pushed them into a quiet corner of the enclosure. "Look Atsia, I still have a few shells. We can eat them later if they don't give us any food. Ores must be hiding, right? Do you know where he is?"

Her mother fiercely pulled the girls to her and sat them all down.

"Stop talking so much, Tar. Keep your head down. Don't bring attention to us. We've got to stay silent to survive here, I'm quite sure. And do not mention your brother again. We could put him in danger. Understand?" Tar nodded, embarrassed at her foolishness.

The next morning, the guard allowed Tar to get water from the well outside the barracks. As she returned, she saw soldiers marching a group that included her father and brothers away from the camp. Forgetting Ma's warning in her fear, she screamed and cried, dropped the water bucket and ran after the procession. "That's my father. We're family. You can't separate us. Where are you taking them?" she called as she collapsed in sobs. "I'm his daughter, his daughter," she repeated, trying to grab at her father as soldiers herded him past.

One grabbed her hair, swung her away from the procession, yelling in his coarse language. Dragging her across the yard to the barracks, he continued his rant. He pushed her inside the building and when Atsia ran to meet her, the soldier slapped her, shoving Tar into her mother's stomach. They collapsed breathless, red-faced, blood at Atsia's lip and her ear. Inconsolable, she stretched her hands through the cold, hard poles preventing her escape.

Ma struggled to her feet and grabbed Tar. "I warned you yesterday," her mother scolded. "Now listen or you'll get us all killed. I need you to help with the little ones. You're almost a woman now so start acting like one. You can't show weakness. And where's the water? We're all thirsty in here."

"But Ma, Father and the boys were marched away. We've got to stay together and get back to the village."

"I know but you can't draw attention to yourself," her mother said. "We've got to find a way out but screaming at them is not it. Be smart." She wiped her bleeding lip and spoke more calmly. "Imagine you are sneaking up on a bird to shoot, or a small rabbit. You must be quiet in your body and mind like that," she said.

Tar looked up, quizzically.

"Don't be foolish. I know your father was teaching you to hunt the little birds. But now it just might help us. You must be quiet like when you hunt. And then we'll attack when they least expect it. Right?"

Tar nodded, admiring her mother's cunning. Maybe Atsia was better than just a corn grinder who gossiped with her sisters all day. She remembered her harvest from that morning. Quietly, secretly, with the fog shrouding her from the soldiers' gaze, she pulled an oyster from her pouch under her skirt. She found a stick to pry it open and eventually got it—her fingers strong from years of practice. She took one tiny bite, gave each of her sisters pieces and the remaining portion to her mother.

"Good girl," Ma whispered. "Now you're behaving like a quail hunter."

The next morning, their stomachs aching, the entire group was forced up and out of the paddock, the women linked together with the heavy rope that clinked. They walked over hills and down toward the river where there were more foreign structures. When they got close to the settlement, the soldiers stopped and removed the shackles, then pushed the group down the hill.

More unusual looking men appeared but this time with long gray robes and hair trimmed round their heads. They had no hair on their faces like most of the other men of this peculiar tribe. Tar searched for women but did not see any. The gray men approached and tried words of native languages. She did not hear anything familiar from her dialect. These men seemed kinder than the soldiers. Perhaps.

While they escorted the women past a construction site she saw her father, brothers and cousins working among the men and boys mixing mud and stones, cutting sticks and carrying large rocks from the riverbed. How odd they looked with brown hairy fabric covering their legs. She seldom saw her father clothed in his deer skin shawl and leggings. He covered up only when the rain or fog fell heavy or when performing ceremonial prayers to prepare for elk hunting or fighting a grizzly.

"Father, father," she screamed. "Let me go to see my father. I'm his daughter. You can't separate us," she yelled at the scratchy gray men. She broke free and ran to her father who was mixing mud and dried grass, shells and pebbles into a giant stew for bricks. He grabbed his daughter in a quick hug and then shushed her. His tone was harsh. "Stop yelling so much. You don't know what they understand."

At that moment, a large soldier with long curling black hair, a mustache and dark beard covering his cheeks, making him look like a bear, grabbed her around the waist and scooped her up. She thrashed and kicked and punched his heavy leather vest but he barely seemed to notice.

"I'm his daughter. I'm his daughter. Why can't you let me be? Put me down you big bear," Tar screamed over and over again. The soldier ignored her, carried her around the back side of the construction site and set her down in large wooden tree trunks which he locked around her ankles, never looking at her or saying a word.

She screamed and thrashed, waving her arms, grabbing at the wooden stocks, twisting her calves back and forth, rubbing her ankles against the thick wood, trying everything possible until she was exhausted. She collapsed, leaning her back against the rough wall, sobbing, realizing she could not escape. Eventually, she ran out of tears. She rubbed her swollen eyes and wet cheeks and pushed the long hair out of her face.

She searched the vista in front of her. From the line of the hills she could see where the river dropped down gently to greet the ocean at the beach so white it looked like soft rabbit fur. She had an idea where she was now but she was stuck. And far from everyone else. Away from the construction. Behind the barracks holding her mother and sisters. Hidden from the round gray men or any hairy soldiers. No one knew where she was. How would she get out of these strong tree trunks holding her legs? She spit on her hands and reached to smear her ankles with the wetness to see if she could wiggle her feet out of the stocks. When that didn't work she searched the ground for pebbles or branches she could use to pry at the wood and the strong latch, like on the mussel shells. No use. As she tried again and again, the fog drifted in past the mission buildings rolling a gray tint over the landscape, quieting the air and depositing a dew on every surface. Tar shivered. She was cold and hungry. It would be night soon.

In those first days at the mission, Tar, skinny and slight at thirteen, was placed with the young girls in the *monjerio*, the nunnery. Mistaken for being much younger than she was, she avoided the work assigned the adult female captives who cleaned the church, cooked giant vats of beans, ground corn meal and cleaned the padres' quarters. She took advantage of the arrangement, immediately sneaking out at dusk when the light receded and the padres were distracted with afternoon prayers before the soldiers locked the monerjio doors for the night.

She gathered acorns and had the little ones help her sneak them into any open pots of boiling water for leeching. She'd then grind them and add the meal into the corn masa prepared for tortillas, adding nutrients she knew her people needed to stay strong. She followed the river to the beach, scampered to the rocks and found seashells for her mother and siblings. Her mother scolded her for sneaking out thinking it was dangerous. Yet other times, she encouraged Tar to escape completely and go live with her brother, Ores, in the hills far from the mission. Atsia's conflicting instructions were confusing but she knew one thing for sure. She could never leave her family. She felt she was keeping them alive with the extra food she brought them and was pretty sure Atsia agreed.

Her mother was exhausted from long days working in the mission kitchen and weak from constant ailments. There was so much sickness around and no one knew what caused the symptoms or how to treat them. The captives no longer had access to the herbs and bushes, shells and animals that had nourished them and provided their shamans a wealth of medicinal cures. No shaman was still alive at the mission by the time her sisters and mother sickened anyway.

Tar didn't know why she didn't get as ill as the others but she was observant and careful. Her stomach seemed to tolerate the corn and bean soup with occasional squash better than the others. She noticed everyone descended into stomach pains and diarrhea when the stringy meat occasionally appeared in their stew and so she simply drank the broth. She avoided the white drink they took from the big animals with the horns, which also made so many sick. Once she had figured out her system to escape, Tar endeavored to bring her family fresh food at least several times each moon cycle.

Her efforts were not always successful. One night, a soldier, not drunk or sleepy like the usual guard, caught her and dragged her back to the stocks. Another time she stayed out too late and missed returning before the padres locked the monerjio door. Stuck outside, she slept by the horses' watering trough and a soldier found her before she woke up. Back to the stocks. Eventually she figured out which building to throw rocks at if she was forgotten there too long. The native ladies or the girls in the nunnery would complain to a padre that she was missing again and some obedient servant would be sent to retrieve her.

As more months passed, she realized that her brother would not be coming to liberate them and she grew bolder. She gathered branches and stones and crafted a bow and arrow, which she hid under her bed mat. Some nights, she'd sneak out late and stay in the nearby riverbank brush through dawn so she could shoot quail and sparrows.

Despite her craftiness, she could not prevent the terrible illness that tormented her tribe with fever and coated them with spots. The little girls succumbed first. Tar was distraught that her efforts could not save her sisters. She told herself to stay strong for Atsia but her mother lasted only weeks after her sisters were gone, dying of grief and measles. Hardened by sadness, so alone, so shocked at the complete reversal in her family's fortunes, Tar resolved to plan an escape with her remaining family members. Her brothers, however, sequestered with Aha'ya and all the men, caught the fever too. Within a year in captivity, she and her father were the sole survivors.

SHOLETA

"**A**ha'ya, *don't despair. Don't betray* our ancestors," Tar called. A guard braced her against a wall with both arms, preventing her running to her father as a priest led him and a group of native men into the church. She'd heard rumors that after almost three years at the mission, her father had agreed to be baptized as a Catholic. Probably in a desperate attempt to stay alive. Maybe this capitulation would allow him an easier job like candle making or sewing saddles. She understood he was sick and exhausted but this betrayal of their native ways saddened her deeply. How could she get to him, to stop the conversion, to reunite their tiny family?

Suddenly, she recognized the guard restraining her. Not only was he a neophyte convert, a native who'd lost his soul as far as she was concerned, but he was a man from her village. The *cacique*, her fellow tribesman, pushed her against the wall hard. "Stop yelling. It's futile, *Sholeta*," he said, calling her the name the padres had assigned her, the Ohlone word for daughter. He knew her real name. "Your father will be fine but you must stay with the girls," he ordered.

Across the plaza her father disappeared into the mission sanctuary. Defeated, she nodded and turned away from the church and Aha'ya. This double betrayal of her father converting to the foreigners' religion and her fellow tribesman serving as her jailor exhausted her. He released her and she turned back to the plaza, looking for one of her favorite horses. Her only companions these days.

Bitter when the padres started calling her *Xolita* with their Spanish accents, she realized she could try to tell them her real name, her tribe, her family lineage but not one priest or soldier cared. Not one baptized native was interested. They had given up their former village life. Why should they help her resist? Now, she was prevented from seeing her father, a convert from her own tribe calling her as the Spaniards did. After years of captivity, the suppression was suffocating. It felt complete.

Yet a spark of defiance persisted every time she spied Aha'ya. Tar screamed his name, pleading with the padres to let her live together with him in one of the family huts since her mother, sisters and brothers had all died. The low scratch of her voice became a familiar sound throughout the compound. She'd damaged her vocal cords. She'd suffered the stocks and the lash. But she refused to stop hoping that some kind-hearted padre would let the remaining family members reside together.

Rules were rules. The padres always kept the men and women separate. Any girl over eight was moved into the monjerio and locked in at night. And she refused to accept their religion so would definitely not receive any special treatment. It was all in vain and did nothing but alter her voice to a hoarse rasp and turn her hard and angry.

She also noticed that the padres' rules didn't seem to keep drunken soldiers from straying over from the presidio barracks to break in on moonlit nights. They'd grab whoever they liked, or could catch, for an evening at the makeshift saloon near the presidio, or worse, a short trip to the stocks hidden behind the mission buildings. So far, Tar had avoided serving as soldier entertainment. She'd never been off the mission grounds to the saloon and had not been raped in the stocks or up against the church walls. But she was no fool. Now sixteen, she knew her luck would not last and she was as desperate as ever to find a way to stay with her father. Or escape.

Yet she could never leave without her father. And where would she go if she left the compound alone? She'd seen what happened to the baptized natives who changed their minds after accepting the priests' religion and then decided to escape to the woods. Once the padres consulted with the presidio *comandante*, they'd send a team of soldiers and neophyte converts to yank back the wayward natives behind horses. Every soul living at the mission was herded together to see the sinners dragged in and given their sentences. She'd often wondered which was worse: the days of whippings or the fact that they'd been betrayed, recaptured and humiliated by their own kind—the native caciques.

After her mother and sisters died, Tar felt completely alone, as if she were an orphan already. Now, watching her father with the baptized neophytes, the loneliness deepened as he appeared completely oppressed by their captors. So few were willing to rebel. It seemed to her that all her former tribesmen had descended into submission to these new lords. They'd been corrupted by the invaders who addicted them to cow meat and the altar's alcohol, distracted them with sparkling beads and bright cloth. Who bribed them by training them to fancy horses and become cowboys. She had no patience for the betrayal.

Over time, the corn and weak porridge and beans made her sick too, but she hid that from the padres' eyes. She could not sleep on the molding straw and was covered with insect bite scabs, infected rashes and plagued by a constantly itchy scalp. Her hair fell out in patches. She didn't want anyone to see her as weak so she continued to care for the young children, cook vats of watery stew and round up stray horses for the missionaries. Once the priests seem to tire of her rebelliousness, she was re-assigned to construction, stirring mud, straw and rocks into adobe bricks all day. The only breaks from work were for the priests' strange rituals every seven days and for daily prayers, catechism and Spanish lessons. But she refused to acquiesce to their religious requirements or accept new beliefs.

She heard from the priests and baptized natives the promises that they would be looked after by a powerful God and his son, the skinny one bleeding and dying who they put up on most every wall. Baptized natives told her the priests promised in death they would go to a beautiful place where little babies with wings took care of you. Tar was not convinced. She would never erase the tribal elder's teachings from her mind. The lessons of her grandmothers were embedded deep as if they were etched inside her. These foreigners could name her but they would never own her Ohlone soul.

⁓

"Sholeta, wake up," the young padre said as he shook her awake in the dark. "Come quickly but be quiet. Don't wake anyone. Sh, sh."

What was going on? She didn't know this young priest but his voice was unusually kind. She picked herself up off the straw-covered floor and followed him. He said nothing more but led her toward the barracks for the baptized single men. Her father was in a small room where he lay on a thin straw mattress atop a wooden bed frame. Sholeta stumbled at the threshold to the tiny room, smelling of stale air and sickness, shocked at seeing her father in such a bad way. She'd been waiting for so long to have contact with him but this was not what she'd imagined. She knelt at his bedside and took his hand.

"We are giving your father his last rites," the priest said. "He asked for you. I hope you too will consent to be baptized. So you can go to heaven to join your father. I mean…when your time comes."

"Aha'ya, it's me, Tar. Can you hear me?" she whispered. She immediately lapsed into an Ohlone prayer, the first one that came to her mind. He stirred but did not speak. She kept praying, then asked the priest who was lingering at the door, "Was he awake? He spoke to you? I can't get him to wake up."

The priest nodded then shrugged. "I'm sorry."

She stayed on her knees for the rest of the night, praying over him, telling him why he needed to live, to not leave her alone. Atsia had her sisters and brothers in the afterlife but she needed him here with her.

"Please don't leave me, Aha'ya. Once you get better," she whispered close to his ear, "I'll take you and we'll go find Ores in the hills. I know how to escape this place. We'll find his village and live with him, together." His fingers fluttered and his shoulders moved. Was he finally waking up?

It seemed to her that she got more response when she spoke of their former life, so she talked about the elk hunt, the quail and rabbits they would find in the hills. And how when it was time to drop down to the coast again, she'd find the tasty mussels and abalone. They'd taste the salt air and paddle their tule canoe out to the best rock outcroppings for shellfish and otters. As she spoke hour after hour, her voice grew weary and even more hoarse than usual. The dawn's light slowly crept in as it rose up over the hills and down into where the river mouth met the sea.

"Aha'ya," she kept saying, "wake up and come with me."

As the pale yellow of the early sun hit the mission compound, Aha'ya stirred, opened his eyes and lifted his hand to her.

"Tar," he struggled to whisper. "Go to the hills." Then he lay back, closed his eyes and his breathing became shallow. She could feel death closing in.

"Aha'ya, stay with me. We'll return to our natural lives together. We'll keep our Ohlone traditions, our beliefs. We'll live as a family with Ores, together."

There was only silence. When soldiers came to remove the body for burial, Sholeta sat mute, unmoving, recognizing both how completely alone she was in the world and the promise that she could never abandon.

REPLACED

As *Nicole drove south toward* her childhood home, she imagined how she would break the news to her father. Great Gram refused to sell the house and was exploring legal ways to prevent any sale. Had he known that was likely when he sent her up there? Dad's motives seemed pretty focused on the dollar, not on what was best for Great Gram. Now that Nicole had been there for over a month, she felt Great Gram could manage living in the big house as long as she had daily assistance. Nicole had grown fond of her great grandmother yet had no desire to become even further alienated from her dad. She wished she weren't stuck in the middle.

As she wound through the final stretch toward the ranch, Nicole mused over ways to make the new information palatable to her father so he'd let Great Gram stay and pay for a caregiver when Nicole got another job. He and Grandpa would inherit the house in the will, right? That should be good—it would be worth a huge amount of money, multiple millions. He should be pleased with the amount the tech guy had offered, even though Great Gram had refused to sell. Probably could get even more when Great Gram eventually passed, she decided to remind him. And lower property taxes in the meantime once the historic landmark designation had been approved. He would love that. Dad hated taxes.

She turned onto the familiar long driveway and took several deep breaths to loosen the knot in her stomach. It would be fine. He'd be happy to see her and happy to hear Great Gram was thriving. Nothing to worry about, right?

"Dad," she called, as she knocked on the door and pushed it open. A wash of nostalgia and sadness swept over her as she smelled the air, a combination of leaky copper pipe and cinnamon apple. Who was cooking apple crisp, she wondered as she peeked into the crock pot on the counter. She called "Dad" again while she looked around noting his computer back at the kitchen table. She stepped down the hallway and saw that he'd moved back into her parents' old bedroom.

She crossed the hall and opened the door to her childhood room. A pair of work boots and two pairs of high-heeled sandals were strewn across the floor, jeans and flannel shirts, denim blouses and a dress lay at the foot of the unmade bed. A picture of her half-sister Missy and Dad was on the bureau. Missy had apparently moved in.

"Dad?" she called again as she returned to the main room, "you here?" Why would her much older half-sister be living there? Thought she and Dad had a bad relationship. Nicole had never even met her. Would have been nice to have an older sister around growing up, she thought absently, still searching the rooms for Dad. The crunch of tires running over the gravel driveway outside caught her attention. A car door opened, then slammed, hard. She headed back into the main room.

"Nicole, it's you, right?" a female voice yelled from outside. "Where the hell are ya? Come out so we can talk. I got something to say to you."

Nicole quickly crossed the living room to peer out the screen door. A blonde, sneering woman with hands on her hips and an angry glint in her eyes leaned against a junker car, taillight broken and back corner smashed in. Her unruly hair stuck out at all angles, curled strands catching in the breeze. She tamed it by angrily popping sunglasses on top of her head.

Nicole opened the door but before she could say anything, Missy continued, "Why're you here? Aren't you supposed to be getting Great Gram to sell that big, old house that's falling apart? Cushy gig. Shouldn't you be working at some tech job? Glad you left the real work, ranching, to me. Pretty easy to babysit an old lady all day. What a racket. Got Dad wrapped around your finger, haven't you?"

"Look, I don't even know you. What's your problem coming here like this?" Nicole said, complete puzzlement in her voice. This was hardly the family reunion she had fantasized about as a kid when she had wanted a sister, a brother, any company to assuage the loneliness of being an only child.

"And I can see online you're digging into family history," Missy said. "What ya looking for, Nicole?"

Now she wished she had made her family tree searches private. But then she wouldn't have found as much information. It didn't matter. Missy had no right speaking to her like this. And why was she living in her old room? Had Dad replaced her with this crazy half sister?

"What? How dare you? My mother just died. Do you remember that? And this is my home. I grew up here, not you." Nicole's voice raised in anger, her heart thumping with adrenaline. She glared at Missy with a reddening face. "Bitch," Nicole muttered under her breath. She took another step forward. She'd never been a fighter in school but she was close to throwing a punch at this insolent woman. She stepped even closer, the woman still leaning against the car. Still glaring defiantly. Missy threw out her arms as if to say, bring it on.

Just then her father pushed open the screen door and stepped out into the parking area. "What the hell's going on here?" His voice was loud and harsh. He slammed the door behind him. Dad was as mad as the last time Nicole had spoken with him but it was a relief to see his anger directed at someone else. The other daughter for once.

He approached the visitor forcefully and got up into her face. "Now Missy, I've told you over and over again. You can stay here to get back on your feet but you can't start anything with Nicole. She's got nothing to do with our issues. Her mom just died, remember? Think about someone else for a change. You gotta buck up and take care of yourself."

He hitched up his pants and squinted at her in the sun, then mumbled, "If you needed help, I still don't understand why you didn't ask your mom."

Nicole was dumbfounded by the whole scene. Here was her long-lost half-sister. Here was Dad acknowledging his grief and maybe even defending the remainder of their little family. But what was Missy doing here?

"I told you before," she said. "Mom's messed up since that drunk driver hit her. She's gotten into pills. I gotta save some money so I can get my own place. Can't live with her anymore." Missy kicked her boot back into the tire and then stood like that, with one knee up, as if trying to project a forceful stance. "Why don't you go on back up to San Francisco, Nicole, and take care of business. You got a job, do it."

What? Nicole was angry and confused. What business was it of hers the agreement with Dad?

He shot both of them a hard look, eyes cold and cheeks red. "Missy, I don't owe you anything. I paid my share for you to grow up. You never lacked for anything. I haven't had a thing to do with your mother in twenty-five years. But I get it, sometimes folks need a little help. I told you you can stay for a bit. Now go on get those groceries we need for the weekend." He waved his hand toward her car in a clear dismissal, then turned to face Nicole, commanding, "Come on in. I gotta talk to you."

Missy opened her car door and got in, then looked over at Nicole through the windshield and gestured with two fingers to her eyes and then pointed a finger. I'm watching you. Nicole just shrugged and flipped her off. Missy turned to Dad, peered at him through the window and said, "I could've used a Dad all those years, so fuck you." She gunned the car in reverse, screeched through the gravel to swing it around and roared off down the long drive toward the highway.

"God damn it. God damn daughters," he said then turned right around and huffed up the stairs to the barn apartment. Guess he'd forgotten the order to meet in the kitchen.

Hands shaking with adrenaline, Nicole went back inside and sat in her favorite chair at the farmhouse table. She was shell-shocked from seeing Missy for the first time. Realizing her stuff was in her own bedroom. Dad both defending Nicole but also letting Missy into their world. Sure looked like Missy wanted to rob her of her father, her family, her home. Was he going to let her do that? Not if she had any say in the matter.

She found some *Progresso* soup cans in the cupboard and heated up a pot of his favorite Beef Barley Vegetable. Then she went up to the apartment to try to coax him out so she could give her report on the San Francisco house, plus find out what the hell Missy was doing here.

Dad agreed to join her with a nod, no words. His boots clacked on the wooden floor as he followed her back to the main house. "Soup," he said. "You should've told me you were coming." Irritation was clear in his dark eyes and pursed lips.

"Nice to see you too," she said sarcastically, then bit her lip. He looked so old, hair now completely gray and thin with pink scalp showing through. He was more angular than ever. "Dad?" she said more softly. She had to make an effort. His hard gaze did not lighten.

"House ready to sell?"

"Smells good, the apple crisp. Missy cooking for you? That'd be good. You're too skinny," she said thinking a little kindness might help.

"She just came a week ago, staying for a few weeks, maybe a month or two. Needs a leg up. Get some savings," he said, sounding matter of fact as if it were a common occurrence.

"I thought you two didn't get along." Nicole wondered if he was acting out of guilt over not being present when Missy was growing up.

"None of your business," he said, a scowl darkening his face.

"Look Dad, I came to see how you're doing. And also to report on the job you're paying me for. Great Gram is amazing." She wondered again why her father had never taken her to visit Great Gram when Nicole was little but thought better than to ask. She didn't want to start out antagonistically. "She's healthy, very active, in all these clubs and stuff. She's busier than I was in college. The house seems fine. The tenants love her, did you know that?"

He glared at her and didn't say a word. Maybe she saw a slight nod. Or maybe it was just wishful thinking that he'd respond to her. She probably should never have come, just picked up the phone. Then she could have avoided Missy too.

"But there is one problem," she continued. "Great Gram refuses to sell. She didn't seem to know about your intent or think it's for sale. And...I'm not sure she should sell. She looks after her tenants like they're her kids. She has her friends and activities in the neighborhood. Why would she leave? Plus, it's her family home, she's lived there for over fifty years or something."

"What the hell? Your job was to take care of her and get her to sell the house. Can't you even do that?"

"Well, I did find a rich tech guy," Nicole said. "I thought he'd be perfect. Turned out he's a distant cousin of ours and he just sold his start-up for a billion dollars. He really wanted the house too but it didn't work out. Great Gram has all these requirements. He didn't like the restrictions. Clearly, she doesn't really want to sell."

"Requirements? What do you mean?" he asked, his head tilted toward her.

"She wants the tenants to be able to stay in the house until they die or move of their own accord. Plus, she wants it to be a historical landmark or something. It's really old, from before the earthquake. Did you know that? It's really cool. She's pretty attached to the place."

"That was the whole point of you going up there. She's in her nineties and can't take care of it. If all is so hunky dory as you say, why am I getting phone calls? One of the tenants called me. Said plumbing backed up in his kitchen sink and toilets. Needed a plumber but the guy didn't show when he was supposed to. Why they calling me if you're doing such a great job?"

"Oh yeah, Great Gram forgot to tell me about that one 'til the plumber didn't show up. I didn't know you were called. Sorry about that. But we finally got the plumber there." She softened her tone with the apology.

"That's why you're there. I've got the ranch," he said. "My Dad is fading in that nursing home with his bad heart. I gotta make sure he's okay, keep the ranch going. Missy's trying to get a fresh start. I don't need my grandmother's big, old house with fifteen tenants and property management issues. Plus, my wife died recently, remember that?"

"What, really Dad? Are you kidding me?" The insensitivity stung. It hurt that he didn't seem to even consider her feelings, her grief. "She was my mother, remember that? How dare you? I'm struggling as much as you. Nice of you to help Missy out. What about me?"

"I gave you that damn job, didn't I? Now just get it done. I thought I'd taught you how to do that all these years." He looked at her, then sighed and said, "I gotta sit over there." He moved to his worn upholstered armchair and sat back, feet splayed out.

Nicole sat down across from him feeling confused and so alone. She felt him slipping from her as if she'd now lost both parents. She had to bring some sense of family back into her life or she'd really be adrift. What now?

"Yeah, I know we're both still grieving and figuring our stuff out," he said. Was there a softening and hint of caring in his voice? "You going down that family tree rat hole—can't understand that one," he said curtly. Then he continued with a more practical tone. Was it even conciliatory? "But you got a good degree and can get yourself a job. Just gotta get over yourself that it has to be for some goddamned do-gooder company. Yeah, I never really understood your fascination with the computer, where you can't even see inside, you know, but I'm not stupid. I know your skills are in demand here and you could make good money at any of these big companies."

"I don't want that, you know," she said. "I want a smaller place working on really important issues. There's a lot of big problems to work on, you know. Anyway…I know you don't understand." She decided to change the subject.

"So why's Missy living here now? You get lonely or something?" she asked.

"Aw, hon, look, I'm trying to help out someone struggling, " he said. "She is family. She had to leave her Mom's place, get a fresh start. She's staying here 'til she gets on her feet. She's cooking for me so that's a help. She's getting her real estate license so I'm trying to support her doing something productive. She and I made our own deal. Anyway…. That's none of your business. Just get Great Gram to sell. And no more of those damn conditions."

"Well, mighty nice of you to help out Missy." She didn't try to hide her sarcasm. "I'm just confused, I guess. I thought you were mad at her. Kinda takes a lot of energy to stay mad at people though, huh? Look Dad, I want to help you out," she said, hoping to show some more cooperation than Missy just had with her curse. But Great Gram seemed more adamant than all of the stubborn family members.

Nicole decided to make one last pitch. Maybe the land trust document would help him see the value of the family's real estate. "Can't we let Great Gram stay and get someone to come in and help her do the property management? Now that I've been there for a while I see how the house, the tenants and her neighborhood are keeping her alive. You gotta have stuff to live for at that age. We're her only family around. Her friends are dying off or moving to old people's homes—"

"Exactly where she needs to go," he interrupted. "We had a deal. Go back up there and get your great grandmother to sell. And make sure you check in every day on the house issues so I'm not gettin' any phone calls. I don't care if she wants to stay. We gotta sell in this boom, at these insane prices before there's a crash. I can feel one coming. Seen it before. Then you can get a real job."

"But Dad, she's adamant. She won't sell. And you and Grandpa will inherit in her will, won't you? And then it should be worth even more. I'll try but I don't think I can convince her to sell. I'll keep taking care of her for a while." Her voice drifted off and they were both silent for a moment. Nicole thought maybe she had an opening.

"Plus the house and our family are historic. I want to show you this paperwork we found in the attic. The original legal document that set up the land trust. That one with the land where you can go camping and stuff."

Dad pulled his glasses out of his brown striped flannel shirt pocket and put them on. "What is this?" he said, staring at the faded paper and flipping through the pages.

"Dad, this shows that the guy we thought was from Ohio and brought our family here, well, he wasn't, either one. He was really Mexican. Born here with Mexican parents. Like, descended from the first Californians, you know from Spain and all, when they set up the missions. You know that DNA test I did, I don't think it was wrong. Great Gram did one too and it showed even higher percentages of Spanish and Mexican and Native American in her genes."

He said nothing, peering at the looping scrawl. "Look at the names," she said and pointed to the final paragraphs. Dad ripped off his glasses and tossed them onto the wooden table.

"I don't care what you think you found but this is ridiculous. The first in our family to come to California was Irish from homesteading in Ohio. Came here for the Gold Rush like tens of thousands. Not many made it in gold. I think he was in mercury mining. That's why there's that land you can camp on near the old quicksilver mines. Native American? Are you kidding? That's ridiculous. We're not Indians, come on. Anyway, why's it matter? Stop wasting time on attics and moldy old documents. Take care of Great Gram's business and convince her to sell. That's what you're up there to do—a year goes fast when trying to sell a house and you can damn well bet I'm not paying anymore after that. Get the job done."

Nicole sat down hard in the chair. He didn't believe her? He didn't care that the house or family was connected to local history. That their family stretched back for generations in this place. He seemed blinded by his long-held view of the past. Any sense of belonging with him, any comfort and love in her childhood home was disappearing so quickly it was gut wrenching. She needed whatever family she could grasp ahold of with Momma gone.

"Oh, and one other thing. Just so you know," he said. "I've got my lawyer working on conservatorship over Great Gram so I can make the decisions. My Dad agrees and he's too sick to do anything. He wants me in charge. So soon I'll have full control over her house and finances and none of this will be an issue. Don't tell her but thought you should know. The house is going up on the listing sites soon. Now get out of here before Missy comes back." He turned and went into his bedroom and slammed the door. Clearly, she'd been dismissed.

Nicole stumbled to her car and drove down the long driveway in a daze. What? Conservatorship? As she turned onto the road which led to the highway, she noticed Missy's beat up car pass her and turn toward the gravel drive to the ranch. That was it. She pushed her foot on the accelerator and sped up with anger, frustration.

She was done with her father. What loyalty did she have to him anymore? He had chosen Missy over her and the betrayal stung. It felt hot, like a burning inside. She had to focus on driving so she wouldn't burst into tears. She swallowed hard and poked her fingernails deep into the palm of her left hand on the steering wheel. She would keep looking after Great Gram, who was pretty great. Maybe she could fill the ache for family right now. She would help her get the historical landmark designation, then figure out what to do. Forget Dad and the ranch. Seemed he had Missy on his side. Didn't seem to need Nicole around for anything anymore but making money off a house sale.

She kept driving, thinking about how she better pay more attention to the tenants' problems. They sure needed to avoid any frustrated renters calling Dad. Then she realized she had an even more important thing to do right away; she had to come clean and confess to Great Gram that her father had sent her to sell the house. That she was the one who found the tech guy buyer and encouraged them to meet even when she understood Great Gram did not want to sell. Sure hope she'd accept an apology for the deceit.

But Dad getting conservatorship over Great Gram, her house and her money? She could not let that happen. I'll be damned if I'm selling her house out from under her. Allowing her to lose control over her money, her own life? I'm on her team now. Geez. How low had they fallen?

THE LITTLE ADOBE HOUSE

Diego threw the polished saddle on his favorite of the two horses he now owned, mounted with spurs clinking and rode away from his new homestead. He looked back at the small adobe with pride as he rode up the hill and down the other side toward the mission. Diego needed a servant and figured he could trade blacksmith work for a girl to keep his house. He nudged the horse and they trotted along the worn path. He bounced gracefully in the saddle, at one with the animal, a place more comfortable for him than a sitting room chair. His chest rose with pride at owning two horses. At having completed his own adobe. He was still troubled by nightmares of the Atlantic crossing and his former Catalonian life, but maybe they'd lessen now.

A few times a year, when he looked out across the bay below, he'd see a ship moored. Despite the curiosity and the excitement that more supplies or soldiers had been dropped off, his entire body instantly would fill with a nausea and dizziness so pronounced that he'd have to stop whatever he was doing, grab the doorframe or hitching post and slide to the ground. He'd feel the rock of the ship again and gulp air, desperate to regain his equilibrium. This is it; my future is here, he'd remind himself. I will never leave. I'm an Alta Californian now. This is where I'll die. The nausea and nightmarish memories of the sea would pass, pushing him to work even harder to make a life in this lonely land.

After his promotion to sergeant several months ago, and with the few silver coins he collected from blacksmithing at the presidio and over at the mission, Diego decided to build himself a house. He traded for materials and a neophyte worker to help construct the small adobe. They built a kitchen and pantry, a tiny sitting area, a small bedroom and an alcove attached to the corral. He included a covered area for his tools and a tiny stable for his two horses. Diego conjured up images from Catalonia. He had big plans.

He imagined fluttering olive groves, lemon and orange trees blossoming, ruby red pomegranates dropping to the ground, their juice dripping down the chins of his future children. He pictured grapevines laden with purple fruit and a full complement of vegetables in the rancho garden of his dreams. So he had the native servant hand plow rows and put in as many corn, bean, fava, barley, squash and tomato seeds as he could scrounge from the presidio cook. He would plant lemons and oranges as soon as he could get the seeds. It was not only Catalonia that inspired his planting but survival. Since seeing scurvy up close, Diego was a fanatic for gardening.

Everyone had their own idea about scurvy but his theory was that the lack of fresh food caused it. He'd heard rumors recently of a ship's captain who gave his sailors lemon juice and no one sickened. He remembered the dried oranges and lemons and the tea he'd lived on during that sea voyage. Even in his years at the presidio, the minute he had convinced his platoon boss to lend him a shovel and let him dig and plant behind the barracks, he'd grown tomatoes. Starting with his own little house, a few rows of beans and corn, his own blacksmith shop and a housekeeper were the first steps toward his bigger goal.

Diego passed native tule huts for those allowed to live with family, the monjerio for most girls and women and the priests' simple dormitories, into the central plaza. Father Juan, a favorite of Diego's for his willingness to barter, greeted him at the church door. He was much rounder than most of the prairie priests and it was rumored that he sampled the homemade sacrament wine more often than just during Mass. He and a crew of neophyte women were finishing a thorough cleaning of the altar stones. Diego hoped he could quickly make a deal for a servant without any hassle or disagreement with the priests.

There was not a lot of love between the presidio and the mission. Padre Serra and Governor falling out had caused further animosity. While the early soldiers conscripted to build the presidio without breaks or much food were no fans of Fages, they also did not appreciate religious leaders meddling in military matters. It was humiliating that Father Serra had been successful in getting Captain Fages demoted from his governorship and removed to Mexico City. The new governor, De Neves, was attempting to give the natives more rights, but Diego wasn't so sure that would work either. He figured there were more conflicts ahead for Padre Serra's fellow Franciscans and his military bosses.

The reality of their life, however, with so few Spaniards living in a remote and vast land, was that they were completely dependent on each other. The padres counted on the soldiers to maintain order, protecting them from horse thieves and native attacks. They sent soldados de cuera and dragoons out to recapture the baptized who escaped. Particularly in the early years, they relied on the soldiers for herding cattle from field to hillside and all *vaquero* activities.

Military protection was essential to continue Father Serra's mission to settle the entire territory.

The padres, for their part, were much more than just evangelists. They proved to be fruitful ranchers and trained the newly converted natives to be Alta California cowboys. They raised the cows, horses and mules. They grew the barley and corn, beans and fresh vegetables. They taught natives to be the work force, to build the feeble buildings and till the land, to spin wool and slaughter and milk the cows. The padres preached constantly that in this rich land where everything seemed to grow abundantly, eventually they could get to a volume where the City of Mexico would send ships laden with furniture, building supplies, cloth, art and finery in return for their produce. But the priests did have to rely on soldiers to further this empire building.

"Sergeant Castro, I'm pleased to see you back safely," Father Juan said. "I heard about your promotion. Comandante Ortega finds you useful." The father clapped him on the back as he dismounted and shook Diego's hand heartily. "Have you secured yet another mission for us? You were helping establish Mission San Francisco de Asís, no? I understand it's quite beautiful there and there's another great bay for Spanish ships. I would love to see the place. But alas, my work is here with God's children. We are so needed. There is so much to do."

Diego greeted the friar politely and started to explain the latest trade he wanted to make but Fray Juan interrupted.

"Have you heard, Captain De Anza has returned? Oh, I mean Lieutenant Colonel De Anza. He was promoted after his first expedition here. This time he traveled north from Sinaloa and Sonora with cows and horses, settler families, not just soldiers. There were babies and young children along."

Father Juan was quite a gossip and always had news to discuss when Diego visited the mission. Diego often found his stories exhausting and of little interest but occasionally the padre had good information.

"They brought hundreds of cattle, more than five hundred horses. Soldiers with wives and children. Did you hear? Oh, this place will grow now, Sergeant Castro. Mark my words."

Diego knew all about Lieutenant Colonel De Anza, having been assigned to protect the new settlers as they headed north from Monterrey, but thought better than to point out the father's forgetfulness.

"Wait, what am I thinking? You were just with them at the great bay. I heard the Lieutenant Colonel found a good site for another mission on your return journey back here. Is that true, Sergeant? Will there be another mission closer to us?"

"Yes, Father, this place will indeed change with new arrivals. You are right about that," Diego said vaguely, refusing to satisfy the father's craving for gossip. "I think this place will change and I think that's a good thing. We need more settlers here. More than just soldiers and priests. But right now, I need a servant girl. I've just finished my own humble house with a shop for my blacksmithing, a garden and a few simple rooms. I need someone to clean it, cook for me and care for the adobe when I'm away. Do you have someone who can do that? Someone strong and reliable. I'm away most of the time, as you know, so this housekeeper must be trustworthy. You understand, Father. Of course you will be my top priority for blacksmith repairs, don't worry," he added.

Father Juan smiled, as if Diego would be doing him a favor as well. "I have just the girl for you. She's a bit low right now as her father recently died. But she's young and strong. Never seems to get the illnesses that sicken so many gentiles, and even our baptized neophytes. She may pretend she doesn't speak Spanish but she understands everything. I think she'll be perfect for you, Sergeant."

The father said something to one of the nearby cleaning women and few moments later, a neophyte arrived firmly gripping the elbow of an unkempt girl in a filthy dress, hair tousled, barefoot. Diego raised his eyebrows but assumed she could clean herself up once she was not making adobe bricks all day. She was so skinny. How had she managed to do the backbreaking work required to build walls? On the other hand, he should probably take what was offered and complete the deal quickly.

"Take this one. We call her Sholeta," the padre said. "She used to say the word constantly when her family was still alive so we figured it must be her name. Anyway, she's strong, doesn't eat much, hasn't gotten sick or pregnant yet so she should be able to help you out, Sergeant. We're pleased you came to us for a maid in your new adobe. Here is a bible for her. Perhaps you can read to her every day," the padre suggested not so gently, as if the girl needed a lot to save her soul.

Sholeta could see that she was being sold off to a Spanish soldier. On the walk over the hill toward the presidio and the larger bay she debated if she should run for the pines. But she had no idea where to go for safety. She didn't know where her brother's new village was, if he was even alive. Perhaps he'd been killed during one of the Spanish raids.

Her father's demise had been devastating, but not unexpected, and she'd been so alone for years. Her survival instincts rose to the surface so she trudged behind the soldier on his horse, her bare feet catching in the pebbles and pine needles. She would follow this soldier now and feign compliance. Just to get away from the mission was a relief. She breathed in the fresh, moist air, and allowed herself to be pleased to be out of the nunnery, which smelled of illness, despair and rotten vegetables.

Sholeta had observed whenever new tribespeople arrived to trade or were captured, they seemed healthy. But if you lived with the padres very long you were likely to sicken and die. Babies were born dead or breathed only a few days. Healthy young men caught strange diseases and perished. Sholeta knew that if she stayed at the mission much longer she too would be a casualty. The place she had slept for three years, no better than horse stables, where she had cradled her little sisters and her mother in death, was a torture chamber for her. She was glad to leave it behind. Here was a new opportunity for freedom.

She was convinced that her father's deathbed words were a commandment to continue the family line. To not die an unnatural, early death. She was to survive, to flourish, to return to Ohlone living. And that is what she intended to do, no matter how long it took. She was patient, a quail hunter, after all.

As she followed the soldier past the rancheria just outside the mission plaza, Sholeta felt ashamed at the squalor of her people as they emerged from moldy huts clutching their bark bowls for the midday *pozole*. She closed her eyes. She conjured up an image of her family's village with its clean, well-constructed huts, the sweat lodge structure, herbs drying in the sun and the seashell waste mound at one side. She smelled her favorite acorn pancakes and thought she could hear them sizzle on the morning fire. She opened her eyes, and her heart ached at how her people had grown dependent on the padres for food, shelter and spiritual direction.

She scrambled along the path to keep up with the soldier on horseback. He never turned to look at her, never said a word. Her hatred of the enemy was deep, all consuming, but she noted this one was not as smelly and ugly and mean looking as some of them, so there could be worse masters. She would have to watch herself at night. Yet, maybe, this soldier could be her path to survival.

With the patient, quiet hunting skills deep in her blood from thousands of years of her ancestors, Sholeta promised herself she would watch and wait, seeking an opportunity to escape to her brother's village. She was sure it was out there in the hills, just waiting for her to return to her natural life.

THE MAID

⚬

Sholeta followed Diego into his little adobe. He gestured to the kitchen with pantry, just off the main house in its own tiny building. He led her through to the living room where she saw a wooden table with two spindle chairs. A few steps away sat a small desk with a tiered candelabra holding dripping white candles coated with soot. A small bedroom was past the sitting area. She looked around, noting the odors and breathed in the scents of candle wax, cooked beans, muddy whitewash and dusty leather.

She followed him through each room. The soldier was not a tidy housekeeper and his bedroom was littered with boots, belts and colored sashes. His chaps stretched across the top of the bed frame. An extra reata lasso hung on the wall and his sweat-stained hat dangled off the back of a dining chair. While not as tangy sweet as the aroma of the briny sea she loved, the adobe's smells were a significant improvement over those at the monjerio barracks.

He escorted her outside to a tiny alcove just larger than the single bed frame inside. The room was attached to a makeshift stable holding two horses. Having observed the Español up close over three years, Sholeta noted that this soldier must have some silver or be a higher rank than most she had encountered guarding the mission. None of them owned a horse. And this soldier had two.

He indicated this tiny space was hers. She had never slept in a bed or had her own room. If her family had still been alive, she would have found her own bedroom an alarming development. But now, an orphan, with only a slim hope of finding Ores in his own village in the surrounding hills, a bed raised off the ground and a private place to sleep with no retching, no stink of blood or air of despair was a relief. And no locked door with soldiers standing guard each night. The room smelled of soap and she wondered if the soldier had cleaned the bed linens and swept the floor himself. The man continued the tour.

Sholeta understood most of his instructions—they were simple enough—but did not let on that she spoke his language. Ewshai, her ancestors, were bereaved. She had a responsibility to them to not give in, to fight. She could not just become a little house slave and pretend everything was fine. He was the enemy after all. Yet, at this moment, she was still unsure of how she could free herself, where she would go. She needed time to analyze her new surroundings.

Diego led her outside and pointed to the few rows of seedlings behind the kitchen building, pulling seed sacks out of the pantry indicating he wanted her to plant more and tend the garden. He took her into the corral and showed her how to brush and clean the horses. She looked up slightly then, showing him she was adept at horse care.

In her three years at the mission, the priests taught many of the natives cow punching skills. When allowed, she'd tagged along with her brothers, pretending an interest. At first, she'd really only wanted to be with family away from the sickness and heaviness of the women's quarters. A side benefit had been that she'd learned how to ride and care for horses and mules. And she'd discovered a new love that filled some of her emptiness.

Sholeta often thought of that horrific day of her village's capture and the end of her family's natural way of life. Horse hoofs pounded in her nightmares still. Ironically, she'd discovered over time at the mission that she was drawn to the beast. Once she suppressed her initial fear, she was entranced by their large, sad eyes, their gentle nuzzling when eating out of her hand, the power of their grand torsos and strong legs, their tails whispering back and forth against the flies. Once she saw a foal born and struggle to stand on wobbly legs while mother mare licked to clean her new offspring, she was captivated.

Her new horse friends understood her sad loneliness and maybe experienced a bit of the same. She imagined the domesticated animals in Alta California also possessed a nostalgia for their once free existence from here. These horses and their ancestors had once roamed wild in thundering herds across the plains of Iberia, unfettered by Spanish masters.

Once comfortable with the animals, Sholeta offered to the priests that she'd keep an eye out for those who strayed from the plaza or munched grasses too far up the hill from the mission. The priests agreed and after years in the role, Sholeta could mount a horse bareback, coax it to return to the mission plaza and occasionally spin the reata. She loved it when a horse wandered and she could flee the mission and the suffocating barracks. Sometimes, she intentionally left their lassos a bit too loose around the hitching posts.

Now, Sholeta nodded in response to Diego's instructions. Horses here would help her adjust and tolerate this new living situation. She was pleased.

After the tour, the soldier spoke to her harshly, "Now get yourself cleaned up. You're filthy. I want a clean maid in this house. Can you keep yourself clean?" He didn't wait for an answer. "After you've cleaned up, then make me *almuerzo*. That's why you're here, to cook and clean. And to take care of this place. I have lots of responsibilities at the presidio. Now go on."

Sholeta nodded very slightly and went to her room where she found a wash basin, pitcher of water and tallow soap. An apron and dress were folded on the small table. She scrubbed and washed as best she could with the one pitcher as she had no idea where fresh water came from. Just removing the scratchy sack of a dress was a relief. She resolved to burn it. She'd had to mend its many tears over three years. It was the only thing she'd worn since her capture, her tule skirt long ago deteriorated, the deerskin shawl worn down to a tiny scrap. She'd kept the deerskin fragment hidden, treasuring it as the only remnant of her first life.

Once cleaner and wearing the new clothes, she entered the kitchen building. She found utensils and supplies and began cooking. She still had some leached acorn meal in her pocket, a survival trick she'd tried to teach other girls in the barracks, so she sifted it with her fingers into the corn masa for the tortillas.

On their journey up the hill away from the mission, she'd observed that the little house was farther from the sea. She'd have to figure out how to sneak out to gather mussels, and her favorite, the abalone. Eventually, once she had her bearings and figured out how to escape the soldier, she would slip away to find her brother, she thought as she stirred the pozole and salted the previously cooked beans. She stepped out the door to tiny garden and selected a few herbs to add to the pot, then patted the tortillas and tossed them on the *comal* to cook. She pulled a plate off the shelf, and a bowl for the pozole, and presented her first meal as housekeeper to Sergeant Castro, dragoon of the Spanish Army and Calvary.

The soldier tasted his lunch then looked up at her with just a tiny hint of a smile. He nodded, "*Sabroso*," he said. Delicious. Good he liked her food, she thought. Now gotta figure out how to poison it.

At first, Sholeta's deep hate of the foreign invader and her grief at losing her entire family was so overwhelming that she interacted with Diego with a profound nausea. She felt she might retch all over his leather tunic every time he left for a mission and gave her instructions. Her dreams were filled with gathering bark and roots to poison his soups or porridge or taking his favorite whip for the horses and using it to strangle him. She still smelled the smoke of her burning village.

At the same time, Sholeta was conflicted. She was desperate not to return to the mission. Her new quarters and Sergeant Castro's simple expectations were far superior to her life in the barracks. He was the invader, her captor and colonizer. But he also was her savior. If she had not been brought to work at this little house, she would have died at the mission like her parents, siblings and most members of her village. The mixture of hate and gratitude confused her.

The soldier was frequently away, she quickly learned. He left just two days after first bringing her to the house. He took only one horse so she used the solitude to get to know the other one. He returned a few weeks later and then left quickly again with both horses. He was gone for weeks. Still weak from the years of mission confinement and with no idea where Ores was living, she decided to get healthy and assess her surroundings before fleeing.

His house was up the hill under the tall pines, some distance from the presidio and slowly expanding simple houses around it. With no horse companions, Sholeta's loneliness deepened in the clearing beneath the wide, flat-topped cypress trees and black oaks. But the lack of a schedule or set responsibility was a luxury she had not experienced since childhood. She returned more to her old ways. She cleaned herself up. She altered her diet to familiar acorn meal pancakes and porridge, small birds and rodents, and she drank in the cool, fresh air.

Unfortunately, she didn't know her surroundings well enough to try to reach the seawater and sand. She had no idea when Diego would reappear and she did not want to draw attention to anyone at the presidio that she was living alone in his house. But she dreamed of scrubbing the salty sand all over her skin and through her hair to scour off the death coating her like a cloak. To return to her former smell, to clean out the toxins devouring her body. To capture a sea otter or small seal for the blubber as she'd watched her brother do. She missed the sea. She longed for the crags and fissures and treasures of the tide pools.

Instead, she used the roughest cloth and best soap she could find in the soldier's house and scrubbed for days. The rashes and insect bites that had plagued her at the mission finally disappeared. She gained a little weight. Her hair began to grow again and shine the deep black it had been in her childhood. She slept through a whole night for the first time in years. She planted seeds in the garden and began to take longer walks to gather acorns. Her strength slowly returned. She didn't miss anything at the mission now that those she loved were gone. She did remember fondly when her favorite horses nosed her dress pockets sniffing for grain kernels. Though it was quiet and lonely up on the hill above the bay's sparkling blue, she felt as if she were returning just a little bit to a newer version of her former self.

Desperately sad, she welcomed the swaying pines, the fluttering quail, the herb seedlings growing taller each day. She had no reason to speak but occasionally would utter a few phrases of her native tongue just to hear a voice. And to remember who she had been. She tried hard to not forget the voices of her mother and father. She sat in the shade of a large oak and forced her ears to hear her sisters' giggles and the shouts of her rambunctious brothers pretending to hunt elk or outrun a grizzly. She must not forget who she was and that this land was her home. She was not the one who was a stranger here.

Each time Diego returned, he gruffly uttered commands, complimented her food, smiled at the growing garden and promptly slept for days before he departed again. His tone could be sharp if she had forgotten something or was not prepared upon his return. But he never hit her or used the lash or put her in any kind of stockade. Sholeta dared to hope those days were behind her but knew never to let her guard down. She noticed that the soldier drank a small cup of rum or whiskey at night. But she never saw him get roaring drunk like so many of the soldiers she'd observed guarding the mission.

After his fourth trip, she began to relax in the little adobe, organizing the kitchen and furniture to her preference. He did not seem to mind, or even notice, as she tidied his bedroom and thoroughly cleaned every surface and item of clothing she could find. She spoke a few more words each time he returned but they did not engage in any extended conversation.

She feared what he did on these trips away as she was not naive and could see that he was a soldier of some importance. At first, when she was so sickly and desperately sad, she put it out of her mind. But often when he returned there were hints of the trail and his exploits. Sometimes his clothes were bloody. He usually spent hours cleaning his musket and pistols the day after his homecoming.

One time she had to sew his arm up from a long gash. As he peeled back his blousy shirt, she saw scars from the arrows of a native tribe on his shoulder, at his hip. She poured a little more whiskey into the wound than really necessary and sewed together the flaps of skin with jerking movements while he grimaced and yelled in pain.

After several months of learning to live this way and regaining her health, Sholeta watched the soldier ride out again on his favorite horse. She was always thrilled when one horse stayed behind to keep her company and allow her to ride up the hill to the oak trees. He had told her he would be gone for a month or two on the current expedition. She knew he was hunting her people, probably as he established another mission with the gray-cloaked priests. Healthier and more confident in her surroundings, she decided it was time.

She waited two nights to make sure he had gone farther than just to the presidio down the hill. Now she was ready.

FROM HUMMINGBIRD TO COYOTE

Sholeta waited until the moon had set below the horizon. It was very dark under the pines but she told herself she ought to be able to find her way toward the river as it wound down through the hills toward the sea. She filled a small satchel with acorn pancakes and a goatskin bag with fresh water. The sour taste of old wine still lined Diego's goatskin and made the water acidic. But she knew the journey might stretch longer than planned. She needed supplies.

She wrapped herself in a dark woolen shawl and slipped past the blacksmith shed and the corral, fingering the barley grains she had in her pocket to silence the horse if he woke. As she passed, his ears twitched, as if to send her off with a loving farewell. She padded imperceptibly on her bare feet, hard as the leather soles of Diego's boots. She passed the garden and walked into the forest beyond the clearing. It felt as if she held her breath all the way to the top of the hill and then as she descended in the direction of the river.

As she approached yet another hill rising beyond where she thought her village had been, she broke into a little jog, a scamper like she used to do as a child. Was this a familiar hillside? The Spanish occupation and more than three years away from her home village had clouded her memory and distorted her sense of geography. Her heart beat fast and her breath quickened and for just a moment she could feel the breeze of her former life touch her cheek. Then she remembered her goal and slowed her pace.

She began whistling the low, soft call of an owl. Her family and tribe had used the specific tone to alert each other to danger, approaching animals or other tribelets in the vicinity. She continued up the rocky terrain, making her bird call periodically. At one point, she stopped, sat down and listened intently. Could she hear the sea breakers? Was that an answering owl? She realized her hope was making her lose focus. Her mind was inventing noises.

She continued in this manner for hours, surveying the hillside, then dropping down to the river and exploring along the bank. She tried to put herself into Ores' shoes. If she were suddenly forced into tribal leadership by an attack from outsiders, where would she go? Where was the safest place to establish a new village? Where would he go to protect his wife and first born?

As she hiked up into the hills and along the river, she left signs for Ores. In torn pieces of burlap from the seed bags, she carefully wrapped an acorn tortilla with a bay leaf on top. She left these little packages below a tree, on top of a rock, at a bend in the creek. When she got to one grassy knoll with the river below and a hilltop not far above, she put another packet down at the base of a giant live oak. This one also contained the abalone shell necklace she always wore. Ores, and maybe anyone else who'd escaped with him, would recognize it as she had been famous throughout family and tribe for sneaking off to the tide pools and keeping the best shells for bowls and jewelry.

Sitting under the oak, she watched the sky turn from black to a deep blue as dawn approached. Fuzzy, barely green moss hung from the tips of the thinnest branches, making her feel as if the bearded woods were a canopy reaching down to protect her. She listened for the ocean but sadly was too high up to hear the waves breaking. She whistled a final few bird calls. Then she filled her pockets with acorns and trudged down the hillside toward the house.

Once back, she collapsed in her small bed and slept for several hours. Unused to sleeping during daylight, she quickly woke and set to her regular chores. Sholeta repeated this search every night until the moon was so high and full there was no protective darkness. She waited several days, then repeated the effort.

One night she finally heard a response to her whistle. She froze. She was near the tree where she'd first left the abalone shell tied to its rabbit gut necklace. She called again and tiptoed under the heavy branches, then climbed on the lowest one and scrambled up into the tree for a safer viewing place, careful not to move. Could this finally be the reunion she'd longed for? The anticipation made her nervous. It was very hard to stay still.

She saw a silhouette approach from slightly above her position. The bird call repeated. She waited silently and watched the shadow move along a deer path toward her oak. Another low whistle. She took a breath and repeated the call back. The shadow changed direction slightly and moved toward the tree, getting closer to its stretched branches. She slowly descended and hopped quietly to the ground after the last whistle. The shadow grew taller and she could sense it was a young man.

As he approached, his features became clear and it was not Ores but a distant cousin who had married a girl from a tribelet down south. She was crestfallen. She held her breath. She heard her language for the first time in almost two years since her father had been the final family member to die at the mission.

"Ores has sent me to find you." His deep voice in the familiar tones reminded her of her father's voice when he'd been a tribal elder. It was comforting and heartbreaking at the same time. "He was impressed with your careful, clever search for him. We've been watching and waiting for a safe time to meet you," the cousin said with the drops, clicks and shushing sounds she so missed.

Her emotions spilled over at connecting with a family member after so long. Her tongue was clumsy at switching to its old ways. Sholeta was silent for a moment as she tried to untangle the syllables anxious to rush out.

"Tar," he said, "I know it is you even though you have grown into a woman since the attack."

"Yes, yes, it's me, Tar. They call me Sholeta now," she said, words now spilling out as if a damn had broken open. "Where's Ores? Can I see him? There is no one left of our family, cousin. They killed them all. I'm the only one left."

She hoped he'd lead her to Ores' hut right away. "I want to leave this place and live with you and Ores in your village. Take me now. Or send Ores to collect me tomorrow. I cannot stay here any longer," she begged.

The cousin took her shoulders gently in his hands. "We are constantly on the run. It is no place for a young girl. We have no village to speak of. We're organizing with other tribelets to attack the invaders. Our leaders are in the church huts of the pale faces. We're no longer a village."

Sholeta was stunned. All these years she had assumed Ores was an important chief, thriving with his wife and babies. No matter. Moving around wasn't a problem. She knew how to ride horses. She could help them. She had to escape and finally live with her brother.

Her words came rushing out. "I can help fight them. I know how they are. I've lived in their strange villages and seen their terrible ways and the death that follows. I can be a soldier for you. You may not know this but my father was teaching me to hunt before the capture."

"Cousin. Be calm. You cannot come to our makeshift village. But Ores does have a mission for you. He asks you to stay in the soldier commander's house and report to us what he plans, where he will go, what the results are of his military campaigns. Ores is giving you an important role. We need you to be our spy."

Sholeta took a step back. "What?" she said, not fully comprehending. "I can't do that. I came here to go back with you."

"You must stay, cousin, and tell us what the soldier plans. Ores is our chief and you must obey. We need your help, don't you see? Your brother said to think of it as quail hunting." She knew her brother was trying to appeal to her, but doubted the task would be easy. She knew nothing of spying or about military plans. The cousin continued.

"We believe the soldier is an important leader who battles other tribelets. He and his cavalry have been invading villages alongside the great bay in the north, south in the mountains above the cliffs that drop to the sea. You must give us information so we can defeat those who are killing our people. We have horses and can get more. We steal guns too but we need to know their plans. I'll tell Ores you want to see him. Meet here tomorrow night. We need you, Tar."

Sholeta left feeling dejected. It would have almost been better to not have seen this cousin at all. She had just wanted to go home. But now she understood there was no home anymore. Not anywhere.

⁓

Under the tree the next night, Sholeta waited nervously. She'd been so anxious to see her brother that she left the house before the moon had fully set. From her tree branch perch, she waited until it was dark to start the soft bird call. At least an hour later, she finally heard the response and leapt out of the tree in anticipation. A shadow came down the deer trail slowly.

"Tar," her brother's voice said sharply, "Don't be a fool. I saw you in the twilight from my perch up on the cliffs. You must only come out at the cover of complete darkness. Do you want to risk us being spotted? Don't you understand that we're at war with these invaders?"

Sholeta was ashamed. Yet could not help herself from spreading her arms to hug him as he approached. "Yes, yes, Ores, I know. I'm sorry but I was so anxious to see you. I'll be more careful. They're all dead. We're the only ones left. All the babies, our strong brothers, mother, Atsia, and father, Aha'ya. They all died in that place. I'm so sorry I couldn't save them." She sobbed into his bare chest, which smelled like home, grateful for the release. He held her, caressed her hair briefly, then shook her and pushed her off.

"Enough. I know of this terrible evil, this crime against our people and I too have been devastated by sadness. But Tar, we don't have that luxury to mourn our dead. We must save ourselves and our people. Ewashai, our ancestors, have no one else to rely on."

He shook her shoulders gently, as if to say do you understand, and she nodded, wiped her tears and swallowed her sobs to get them under control. Enough. He was right. Ores was finally here with her, as she'd dreamed about for years, so she needed to pay attention.

"I need your help," he said. "You were a little hummingbird last time I saw you. But you are grown now. You must transform yourself. You must become coyote, the tricky one. *Umun —Tatikimátean*. From hummingbird to coyote."

Ores opened a deerskin pouch and handed her a tule woven packet of elk meat, quail, mussel shells and acorns topped with her abalone necklace. "Put this necklace back on to remind you who you are, what your role is in this fight. Our cousin will meet you here and bring you traditional food, *mak-àmham*, at three nights after the new moon. And when the soldier chief returns, then listen, learn to speak their tongue well, talk to him, go over to their village. A spy must become one with his enemy. And then you will tell us everything. I know they call you Sholeta. Now go be Sholeta."

He gave her a quick hug then turned and climbed up the deer path. He had not given her a moment to reply. She realized she had no say. But, of course, she would comply, for the sake of her parents, her sisters, her brothers, her burning village.

Sholeta walked back to Diego's house with a mixed sense of dread and elation. She had always suspected Ores was alive but she couldn't believe she'd finally embraced him, spoken with him. She had some family after all. But now, her duty to learn the soldier's secrets and missions was overwhelming.

She knew little of Diego's work except that he sometimes came home wounded by other natives. She had no idea how she would get military plans but resolved to try. She'd have to pay more attention, listen harder, start asking questions as if interested. Perhaps she could get him to invite other soldiers to the adobe.

It would be risky, but she had made a sacred promise to her father. She had vowed to honor their ancestors by surviving, by not dying, by not succumbing to the invader. By not accepting their strange beliefs. And so now, Sholeta—captive, native orphan, unbaptized mission rebel, servant girl—became a spy.

When Diego returned about a week later, Sholeta was careful not to change her habits to arouse suspicion. She chatted a little more than before in an attempt to improve her Castellano. She casually asked about his trip and made more efforts to mend clothes while he wrote at his desk or ate his dinner, and not just retreat to her private space near the horses. She stretched cleaning up from supper into the dark while he read by candlelight.

As the atmosphere of the little homestead relaxed from the previous tense silence they'd managed, Sholeta asked about what he'd seen on his expeditions. Did he ever ride to the great bay in the north? She had heard about it but had never been there.

"Yes, Sholeta. It's magnificent," he replied. "I was with Father Crespi and Captain Ortega when we rode up the hill and looked over the great bay the first time. No Spanish ships had found it before. It's a bay like you've never seen. Perhaps someday you can visit the mission there," Diego continued. "That's where I've been these past months. We now have a mission—San Francisco de Asís—not far from the water's edge. And we built a presidio on a hill overlooking the entrance to the great bay, like we have in Monterrey. Padre Serra keeps us very busy. Slowly civilization is coming to this land, your land, Alta California. You should be proud to be a part of it."

Sholeta cast her eyes down at his last statement and pretended to pick up something off the floor. How could he say that? Think that? Did he not know what she'd suffered? All that she had lost at the hands of his people? Anger burned and she wondered if she should poison him after all. She grabbed the broom and began sweeping so that she didn't have to look at him. She didn't know if she could do this spying job.

At the mission, she'd been young and foolish and headstrong. She'd yelled at the priests and soldiers who made her angry. She'd stolen extra food for her dying mother and snuck out to shoot quail to keep her sisters healthy. She'd refused to read a bible or recite catechism or be baptized. She'd spent plenty of time in the stocks as a result. Here, however, here in the soldier's house, she realized, if she was to become a spy, she could not be disobedient.

So she swept and channeled her rebelliousness into duplicity and manipulation. She watched obsessively his every move, what was important to him, what motivated him. How he liked his clothes and food. His garden and tools. She learned the seeds he wanted planted and how to clean the tools in his tiny blacksmith shop. She watched as he dressed himself with his elaborate costume before leaving on mission establishment expeditions. She peered secretly through cracks in the flimsy door between the stable and the kitchen to spy on how he cleaned his pistol and rifle. She memorized his weapon collection so she could report to her cousin. Probably most of this information would not be particularly useful to Ores but she didn't know what else to do. So she observed carefully to learn his every move by heart.

After some time and several visits to the live oak to report her findings, Sholeta realized she was not much of a spy. Diego told her little about upcoming ventures, and in any case she began to suspect he was not as important as her brother had thought. He talked endlessly about his hero Captain Ortega and Sholeta determined that Diego was not a chief but maybe an assistant chief at best. He did not seem to be the one making the decisions but appeared to go on all the major campaigns. She mostly heard stories after the scouting was complete or a new mission established.

How was she ever going to gain information about upcoming expeditions or mission building plans? A few times she would hear him having a nightmare and hide outside his bedroom to listen. But there was never any new information to report to her cousin. He just feels guilty, she decided. Good. But she kept listening to see if he'd reveal anything significant in his sleep.

When a supply ship arrived in the bay, she would make a quiet trip to the presidio to get supplies for the adobe. She hid in the shadows and eavesdropped on any gossip she could hear. Disappointed, she usually returned with little but the boasts of drunken soldiers, sightings of native women at the saloon and stories of more baptisms at the mission. Those seemed to correspond directly with the number of babies that died each month, she noted wryly. She reported what she could to her native handler but to little avail. No grand rescue, no well-coordinated attack from native groups materialized.

After one long stint away, Diego told her how they set up the mission in Santa Clara just a long day's ride up the El Camino. Another time he talked about the original presidio many days ride away in San Diego located on another good bay. After that journey, he returned with open, festering wounds from poison-laced arrows, which told her he was indeed on native elimination campaigns, not just trading expeditions or mission-building in peaceful areas. The natives around San Diego did not seem to like the mission, he noted as he grimaced while she cleaned the pink, oozing holes. Sholeta pretended not to understand while she swabbed the open wounds across his shoulders, back and chest, letting her hair fall across her face out of embarrassment at the intimacy of the act. Again, applying a little extra whiskey for torture.

After she had dressed the arrow punctures, they avoided each other and did not speak for several days. Sholeta felt confused by her emotions; she detested the man for his work but she did like having someone to talk to when he was at home. In the little house, Diego continued to be a tolerable master. He did not beat her and allowed her great freedom. She could ride a horse into the pueblo with his silver to trade grains, beans, blacksmith tools or seeds. The time she told him about some drunken soldiers grabbing her at the hitching post, he hopped on his horse and rode angrily into town to defend her honor and tell his underlings to leave his maid alone.

She was frustrated at Ores' refusal to bring her back to his village. And having someone treat her kindly and defend her at the presidio was comforting. Figuring Diego was still the only path back to a native life, she would always put some of her acorn meal into his tortillas, even some of the precious seal blubber or oysters her cousin occasionally gave her, into her stews and plenty of garden vegetables on his plate.

THE CRUSADER

*Q*uina, *age eleven and barefoot* poor, began her ascent to the matriarchy of an important Californio family by walking eighteen hundred miles across New Spain's northern frontier from Sinaloa to bahía de San Francisco.

As she stumbled in the first huaraches she'd ever owned to cross cacti-covered deserts, Maria Joaquina Altamirano Pacheco was distraught at her parents' decision to uproot the family on what seemed a misguided enterprise, leaving the only home she'd ever known. The life Quina's family had abandoned in Sinaloa was not much to miss but it was what she knew. Quina liked the familiar and predictable.

Her father, a Spanish soldier and farmer, worked hard to scrape a living by tilling the hard soil but was barely able to feed his growing family or even the pig. The soldiering provided little extra but his uniform and a pistol, sometimes another chicken or two or an extra jug of wine. Occasionally, his commander stopped at the shack to demand he ride out to even more remote locales to fight Yaqui or other native intruders. But mostly he scraped in the dirt, hand plowing rows of beans and corn.

Each dawn, Quina's first task was to gather sticks for the smoky fire at the center of their dirt-floored hut. Once the coals were ready, she'd pull out the comal from behind the wash bin and place the patted round corn balls to sizzle, turning the tortillas as the masa hardened and a brown crisp formed on the underside. As the eldest of six children, she often had a baby at her hip or swaddled in a *rebozo* on her back throughout the morning routine. Days filled with carefree play were a distant memory. In reality, they had never existed.

When Colonel Juan Bautista De Anza rode in to the impoverished pueblo's plaza amid a cloud of dust from his soldiers' horses, flags flying, his arrival got the attention of every *campesino* within miles. That Sunday he spoke to the parish from the church's simple altar with grandiose language and sweeping gestures. He promised the impoverished farmers lush land, plentiful hunting grounds and a more temperate climate in the lands to the north. "Join me on a sacred journey to settle Alta California for God, King and the viceroy," he told the assembled.

Quina, who never sat still except when required to during Sunday mass, squirmed in her seat during the colonel's speech, bored with so many adults talking longer than usual. She had admired the colonel's colorful flags and thought back to the picture books of the Crusades she'd seen in Sunday school a year before. Her stomach grumbled. When would they get to leave so she and her sisters could see if any of the church ladies had brought *pan dulce* for an after-Mass treat due to the special guests? They were always a little bit hungry.

"We need Spaniards to populate all our lands," De Anza continued, his voice louder now with an urgent tone. "The Russians are threatening our sovereignty. English pirates raid our coasts. There is no greater service to your King, and to God," he said with a nod to the humble priest in the decrepit church. "If you join this sacred mission northward, the Crown will provide all basic supplies and your families' clothes and food for the first five years," De Anza declared.

Even Quina sat straight in her seat and paid attention at the colonel's grand promise. She noticed her parents glance at each other above the heads of her young siblings. Her father reached over and caressed her mother's cheek, a shocking sight in a family so focused on survival that affection was rare. Whoever this De Anza was sure grabbed the attention of the parishioners. Would her family leave with these soldiers?

After Mass, while the colonel gathered the men around him and spoke loudly of adventures and riches, the wives gossiped among themselves. Quina, in that tenuous space between child and woman, stood at the edge of the group, trying to catch the theme in their words. Her mother debated with her sisters, cousins and friends trying to make sense of this unexpected development in a life where little changed even from one generation to the next. Nothing like this had ever happened before in their remote corner of Sinaloa.

Quina thought they sounded suspicious of the flamboyant colonel and his promises of food and supplies and a distant rich land. Wasn't it possible that life in the new territory could be just as hard as in this one, they said to one another? Weren't there even hotter deserts, high mountains and rivers along the way? Weren't there native tribes who didn't want to give up their lands? Quina sidestepped closer at that. What were they talking about?

Several of the ladies told stories of Yaqui attacks when they were children. They did not look forward to facing other hostile native groups. Her mother mentioned that the soldiers would be obligated to protect the Franciscan priests in the party. Were the settler families going to be protected? And just how far would they be traveling with Colonel De Anza and his men to get to this promised land? There was a lot of skepticism among the wives.

Quina's preference for a stable life with her parents and siblings was exacerbated by stories of flying arrows and traversing scorching sand. It all sounded dangerous and difficult. She was quite sure her father would see sense and stay put in Sinaloa.

That night, Sebastian Altamirano announced to his wife, Quina and her five younger siblings, "We need a new start. This land is no good for farming." He pointed to the dusty soil outside the shack's opening that served as a door. "You children can grow up to be the stewards of this new frontier. Always been proud that we're not mestizo. We'll go with Colonel De Anza to settle these Las Californias with our pure Spanish blood."

Papá was always telling them that they were true Spaniards who had not been tainted by mixing with natives. She didn't quite understand what he meant or why it was so important, but it clearly was to him, so she figured Spanish blood must be a good thing. Dismayed by her father's sudden announcement, she was surprised that he'd been taken in by the colonel's bright flags and finely outfitted troops. The thought of a perilous journey filled with the unknown frightened her. She noticed her mother said nothing.

The next day, her father called the children and his wife together and had them kneel in the dirt outside their hut to pray for their safety on this sacred journey. He made an impassioned speech quoting De Anza's promises and description of the mission's importance. He compared the expedition to the Crusades. He cited their role in civilizing the natives, in bringing God to the north. Then he sent the older ones off to their usual chores, explaining what was needed to pack and prepare to leave.

Each night after that in the few weeks before they departed, he read bible passage after passage stressing the importance of their role in this settlement mission. Quina sat dutifully and listened, terrified, but getting more and more drawn in by her father's readings and passionate speeches.

She knew every story of the Crusades by heart. She pictured the one storybook she'd ever seen at the pueblo church when strangers from *Ciudad de México* had donated supplies to the tiny parish. She'd fawned over the sketches where splashes of color ran outside the black lines in a tableau of religious fervor. She had so wanted to take the book home but the priest had explained that they must be kept at the church for other children to enjoy. Quina had run her fingers across the black markings under each drawing and, for just a moment, understood that there were worlds beyond hers. She tried to imprint each drawing onto her memory, drinking in the luscious colors and sense of glory in every picture. She had paged through the entire book again and again, then reluctantly handed it back to the father. Life in Sinaloa was mostly a dirty brown save for the desert bloom each spring. The colorful images stayed brilliant in her mind.

The day arrived for the family to leave Sinaloa and head toward Tubac, a thousand miles to the north, where Colonel De Anza was assembling settlers and soldiers, priests, livestock and provisions. Sebastian marched ahead, followed by his wife carrying a baby on her back and young ones at each hand, trailed by Quina with her younger brothers at her side. The entire family stomped clumsily in the new huaraches he had acquired by trading the belongings they could not take on the trip. None of them had ever worn shoes before.

As she traversed through Sinaloa to the parched Sonoran desert, forded rivers, crossed mountain ranges, bushwhacked through sagebrush, blisters bleeding from the unfamiliar sandals, Quina reheard her father's nightly readings. She began to accept she was not likely to ever return to her childhood home. In her homesickness, influenced by those glorious stories, during the long days of endless walking, she replayed the Sunday school storybook images in her mind.

A slight, malnourished girl, Quina pictured herself in full knight's uniform leading the cavalry as they traipsed through the desert. Yes, the original crusaders who rode from Rome to bring Christianity to the heathen Arabs and save Jerusalem in the Holy Land were swarthy soldiers of the cross, clinking in their chain mail atop snorting horses. Lances at the ready. But she imagined herself just like them, astride a cantering horse, flags fluttering, as the crusader army followed her on the most glorious of quests. Picturing herself galloping through the sketches of that Crusades storybook, she really thought she was headed to Jerusalem rather than Alta California.

As they finally approached the Tubac meeting site, they met soldiers on horses with families looking as destitute as their own. Once Quina, her parents and the children descended a dusty hillside into a wide plain they all stopped to stare. Below them were seven hundred horses and mules, four hundred longhorn cattle and at least two hundred and forty friars, soldiers, settlers with families and native guides. The dry valley was awash in noisy commotion. Horses whinnied and shuffled. Soldiers' spurs clinked. A crack of the reata popped above the assembled here and there as soldier vaqueros rounded up the cows. Horse hooves pounded the ground in the pursuit. The valley smelled of manure, sweaty travelers and cooking smoke. Gray columns swirled from family fires throughout the throng. The faint aroma of sizzling tortillas rode across the breeze.

The air was electric with anticipation, anxiety. Rambunctious kids chased one another through the field and around the mooing cows. Shy children hid in their mothers' skirts. Babies fussed and women chattered. Men double checked the mule's packs while wives held on tightly to as many children as possible, assigning older kids to grab the little ones' hands. Mothers looked askance at the almost naked native translators and cautioned their children to stick with familiar adults. A loose child could get stomped to death by the animals or disappear with strangers, lost to their loved ones.

For Quina, at that moment, drawings and reality merged. The sight was right out of one of those church picture books. She had never seen so many people or animals ever. Indeed, had not even understood that so many beings existed in the world. Astounded at the sounds and colors, the smells and sheer force of a mob of humanity, Quina sniffed the air. She drank in the excitement as if it were honey flavored hibiscus nectar. Her favorite. She found the communal energy intoxicating. This was by far the most exciting thing that had ever happened in her young, impoverished life. Perhaps her parents were not so crazy after all.

She strode up a little knoll to get a better view. She stood completely still, eyes scanning the valley, absorbing the scene with an astonishment that opened her heart and head to new possibilities. Quina suddenly understood that perhaps she really was a crusader. She really was on a holy mission. That her life had just become so much bigger than she had ever imagined. That perhaps a life beyond caring for babies and coughing over tortilla fires existed. She was overcome with the possibilities and dropped to her knees to pray thanks to God for trusting her family with his mission. Papá must be right. God had chosen them and now they had to deliver.

Colonel De Anza rode in with his favorite soldier escorts, more native translators and the padres leading the religious mission. Quina was enthralled at the respect the crowd paid him as the enormous group shushed to only the soft thuds of shifting horses, an occasional mooing cow. Flags snapped in the breeze. A baby cried, then quieted as his mother must have put him to her breast. De Anza launched into a flowery speech about their campaign, the sacrifice expected for God and King, for their love of Spain. He reiterated his promises of fertile abundance in the north, a land lush and flowering with plentiful streams, fat elk and a seashore brimming with fish. It was still almost a thousand miles ahead and it would take some time to tame the new territory. But the Spanish Crown would provide a steady supply of food and animals until they fully conquered the northern lands. They would prevail.

As the large group moved north slowly, they climbed mountain passes and scrambled up dry river beds jumping from stone to stone with no solid path to navigate. Quina perfected the skills she'd developed on the family's long walk to Tubac. She had learned to hunt for ground squirrels and desert lizards to roast over the weakest flames of sagebrush and cactus needles. She'd squeezed drops of precious water from guaro and barrel cacti and could do so without pricking her fingers. She had learned to tend sick children who had to keep moving. To bind blistered toes. To chisel the cement-like desert floor with a pickaxe to dig a shallow grave for her littlest brother who died after a snake crept into their camp at night and bit the boy.

Now on this long walk with whole villages of people and animals, no longer just her family, Quina developed a new goal. She still missed home but it was fading in her memory and she began to see the journey as an opportunity. She wanted to learn everything she could to be the best servant possible for God on this mission. All she'd done in Sinaloa was gather firewood and cook and take care of babies. Maybe now she could do more for God.

She couldn't wait to read the word of God in the bible herself. She pestered a friendly priest to teach her to read the black scratches in the great book. She convinced the vaqueros to teach her to ride and care for horses and cows, watering them and cleaning hooves at rest stops. She was determined to not let the arduous nature of the journey hinder her family's progress. They must all stay strong for Colonel De Anza, she lectured to the little ones if anyone tired. The mission was too important for any one individual to forestall it. Her friend's mother had died in childbirth the first days of the journey but they kept on. The Pinuelas did not turn back. They scooped up the motherless infant and just kept on walking.

"Let them be an example to us," Quina preached. Her family listened and complied. There really was no other option anyway. No one wanted to be left behind in any of the desolate deserts or mountain passes along the way.

Maria Joaquina grew sinewy and dark brown. So muscular that she could scale any sand dune, rocky cliff or mountain pass with only an imperceptible shortness of breath. Her father called her a mountain goat. But she knew what she truly was. She was a *pobladora*. Just as her parents lectured and prayed, reciting bible passages daily to encourage fortitude. She was a settler, a pioneer, a crusader for God, for the King, for Colonel De Anza, marching as if she too were a soldado de cuera sporting the heavy leather vest of armor, populating and civilizing the northern frontier of New Spain.

The settlers crossed the mighty Colorado River and the endless, arid badlands. They kept moving even when parched with no freshwater stops. They persevered through snake bites and native arrows.

They waited patiently while Captain De Anza detoured slightly with a small contingent to support soldiers defending the San Diego mission against native attacks. When deserters stole the best horses and supplies while they rested at the San Gabriel mission, they sent their fiercest out to capture the miscreants. They said farewell to fellow crusaders as some were assigned mission protection duty at San Gabriel. Then, finally, the De Anza expedition reached the edge of the continent.

Most of the pioneers had never seen the sea. They marveled at whales spouting and birds soaring above the blue. They splashed in the breakers and scooped up handfuls of white sand. The colonizers noted the fertile land and many native villages along the coast as they surged north. In many hamlets the locals were friendly and willing to trade beads, cloth and tobacco for fish, baskets and cups made of reeds and bark. In a few others, they were shooed away by flying arrows with sharp obsidian points.

Would they ever stop? How much farther must they walk? Quina often wondered. Several of the native villages were in beautiful areas that seemed a perfect place to build a settlement and convert the poor, naked heathens. Sometimes she was afraid of possible attacks but mostly she felt sad that these people did not know God or Jesus. She pestered her father one night around the fire that she liked the gentle breezes and upward sweep of the mountains close to the sea alongside the Channel of Santa Barbara. Couldn't they just stop here? Papá said he agreed and had even asked his superiors the same thing. But his sergeant had told him they had to get to Monterrey and the *Puerto* of San Francisco.

"He said we could return to join the guards at that little San Gabriel mission. But it's too dangerous there. We need to stay with the colonel's party. But don't forget this place. There's a future here for us someday," he said. Quina noticed the gleam in her father's eye and the determination in his voice. She hoped he was right. There was a beautiful lagoon and white sand beach and the soft air was so much more inviting than her memory of Sinaloa. She was tired of walking but she realized she didn't miss her old desert home much anymore. They needed to make a home somewhere in this new land.

⁓

"There's the fog again, Mamá. Coming in from the ocean. No sign of the supply ship," Quina said. She had given the same report most every morning for months, that stretched into years, after gathering firewood, her woolen shawl wrapped tight around her shoulders, threadbare from overuse. Their willow branch hut was too small for a fire pit so she stoked the coals cooled by the drizzle, her eyes searching across the large bay to the islands, out along the Eastern shore, then the West at the bay's great opening, hoping for the arrival of the *San Carlos*. The little colony perched above the enormous bay needed more food, tools and supplies to build stronger shelter, clothe and feed the settlers.

Once depositing the group to establish a settlement alongside the bay, Colonel De Anza left for a new campaign. His lieutenants and the priests took over to build a fort and establish a mission. But the De Anza settlers found the little Yerba Buena settlement was not a home but a freezing, windy hilltop. The land was rocky with few flat meadows, nothing but milk cows and sheep could survive there. Unaccustomed to the chilly weather, the entire party was frozen. They grew resentful and sick. Mothers were coughing. Children had constant runny noses. Strong soldiers were weakened by the need to divvy up shrinking food supplies. No crops grew. The frustrated and destitute settlers clung to the frozen hillside dependent on the supply ships from San Blas and Acapulco, unable to become self-supporting.

Quina and her mother struggled to keep the children fed and healthy. She was angry. Where were the promised lands they could plant? Had they just traded the hot desolation of the Sinaloan desert for a cold one by the sea? Yes, the bay was spectacularly large and surrounded with good alcoves for ports and anchoring but it was not the place for the Altamirano family, she thought. They needed flat land, warmth and rich soil for crops and animals.

The shores of the bay did not seem particularly promising either. Papá often went with Lieutenant Moraga to explore the bay's winding shoreline. Each foray he returned with stories of yet more native villages, some friendly who exchanged elk and fish for beads and sashes and held elaborate dances around the firelight. Other times he told stories of natives attacking with arrows from the brush, hidden in the tall grasses. She was always glad when he returned safely. This family needed every one of its members to survive. Losing her brother in the desert had been devastating to all of them. They had to stay together.

Quina grew discouraged. Was this what it meant to be a crusader? To suffer in cold instead of in heat? By fourteen, she was growing into a young woman, obedient and devoted to her parents since survival with them was all she knew. She was as devout as they were, determined to fulfill the goals of the Church and Crown. But the tough mountain goat who was not afraid of crossing rivers on terrified horses or drinking water from prickly cacti had just enough rebelliousness to speak up to her parents now and then.

"Papá, can't we serve the King better in that meadow and lagoon by the Channel of Santa Barbara?" she asked gently after bible readings one night, wind whipping at the flapping sail fabric serving as their front door. Papá nodded and told her he'd been thinking the same thing. Las Californias was vast the Spanish had discovered. Soldiers and settlers were needed in so many locations. Including in warmer ones.

Moraga had just announced he was finally allowing some of the soldiers to venture south as scouting parties for future presidios and missions. The military leaders had determined the coastline between Monterrey and San Diego needed protection. The next presidio was planned for that plateau between sharp rising mountains and the beach. There were villages around for the priests to convert. Someday they'd build a mission there. Quina's father told the family he would ask permission to leave. She was elated. Maybe finally they could settle in a place as plentiful as De Anza had promised.

Within a few weeks, Quina's family said good-bye to their fellow crusaders—the Peraltas and Bernals, the Berrellezas and Alvisos—with whom they'd walked almost a thousand miles from Tubac. Together these soldiers and families had built the adobe and brush walls of the presidio and the Misión San Francisco de Asís. They'd explored the shores of the great bay. They'd established the northernmost outpost of the Spanish empire in the Americas. As Quina and her family headed south to continue as pobladores for the Spanish King, and God, they left behind a cold and desolate Yerba Buena, no more than a lonely cluster of makeshift buildings perched on the edge of the continent looking to the sea for supply ship salvation.

She and her family once again walked, as the two horses, two cows, two sheep and a mule the army had granted them were loaded with supplies. Sacks of seeds, grains, beans, dry corn kernels and a few farm tools bounced atop the animals. She held on tight to the ropes around the cows' necks as she walked in her now worn huaraches and mused that the Crown must have realized how difficult a frontier Alta California was when they'd promised five years of supplies. After almost four years since departing Sinaloa, they still needed provisions to survive. She was not one bit sorry to leave the miserable place. Maybe now they could find a place to settle with some actual promise.

Yet as the sky turned navy then dark at dusk on that first long day, Quina realized there were many dangers and uncertainties ahead. Her family was alone on this expedition, told by the army commander and priests to find a sound location for the presidio, set up a homestead and grow crops to prepare for others to come. In years. There were no soldiers to protect them, no other families along on the campaign for companionship or to share the burden. Quina marched with trepidation, yet with purpose. The Altamiranos were crusaders once again.

CHANGES IN THE LITTLE ADOBE

Diego rode back from a broad southern beach, Santa Barbara they called it, where he'd been with Captain Ortega scouting the final site for a fourth presidio. He should have been elated at this latest development as Alta California continued to grow. Padres Serra and Crespi had plans for another mission on yet another lovely bay. He'd been promoted to lieutenant and should be heading to the presidio in Monterrey to celebrate with his comrades. But he aimed for his little house. He had a bad tooth. He feared it was horribly inflamed and mentioned it to Sholeta when he first arrived. He was in pain.

By that evening, his face had swollen and his cheek was hot. His skin was pink from his forehead down his neck to his collarbone. He could not stop sweating. He put a cold compress on his cheek and lay down. Nothing helped. Sholeta returned to the house after cleaning up the exhausted horses from their long journey away. Moaning on his bed, Diego gestured to her to sit and she looked inside his mouth. She told him to wait while she left for his work area at the corral. She returned with a blacksmith tool for hoof care. She gave him whiskey to drink and waited a bit until it took effect. She poured some into his mouth over the infected spot.

"Sit still," she said while she tied one hand to the chair with rope. She poured whiskey on a handkerchief. "Hold this to your nose. Now don't move."

She put her foot on his knee, opened up his mouth, put the blacksmith forceps in and yanked that tooth right out. She had to twist and pull a few times but she got it. Diego cried out in shock and pain. What had she done? He almost passed out. She untied his hand, pushed him to lie down on the bed, put the soaked handkerchief over his mouth and nose.

"You'll be fine soon," she said as she returned to cleaning her kitchen pots and preparing a soup for supper. He wouldn't be able to chew anything for a meal or two.

In his feverish sleep of recovery over the next few nights, his dreams of Isabela became more mixed with images of Sholeta. The two blended and twisted, floating over the tossing ocean, above the leaky ship with sails whipping and the captain yelling as water poured over the bow and a gale howled.

Since the padres took away the tule skirts and deerskin tops of the native women long ago, they covered them up with rough burlap, wool and poor cotton shifts. There were no seamstresses around to make a proper dress or mend tears. Sholeta always wore a baggy, burlap sack of a dress with no shape. Nothing showed except ankles and arms from the elbows. Diego had often noticed her fine wrists and in his feverish dreams he saw wrists and ankles swirling through the ocean.

Once his fever subsided he resolved to rejoin Captain Ortega in San Diego, where they always seemed to have problems with native attacks and thievery. The night before he was to ride off, Diego cornered Sholeta in the pantry as she reached high for a pungent salted meat. He grabbed her from behind, spun her around and kissed her, pushing her up against the shelves loaded with sacks of seeds, corn meal and beans. He caressed her wrists, one at a time, gazed into her eyes, then grabbed at her rough shift. He kissed her again as he pressed into her and started to pull her dress up to her thighs.

Sholeta never resisted, surprising him with an impassioned kiss, raising her arms for him to remove the scratchy fabric. He never stopped kissing her mouth or her wrists as he took her in the pantry, their shyness covered by the damp darkness, their bodies pressed up against the hard sacks of corn and barley.

Diego had never wanted to overly force her. His memories of his father beating his mother, dragging her into their bedroom and whipping the sheet closed behind through which he could hear her cries had never left him. He knew he held the power, but he did not want to ever take a woman that way. His father's behavior had led him to limit his drink and not force women the way he knew many soldados did. He'd heard the screams of gentile women in the mission nunnery when soldiers broke the locks to get in. Or out back of the newest saloon in the pueblo where off duty soldiers drank with native cowboys. He never especially liked hearing men force themselves on women, and tried not to think of Isabela, or his sisters left behind in Barcelona, as possible victims. The women he'd been with were prostitutes in the port towns like Veracruz and San Blas and he'd always paid, selecting girls who were outgoing and vivacious and seemed to enjoy the work. Any who he suspected were forced into the trade were not appealing to him.

At the same time, this native woman was his, after all. His for the taking. And it was not really his place to judge others. There were so few women in Alta California, although their numbers had definitely increased since he'd first arrived ten years ago. So he pretended not to see or hear when a soldier forced a native woman. But he did not like it.

With Sholeta, he was pleasantly surprised that she succumbed easily to him and even seemed to want to participate. He never got her to his bedroom. They fumbled with each other so furtively and passionately, almost as if someone outside were listening, that they never left the dark pantry, their clothes tossed across the sacks of grain.

Afterward, their bodies still entwined on the pantry floor, Diego realized he was somewhat ashamed that he couldn't remember what Isabela looked like. A little embarrassed at this change in their relationship, he caressed Sholeta's wrist and arm up to her shoulder with a single finger, quietly. Her skin puckered slightly; she shivered and her nipples tensed again. He realized he liked not only having sex with her, but this moment of tenderness afterward. For just a moment, Diego had a sense of a real home, perhaps even of family. Sholeta touched his cheek.

"Is the pain gone?" she asked. It was the first time either of them spoke. He laughed and nodded, appreciating her young, firm body, her strong arms, her supple hips. He caressed her wrists, kissed each one, then pushed her away to grab his shirt and pants, boots and sash. He quickly cleaned up and dressed in his room, grabbed his bag and the food she had packed and strode out the door. He did not return for three months.

When Diego rode in, Sholeta had the house spotless, the clothes mended, the garden flourishing and a mini-orchard started with tiny orange and lemon saplings swaying in the mist. She was heartier and browner than ever. He noticed she seemed to be happier too, with a little less of the heavy sadness on her brow and shadows below her eyes. She must like it when I'm gone. She has the run of the place, he absentmindedly thought as he watched her prepare a meal. He noticed she did not ask many questions at first but seemed to focus on the cooking. Perhaps she was still shy from making love in the kitchen pantry. He did realize it was possible she'd had little experience with men, despite being at the mission with other neophytes and natives, vaqueros and soldiers for her early teen years. Sholeta seemed to be pretending their encounter had never occurred.

Exhausted from the trail, stuffed with her delicious food, which he had missed out on the camino, he stumbled into bed after supper, simply throwing his guns, chaps and heavy cuera armor on the floor. Sometime later he awoke and felt her next to him, smelling of soap and sweet jasmine flowers. She was asleep but he could see that she had brushed her hair, cleaned herself up before creeping in beside him wearing only her light gauze nightgown. He rolled over and began caressing her.

Afterward, when they both fully woke up, he smiled at her, touching her wrists relieved to find that she still wanted him. He was gone so often that he had wondered if she would find a native at a nearby rancheria to keep her company. Every time he returned to the adobe, Diego was always a bit surprised that she was still there. He was pleased that the pantry encounter had not frightened her away.

Without a word, she slipped from under the blanket and heated a pot of water in the kitchen. She returned and led him to sit in his chair while she mixed the hot water with cool from a silver pitcher. She threw mint and salvia in the warm water. Then she lathered him with the best soap they had, scrubbing his back, his chest, his muscular arms, touching the scars as she washed. She soaped his hair then used the pitcher to rinse him. After he was clean and dry, she climbed on, straddling him, and made love to him right there. Diego was surprised, but not disappointed. Though neither said a word, he silently agreed that it was far superior to have intimate relations when refreshed with sleep and a good hot bath.

That night, Diego waited until she'd cleaned up the dinner plates and he'd written in his journal and read a few passages from the tiny bible he'd carried with him from Spain. Then he approached her in the kitchen and invited her into his bed. During the cold, lonely darkness of nights out on the trail, he had thought of her often. He found himself hoping she would be a willing partner in the little house, not only as a lover, but as a companion. In the shadows dancing on the candlelit clay walls, he took her hand and led her into his small bedroom, clearing chaps and sashes off the wool blanket.

Diego, slowly this time, kissed Sholeta's wrists, then her lips, then pulled the coarse dress up over her head. He admired her in the dim light, then caressed her breasts, her firm stomach and strong legs. Then with greater ardor he pulled her to him, wrapping his arms around her in a firm embrace, kissing her deeply. As he gripped her back, he felt a strange roughness on her skin. What was that on her back? He grabbed her shoulders and pushed her away, then looked deeply in her eyes, questioning. He turned her around. Long scars crossed her shoulders and her back, crisscrossing and twisting in an angry tangle of raised skin, puckered lines, gaps like troughs, between other lines. He was horrified at the damage, shocked and ashamed that he had not noticed before.

Sholeta was so young, so strong and beautiful in a natural way. She was never sick and seemed so comfortable on the land, as if she were a part of it. As if they were one. Never trying to tame it and control it as he knew he and all the Spaniards were attempting to do. To make the earth their own possession. The horror at what his comrades had done to her exposed Diego to a truth he often denied himself. That he was an invader, taking land and people who did not necessarily want to be colonized or converted to the ways of the Church. He felt protective of her and wished he could heal the scars and her suffering. But Diego rarely allowed himself to question his work and face that he too had subjected many natives to pain and loss. It was a conquest after all. It was his job to ensure that the Spaniards always won. Questioning would not solve anything. He determined that his job was to just protect those in his orbit.

"Oh, Sholeta. The lash? They whipped you? A young girl?"

"The mission," was all she said. She looked down as if embarrassed by his discovery.

"You're with me now," he said. His voice was firm, strong. "That part of your life is over." He tipped her chin up to look at him. She nodded so slightly he almost didn't see it.

"Now come here," he said, so softly and gently that Sholeta looked at him directly and leaned in to kiss him, wrapping her arms around him.

❧

Although he was her captor and she was supposed to be spying on him, she had come to care for this man who never treated her badly, who was a companion in the loneliness of having lost her family, village and familiar life. She'd been pleased he'd made love to her in the pantry as she felt connected to him more each time he returned, indeed, realized she missed him when he was gone. She ached for affection and her womanly body now ached with passion as well. With no mother or aunts, grandmother or sisters remaining to discuss love making, she felt she was fumbling through but instinct guided her to clean herself with fragrant flowers and seduce him as soon as he returned home. But the scars. She'd almost forgotten about them, or at least they'd become such a part of her that she pretended to forget them. She was mortified in some ways that maybe she was damaged goods to him. But his people had done this to her after all. Best that he know the truth.

His shock and tenderness touched her deeply. She had not heard words of kindness, was it perhaps love even, in years. Not since she was a child, she noted absently as she pressed herself into this man who would protect her. She was a woman now and perhaps this man would help lessen the weight, the pain, the loss her scars represented. The isolation could be excruciating. Since he'd discovered her scars, Sholeta found Diego desirable in an exotic way, as if he were from a distant village, maybe one farther south. As if he were from where the men were rumored to be extra handsome and strong from living along the cliffs where the waterfall splashed to the sea.

After that, Sholeta welcomed him home from the presidio each night with a hot meal spiked with acorn or game birds. She added fish and shellfish into her stews. He told her it made him nostalgic for Catalonian dishes. Then she slipped into his bed. Once they were sleeping together regularly, she showed him how to wash, with which plants to scrub to remove horse hair and hoof residue. To lessen the foul stench of sweat-soaked leather and wet wool. To cleanse the heaviness of oils from his hair and limbs. Their bed became a warm, clean respite from the harshness of frontier life.

At the same time, she was often disgusted with herself, with her betrayal of her people. And she still wanted to help Ores. She continued to feign interest in Diego's campaigns for information. Combining it with what she heard in the pueblo she sometimes had something to tell her cousin in their midnight meetings. But Diego was not a useful source of information. He was not a politician and most likely would never be a comandante. He could rise through the lowest ranks, as he was so focused on doing, but he was never going to be the supreme commander. A ferocious el fantasma warrior, perhaps a capitán one day with his own small unit. He even told her that was what he aspired to. That he was not a glad-hander or dealmaker. He was a blacksmith, a magician with horses, and above all, an order-following soldier. Would Ores ever take her back to the woods if she couldn't provide more valuable insights into Spanish plans?

She also wondered how she would adjust if she did return. The Ohlone ways were buried deep within her and they would always be her preferred manner of living. Yes, she'd proved to be adaptable, a survivor, as she'd promised her father. But it was as if her parents had branded her at birth, the way she'd seen the vaqueros do to the cows. Her instincts, the songs of her childhood, the sense of earth's electricity under her callused feet, her ability to smell the animals and read the winds were burned into her over thousands of years. Her Ohlone ancestors still stirred. She felt compelled to honor them. But she started to wonder if living with Diego in the simple yet comfortable little adobe had corrupted her. Sometimes she felt guilty at the comfort their life almost as husband and wife gave her in the empty land. Perhaps the loneliness had pushed her into this twisted relationship with the invader.

Diego had excelled since his promotion and was aiming for the captain sash. As Las Californias grew and transformed into a Spanish settlement, his newest goal was to become not only a higher-ranking soldier but to have a larger, comfortable home with his own produce and animals. He took on more blacksmith jobs whenever he could convince the commander he was needed in Monterrey. His hidden stash of silver grew. He negotiated with the priests and vaqueros and acquired a cow, building materials, a sheep and some chickens. He expanded the corral to add a little barnyard and he made plans to add rooms on to his adobe.

Occasionally, he'd grow nostalgic and wish his mother and Catalonian family could see him now. But mostly, he followed his commander's orders and took advantage of his growing wealth and status to expand his mini homestead. Perhaps he should marry he thought now and then. Comandante Ortega was always after him to find a Spanish wife from among one of the new settler families. But being continually on the trail with the soldiers and padres, he didn't spend enough time at home to court young ladies. In fact, Diego was quite content with Sholeta and his little home in the pines above the presidio. He had little interest in making a change.

THE BABIES

The blood had stopped now for two moon cycles. What now? She said nothing to Diego nor to her cousin in the shadows below the live oak. "I've been feeling weak lately. Their food often makes me sick," she told her cousin one night. "Can you bring me more mak-'amham next time?" She tried to get his sympathy by describing the strange food of the Spanish.

He grimaced. "We have little ourselves. You must be used to it by now, Tar. You've been with them so long. We're just a little group of warriors on the move. But I'll do what I can."

Although her blood had not flowed until after she was a captive at the mission and she'd been denied the ritual ceremony and tattooing associated with womanhood, she instinctively knew she needed to nourish the baby growing within her. Losing her mother so young had denied her the traditional knowledge of sex and pregnancy, birth and child rearing she would have learned in the tule and willow branch huts. She often felt cheated of that instruction into womanhood and it made her miss her mother even more.

Sholeta felt naked without the tattoos which identified her as a grown woman, ready for adult pursuits. To not have had the formal shaman blessing and rituals welcoming her to womanhood was serious and she feared it could lead to problems. Would she have a healthy baby? She was just guessing at love making with Diego, at how she should care for her growing belly, and she had no idea what she would do when the baby was ready for this world. Childbirth was frightening. Would she give birth alone in the little house? What if there were complications? As she had grown accustomed since her capture, she would just have to figure it out on her own.

Diego returned when she was about four months pregnant, but as with so many men, he did not notice any difference in her shape. She greedily kept most of the native food she'd collected for her own meals and spiked his food a little less with the shellfish he loved. He didn't notice that either and just seemed happy to be home with her.

"I have to leave again soon," he said to her one night in bed, his voice husky with post love making emotion. He leaned in to kiss her. "I don't want to go. I'm trying to get Comandante Ortega to put me in command here at the presidio so I don't have to ride out with him so often."

She was surprised and said nothing but couldn't help but raise an eyebrow. While she believed he did like their cozy house and growing set of crops, she knew him well enough now to know his life was in the saddle. He was built for adventure and the military life on the road with the soldados and a clear mission. He would be restless if he were assigned to stay in Monterrey too long. And of course, he wasn't. He left several days after telling her he wanted to stay.

A few weeks later, Sholeta awoke in the night with sharp pains and blood pouring down her legs. Alone, as always, she got herself up as best she could, stumbled and grabbed at the bed frame and table and tried to sit on the chamber pot. She told herself to imagine the trees above the house protecting her, to breathe with their rustling needles in the wind. She calmed her body as if she were silently waiting and stalking a deer. She breathed the strong but imperceptible breath of the patient hunter. She got the pains to subside in this manner and the blood eventually stopped.

As she cleaned up, she could see that a tiny figure was part of the debris that had oozed out from her body. She began to cry as she accepted that she'd lost the baby. What had happened? This was what she'd feared without her mother and a shaman to guide her through pregnancy to successful childbirth. She must honor the traditions and protect the baby as it moved into the afterlife.

Once she could walk, she collected every sheet and cloth coated with blood and took them out through the garden, past the tiny orchard, up to the base of the largest pine and buried them beneath it. She said Ohlone prayers of loss and longing for family and wishes for sending her child to the spirit ancestors. The pine would protect the baby. The spirits would whisk away its tiny soul so it would not be alone in the spirit world. She said more prayers to send the baby to her mother and father and all her siblings. They would be together there. The baby would not be an orphan, alone, as she was.

She said nothing to Diego. The sadness dwelled deep inside her in a private place connected to her past, her Ohloneness. While their relationship grew more comfortable and affection slowly blossomed within her, Sholeta still saw him as the other, as unable to fully understand her, as the foreign invader.

She did tell Ores when she saw him one night at the live oak. He was sad at her loss but did not ask who the father was. Sholeta realized that perhaps Ores had expected all along that she would get the best information from the soldier if she lived with him as his wife. She asked again, as she did every single time she saw him or the cousin,

"Please take me with you back to your village. I'll help you defeat the Spanish. I can help your wife raise your children. Don't you want us to be together, as family?" She begged him out of habit but also afraid that if she lived much longer with Diego as his wife, she would eventually have a baby, they would become a family, she would no longer want to return to her Ohlone roots. That terrified her as well.

He was unflinching in his rejection of her proposals. He needed her where she was. "No begging. Don't be weak. Help your people," he'd repeat each time with what she felt was a callous disregard for her loneliness and isolation.

She felt suspended between two worlds and not able to move much in either one, as if she were a bear trapped by the cowboys with a lasso on each leg as they did to grab a grizzly before the bear and bull fights. Sometimes, Sholeta did not ask Ores too forcefully about going back with him. It seemed that when she did, he sent the cousin more often, and there were longer periods without seeing her brother. She was desperate for family and didn't want to jeopardize any interaction he was willing to have. She tried not to beg. She tried to uncover useful information but usually had little to offer.

After the miscarriage and Ores' refusal to rescue her, Sholeta grew quieter and less energetic. She missed the baby that had not even fully grown and that emptiness merged with her loneliness to consume her days. She noticed Diego seemed to stay at home for longer stints and was more tender with her. Perhaps he noticed. After a few months, Sholeta was pregnant again.

Diego left before she was showing and did not return until she was eight months along. Nervous about the birth, she was relieved to see him ride in as she must be getting close to delivery. He eased her anxiety with his delighted surprise at the prospect of a baby in the little house. She heard him start to ask if he was the father and then stop himself. Did he think she ventured out to the tiny saloon at the presidio when he was gone? She did not reassure him one way or another. There was so much they didn't say to each other.

The real problem was that Diego returned sick. He told her that many natives had died at the Mission San Francisco de Asís where he'd been. She was terrified of the horrible pox she'd heard stories about and stayed far from Diego in her tiny room. She did not eat with him but simply cooked and left the food at his table. His sickness was mild but he'd have to care for himself this time she told him.

"Next time, don't come back home until you're well," she said. She was furious that he hadn't left the moment he saw how pregnant she was. As she feared, she came down with the pox. She became violently ill and could not eat. She had fevers. Pus-filled lesions covered her torso and legs. Her body ached constantly and she had to fight to not cry out in pain. She was delirious so barely realized that Diego, weakened by his less serious bout, struggled to care for her. He told her he could not ask an army doctor to assist since she still had the pox and was covered with sores. So Sholeta and Diego had that baby by themselves. He brought her broths filled with meat and vegetables and coaxed her to eat. He covered her body with rough cotton cloth soaked in cool spring water and brought her into the main house. She was touched that he moved her into his bedroom and took charge. Though she suspected he knew as little as she did about childbirth. And then the baby was ready for the world.

Somehow the mistrust, the tangled web of animosity and appreciation between them, the protection and betrayal, and maybe a little growing love, seemed to lighten and fold together as they worked to birth the baby. A little boy did make it into the adobe but he quickly sickened with fever and spots and died three days later. She held him in her arms almost constantly those few days and felt the love she'd so longed to express to her own parents and siblings come through to this child. And then a deeper sadness that threatened to drown her completely poured in and consumed that love after the baby died.

Exhausted and distraught, Sholeta led Diego up to the pines above the house and suggested they bury their child under the second tallest tree. Diego was strangely quiet and passive and she assumed he just did not know what to do. She took charge naturally. "The biggest pine watches over our hill and home," she said, pointing to it. "We will bury him here. This second tallest can protect our son."

She held his arm for strength and began to cry quietly and say prayers in her native tongue. She noticed his quizzical gaze at her and understood he had not been completely sure he was the father. When she stopped praying, Diego said The Lord's Prayer over the tiny mound under the swaying trees. She'd heard the prayer in her mission years even though she'd never uttered it herself. She squeezed his arm and nodded. Even though she was not a believer, she realized he was sending the baby off to his God and ancestors in his own way. For some time, they stood together, holding on to each other, as the whisper of the wind rustled the pine branches and needles far above their son's grave.

Sholeta retreated into herself even more than a lonely woman who lived almost a hermit's existence could. She was so sad over dead babies. She barely ate. She lost interest in the garden and let it go to weed when Diego was away. The horses seemed to read her pain and were extra persistent about nuzzling for a barley or vegetable treat. But other than them she had no one to confide in, no one for comfort, no one who could share her grief. After that tiny window of union during childbirth and the burial of their son, Sholeta had nothing but anger and blame for Diego.

The hate she'd born when she first came to his house returned. He was responsible for their baby dying. He returned with the pox and stayed there. The minute he saw her bulging belly, he should have turned and moved in to the presidio, having a military doctor care for him. Sending a well doctor to help her give birth. She shouldn't have had to ask him to do that. He should have figured it out. Furious, one night a few weeks after the baby's death, she let him have it.

"You killed our baby. And I know what you do on those expeditions when you're gone for months and return with infected arrow wounds. You kill my people. Maybe you would stop having nightmares if you stopped killing the native peoples of this land. We are peaceful and your kind, those you call *gente de razon,* are the most unreasonable of all. Don't fool yourself Diego, all you Spanish gente de razon are just a bunch of murderers. You're not saving us with your religion. Do you see all the ones the Padres baptized? Are their babies living? Are they thriving? Not too many of them." She stopped and fled to her room. She didn't make food or clean the house for days.

After a week of her self-imposed exile, she heard Diego return from the presidio one night, banging chairs and pots around the dining area. The noise was unusual. It sounded angry. He stormed into her room, pulled her up off the bed and marched her into the main house. She was light headed and weak and felt like a shell of her former self. He pushed her hard into a kitchen table chair. She could barely sit up but she could see his glare was dark, fierce.

"This is the life you have," he said. "Don't you lecture me." What? She was confused at his angry tone but then remembered how she'd blamed him for all the death around them. "I know you're not baptized. You should be grateful to be alive, living here peacefully, not at the mission. You know perfectly well they beat natives there if they flee to their villages, if they don't work hard, if they steal food. Do you want to go back?" he threatened. "I'm not responsible for all the sickness at the missions, for your family dying, Sholeta. You're better off staying with me. You too might die if you returned to the mission. And if you go back to the woods with your people? I can't protect you there. You know that."

She couldn't respond. The foreign words stuck in her throat and all she could think of was expletives and disbelief in her native tongue. "Back to the woods?" she managed to get out. Just a croak, her voice unused to talking.

"I know about your visits up the valley," he said. Accusation in his tone. "Who is he? Why do you go all that way in the darkest hour and then return? Are you planning to run off? You've been here a long time. And you keep coming back."

Sholeta sat straight up in the chair, shock and fear causing a tingling in her blood and a hotness in her cheeks. She put her hands to her opened mouth to prevent a cry from escaping. How could he know? She was always so careful. She stared at him, looking deep into those dark eyes she now knew so well, that she despised and found comfort in at the same time.

"I followed you on several nights," he said. "You think I'm dead to the world in our bed after we've made love? But you forget, Sholeta, I'm a dragoon above all else. Mostly I sleep out on the ground listening for grizzlies to come steal our meat or enemy horse thieves sneaking into our camp. I'm never fully asleep. After I awoke several times and found you gone, I had to follow you."

She was too surprised to say anything before he continued. "Perhaps you could tell me if the local natives have attacks planned for horses at the nearby missions? Or if they plan to lure baptized neophytes away to the woods. I will keep your secret visits to myself. Let you stay here, but you must give me something in return."

Sholeta nearly choked, aghast at what he was suggesting. But did she have a choice? Diego was right that she would likely die if she returned to the mission compound. And she realized that a life hiding out on the run in the hills above might not turn out very well either. Her people were under attack and dying everywhere. The little adobe was safe for now. Even though now it was filled with as much sadness as she had endured at the mission barracks, it was more of a home than she'd had in the past nine years. She would stay. And she would have to figure out how to appear to spy for Diego. Could she get away with being a bad spy for both men? Fortunately, he was gone a lot.

"Sholeta, please don't forget that I lost the baby too," he whispered. "I too am grieving. We have a life here, together." This sudden change toward tenderness moved her. She did care for this man, her only companion in a precarious place, but she was not naive to the complexity of their dependence on each other, their power imbalance, her imprisonment of bad options. To stay safe she would have to continue in survivor mode.

"I only go to my people for better food," she lied. "The Spanish dishes make me sick. When I was pregnant I needed to stay healthy with my own food. My body is still not accustomed to your grains and beans and cow meat. I went to keep our baby healthy." She began to silently weep. He put his arm around her and led her to his bed where he held her close through the night.

In the morning, she rose before dawn to clean the adobe and prepare breakfast as before. It was a mess after weeks of her strike from household tasks. She had never promised to spy on Ores and his rebellious band but an implicit agreement now existed between them. Diego would not send her packing and she would report on native movements in the area. What have I become, she thought, as she took a break from cleaning to find some measure of comfort with the horses.

Her favorite whinnied at her approach and licked her palm where he found the barley grains. The horse leaned his vast head into her body as if to say, I know, I know, we are both captives, locked into a contract for survival. Maintain some dignity. I am a fine stallion and serve my master proudly. I know you are strong too. Sholeta gazed into that large brown eye with the frame of long lashes, felt his immense power and contradictory softness and swallowed her pride. She would spy for both men and remain in the little adobe.

When they had stood under the tall pines to bury the dead baby, Diego also was grief-stricken over losing his first child, a son. He had been astonished at Sholeta's calm and strength after a birth filled with sickness and pain. He had decided to let her say farewell and grieve in her own way. Surprised at hearing her speak in her native language, he realized that in many ways, he'd come to think of her like himself. As if she had no ethnicity, nationality, no other life before him. She belonged to him and the little house and the wooded hillside. They fit together. He knew that was not true, of course. He touched her scars regularly. But he refused to let himself think too much about the lives the natives left behind when they lived away from the woods.

After their baby's death, at first, he left her alone. But when she lashed out at him in anger, blaming him for all the loss in her life and then retreated to her room to lie comatose on the bed, he decided enough was enough. She had never said so much to him at one time. It had been so hate filled it anguished him. Everyone grieves differently, he reminded himself. He knew how powerful grief was and that it could make you behave in unusual ways. He remembered how he was so numb and confused with grief after his mother's death from tuberculosis that he'd joined the military, left his siblings with his aunt and fled Spain. The anguish of loss could push people to extremes.

Exasperated with her, saddened by the loss not only of his son but also any closeness they'd shared, he'd tried to shock Sholeta out of her incapacitating grief. He was still in charge and she should not forget it. It wasn't his fault the little boy had died. He wouldn't report her contacts with rebel natives to the presidio if she stopped blaming him for the evils of the world.

Diego knew he'd pushed her hard, acting like a controlling patron. Deep down he realized he couldn't let this woman, a comforting companion, the mother of his dead baby buried up under the pines, leave him. He too struggled with sadness over losing their son. A loss of family in his new world—Alta California. He longed to make this place, his new Catalonia, a real home. She was an important part of his life in the little house under the pines.

At the presidio, Diego continued to be a loyal and efficient solider for Comandante Ortega, who the army moved throughout Alta California as needed. Diego followed him, ambitiously seeking his own promotion to captain. His El fantasma reputation as a tricky opponent to horse thieves and mini-bands of rebels grew. Little did his enemies suspect that when not on the trail hunting them he was actually becoming domesticated. A promotion would give him more silver and perhaps a chance at a grant of land from the viceroy. His new goal was land for ranching. Funds to build a bigger adobe.

The tiny Monterrey pueblo's population was growing and the mission expanding its agricultural production. He felt sure the future was in land. Whenever stationed in Monterrey, he increased his blacksmithing business to trade for seeds and timber, tools and animals. Slowly, he expanded the adobe, adding on rooms, improving his blacksmith shop, buying more horses and investing in sheep.

Within a year, Sholeta was pregnant again. He was thrilled. When she was clearly close to giving birth with an enormous round belly, he returned from a campaign sick and she picked up the illness. They were both desperate to keep her healthy and protect the baby.

Late one night when she'd fallen asleep early, Diego snuck out in her place to meet the secret contact in the forest. He'd learned the signs of her preparations for the visits and expected the contact would be there. He took her tiny deerskin, bay leaves and a favorite abalone shell to cover his scent and have proof of his connection to her. He slipped on the deerskin boots reserved for El fantasma strikes and climbed silently up the hill and over into the next valley.

He waited on the tree limb that she used as her watching perch. He controlled his breath to move through him without any sign of inhaling or exhaling. A figure approached the tree and slid under its branches. Diego, as quietly and unthreateningly as he could, murmured almost imperceptibly, hoping this native knew some Spanish,

"She's not coming. She's very sick and very pregnant. Can you bring her more of the best of your native foods to nourish her? We must keep her strong so she and the baby both survive. She has already lost one baby," he said to the shadow.

There was a sudden movement as the native realized he'd been tricked but he seemed to regain his composure quickly and spoke in a broken but understandable Castilian. "No, you are wrong," came the reply through the dark. "There are two graves on the hilltop. Why should I help you? You are her captor.".

Diego could just barely see the man's shape but no distinguishing characteristics. Who was he? Her lover? A relative? "Who are you?" he responded. "Are you her husband, her brother? What do you mean she lost two babies? I would know about that." He was aghast at the man's accusation. Was her life more secret from him than he even imagined?

"You were away. You're quite audacious to come here. I assume she doesn't know. I'll bring her favorite foods and leave them under the pines where the babies are buried. Do not come back. Do not look for me. Do not tell anyone, least of all Tar, uh, Sholeta, we've spoken. I know whose baby this is, but don't let anyone else know. That will only put her in more danger, from all sides. Now go."

Diego, unaccustomed to taking orders from anyone but Ortega or his commanders, flinched at the direct order. But he complied as the figure disappeared as quickly and mysteriously as he'd arrived. He proceeded slowly, silently as he'd come, listening intently for an approach behind him. Why wouldn't this native attack and kill him right there on the dark mountainside? Presumably he loved Sholeta too, and also wanted to see her give birth and thrive. He realized the errand had been foolish. But he was desperate.

He returned without incident. Several days later he ascended the steep incline to the pines and found small piles of shellfish, seal blubber, bird meat. There was a basket filled with acorns and roots he did not recognize. As he scooped up the Ohlone food, he realized that the first dead baby must be buried under the largest tree. That was why she'd wanted them to bury their son under the second tallest. He realized he had no idea of Sholeta's life in his absence and perhaps this native figure was the father of the other dead baby. Maybe he came down from the hills to be with her when he was gone. Maybe she had an Ohlone husband who was a fugitive and she was balancing conflicting lives as much as he was. There were strong walls between them he hoped a healthy child could help tear down. He told her he'd obtained the native food she liked from a nearby rancheria.

Out in the pueblo or at the mission as he traded sacks of seeds or repaired vaqueros' saddles, spurs and bridles, Diego told everyone that his maid had been raped by a soldier at the presidio in the dark and was terrified to go down the hill to Monterrey. He'd been away, they didn't know who it was but now he had a pregnant maid who didn't want to leave the house for errands. What a hassle, he implied in all the conversations. The padres or vaqueros, even the soldados, would nod in understanding. Yeah, gotta watch out for the neophyte women, but the unbaptized ones are even worse, they'd say. They get into all sorts of trouble when you're not watching them. Can't let these native women out of your sight. They've got no morals. Get them over to the mission and get them baptized, they said.

At the same time Diego strove to keep Sholeta healthy and protected from any outside intrusion, he was under increasing pressure from the comandantes, any governors he met, and his own beloved Commander Ortega, to get married. The number of women in the territory had grown significantly over the past fifteen years, especially after the De Anza party blazed a trail for settlers to come north to homestead. Many of the original settlers had large families whose daughters were growing up and as more pobladores arrived from the south, and even from Spain, the collection of candidates increased.

Several of the ever-changing governors and military elite were establishing themselves with larger homes. The hospitality famous in the great houses of the Spanish steppes and in Mexican New Spain was slowly making its way to the northern territory. Spanish fashion and taste for fine wine, food and a good party was slowly coming to Alta California. Men ordered furniture and luxurious cloth to impress their wives, hoping to convince them to stay in the barren territory, still mostly populated with priests and soldiers. A few of the longtime commanders had just been granted land concessions from the Spanish king. After a good rodeo to show off their horses and cow punching skills, the cowboys and their bosses found weddings and holidays a perfect excuse for guitars, castanets and dancing. The Spanish elite brought the great *fandango* tradition to the northernmost Nueva España frontier.

Diego watched the changes coming to his adopted homeland. He listened to his leaders and observed some of them becoming more prosperous with ranches, larger adobes, growing families and additional ways to increase their silver stash. He coveted land that would be his now and then he could pass on to his offspring. And to get it he would need a pure blood Spanish wife to make himself presentable to the Las Californias governor, the viceroy and the King. He needed to find one. And quickly. He wanted a land grant before the best pieces were gone or the King and viceroy became distracted with other Spanish business. Alta California was so far from the great cities and government palaces that most of the time it was a forgotten corner of the empire.

KIDNAPPED

∞

Nicole climbed the stairs to the top floor of the San Francisco apartment, reliving her visit to the family land. She was anxious to tell Great Gram about her hike, where she'd climbed and explored. Great Gram had told her to look for an old shack crumbling somewhere in a glade on the property. Great Gram and her cousins had discovered it as kids and found some old cups and pots there. Maybe Nicole could find something useful for their historic landmark search. But mostly, Great Gram said go get acquainted with this wonderful family property that she'd never been introduced to in childhood.

She'd found a creek, lots of brush, steep terrain and some old mining equipment at the base of a waterfall. A rusting hunk of metal piping and possibly remnants of the mine's railway system were exciting but revealed nothing about the family, just that the land did have a connection to New Almaden quicksilver mining. Disappointed that she'd found no sign of humans beyond the mine equipment, Nicole planned to go back the following weekend. She wanted to hike farther up the waterfall and over the ridge. She'd felt at peace there, at one with the earth, the ferns along the brook, the sycamores and maples. Most of it was hot and dry but she'd found a small redwood grove. She'd sat in the cool of the shade beneath the majestic trees and smelled their bark, the damp soil. Her skin had prickled and she shivered with anticipation. She felt connected to the place, as if ghosts were watching over her. Something was there waiting for her. She just knew it. She couldn't wait to tell her great grandmother.

She knocked again. What was taking Great Gram so long to answer? The door opened and there stood her father. She almost didn't recognize him. Gone were his hat and dirty work boots. Here, in the city, he wore a pressed shirt, clean jeans and the new boots he saved for off ranch business, which he avoided at all costs.

"Dad. What are you doing here? Is Great Gram all right?"

"Nicole, come in and sit down. She's not here but she's fine"

Nicole's pulse sped up. What was going on? Dad never came to the city. She sat on the sofa and he took Great Gram's armchair. She rustled in the seat. Her stomach started to feel queasy. She swallowed. Dad looked as uncomfortable as she felt. He ran his hand through his close-cropped hair and sighed.

"Your great grandmother doesn't live here anymore. Grandpa and I moved her into a care facility in Oakland. She can't take care of herself alone. She's not in her right mind to make decisions about this house. We're going to sell it now."

"What? What are you talking about? I've been taking care of her. It's not even close to a year yet. She's totally with it. She's got friends and activities here. Like I told you." What did he do to her? Did he drug her to get her out of here?

Nicole continued, enraged. "She doesn't want to go into an old people's home. She's told me that many times. Oakland? She won't know anyone there. How can you sell against her will? It's her house, not yours, not Grandpa's. Great Gram has a lawyer. Does she know about this?" Nicole was so angry, she couldn't look at him. She got up and paced in front of Great Gram's window.

"I was very clear with you," he said. "Get it done. Told you to get rid of her restrictions. Great Gram and you won't take care of selling it so we're doing it."

"But Dad—" Nicole squawked.

He held up his hand and kept on. "I've got a lawyer almost done with my conservatorship status for her. She really can't take care of herself and make informed decisions. Clearly. She's ninety-four. We're selling the house now, not waiting for the will to go into effect. The market might tank by the time she dies. Don't you see?" He stood up too and came over to the window facing Nicole, forcing her to look at him. "Missy got her real estate license," he said. "I want to support her doing something productive so she's gonna be our realtor. As soon as we get the paperwork in order it goes on the market. Missy already told the tenants they have three months to find a new place."

Nicole felt the blood rush to her face. "What the hell? Why's Missy involved? You still feeling guilty for not being there for her childhood? Did she put you up to this? I don't trust her one bit. And you didn't used to either."

He looked down at his shoes and shuffled. She grabbed his arm and shook it to make him look at her. "You think you'll get control of her estate? She and her lawyer had an idea this was coming. I heard her on the phone before saying she didn't want you to do this exact thing."

Dad pulled away, ran his hand across his scalp and sighed. He looked older than she remembered, lines etched now into his forehead. "It's done. She in a good home for someone that old. It's time to sell the place. It's become a burden, what with the repairs and managing so many renters. She couldn't keep up, even when you were supposedly helping her. Time for someone else to take over."

Later that afternoon, as Nicole pushed the large glass door with a handicapped sign, it came to life with a buzz and swung open, startling her. Already on edge, the automatic door and the smell of bleach that stung her nostrils made her stomach churn. She introduced herself to the front desk staff and was escorted across a courtyard to another building and an apartment door. She pushed the glowing doorbell. After an extended wait, Great Gram opened the door. Nicole was shocked. She was wearing a pale blue bathrobe and her favorite comfy Nike's. Her hair was in disarray as if she hadn't brushed it for days. Upon seeing Nicole her face crumbled. Nicole hurried in, slamming the door in the orderly's face.

"Oh, Nicole, I'm so glad to see you. See what they did to me? Can you get me out of here? I hate it. The food's awful. They make me take these pills. I don't know what they are. I try to hide them or spit them out but they catch me a lot. I saw them grind them up one time—think they might be in my food." She spoke so fast Nicole wondered if she hadn't talked to anyone for days.

"The people are all in wheelchairs and mope and drool. I've no one to talk to. I'm so bored and lonely. Come to lunch with me and you'll see. Will you help me get out? The only problem is I don't know where to go. I've got my lawyer working on getting my house back but that might take some time. They changed the locks." She shook her head. "Goodness me, where are my manners? Sit down and I'll get us some tea."

Great Gram walked into the kitchen where she caught sight of her reflection in the glass divider between the breakfast nook and tiny living room. "Oh my, I look awful. Can you make the tea, dear? I need to freshen up and get dressed. See what this place is doing to me? I forgot to get dressed for the day." She stepped into the bedroom muttering to herself, "Gotta get out of here. Where am I going to go?"

Nicole made the tea, feeling confused by her father's actions. Great Gram returned, wearing a skirt, blouse and sweater. She carried their tea to the back patio, where Great Gram told her about how Dad had barged in with the news he was now in control of her finances and estate and moving her out, putting the house on the market.

"I was completely blindsided. No warning and I couldn't reach you. Were you out at the land? Did you find anything?"

"Okay, calm down a bit," Nicole said. "Let's figure out how to get you out of here. He can't just take over control of your accounts, can he? Don't you have to sign off on a deed to sell your house?"

"Yes, but he's trying to get me declared incompetent. To get conservatorship so they can make all the decisions. With my money. It's appalling. Some doctor came to interview me. I think there's another one coming. It's all so exhausting. And my tenants are calling me, very upset. Mrs. Sanchez told me I'd betrayed them. That Missy is something else, isn't she?" She barely stopped to take a breath. "She's got her claws into your dad, that's clear. But I have a plan with my lawyer. We're fighting it. You just need to get me out of here. I'm getting depressed. It's like jail or something. You've got to help me escape."

A few hours later, Nicole took a small suitcase and a travel bag out through the patio's back entrance to the parking lot. Great Gram called the front desk telling them she was going out for the rest of the day with her great granddaughter. She might stay over at her new apartment.

"Oh, how nice of her, Mrs. Sinclair," said the receptionist. "Don't forget you have a doctor assessment on Thursday. We'll see you soon," she said and hung up.

"Thank goodness your dad couldn't put me in the assisted living where you can't come and go as you please," she told Nicole when she returned from the parking lot. "I think he might've tried but this place said I was too independent and should be in my own apartment."

"Yes, thank goodness for small favors. Now let's go out by the sidewalk. Act natural," Nicole said and she giggled just a little. Great Gram looked up at her and smiled.

"Oh Nicole, I'm so glad to have you back by my side. You're such a help and you make me feel like a girl again. Now let's ditch this place." She smoothed her skirt, patted her hair, as if checking to see that she had indeed brushed it after all, put her arm through the crook of Nicole's and winked. They strolled to the car as if headed out for afternoon tea.

As Nicole drove to the three-story Berkeley Hills home where she rented a flat she felt just a bit guilty for planning an escape from the senior home. But her anger at her father was so blinding she had just jumped in to help her great grandmother without hesitation. Her loyalty to Great Gram was complete now. Dad would be furious but she was past caring about him.

They unloaded Great Gram's suitcase but left the smaller travel bag in the trunk. Nicole packed up her own weekend bag, then they set off, driving south, aiming for an inn tucked alongside a winery in the Santa Cruz Mountains. Great Gram's distant cousin had opened the place decades before and it was now run by the cousin's grandson and his wife, a young couple with two babies. Thinking it was best to hide out for a few days, they'd selected the place for its privacy and the discretion of its owners.

They called Great Gram's lawyer to schedule a phone appointment for the next day. The lawyer's office had set up a doctor assessment that was legally neutral. Irene said she did not trust who her son and grandson might have selected but was willing to have her mental acuity tested by a professional.

Once settled into their adjoining guest rooms, they moved to the patio where they watched the sunset turn the eastern hills across the valley pink and orange. A half-moon dangled in the darkening purple sky. For a moment, they held hands. Nicole knew she'd crossed a line helping Great Gram leave the senior facility, an act that would probably destroy her relationship with Dad. But Dad had been the kidnapper. Great Gram should be in her San Francisco home. It was not up to him when she moved or sold. Fury at Missy burned like indigestion below her sternum. She was after the money, like Dad seemed to be. She hoped the lawyer would be able to put a stop to all of this mess.

After dinner, Great Gram retired early and Nicole returned to her computer where she was continuing her research into family trees. With no access to the records in the San Francisco attic, online was the only place they could search at the moment. Great Gram's DNA test results had provided more connections to explore. And messages to respond to. It looked like some distant relatives had also gotten to Joe Brennan, possibly alias Joaquin Castro, in their trees.

Determined to find additional proof of Mr. Brennan's dual identity, Nicole had found a death certificate dated 1909 in San Francisco. She was still searching for a marriage license, maybe property records. She combed through San Francisco newspapers,

New Almaden mine records, deeds and land sales, probates. No other distant cousins in her trees had gotten any farther than Joe Brennan either. It was like he was a brick wall enclosing their family history in a tight fortress. His mother, Juanita Castro de la Cruz, was nowhere to be found. And what about her parents that were mentioned in the land trust. Who were they?

THE WIFE

❦

"**P**apá, *I mean no disrespect,* but how can you force me to go far away to marry some stranger?" she asked. "And he's so old. You know, I always follow your orders. But this is my home, with you and Mamá. After all we've survived together, how can you send me away? I won't leave."

"Maria Joaquina, do not argue with me. It is not proper or becoming. This is your destiny," her father said. "Diego Castro Cardona is a good man, a fine soldier, a respected lieutenant in the military. He's been at Comandante Ortega's side establishing the presidios and the missions. He has saved many natives. He is a servant of God, just as we are, and will make a fine husband for you. Now stop simpering and go get ready." Quina, all the ferocity of her eighteen years packed into her lean body, glared at him.

"This is your duty. Enough," he repeated. Seeing no weakness in her father's eyes, she whipped her skirt around and marched off, fists clenched in anger, teeth jammed into her jawline. This was not what she had in mind for her future.

Although she always obeyed her parents' commands, she'd been given quite a bit of free rein on the growing rancho. They allowed her to ride, to work in the stables as well as the kitchen, to contribute to the little hacienda in ways uncommon for girls. The family and only a few native servants and soldier cowboys had lived for years with nothing but the parched, hardscrabble San Gabriel mountains rising to the east and the sun setting over the breakers crashing on their shore. They tilled the land, built small adobes, raised cows, sheep and horses. Quina had no friends but her siblings, the wild animals and the cowboy soldiers who worked for her father to build the fort and prepare a mission site.

The De Anza journey and frontier life on the frigid slopes of Yerba Buena and desolate Santa Barbara so shaped young Quina that she remained dark skinned from outdoor work, sinewy and lithe, hair always pulled back in a bun or braid. Fiercely independent, she would dig her own holes for corn, beans and fava, and eventually oranges, lemons and grapes. She rode horses like a man, even though she had to do it side saddle in long skirts. She could outfox the best of the ranch hand cowboys and they knew she could outride and rope them if she really wanted to humiliate them. She had a life of backbreaking work to build a viable ranch homestead but she saw it all as her God given duty and life's mission.

She was not naïve and knew she would have to get married someday. But she'd always imagined she and her husband would stay at her parents' home, maybe in their own little adobe on a small plot near the main house. Why did the girl have to go away to her future husband's home? They'd worked so hard to develop Santa Barbara into a presidio site and now the new mission and its chapel were signs from God. They finally had built a family home that had a glimmer of promise. Quina had assumed she would spend her life there.

When they'd first arrived in Santa Barbara, her father had been strategic in planting desirable crops and trading the ranch produce well, not just with the Spanish supply boats but also with the occasional foreign ship that anchored in the bay. Though trade with foreigners was prohibited by Spanish law, Don Sebastian ignored the limitation in an effort to build a thriving outpost. Contraband was of value to both those lonely on the seas and those on the empty land. Sailors needed food and the settlers needed supplies. He expanded his crops and added on to his adobe year after year. They now had comforts the family had never experienced before like a tile floor, wooden bed frames and packed cotton mattresses. And Don Sebastian had risen to a level of import in the King's Alta California army. Quina did not want to start over yet again, and she could not even imagine leaving her parents and siblings, the only companions she'd ever known.

Her mother was waiting in her bedroom with a hair comb she'd secretly brought on the long journey from Sinaloa for an important day such as meeting your betrothed. It would have been a touching gesture, her mother planning so far ahead over seven years ago when they were dispatched north as settlers. And when they'd been destitute in arid Sinaloa. But Quina felt so betrayed that they would marry her off to a military leader who was stationed far away that she barely noticed her mother's kindness. Now, Mamá was able to dress her in soft linen recently purchased off one of the pirated supply ships. But it didn't alter the situation. In a daze of grief that she'd have to leave the new rancho adobe her father had just built, she let her mother wash and comb her hair and fit her into the finest dress she'd ever worn. She lifted her gaze to her mother's eyes. "But Mamá how can I leave you? I'll miss you and Papá so much. I don't know how to live without you." She felt a tear glide down her cheek.

With a movement so swift Quina was completely unprepared, her mother slapped the damp side of her face. "Don't be foolish, Quina, you're always in the stables, stronger than half the vaqueros," she said. Quina gulped and suppressed more tears and complaints. She sat up straight. "You're no longer a girl who needs her mother's care. You're a grown woman, ready to settle the north and continue our mission for the Crown. We've been chosen for this sacred journey, this life bequeathed by God. You must not falter now. God needs you to go north with this lieutenant in the King's army. You'll have many children and settle the northern parts of the territory. Go with grace and respect, Quina. We'll have a big wedding here at the rancho and invite all the soldiers and settlers from De Anza's expedition. Do not disappoint us."

It was a long speech for Quina's mother, who usually sat motionless and silent as her husband read the bible, entertained visiting governors or negotiated with priests for cows, horses, native servants and materials. She had made her point.

Quina sighed as she saw no way out of this fate. She nodded at her mother, forced a slight smile and twisted her hair into a thick, dark braid reaching below her shoulders. Then her mother swooped the braid up into the comb, Spanish style. She adjusted the dress at her slight hips and thin waist, pulled the sleeves to her wrists and swept out of the room toward the courtyard to meet her future husband.

Diego was sweaty and dusty from several days heavy riding on the trail to the Altamirano Santa Barbara rancho, the grandest building outside of the presidio compound. As he rode into the rancho's imposing gate, he straightened his rounded sombrero, adjusting the neck strap below his chin, brushing the dust off his chaps, polished specially for this introduction. He tightened the Spanish red sash at his waist and touched his reata, wound at the back of his saddle, absentmindedly confirming that all pieces to his soldier-vaquero ensemble were in place. He sat up tall in the saddle telling his stomach to settle. A temporary nervousness surprised him and the image of beautiful Isabela splashing in the Catalonian waves surfaced briefly before he scolded himself. His past was now almost like a dream, as if it had belonged to another. Diego's life was here now and this woman would be at his side as he forged forward.

He'd coveted Maria Joaquina for some time, but only by name and reputation as he'd never met her. Diego knew Captain Altamirano as a leader who'd made his mark since arriving with the bedraggled De Anza party. The survivors were highly respected and he knew their walk had been as arduous as his trip north with Governor Portola. He deeply admired anyone who had survived the brutal journeys with a vision of Spanish dominance over the northern provinces of New Spain. Captain Altamirano was a loyal soldier who'd helped to establish the San Francisco de Asís and Santa Clara Missions. He'd been willing to almost singlehandedly do the work to homestead and now lead the development of a fourth presidio. A wife from Santa Barbara, and a daughter of Captain Altamirano, seemed an auspicious statement.

This Maria Joaquina, Diego had heard other soldiers gossip, she might be from a good family but she's a bit rough and not proper Spanish wife material. "Can you imagine?" a soldier said around the trail fire one night. "She rides horses almost like a man. She'd probably try to play *carrera de gallo*, catch the rooster, with us cowboys if her father let her." Diego chuckled with the other soldiers all the while thinking that she sounded like the perfect partner.

He coveted a large tract of land, hundreds of cows and sheep, a sprawling adobe hacienda with orchards, all while continuing to ascend the military's ranks. He needed a strong, healthy woman who could bear him many children, lead a big ranch and not fear the lonely life in the remote province. If she'd survived the De Anza party as a child and had parents committed to Alta California, then she was a great candidate. If she cared more about horses than coveting fine cloth from Mexico City for elegant dresses, then perfect. If she too saw populating the northern region as her destiny, then she sounded like the right Spanish wife for him.

Diego had approached her father privately one night at the end of the Santa Barbara campaign. He'd been nervous, putting the conversation off, but was headed back to Monterrey's presidio with Comandante Ortega early the next morning. With plenty of rum flowing as the soldiers celebrated establishing a fourth presidio, Don Sebastian seemed more approachable than usual. Diego scolded himself for having the nerves of a schoolboy at the age of thirty-one. There was no time to waste in this matter. His fortitude paid off when the elder soldier seemed open to the proposal. "When you finish up in Monterrey, come to my adobe here in Santa Barbara and meet her," he'd loudly invited. Despite the shortage of women in the territory, Señor Altamirano seemed relieved that anyone was interested in his eldest daughter.

As he rode back to Monterrey the next day, his nerves calmed somewhat but not completely. With the captain he'd been anxious because he hated to be in any position of weakness and one never know how a man would react to a soldier wanting to marry his daughter. In reality, he had hesitated to take this step for years because he knew his quiet life with Sholeta would change dramatically. And he'd not told her about any of his plans or ambitions, save from wanting to enlarge his land, crops and lifestock holdings. How would she react to him bringing home a wife? He hated to threaten their life on the hill above the bay. She was a welcome, warming presence in his bed each night. Really the best part of his home.

And now there was a child. His first born. A son. Finally, a Castro heir, a native born Alta Californian. Diego was surprised how proud and excited he was at delivering a Californio to the territory. His destiny would continue into a new generation.

But Sholeta was a native. Marrying her would be foolish. Diego had seen in the overland journey from Veracruz to San Blas that many Spanish and natives had intermarried over two hundred years since Cortez. Indeed, he knew soldiers with native mothers and Spanish fathers. But Alta California was different. It was so remote, the natives so weak and savage, their ways so far from proper Christian manners of being that intermarrying was an outrageous thought. Most of his fellow soldiers just took neophyte women from the mission nunnery to join in drunken evenings at the pueblo's saloon. Or even to force out behind the barracks. He knew a few soldiers who lived quietly with native women but only the lowest soldados de cuera married a neophyte with Father Crespi's blessing. And no one married an unbaptized native woman.

As Diego slowed the stallion to a polite trot to approach the grand adobe house and Sholeta appeared in his mind softness alighted on his heart when he thought of her care when he returned home from long campaigns. Her delicious meals and the expanded vegetable garden. With her in their little house, any ailments from the trail seemed to disappear. However, for his ambitions, marriage to Sholeta, despite her many fine qualities, was impossible. She was a servant girl after all. He hoped to become a captain soon. He wanted a land concession from the governor. He must be a Spaniard bringing Spanish ways and blood to northern New Spain. He needed a Spanish wife and pure Spanish children for the cause.

Trotting into the hacienda courtyard, Diego decided right there in front of Captain Altamirano's hacienda that he would have Sholeta's baby raised as a Spaniard. Maria Joaquina would surely be acceptable and marry him in the coming months. As soon as she moved in to his adobe as his wife, one of her first tasks would be to raise his half-breed child as her own.

Diego left his prized stallion with Don Altamirano's stablehand. A neophyte servant ushered him to the grand door with wrought iron handle and bands crisscrossing the heavy wood. Both from Spain, he noted, impressed that Don Altamirano was using the finest materials probably secured from one of the few merchant pirate ships stopping at Santa Barbara's harbor. He asked the servant stuffed into a burlap dress, her shoulder tattoos visible as the ill cut *vestido* fell from one shoulder to the other, could he please wash up before meeting el patron? It had been a long ride.

Diego splashed cool water from the large silver bowl she provided, perfumed with salvia stalks. He grabbed the herbs from the water, crushed them in his calloused fingers and swiped beneath his billowy blouse under his arms, across the top of his tunic, through his perspiration filled hairline and across his taut torso. He re-tied the sash over his blousy shirt, put the salvia to his nose and inhaled. He stepped out from the private guest washroom near the entrance, noting that he must have one of these in his grand adobe one day, and strode, boots clicking under his purposeful step, to meet his bride.

"Capitán Altamirano, it is an honor to be in your grand home. I think it must be the finest in all of Alta California. Thank you for inviting me to visit. I have brought you fresh herbs and some grapes we are trying out in the garden at my adobe. Like Spain, we are so fortunate we can grow fruits and vegetables in this fertile soil. Don't you agree?" he said with a low bow to the gentleman. "Señorita, it is a true pleasure to finally meet you. I've heard high praise of your many talents." Diego took Quina's hand. He bowed to kiss across her knuckles, raising his eyebrows in surprise that it was equally callused as his own.

Quina seemed embarrassed for a moment, before regaining her composure. "I very much doubt you've heard of me, Don Diego. But I certainly am aware of your exploits for the Crown. I believe we are both colonizers for King Carlos, settling Alta California on God's Sacred Expedition to civilize this remote land." She pulled his stooped torso up, changing the handshake from one offering a genteel kiss to a firm grasp.

Diego raised his eyebrows yet again at this young woman's gumption, noticed her dark complexion, so unlike the fair women he'd fantasized over in his teen years. She was not effervescent like the Isabela he'd imagined would be his wife back in Spain. But she was not unattractive. Her confident posture, her thick hair and strong jaw made her a formidable woman. She surprised him further by continuing boldly, "The honor is mine. I look forward to hearing about your adventures settling the San Francisco presidio, and of Monterrey years back, and the many missions with Padre Serra." She looked directly at him.

Diego, a good thirteen years older and more wizened from soldier and prairie life than Señorita Altamirano, caught her eye. Staring into the dark brown, he saw only his reflection. No other emotion. No flirtatious glint like from Isabela who still haunted his dreams. No soft affection which he saw in Sholeta's eyes when he took her into his bed. Quina's countenance showed simply the practicality of required partnership, of a mission-focused approach to the hard-scrabble life of the frontier. He had found a fellow settler. He felt no warmth from Quina but in that moment the zealot in him fell in love. He was entranced by the notion that their ambitions converged. They were pobladores and they would conquer together.

"You plan to settle at the presidio of Santa Barbara, Lieutenant Castro?" she asked.

"Oh no, Señorita. I am based at the presidio in Monterrey and have my own adobe just outside the pueblo. But I frequently travel throughout the territory with Comandante Ortega and the padres, Fathers Serra and Crespi. Oh dear, God rest Father Serra's soul. I am still getting used to the fact that he is gone. There has never been a more dedicated servant. But they continue the work without him—civilizing the natives, you know. I protect the fathers as they bring Christianity to the locals. It is a noble mission of the utmost importance."

"Indeed." Quina nodded with a slight exhale. "It is, indeed, Don Diego. The most noble of missions."

THE FAMILY

*D*iego *heard the familiar clip clop clip clop* even before Sholeta did. He had survived this long in a hostile land via heightened senses. He stood up from the candlelit table and moved quickly through the back of the cool clay building to the stables. "Sholeta," he called. "She's coming. Did you get everything out of my room? How's baby Pedro?" his words came out in a rushed torrent, so unlike his usual calm, commanding tone. He felt bad about moving Sholeta back to the stable apartment. Yet he was also excited to greet his new baby daughter, the first-born Spaniard in the family, and to see Quina who had gone to her parents' Santa Barbara rancho several months prior to give birth and recover.

Sholeta was rocking the baby to sleep in the rocking chair Diego had a local woodworker craft for her. She had appeared touched at the gesture and told him she found rocking little Pedro to sleep in the chair a welcome comfort. It was such a relief when their son was born healthy. The little family gave him some sense of peace. But the decision he'd made to marry quickly thereafter and move in a Spanish wife altered everything.

He could see the grim line of her tightly closed lips and knew she was angry about her demotion back to servant for Quina's return. He thought she'd accepted this new reality some time ago after his marriage but she clearly had mixed emotions, as did he. To a point.

"Everything's fine. Now leave us alone. Go meet your wife," she said coldly. She refused to look at him and fussed over the baby. "I'll have supper ready for you two, oh, I mean, three, at the usual time."

Diego could hear frustration and sorrow in Sholeta's voice. So confident and commanding in the rest of his life, he found home life bewildering. It was confusing the emotions that roiled through his usually hardened heart, toughened by years on horseback, taming the uncooperative natives. He could reveal to no one that his gut was torn up by the situation he'd created. Probably he shouldn't have waited so long to marry a proper Spanish wife. He'd fallen into a family way with Sholeta unintentionally but he cared for her and was thrilled when they finally had a healthy child. He realized it was hard on her now. But didn't she understand that his first duty was to his military obligation to settle the land for Spain, with Spanish settlers?

He left her without a kiss or touch for even the baby as it was clear she would not tolerate any sign of kindness right now. He understood she felt betrayed at his marrying Quina, at getting her pregnant immediately, and at agreeing to welcome her back after she'd fled south to her parents for several months to birth their first child.

After his surprise at Quina's departure, and his failure at luring her back to Monterrey to give birth, Diego returned to the little house and fell into old habits. He took little Pedro riding with him wrapped snug in a rebozo at his chest. He padded in bare feet out to Sholeta's room at night and told her to bring the baby and come sleep with him. It was his house and he'd run it the way he wanted. Sholeta didn't argue but she also held forth on her view of the new situation, telling him Quina was emotionally weak.

"She's cold-hearted, that woman, Diego," she'd told him one night in bed. Sholeta's voice had an angry timbre. Was she jealous? Sholeta had his affection, he thought she knew that, but Quina was his wife now and he had obligations to her.

"It seems her heart only has room for her parents," Sholeta continued, uncharacteristically talkative. "Why'd she leave here for the birth? How will she be with a baby? As the children grow? A mother must build character with love, not only discipline." Diego had stopped the conversation right there, leaning in to kiss her and envelope her small frame in his strong arms.

"Let's not talk about Quina right now. She's not here and we are," he had said and began to caress her wrists while he kissed her deeply, distracting her from the uncomfortable topic.

He'd found a measure of success by compartmentalizing the facets of his life. He kept his soldiering work separate from his little homestead. Ever since he and Sholeta became lovers, suffered the sadness of dead babies and managed to find some stability in their unbalanced positions as conqueror and conquered, it felt like a home to him. He got indigestion thinking about managing two women in his life yet he felt no rancor or guilt over the complications. Sholeta was a native servant who had to do as he wished. His Spanish wife had a duty to help him grow their home and provide him with children. There was no need to let her know about his relationship with Sholeta or that he was the father of her baby. Each of them would need to acclimate to the situation. It was that simple.

Now Quina was returning, he realized he had missed her in a distant sort of way. They were not affectionate or close as a couple, but, of anyone, Quina was with whom he could discuss his ambitions, his plans. She too coveted a larger adobe, more land, a higher position for him. She was not shy about her desires for a Spanish-influenced lifestyle with the increasingly luxurious amenities which were just beginning to arrive on the supply ships. They both sought respect from the governor, military leaders and the head priests. Diego found their connection motivated him to keep his young wife reasonably happy.

And so Quina rode in with a darling baby girl with light skin, long dark lashes and curling, thick hair. He noted immediately that his wife's true skin color must be a pure Spanish white after all. The baby, Beatriz Victoria, was as light as a pale pink rose. Diego's heart palpitated when he first held her and kissed her tiny forehead. His wife looked her former self, having returned to her slim strength during the three months post partum at her parents' hacienda. He greeted her warmly with an attempted hug and kiss but she pushed past him.

"So what's happened to this place since I've been away?" she demanded. "Any expansions, Diego? You know we can't all fit in this tiny adobe for long. What's the news of Monterrey and the northern missions since I've been south?" Immediately, they were all about business, which helped settle Diego's stomach as that was his domain too.

He escorted his wife out to the expanded vegetable garden, the additional grapevines and the mid-sized lemon and orange trees. He took her into their bedroom, which of course had been his and Sholeta's only the night before. He tipped the wooden rocking cradle the woodworker had made for their first born.

"Oh, the cradle is beautiful. Thank you. Baby Beatriz thanks you too," she said, and a shy smile crossed her lips, finally.

"Sit, my dear. It's wonderful to have you back. This is your home, Quina, don't forget that." He'd contemplated using the word please but quickly decided against it. He was a commander and never used such words. To start now with his wife could only lead to more trouble. "First the news." And Diego updated her with the local gossip. The fact that the maid's baby was getting big, the priests seemed to be baptizing more neophytes, the pueblo was growing with a few businesses, and saloons, of course, and the governor was giving out land concessions. Quina rocked the baby to sleep in the new cradle as she listened.

"My darling," Diego said, as he took her hand. Still callused but softened somehow—perhaps from mothering he absently thought. "I have two pieces of good news for us. I was named captain in the King's Army for Alta California just after you left for Santa Barbara." Quina looked up at that, raised her eyebrows and really smiled for the first time since she'd entered the house.

"Well, Don Diego, that is something now isn't it? Comandante Ortega finally recognized how indispensable you are to him." She continued pushing the cradle gently with her fingertips. "There's something else?"

"Yes. The most important of all. Governor Fages has just granted me a concession, to ranch, plant and herd on five leagues of land out east of here. It's beautiful. I've surveyed it on horseback. As a captain, I get more silver and with my blacksmith trade increasing we can begin to build our rancho. We'll start with a larger adobe for the family. We'll plant a real orchard and raise herds of cows and sheep. This is the beginning of our dreams."

His eyes shone as he spoke and Diego surprised himself with a catch in his throat as he pictured the two of them and their children in the courtyard of a large hacienda surrounded by corrals, stables, orchards. Quina stopped rocking the cradle, looked up with surprise and stood up.

"Oh, that is wonderful news," she said. She approached him with arms open and stood on tiptoes to kiss him. He pushed her long braid to the side, caressed her cheek and wrapped his arm around her waist, pulling her to him. Quina deftly unlatched the bottom of her braid and slid her hand through it to release her hair. It cascaded over her shoulders and down her back as she embraced him fully. Diego was taken aback by her interest but delightfully surprised at her ardor and he continued kissing her deeply as he worked at the many buttons on her dress.

"Oh, Capitán Castro, take me to our rancho. I can't wait to see it," she murmured as she fully surrendered to her husband after many months apart.

The next morning, Diego saddled up Quina's favorite horse and guided her out to the concession land. He showed her the Governor's letter and map and they galloped from its southern to northern border. Diego stopped at the site he'd selected for their house, had her dismount and they walked through the clearing pointing out where the kitchen would be best suited and the stables and the vineyards. He explained his vision of orchards bursting with oranges and lemons, vines of table grapes and trees laden with red pomegranates and black olives like where he'd grown up along the Spanish coast. He took a stick and outlined the rooms of the house, an actual courtyard for guests to enter and tether their horses.

Quina was as animated as he'd ever seen her and he was delighted with her enthusiastic return. He hoped her homesickness for Santa Barbara had waned and this would be the place where she could take the reins as mistress of the household. "Take my hand. I want to show you something," he said. He led her up the rocky slope to a cluster of oaks with low hanging branches shading a small clearing. "Look. From here you have a view of our new adobe, much of the rancho and the valley beyond. Isn't it beautiful? Can you imagine the house? I hope you can feel at home here, Quina."

He turned to her, looked in her solid brown eyes and leaned in to kiss her. And he made love to her in the shade of the ancient oaks, overlooking their new homestead. Afterwards, as they reassembled their clothes and pulled prickly oak leaves from her hair, Diego knew he would have no better opportunity than this. "I want to talk with you about something," he said. "Here, sit by me. Look at our view," he coaxed hoping the prospect of a rancho would ease this conversation.

"You know the native maid, Sholeta? She's worked in my home for nine years now and has always kept it clean, fed me well, and cared for the house and garden and horses when I'm away. Which was most of that time, you know. She's loyal. Doesn't steal. Unlike so many at the mission, she doesn't get sick. I'd like to keep her on with you at home. Her food is delicious and she can help with the baby. You'll be busy working on building the adobe and rancho," he added quickly. Quina smiled at that.

He went on. "She does seem to have had a bit of trouble at the presidio and got herself pregnant with one of the vaqueros. But no surprise. Anyway, I want that baby raised in our household. That baby has no chance as a native. If the maid returns to the mission, the baby might die. If I put her out, she can't return to her village. She has nowhere to go and we must Christianize these heathens. We have an opportunity to bring this child to Christ, to the Church and to raise him as a Spaniard. He'll become part of our family. She'll help with both children, but little Pedro will be our child too, along with Beatriz."

Quina looked at him for some time with a quizzical eye. She looked out at the view, smoothed her skirt. Diego fidgeted waiting for her to reply. Did she have concerns about this arrangement? Was she suspicious of his relationship with the maid?

"I understand you are loyal to this servant," she said. "And we do have a duty to bring all the children here to God. This is an opportunity.

Has this woman accepted Christ? Has she been baptized? Does she read the bible? When I was here before, I don't remember seeing her with a bible. I do recall she had a good command of Spanish. We must attend Mass with the padres with both children, immediately. And have them baptized together." She paused.

Diego looked sharply at her long speech. "But listen," she continued. "If I am to raise her son, then I will do exactly that. I will be the boy's mother. He will never know his birth mother. She can no longer treat him as her own. She can come into the house but only for the kitchen and cleaning. The children will learn Spanish and the bible together. Once we are in the new house, they will share a room as siblings until they are too old for that. They will remain in my care and I will see to their education. Is that clear?"

She stood up to walk down the hill. Diego followed, surveying the view he could not get enough of, as he listened to his wife state her position on raising the baby. He felt some relief that he'd finally presented the situation he had worried about, yet what was she really saying? Did she suspect that he was baby Pedro's father? Would Quina say anything to Sholeta or ask about the father? He didn't think so but he'd move the baptisms along quickly. He needed to get everyone accustomed immediately to the new arrangement. But he had a nagging feeling that this was not over. It might just be the beginning actually. And he still had to tell Sholeta, of course. He was not looking forward to that.

"Of course, my dear," he managed, walking quickly to keep up with her. Women and children were so damn complex. Just give him his horse, his soldiers and a clear mission to recapture stolen horses and he could get the job done. But a family? That was much more complicated.

RANCHO CASTRO

Inland from the Presidio de Monterrey, Alta California
1785—1796

"**S**holeta, *come sit with me.* I need to talk to you," Diego said one afternoon. The half built larger house was empty save for the two napping babies. Quina had insisted on going over to the mission for confession with the new padre in charge, Father Lausen. Sholeta wiped her wet hands on her apron and sat in a side chair. She looked at him coldly, remembering the days when she could caress his cheek and run her fingers through the long dark hair. She was a servant girl again, she told herself, dropping her gaze to the table.

"Sholeta..." He hesitated. Then he spoke forcefully. "I want our son raised in the Church, taught Spanish. Pedro will be raised with Beatriz. We are going to baptize them together."

Sholeta glanced at him hard. She raised her brows and squinted at him with concern, then looked at the floor in confusion.

"Quina will be their mother. Officially. I mean, you are always here. You love and care for those babies, both of them. That's very clear. But Quina is my wife. She must be the mother. Do you understand?"

She couldn't speak. As if her tongue was paralyzed. What was he saying? Pedro was her baby. Her darling son. The one good thing she had now. Really, her only family. The village life she craved with

Ores was a mirage, an unlikely dream. She had to make this her home. Diego had slipped away since marrying Quina and bringing home baby Beatriz. At least she had Pedro. And the two babies were adorable and sweet together. She loved them both.

"Do you understand what I'm saying?" He reached out and raised her chin with his hand. She jerked back at his touch.

"What? You want to take my baby? How could you? You know what I've lost. What we've lost. Don't forget that. No, you can't have him. I'm his mother. Don't forget, we ba—"

"Sholeta," he cut her off. "You will still raise him and love him and be with him as much as you want. It's just that we need to baptize him with Beatriz, with Quina as his mother. Officially. Don't you see my predicament?"

"Your predicament? And what is that? Having two women and all the babies you want? No, I'm not giving up my child. I'm quite sure you and Doña Joaquina will have many more babies. You'll have plenty of children to work your rancho. Don't worry." She moved the chair and started to get up. He abruptly pushed the chair back to keep her from leaving. He slammed his hand down hard on the table.

"No, this is the way it'll be. Pedro will be raised as a true Spaniard with his sister Beatriz. They will be baptized together at the mission in a few days. Now listen to me. If you don't comply, if you raise a fuss, if you complain or create a problem, I'll send you right back to the mission. To work for the fathers. You'll never see Pedro grow up. You'll never see me or baby Beatriz ever again. You'll die there most likely." He hesitated, then his voice softened. "Look, I do love you. But I need a Spanish wife and a Spanish family. It's that simple."

Sholeta's heart raced. The pattering got louder and louder. It moved into her throat, up to her cheeks and eyes. It shushed and pulsed in her ears. She felt like her head would explode. She coughed and tried to catch her breath. She was dizzy and swayed a bit in the chair. She pushed away from the table and ran out to her tiny servant room and vomited into the chamber pot. She splashed water onto her face from her washbasin, then tiptoed back to the main house to the nursery to spy on the sleeping babies. She peered into the cradles with tears trickling down her cheeks. What was he talking about? He loved her? This was no kind of love she'd ever experienced. She'd never leave these babies. She'd sacrifice her son in order to remain with him as he grew up. That was real love.

Over the next ten years, Quina complied with her new role and rolled out a steady stream of babies to take on the Castro mantle and provide workers for the growing rancho. She always seemed to be pregnant or nursing an infant but she never complained, never got sick and managed the growing household with a fierce efficiency. She was tough as a mule. But in reality, Diego discovered, emotionally, she was frail.

"I need my own mother to teach me how to become a mother," she had lied when she was first pregnant and fled to Santa Barbara. Diego had visited her there repeatedly and begged her to return to the little adobe he'd furnished for her and the baby. She refused. He realized she'd used an excuse to flee.

It became clear to him that she had some deficiency. She seemed unable to show affection or accept support from anyone other than her own parents. And, as if still a child, she couldn't imagine living at a distance from them and her siblings. It became a pattern. Each new pregnancy, after about six or seven months, she'd descend into a melancholy so deep it frightened him. He'd pack her up on her favorite horse, sometimes with the youngest child still at her breast, and escort her back to Santa Barbara into the familiar comfort of the home of her adolescence. Any toddlers and young children were left at the rancho with Sholeta and the increasing staff of servants and ranch hands.

Perhaps, Diego thought, Quina and her family were so bonded by the horrific journey north that they could not live without each other. Could not function in the harshness of the remote territory without the care of family members with whom she'd survived great hardship. He thought back to his own voyage to New Spain, to a life at sea that could never be anything but a foreign hell for him, to the siblings he'd left in Catalonia, to the pouting lips of Isabela that he'd sacrificed for the new world. He realized that if he'd had family on that rolling ship perhaps he would be as bonded to them as Quina was to her parents. But Diego had had to make it through the horror of the sea on his own. One purpose of his life was to become anything but the monster he saw in his own father. Memories of his mother were faded and sad. He could barely picture her anymore. Remembering his siblings just made him feel guilty. Diego could not fathom the powerful attachment Quina had to her family.

As she disappeared each pregnancy to her father's rancho, leaving more and more children behind, Diego slowly accepted that she was unlikely to change. He certainly didn't want to lose favor with Señor Altamirano, who had become the commander at Presidio Santa Barbara. So he accepted his marriage fate, the fact that he had healthy, devout, productive children and, in reality, a business partner for a wife.

For his loneliness he sought solace in Sholeta. She became the loving, nurturing mother of the children, though he suspected she was resentful. She cooked them healthy fare, surreptitiously slipping mussels, squirrel, quail or seal blubber and homegrown herbs into their stew, as she had done for Diego since her first days at the adobe. She treated their wounds, mediated disputes, noted the shine in their eyes as they mastered horse riding or the disappointed frown at their mother's coldness. Diego took Sholeta into his bed each night Quina was away and they lived as common law husband and wife.

As the older children grew, Diego suspected they noticed the arrangement but were so attached to Sholeta as a maternal figure that they had no motivation to tell their mother what occurred in her absence. The children loved Sholeta's delicious food, her common sense and affection. Indeed, they would complain to him when Quina arrived back at the rancho with yet another baby on her hip. Their chores were more demanding, their lessons stretched long and they'd bear the brunt of Quina's harsh scolding. Sholeta would return to the kitchen and her small room behind the stables, back to her servant role, focusing on cooking dishes that Diego thought were even more delicious than when Quina was gone. Was she pouring her love for his children into each tortilla or stew because she was forced to suppress the truth of her relationship with the family when the *doña de la casa* reappeared?

The increasing number of native servants and stable hands said nothing about Sholeta to Doña Joaquina because, he was quite sure, she treated them as inferior. He knew she looked down on the natives as unbaptized heathens. She never tried to learn their language or respect any of their customs. She insisted they dress modestly in scratchy wool and rough cotton. She demanded they pray daily in the small family chapel she'd insisted Diego build above the hacienda compound. He was relieved that no one ever asked him about Sholeta acting as the mistress when Quina was gone. And

Quina never complained when she returned, so Diego convinced himself that the arrangement suited everyone. Most of all himself, and the children.

Pedro, the eldest, was clearly a favorite of the growing brood who loved him as the leader of their Castro Altamirano band. Diego adored his son and was pleased to see that with so many girls—the Castro Curse it came to be called—Pedro became the junior head of the family.

El fantasma had grown a little less ferocious and Diego was secretly pleased when a new mission's padres were able to manage the native converts without conflict and need of military assistance. As Pedro grew into a teenager, Diego became more interested in staying at the rancho and teaching him the trade, working side by side with his son. But too long at the house with primarily a pile of young children and native maids and vaqueros as his companions, he would grow restless, anxious to get back out on the camino. Diego remained a soldier above all else.

To Quina the best kindness she could show her children was to imbue them with a sense of purpose, a devout faith and practical skills for survival and financial success in the remote territories. She knew well that no one, not even her own children, ever described her as particularly kind. She was not interested in being a warmhearted person. She was a practical survivor. A life on the frontier did not allow for any weak emotional distractions. She had survived without comforts and she expected everyone else to operate in the same manner.

Ever since her little brother died in the Sonoran desert, Quina had shut herself off from the pangs of love's trials and heartbreaks. While she loved her offspring, as a mother naturally does, it was in a distant manner. She did her duty. She raised her eleven children to be strong, independent survivors, just as she was raised. This was a Crusade for God and all were expected to comply with no complaints. "Coddling is for fools who want weak offspring," she'd tell anyone who asked.

Quina, however, was not so naive to be completely unaware of human feelings and frailties. She realized from that day Diego made love to her under the large oak tree on the hill above their land that Sholeta's son was his. She was not pleased with the fact but did her duty and raised Pedro as her own, as Diego had insisted. Admittedly, she was never as giving to Pedro as all the others. In reality, she was harsh with everyone so her hardness toward Pedro was a subtle distinction from the manner in which she addressed all of her brood. Yet she wasn't heartless either. She was sympathetic that Pedro's parentage was not his fault but her heart could never love him as her own. She never told him who his birth mother was nor denied she was his mother. And no one seemed to question, in an era when many babies were born on the plains of old México and valleys of Las Californias without birthdates, that Pedro and Beatriz appeared to be the same age but were not twins.

In the lord's year of seventeen hundred and ninety-five, when he had seven children and another on the way, Diego received another land concession from the viceroy and governor and more silver for his captaincy. For four years in the late eighties and early nineties,

Ortega was stationed as the Comandante of Presidio Monterrey. As one of his most trusted lieutenants, Captain Castro was posted close to home for more than a few weeks at a time. He was able to spread his reputed skill with horses and bring in more blacksmith work to supplement the military wages.

He celebrated by designing a sprawling, beautiful adobe in the hopes of luring Quina to have their future babies in the grand home. Once he had a large Spanish style hacienda sufficient for entertaining the growing number of travelers along the El Camino Real, that wound through the hills and valleys between missions, it embarrassed him to have his wife gone so often. He needed to entertain with a hostess, traditionally the wife, at his side. With no schools in the territory, he also worried that the children needed their mother's strict religious instruction to become educated citizens, and leaders, of the growing colony.

He could now afford to build enough rooms to encircle an entry plaza where horses were watered and tethered. He installed a courtyard at the center of the sprawling estate, complete with a trickling fountain, and for the first time ever had a tile floor—*azulejos* from Spain he bartered for when the Manila to Acapulco galleon anchored in the bay. He built arches and long bricked hallways, and a tower with a bell. Bright magenta and purple bougainvillea draped over the doorways and clung to the railings. The thick adobe whitewashed walls kept the rooms cool in the summer heat and warm when the fog drifted inland. He strayed from the tradition of putting the kitchen in a separate building and built a large cooking area attached to the main dining room, with two fireplaces, long work tables and generous counters. Everything was constructed from heavy adobe bricks to prevent kitchen fire danger. Only the furniture and ceilings were carved from local redwood, pine and cedar.

Quina told him she loved it as a beautiful place, noting that it was more elegant than her father's adobe which had been one of the first big homes in the territory when luxuries were nonexistent. Even though she would never admit it to anyone, he knew, as one who also came from nothing, that she enjoyed the big kitchen filled with servants, far from the smoky fire she'd tended as a child. She luxuriated in private quarters for herself and plenty of bedroom space for her large brood to share with only a sibling or two, not an entire family crushed into the corners of one room. She had told him she was determined to never be impoverished again. Her children would be dutiful and hardworking, but they would not know hunger and hopelessness.

She convinced Diego to build a chapel just up the hill and to enlarge the servants' quarters. They needed so much help with all the children and the additional land. Now she was busy furnishing the new house, planting more fruit trees, helping the vaqueros to break new horses and praying in the chapel, she stayed around just a bit longer than before. But then once another baby was stretching her skin so thin it turned pale, blue veins pulsing at her hips, she fled south yet again.

Diego was furious and thought it dangerous for her to travel. Didn't she appreciate their grand home? All the work and expense he'd put into creating a rancho? How ungrateful and unfeeling could his wife be? He needed her to educate the growing number of children and be a gracious doña at his side. Apparently, her capacity for disregarding his efforts was limitless. But once she sent word, via a soldier breathlessly riding in to the plaza, that they'd finally had a second son, he was just relieved everyone was healthy and a boy was coming home. Finally, a boy.

THE LONE SURVIVOR

RANCHO CASTRO, ALTA CALIFORNIA

1795

Sholeta *noticed the two housemaids* whispering furtively that morning as she helped them finish the laundry. Their tones so dark and eyes lower than usual, she suspected she was their subject. Maybe they finally would reveal to the señora that the patron slept regularly with the kitchen maid and children's caregiver. Maybe Quina's cold hand of authority would finally crush down on her as she had anticipated for years. She was rumored to be heading back after burying her sister in Santa Barbara and her grief might make her more hard-hearted than ever. It felt as if the whole structure of strong adobe walls were shuddering at the thought.

But no. Sholeta overheard "her brother" and caught a glance in her direction. "What's going on, girls?" she asked. "There's lots to clean before the señora returns. What new gossip is so interesting to distract you from your work?"

The young natives clapped their mouths shut so quickly it looked was if they were frogs chomping flies in the pond at dusk. Sholeta would normally have just scolded and moved them along but the alarm in their faces was palpable, and a bit frightening. "Girls. What is it? What's happened?"

"There's a head on a stake in front of the mission church," one of the girls whispered, beginning to cry. Sholeta's mouth opened in shock. The girl continued so quietly Sholeta had to tilt her head down close to hear. "There's talk of soldiers raiding the rancheria up the river. They found horses and guns. They shot some of our young men in the village."

Sholeta, accustomed to this violence after almost twenty years of captivity and living with the Español, shushed them to return to work and stay out of trouble.

"But ma'am," the one girl gulped. "I heard some of the old timers say it's your brother. The one on the stake, I mean."

"What?!" Sholeta yelled. "Watch the children!" She threw down her pile of unfolded wash and rushed to the stable. She grabbed the closest horse, threw on a saddle, strapped him up and rode off toward the rutted El Camino Real. She had not seen Ores, or even the cousin, in some time as she rarely had news to share. It was unspoken but she felt they must be disappointed. She felt guilty at times but they knew she was just a maid, now in a large house with many responsibilities. Her anger that he had never rescued her had dissipated into a nagging annoyance that she rarely had time to contemplate. Fearing that the rumor could be true she kicked her boots into the horse's flanks to gallop at a steady pace.

The Castro Rancho was much farther from the mission than the little house under the pines where she had first lived with Diego. It was a hard ride. She finally crested the knoll just above the *río* and the mission, then stopped suddenly. Her heart pounded. Her face was hot and the *whishing* sound of wind filled her ears. She trotted toward the entrance and saw the girls were right. There was a martyr's head on a stake in front of the plaza leading to the church.

She felt nauseous but proceeded forward, encouraging the horse, who sensed her fear and was reluctant to move beyond a slow walk. She stopped him, dismounted and walked forward staring at the decapitated head. It was Ores, his strong jaw so recognizable, his dark hair flopped over one eye. She gasped, collapsed to her knees and vomited. She screamed in her native Ohlone as she grabbed the stake and tried to remove it from the ground. Several neophyte men heard her cries and ran from their crumbling huts to grab and stop her.

"No, you can't leave him here. Have you become that heartless? We've got to bury him. Where's his body? Help me get him down. ......bury him!" she screamed while fighting them off and trying to yank the stake from the ground. The neophytes could see she would neither calm down nor give up. The leader nodded to the others.

"We'll bury him in the cemetery," one said.

"Are you crazy? You'll have to kill me first to do that," she said. "Tell the fathers and the soldiers that. He never lived here. He's no neophyte convert. He needs to be buried in his home up the river. In the proper way. Get some rags to wrap him up. We must find his body. We've got to bury him."

Sholeta's shock led her into a frenzy of activity. Ores had to be buried with respect, or preferably burned on the funeral pyre as was traditional for leaders. She would never leave him to rot in a mass grave. The men somberly dug up the stake and pulled Ores' head from the top of it. Another native ran up with the coarse woolen fabric the mission women spun and helped her wrap the head. Sholeta vomited again as she looked at the bloody package. She hefted it into her leather trail bag, mounted the horse and rode off. She could see soldiers running toward her from their posts at the courtyard and church door.

She kicked the horse from a cantor into a gallop and headed to the river and then eastward up its banks of willows and scrub brush toward the hills. She didn't know where she was going but some deep instinct, some ancient voice lured her up the river's banks. It was as if she were a homing pigeon with an internal compass guiding her. The horse smelled the blood dripping through the bag and tried to buck and whiny in protest. Rabid with anger and grief, incredulous at this new transgression, she rode on, digging her knees and boots into the horse's sides. Where was that village she'd heard about but never been to? Was that where Ores had been based in recent years? She knew so little about him. She felt guilty for having doubted his commitment. Maybe she'd erred in waiting for his lead. Maybe she should have just fled there herself. None of those questions mattered now.

Now she truly was an orphan. No real blood family save for her son Pedro. And none for the baby she was carrying. It was maybe four moons in but she knew a child was growing in her belly. What to do about this baby? How could she tolerate losing another child to Diego's cold, Spanish wife? She refused to do the work to help raise another baby that did not know she was the true parent. That did not gaze upon her with that unique love for one's mother. She galloped on looking for signs of native life along the creek bed pushing babies out of her mind to remember Ores. She must find his family, his body and send him to the afterlife and their ancestors with the greatest of reverence. He deserved that at least.

Days later, Sholeta returned on horseback to the rancho courtyard at the slowest *clop clopping* a horse can execute. She had not sent word of her whereabouts. Her body swayed as if she were going to fall off any moment. The young children called to each other and scampered around her.

"Where've you been? We missed you. Sholeta. Everyone was worried about you. Are you okay?"

She dismounted, patted a head here and shoulder there as she stumbled through the little crowd, in past the bedroom she usually shared with Diego and into her servant quarters out back. She closed the door and waited until they left her alone. Until they told their father she had returned.

Hours later, Diego burst in with great soldierly bravado. She could smell whiskey on him. She was surprised because he usually didn't drink when he was on duty. "Sholeta, my darling. Where've you been? The children have been sick with worry. No one could find any word at the pueblo or the mission or any other ranchos. Pedro and the vaqueros were out looking for you." He tried to grab her in an embrace but she pushed him back hard into the spindle chair, the single piece of furniture in the room beside her small bed.

"Diego, you murdered my brother."

He stared at her, dumbfounded. "What are you talking about? I've been away."

"Well, it doesn't matter, even if it wasn't you personally," she continued. She took a breath. "You did. You killed him. You and all your soldier compadres. You and your gente de razon. You Españoles who think you are better than us native Californians. We're the ones who've been here for generations. You're a murderer. You all are. Plain and simple."

"What are you talking about?"

"Don't you know they killed natives up in the village who supposedly stole guns and horses? They put a head up on a stake to warn everyone. Didn't you do that, Diego?"

"No, I wasn't in town. I was over at San Juan Bautista. And then they had some problems up at Santa Clara. What happened?"

"They said it was El fantasma," she mumbled amid tears. "I know some call you that." His surprise seemed to deepen and his mouth dropped open. "It was Ores," she whispered, pushing down her sobs, gritting her teeth so she wouldn't cry. She so wanted to collapse into him and feel his warmth and strong arms. But no. Not now. No more.

"Who? The man from the oak tree? Who is he? I've never known."

"He was my older brother. My only family member left. The one who would have been a tribal leader like my father. He was a great man, Diego. Trying to defend his people against yours, against the invader, the colonizer. I blame you for robbing me of my family. Of killing my people. The padres and soldiers and Español settlers say they just want to pacify us with their religion. But those natives at the mission mostly die or live in squalor. Let's be honest. Now, you all need us as your vaqueros and maids, your farmhands and nannies. Your baby makers."

He'd been shaking his head, "What did you say?"

"That's right. I'm your baby maker. Well, no longer. I took care of that. I took the herbs one of my aunts taught me to get rid of a baby. I bled it out, like the first time but this time I did it. Not the spirits."

"What are you saying? You were pregnant? You poisoned our baby? How could you? That's inexcusable. You should've told me you were pregnant."

His face reddened and his hand shook as he reached out, not really pointing, not really grasping for her, just reaching. "How could you do that to our child? That's murder, Sholeta. That's a sin. The Church says so."

"Your church *this* and your God *that*. I'm so tired of it. If your God tells you to be a good person, then why aren't your people good to us natives? You and your mission-building campaigns. I know you just kill natives in the way or put them in the missions to work for the padres." Tears poured down her cheeks as she spoke but gazed at the tile floor. She couldn't look up at him.

"You know I love you and Pedro," he said. "And that I love how you are such a good mother to my children when Quina is gone."

She said nothing. Just stared at the floor, breathing hard as if she'd just run all the way from the mission to the rancho. She hoped he felt the pain now, as piercing and hot as hers was.

"How could you take that poison? That's a mortal sin. And our baby? We've lost too many. How could you?" he demanded.

She looked up at him. She spoke very calmly now. Ice in her words. "Foreigners with big ships are stopping in the bay now. This land is so rich, once they tell their countrymen, more will come. Once more are here on our coast and see the good soil and plentiful sea, they'll stay to farm and build. The more there are of you, the more you'll need us to be your workers. Then, after we've worked to help you develop the new Californias, you'll want us out of the way. Off the land that you want to control. Gone, so there is no reminder of what you stole. Disappeared, so you can forget the murders, and pretend we were never here. The destruction of a good people. You'll kill us all, Diego. Mark my words, you'll kill us all."

Diego abruptly left the room upsetting the chair and slamming the door on his way out. Sholeta collapsed on the bed. She'd never said so much at any one time. She was an empty shell. She felt as if her core being was evaporating into a vapor of only memories, filmy, translucent with no hard center save for sadness. As if her body encased the ghost of a soul. No personal strength, no drive left to live.

She heard a quiet knock at the door and Pedro's voice, "Sholeta, are you are all right? We're all so worried about you. Everyone's glad you came back. What's wrong? Can you let me in?"

His strong voice, that reminder of the ultimate self-betrayal and sacrifice to the pale face destroyers, that reminder of giving up her only living child to become a Spaniard, pushed the pain in even deeper. She listened to the soft voice behind the door and suddenly understood what she needed to do to avenge Ores' death, to keep that promise to her father. The shock, the audacity of it, cracked her being like an earthquake jolt and she passed out.

RETURN TO THE FOREST

RANCHO CASTRO AND INLAND OF BAHÍA DE MONTERREY,
ALTA CALIFORNIA
1796–1804

After storming out of their most heated conversation ever, that day in her tiny bedroom, Diego observed Sholeta's transformation with concern. Since her brother's death, after she'd swallowed roots to expel a baby from her womb, she was no longer the same. It was as if the herbs had sapped her energy. She lost weight and grew slight, almost as skinny as when he'd brought her home from the mission. Her eyes turned hollow with deep shadows beneath. She spoke even less than before. Her force diminished. Was this still the woman of his heart, maybe his true wife, the one he really loved?

Always a dutiful worker, Sholeta continued to care for the children, keep the house, manage the servants and the vaqueros who tended the gardens and cows. But her light had faded. The vibrancy and feistiness that had driven the mission priests and soldiers crazy and kept the children entertained were gone. The care Diego found so endearing each time he returned home was not as prevalent as before. She mostly seemed to avoid him.

However, eventually, as had been his habit for over a decade, when Quina disappeared south to Santa Barbara for yet another birth, he crept into her room a few days after his wife had departed and asked her to join him in his bed. He expected he'd have to cajole her out of this new passive state but she looked up at him, nodded, followed him to his room and embraced him enthusiastically. As if she'd been waiting for his summons. Relieved, he felt like maybe things could return to normal. This woman soothed him at night.

About a year after Ores' death, one night in bed, Sholeta revealed that she was probably six months pregnant. He had not noticed the changes in her body and was slightly surprised but cupped her chin, tenderly, and smiled.

"I'm so pleased. This child will want for nothing. The baby will join our large family and—" She cut him off.

"Diego, this time it will be different. I will raise this child as an Ohlone. My final chance to make things right. For my father, my brother, my people." He had just put his pants and shirt on and stopped with half his buttons still undone. He felt his face go red, he inhaled deeply. What craziness was this woman going on about now? He tried to protest but she kept on, holding up her hand, hard, palm facing him, as she continued.

"Don't try to stop me," she said as she climbed out of bed. "You're responsible for Ores' death. For our babies dying. I gave up Pedro for you and that cold Spanish woman. But this baby will be Ohlone. You'll not stop me this time. I'll be leaving for the villages soon."

"What? Don't be crazy," he said. He grabbed her shoulders, forcing her to look closely at him. "I'm thrilled you're well enough to get pregnant again. The children are good workers because of Quina's discipline, you must admit." He saw a foreboding look in her eyes, the hard set of her jaw and realized she was serious. He could not let her leave. Pregnant, alone, where would she go? He had to stop this nonsense.

"Diego, you pretend she treats him the same as the others but you don't see. You're gone so much. She's even harder on Pedro than she is on the rest. But why am I arguing with you? This time it's my way. I have to honor my father's wish. I made him a promise. This is the only thing I can do now to keep our people from disappearing. I must raise a native child, not a Spaniard. You cannot stop me."

Diego wrapped his arm around her and drew her in to him. He had to make her see sense. He spoke into the top of her head, pressing her firmly into his torso. His voice more tender, but firm. "What are you thinking? You've lived with the Español now, with me, for over twenty years. How can you go back to village life? You were just a child when you lived at the mission. Be realistic. Let's raise this baby here close to us both, to Pedro, to the other children you love as your own. How will you survive out there?"

"I'll have the baby here at home. Then I'll go."

Diego shook his head. He knew her too well. He sensed a lie. He pushed her away from him. "I'll not let you leave. We have a life and a family here. You'll miss the children, and me. Don't deny it. I know you feel as I do."

"Then why didn't you marry me in the mission in front of the father? Like some of your soldier comrades did? You lie to yourself. You always have. You're an ambitious coward who just wants the blessing of Comandante Ortega."

Her words cut deeply. Was he just fooling himself that he'd become more loyal to family as he'd had more children? He did drop everything to do Ortega's bidding, to remain on favorable terms with his military superiors and the governors. To get promoted, to get another land grant. That was true. He had soldiering responsibilities. She knew that, right?

Sholeta pressed on. "No, I'm not living this way anymore. I've been a coward too. But no longer. Time to think of someone else besides myself, you, these children who are not mine. You're a hypocrite, Diego. Now go pray or confess or whatever to make yourself feel better. But I know who you truly are."

The cruelty of her words stung. Why was it that those you love the most can say the most hurtful things? He'd tell her, finally. Was that what she wanted? To hear it out loud?

"Sholeta. You know I love you. I had to have a Spanish wife. But Quina, she's like a business partner. Nothing else. You have my heart. And that hasn't changed in all these years, through the difficult times, or with so many children. You know that."

She looked up at him and smiled weakly. She touched his cheek.

"Good. You'll have the baby here," he continued. "I'll talk to the doctor. But you've got to stay here with your children...all of the children. We're your family. You can't deny it."

That night, Diego made love to her with more tenderness than usual. He caressed her hair and cheeks, her shoulders and breasts with the gentle touch of a shy, young man. He kissed her scars and wrapped his arms tightly around her from behind, fingertips running up and down her stomach. He was relieved as she fell asleep curled into his grasp. He was glad she'd be staying for the birth.

Next he had to convince her to stay beyond that. He could do it. They'd been like husband and wife for years. He'd finally told her he loved her. Of course, she would stay. He nestled in to her warm back and neck and drifted off, lazily imagining another baby joining his large family.

When Diego awoke the next morning, Sholeta's side of the bed was empty. He touched the rumpled sheet where she'd dreamt next to him. It was cold. She must have been gone for hours.

⁓

After Ores' murder, after she rashly, in a fit of rage, had aborted her child with the poisonous herbs, and upon hearing her son calling for her that day, Sholeta had decided only one path lay before her. She would get pregnant again and leave to raise the baby in the traditional manner. She was determined to honor her ancestors, to do something right for her people for once. To keep the deathbed promise she'd made to her father. Her son was now a Catholic Spaniard who had no idea who his real mother was. That was the ultimate betrayal. She would not do it again.

She'd been disloyal to her people by acquiescing to stay with Diego. To help raise his Spanish children. To provide almost no information for Ores and his band trying to attack the invaders. By tacitly agreeing to spy for Diego on her own brother. The list of her transgressions was endless. Her child would help the Ohlone persevere. Continuing her race became her sole focus. Her only reason to endure the injustices of rancho life just a little longer.

Once the path was clear to her, her enthusiasm for Diego's household waned. She was depressed and empty at the loss of Ores. At watching Pedro grow into an adolescent who did not know her as anything but the cook and maid. The only thing that kept her going was staying focused on the goal. Eventually, Quina got pregnant and fled for her parents' home for the birth yet again.

Sholeta set her plan in motion immediately. It was hard not to be consumed by the disgust and pity that overshadowed her view of Diego now, but she still had affection for him after all their years together. She quickly returned to his arms and his bed. The plan worked.

Once pregnant, she decided to leave before she was showing. She sent word via a native maid out to the village where Ores' widow lived that she would be moving in and would soon be giving birth. She did not provide an opportunity for anyone to say no. They were loyal to Ores and she assumed, without question, they would take her in.

When she finally told Diego that she was leaving him, he was angry and shocked and clearly didn't believe she could return to native living. Sholeta would never admit to him that she had wondered the same thing. Could she really go through with it? After all, how would she survive after more than twenty years living with the Spanish? And could she leave him, Pedro and the other kids she adored?

He was right. They were a family in many ways. But not in the most important ones. Not in honesty. Not in raising a child together with united, loving parents. There were too many secrets, too much unsaid. Pedro was a good boy who she had confidence would grow into a principled young man. Her heart would break even further when she left him behind, but she had no other options. She must raise an Ohlone child.

❧

"There are scouts looking for you, Sholeta," one of the young men said at the entrance to her hut. "They say Capitán Castro is looking for you. That he needs his best maid back."

"Tell the villagers I'm not for sale. I'm Ores' sister. They must respect that, honor my wish to stay. I'll not return to the invaders' home," she responded in her awkward Ohlone. It felt as if she had a tortilla in her mouth as she tried to move her tongue around the old sounds. But she made sure the harsh tone of her voice and the coldness in her eyes would leave no doubt to this native lookout that she was determined. "Now go. Tell them and chase away any scouts. I'm staying here with Ores' wife and my nieces and nephews." She shifted her weight to get more comfortable nursing the baby as she sat on the hard dirt floor of their willow branch hut. Another son.

The spirits and her ancestors were protecting her just this once. Already the baby looked like her—like a native, not an español. His eyes had the slope and his jaw the roundness of her people. Yes, she had lost many babies. She had lived through the deaths of her closest family members. She had been a prisoner in captivity away from her people for two decades. But her two living sons each had the countenance that would help them survive. Perhaps the only good providence that had come her way. Pedro looked so much like his father that his true maternal line was unclear. This baby at her breast favored her. Diego's Spanish blood was hidden in this child. She prayed to her ancestors that his look would not change. She would raise him as pure Ohlone, but it would be an enormous advantage if he looked the part as well.

The transition was not easy. She had lived with the Spanish ten years longer than she'd lived with her parents in the village. But the fortitude of her race, her determination to give this child an authentic life was all consuming. It fueled the difficult transformation. She'd been adamant about keeping as much of the traditional food in her diet as possible and that eased her physical adjustment. But sleeping on the ground in the hut next to the open fire, cooking over the flame, gathering firewood, roots and herbs was challenging. For years, she'd been flapping sheets to cover cotton and straw mattresses, ordering others to stir cauldrons and shake iron skillets over well-tended fires, harvesting lemons and oranges from straight rowed orchards. Returning to the hunter-gatherer existence was arduous.

Never loquacious as a captive, back in her home territory, conscious of her slight Spanish accent, she spoke even less. She was aware of how her presence reminded people of the changes in their homeland and status. In the years she'd been gone, the depleted elk population and reduction in shellfish on the rocky shoreline forced the natives to adjust their nomadic patterns. Rapidly expanding herds of cows ate much of the lush grasses. Spanish hunters had already diminished the fish and otter populations. Rumors of possible Chinese interest in otter and seal pelts trickled in via the latest foreign sailing ships. Native fishermen now had even more competition in the bays and harbors.

Meanwhile, the Spanish population was beginning to spread beyond the coast to the inland areas. They were farming great swaths of valleys and hills. It was getting difficult to avoid the Español. They seemed to be moving in everywhere; so the native peoples adapted. Many went to the missions for food and trade and eventually were conscripted to stay. Some escaped and then returned to the mission system in a steady stream of dependence. Many tried to keep the villages true to their traditional ways. But that too was complicated. Horses and guns, mules and cows, new grains and greens planted in rows had taken hold in the lives of the natives, even in many villages.

Sholeta could see the difference clearly, even though her memories of native homelife had faded with time and grief. So with the guidance of her sister-in-law and Ores' children, she raised her son in the modified traditions of her people. She ate only native foods. She strapped the baby to her back and took him to gather acorns and slice reeds for making baskets. She crept behind the teenage boys as they worked to master the hunt of quail, rabbits and eventually elk and deer. She traded her knowledge of cultivating crops and utilizing horses. Her older body groaned inwardly as she tried to get accustomed to sleeping on the hard ground and digesting the elk meat she hadn't eaten for years. But it was all for her son. For her promise to her father. For the survival of her people.

In those first baby years she was overwhelmed. Had she made a mistake? Though she confessed to no one, she did miss the rancho. Longed for news of Pedro, and of all the Castro children she remembered fondly. Had Pedro grown into an honorable young man as she believed he would? Was he learning from Quina and the vaqueros how to be a rancher? Or would he become a soldier like his father? Even though she was conflicted and had a bottomless well of anger for Diego and all he represented, she missed him quite often. She longed for a warm, soft bed, her skinny hips and shoulders never quite getting comfortable on the ground at night. And then of course she would think of him under the blankets with her.

She missed the children sitting on the long benches lining the wooden table mumbling their prayers before devouring her cooking with enthusiastic exclamations, their round, brown eyes looking up at her with appreciation. She missed even the style of cooking she'd invented, mixing native herbs and shellfish into the traditional Spanish dishes. She missed her horses sorely and how she had learned, as the Spaniards did, to ride most everywhere, to become one with the horse. She longed for the garden and orchard she had cultivated. Even for the sheep shearing and the never-ending work of raising cattle and horses while feeding eight children and keeping their large house clean.

As her baby grew into a spirited little boy and spent time learning with the elders and the older children, she had moments when she could reflect on her rather unusual and difficult life. Now, looking back from this strange vantage point, Sholeta could see that she really had become a ranch woman. Yes, Quina also could do the ranch work but mostly she'd been busy having babies and disappearing to Santa Barbara. Diego was first and foremost a soldier, convincing himself he was protecting all the pobladores in their new land, riding from mission to mission, rancho to rancho.

Sholeta had been the one who worked the ranch and the adobe homestead with her hands every day. Who braided the girls' hair and scrubbed the boys' long pants. Who decided when the sheep had to be shorn and taught the children how to do it. Who managed the stable hands to care for the horses properly. Who taught other young native girls to be maids and cooks. Who picked the garden greens and pruned the fruit trees and grapevines with the pack of children as her assistants. She knew she had been the heart of that rancho and it broke her inside, just a bit, to think of all of them there now. Without her. Diego had been right, she begrudgingly admitted to herself. They had become her family.

However, she would quickly remind herself, she had a new purpose now. To create a native family for her youngest son. Pedro and Beatriz and the others would grow and thrive with the foundation she'd established. She had helped shape them into Californios and they would succeed in the new Alta California. Now, she had to do the same for *Asatsa*. She had named her son Morning for her relentless belief that each new rising sun came with possibilities.

As Asatsa grew, Sholeta taught him Spanish. Secretly. She whispered to him that it was their private language. That no one knew it but the two of them. And he was so young, so bound to his mother that he listened with rapt eyes and whispered the words back to her, rounding his lips to make the sounds. He asked about his father and clearly longed for one, but Sholeta would just shoo him out to play with his older cousins. She sent him to learn from a village elder who told her he admired her gumption at returning after living with the Español for so long. The boy eventually stopped asking about a father. His cousins didn't have one either.

As Asatsa grew older and more aware of the environment around him, Sholeta taught him about the world their people now inhabited. Though she told him the story of her capture, she omitted the worst parts. He was still so young. She told him about his grandparents and aunts and uncles but focused on their skills and strengths, not their deaths from disease at the mission. She described her life with a Spanish family for many years but she neglected to mention that she had essentially been a slave with no independence or ability to live with Ohlone customs.

On his eighth birthday, she decided to tell him just a bit more, to begin grooming him to take on the role of rebel like Ores and her cousin had been. To prepare him for the world beyond their small village. She told him, "Even though that Spanish family did not treat me too badly, our natural life here in the village is much better. We have less sickness. We're not so violent. The Español brought those horrible guns into our land. Our arrows are no match. So we need their guns. While they are terrible, you must learn to use them. You must use your hunting skills someday to get their pistols and rifles. You must wait patiently and then quietly sneak in to their strange houses for weapons and into corrals to steal horses. And you can understand what they say, so listen carefully."

"How will I understand them if they speak a different dialect?" he asked.

"Our secret language, my dear Asatsa, those are the words of the enemy. So listen hard to find the guns and bring them back to us in the village. Our leaders want us to have weapons so we can defend ourselves if needed."

"I can do that," he promised with youthful enthusiasm.

"Become the best hunter of all," she said. "But you must be quiet and careful because you must always return to me."

"Don't worry. I'm learning from the older boys. Of course, I'll always come back. And our secret language will help me. I'll be the best Ohlone gun thief. I'll make you proud, Atsia."

A RANCHING WOMAN

RANCHO CASTRO, NEAR THE EL CAMINO REAL, ALTA CALIFORNIA
1804

"Oh, *no, no," Quina moaned* one night, candle shadows flickering on the library walls. In the evenings when he was home at the hacienda, Diego typically sipped whiskey and read in his large upholstered chair. Quina flipped through the bible or wrote letters at her desk across from him. In the eight years since Sholeta had disappeared, whenever they were both at the rancho, they had developed the habit of spending the evenings together in the library. They discussed ranch business and the religious education of their many children. They gossiped over the growing number of neighboring land grant recipients and whether their haciendas were as grand as Rancho Castro. They debated Alta California politics, constantly in upheaval and much neglected by the powerful in México City. It was a library filled with business each night but Diego could not deny there was a comforting companionship in it as well.

"What is it?" he asked. His voice rose with alarm. Quina never cried but her voice cracked and choked as if tears were on the way.

"My mother died in that measles epidemic. I must go home immediately," she said, staring down at the tiles. The parchment letter dropped to her lap, then to the floor as she stood up and began to pace. "My poor father, what will he do? I've dreaded this day. My parents leaving us for heaven. With all we've been through, I could never imagine them passing on." She dropped her head and covered her face with her hands, shaking her head back and forth, a low moan continuing.

Diego crossed the library to comfort her, trying to push the annoyance scratching his throat down into his gut where it resided pretty much permanently. He was torn. Comfort her? Of course. But come on, she had eleven children, a husband, a growing ranch and many servants. What would her father do? Really? What about him? What would he do if she left again? This time there was no baby on the way. Just another excuse? Go home? This was her home for God's sake. And the big family and rancho needed her to help him and Pedro guide it. As alone as he suddenly felt, duty flooded in.

He scooped the letter off the floor and gently put his arm around her shoulder, leading her to the sofa. Awkwardly, as affection was not comfortable for either of them, he sat her down, pulling her toward him as if to put her head on his shoulder. But Quina, stiff, even in her surprise and grief, did not bend that way and their heads tipped into each other. They sat for a few moments, heads pressed together, Diego patting her shoulder.

"Oh, my dear," he said, using the most comforting voice he could muster. "I'm so sorry. I know how much you loved her, protected her. Comandante Sebastian told me stories of your strength during the journey, in the cold of Yerba Buena and at Santa Bárbara before the presidio."

Quina shifted her head to look into his eyes. Diego realized he'd moved into unusual territory. They did not speak of their pasts, of the hard years before their marriage, or before the rancho even.

Intimacy was not a part of their lexicon or gestures. It was all cows and planting, children, servants and hacienda construction, and now, even guests and entertaining.

Quina patted his hand and gave him a peck on the cheek. She sat up straight, smoothed her hair, then her bodice. "I have to go to my father. Oh, and my poor sisters. I'll pack now and leave at dawn. Have two horses prepared and that strong stable boy to go with me. I'll need to fill all three sets of saddlebags. I don't know when I'll be back. The boy can return with two horses."

"But your duty is here," he said. "You're not pregnant. Pedro and Beatriz can't always run the household and the rancho for us. I'll check on your father. There's a mission planned for Santa Ines in the hills above. I have to leave soon anyway; I'll head down there early."

"Don't be a fool," she said. Her tone harsh, biting. "My mother's just died. Have you no sympathy? This is my father we're talking about. He's alone. My sisters have their own families. Who'll care for him? I'll leave in the morning. Just get the horses ready. Good night."

The next morning, after she'd barked coarse instructions for their eldest daughters and left on horseback, saddlebags flapping, Diego wondered if she'd ever return. This time neither of them could blame her departure on pregnancy or post-birth melancholia. He knew she was done with that. No more babies she'd said and openly drank a root tea after they made love. Quina, who'd never learned any native words, who never interacted with their staff beyond barking orders, must have bribed one of the housemaids handsomely to get a recipe for a pregnancy preventing concoction.

He was angry and confused but suppressed his frustration. *My sisters have their own families?* Of course, but so did she. Now, he wondered, would she abandon her own children to care for her father? Maybe now she was done with childbearing she felt her duty to him was complete. Sadly, he had no confidence in the answer to that question.

Yet, Diego had not demanded she remain at home. He lacked the courage, or heart, to play the forceful role and require her to stay. A practical husband, he knew she'd just make them all miserable. She'd be a mess. She might try to flee and run off without his permission. He'd decided to let her do as she wished, as usual.

Despite being in a house filled with noisy children, he felt very alone. He ached for warmth, for companionship and absently wondered what ever happened to Sholeta. Since her disappearance and his inability to locate her whereabouts, he often was lonely. The fact that he, El fantasma famous for his stealthy tracking skills, could not find her made the pain of realizing she never wanted to be found even more difficult to bear. His only solace was the new relationships he developed with his children as they grew into young adults.

For once he felt fortunate for "the Castro Curse." With their parents often away, the oldest girls had grown up caring for their younger siblings and managing household chores with the assistance of the native servants. Most importantly, Diego reminded himself, he had Pedro. His eldest had grown into a capable ranch hand who had an easy manner with the vaqueros and adeptly absorbed estate management. As always, Rancho Castro would survive without its doña.

⌒

Three months later, Don Sebastian mounted his horse in the plaza of his Santa Bárbara home and instructed his eldest daughter to ride next to him as they headed for the cemetery to pray at her mother's grave. The bare mountains rose steep at their backs. September heat pressed into their shoulders, their lungs. They clopped down the path. The mission glowed white as they rounded its corner for the grave-yard. A light breeze blew in from the ocean, rippling the lagoon's sur-face. Don Sebastian mopped his forehead with his handkerchief. He slowed his steed to a trot.

"Quina, my darling, it's time. You must go to your children, to your husband, your rancho. You've been coming here for twenty years and now, for some reason with your mother gone, I finally realize what you've sacrificed to be here with your mother and me."

"Papá," she said. "What? My duty is to you."

"No, you're quite wrong. Your duty is to your husband. You're forsaking your responsibilities. Who's raising your children while you're gone? The heathen servants? And Don Diego is on the trail so much—I know—I see him out there. We're on campaigns together. Who's managing the ranch? Pedro? He's just of age now. He needs your guidance."

"But Papá..." She didn't want to leave him. The familiarity of her old home. The comfort she found in supporting her parents and sib-lings. He didn't let her finish.

"What kind of pobladora are you if you're emotionally weak? If you can't manage your own household and have to run home to your parents? We've survived a lot. I've got the girls and their husbands close by. I'll be fine. I'm sending you off tomorrow. No arguments. But I want to talk to you about something else. Move along, now."

Quina had stopped her horse at her father's words, which felt as if they were stabs at her heart. Her purpose. She'd been shocked upon her arrival that her father's hair had turned gray since she'd last been here for the birth of her youngest. New wrinkles etched his forehead. Her mother's sudden illness and death had aged him.

What was he saying? He needed her. Diego certainly didn't. The children were well cared for by the servants.

"Listen, Quina," he said. "Besides your duty, there's an opportunity there. Get a concession from the governor. Trade is the future. Spain is distracted. Many here don't realize it because we're so far from the capital but the Mexicans will revolt eventually. They'll kick out the Spanish—just like the American colonies did to the English. It's inevitable. Spain has too many of their own problems to keep control of Nueva España. That little troublemaker in France, Napoleon, he's already stirring things up in Iberia.

"Soon the Americas will be rid of the Europeans and we'll govern ourselves. Look at the *Yanquis*. They're prospering without English control. That's who we need to look to next. They're expanding. Heading our way with that new territory. They'll want our meats and hides, our seeds and vegetables before you know it. Just the tallow alone from a high producing cattle population is valuable to any growing nation.

"I can tell you now that I've traded for years with the ships from the Sandwich Islands, with the Manila galleons. The Callao route ships stop here occasionally, English and French sometimes too. I always have hides, fresh vegetables or milk for them. They look the other way while I take some furniture, fine linens and silver for the table."

Quina stopped again and raised her eyebrows at her father's admission. The Spanish had always limited the colonists to obtaining materials and foodstuffs they couldn't produce themselves from the Acapulco and San Blas supply ships. Foreigners and trade were strictly prohibited. Well, maybe she had suspected but she'd looked the other way, never allowing any negative views of her father to take hold. But he seemed proud of his illegal trading.

Papá continued. "How do you think I dressed your mother so finely these last years? Where do you think my cigars come from? I keep a few trinkets on hand for whoever is the current governor when he visits and I have no problems. Cigars, porto from Portugal, silks from the Orient, scarves and combs and decent chinaware for the wife if he has been fortunate enough to get one to stay here.

"The Boston merchants will come soon, you watch. They'll need new markets and everyone needs hides and tallow. We are perfectly situated, my dear. I'll keep Santa Bárbara visitors satisfied. You have an opportunity in Bahía de Monterrey with your large ranch so close by. You can do the trading there."

Quina listened to her father with both a pain in her heart and a gnawing interest in his suggestion. It was as if he were throwing kindling on a fire smoking inside of her. In reality, she was itching to be done with babies and nursing. Papá didn't want her, didn't need her, Diego never had, but Rancho Castro did need her. Maybe he was right. She gazed at him with love, admiration. Trepidation.

"I don't know, Papá...I will miss you all and the rancho so...." Going home, to stay, to Diego, who she'd always known never loved her, was cold and uninviting. Toddlers and young children weren't interesting and quite a lot of work. But they were growing older now, perhaps they could be useful. She was a missionary, a crusader. Papá was right to remind her of that. Settlers could not be weak.

"Stop being a baby, my tough little mountain goat. Remember you are a pobladora, you have strong children, a faithful soldiering husband, a good-sized land concession. We have come so far from Sinaloa, Quina, don't forget that. Do not squander the opportunity God has given us. Leave now and don't come back. When Pedro and Beatriz and the others marry, we'll come to the fandangos. But don't you come here, you're no longer welcome. My mistake letting your mother take you in for all those babies. I let her coddle you. There is no room for coddling on the frontier. But you made her happy so I looked the other way."

His words stung. She had always been convinced she'd been doing her duty by having babies and also supporting her parents. Suddenly she saw that both Papá and Diego had allowed her to never really leave Santa Bárbara and establish the Rancho Castro as her true home.

"But now I think of Diego," her father said. "I see him on the trail—he's lonely. He's burdened with the cattle, a big house, the servants raising his children. Go home, go be a *ganadera*, a ranching woman. Duty to God and King. We are missionaries above all else. Never forget that."

Later that day, as she bounced in her saddle riding north, Quina was torn. She was distraught at her father's unceremonious dismissal. Papá's words pained her but forced her to look at herself more honestly, from an outsider's point of view, as if she were high up looking down from the clouds above. He probably was right. He was now one of the wealthiest men in Alta California. He had a large adobe with many native servants and her sisters lived nearby. He owned plenty of horses and cattle. The governor had given him a land concession. As commander of the presidio he had important responsibilities. Spanish emissaries from Mexico City and Spain, military leaders and the Alta California governors visited him regularly. Papá would be fine.

And Diego? Would he be irritated at her returning and staying? He'd never seemed to want her around much. Always seemed to be hankering for that servant girl even when they were together. Had she fled south for her parents and the familiar home or had she been fleeing her own marriage? Maybe Papá was right that after twenty years of births and newborns, toddlers and child rearing, she should focus on the business of their land.

Although they never spoke of it, it was as if she and Diego had reached an understanding. She had done her duty as a wife to bear him many children and help him build up the ranch. She purposely forced herself into his world and his bed when she was at home. But when she was south in Santa Bárbara it was as if she lived there permanently, with no other home to consider. She'd chosen to ignore any infidelities that likely occurred when she was away but she was not naive. She felt the emptiness between them when she returned with another baby wrapped in her shawl.

But enough of that. She must move her duty to the future, to her land and her children. She must protect her family's legacy. She must keep the Rancho Castro purely Spanish and make it a profitable enterprise. She took her father's admonitions and squeezed her mind hard to imagine a future, the one he was predicting. The children were much more interesting and helpful as they'd grown. She would assign them additional chores to make the place more efficient, more productive. And to build what she started picturing, she would need full control.

When Diego returned from the trail several days later, Quina was prepared to tell him her plan. She'd spent the time assigning the children new tasks, rearranging the house and barns. She'd re-established herself to the servants as the *patrona* in charge. Yes, Pedro and Beatriz ran things when their parents were gone, but now she was back and everyone needed to pay heed to her commands.

Once in the library that evening, she updated Diego, almost casually. She'd be there from now on. No more Santa Bárbara visits. She'd be looking to trade their hides and produce with the visiting ships. Her son would run the rancho when he was ready. He'd be the heir.

"Well of course, my dear," Diego said rather absently, reading through the latest pronouncement from the viceroy which had just been delivered to Monterrey by an *aviso*, a quick moving news delivery ship. "Pedro is already moving into that role. He's such a help when I have to be gone for weeks."

"Put that down. I'm talking to you. Not Pedro. My son. Our son. Francisco." Silence. Diego put down the paperwork and pushed his chair back from the desk. He stretched back, tipping the chair, combing back his hair with a gnarled hand. His dark eyes squinted at her.

"Pedro is our son," he said. "He's the oldest, he's already ranching. He's the heir. What are you talking about? Francisco is only eight. Let him grow and learn. He can be a rancher too." His gaze did not drop from her eyes. She did not flinch, flashing on the image of herself in full chain mail leading the Crusades, the vision that had fueled her eleven-year-old legs to walk two thousand miles to reach Alta California.

"No, Pedro is your son. Not mine," she said. "I've always known that, that we didn't just adopt him. I don't know why you lied to me. Francisco is the rightful heir. He'll inherit the concession. I'm sure the Crown will grant them on into the next generation and not reclaim them as the law says now. The Californios are the stewards of this land. Either way, Francisco is the rightful heir."

"Darling," Diego said. She noted the softer tone in his voice. She had to be on her guard. She would not let him convince her otherwise. "The children told me about your prayers at the chapel the night you returned. That you announced to all of them you'd be staying here from now on. I'm delighted you'll be staying, that you've accepted this as your home. I've been waiting for that all these years."

He moved to sit next to her, taking her hand. She did not pull it away but sat perfectly still, staring across the room at the fire in the stone fireplace. "But Pedro is our son," he continued. "We raised him together. He's already helping me. You'll see what an important role he has here. I know you'll be pleased. He's grown into a good man. You should be proud. I might have wanted a soldier for a son. But that is not him. He understands the land, just like you."

"Well maybe that's from his heathen mother," she said. A cold darkness entered her heart. This man would not take her son and his rightful inheritance from her. "He's not my son. I'll not have it. Francisco can learn from you, from Pedro and me, but he'll be the heir one day. I'll see to that." She pulled her hand away from his.

"Don't count on it," Diego said quickly. "I'm glad you've come home. But this is my house, my rancho, my way. I'm your husband and your duty is to me. I've let you do everything you ever wanted. I never complained or brought you back home all the times you left us for Santa Bárbara. Choosing your parents over us, over me, over your duty here. I've been very flexible with you, very understanding. I built you a big house, even while always on the trail, to provide you the comfort you never had as a child. Don't you forget that. But this. I'll never relent. I'll not give in to your stubbornness on this. Pedro is our son and he will run and inherit the Castro Rancho."

"He's a half-breed," she whispered. "I know he's actually your son with that heathen maid you had when we married. You made a mistake getting attached to one of the natives. You've always favored Pedro. But he's not the only boy now. We have two others and Francisco is rightfully entitled by blood to take over. Perhaps I need to take this problem to confession or to the governor when Francisco is fifteen." Quina stared straight ahead. Diego slapped his hand down on her desk.

"Don't forget we had Pedro baptized as our own when Beatriz was baptized. The mission priests keep careful records. You'll never win this argument. Your duty is to me and Pedro is our son. Period." He got up abruptly and walked to the door, pulling it shut, hard.

Quina let out a breath, curling her hands into fists. She would not relent. She might have looked the other way during his relationship with the native maid. But this, this was different. Duty would prevail. She would make them all into ranchers and her natural born son would inherit a fine cattle estate. She left the room and headed toward her private study and the small sofa there, far down the hall from the master bedroom she usually shared with her husband.

FANDANGO

*S*he was the most beautiful girl in Alta California. With the translucent skin and fine features of a delicate lily. Everyone commented on it. Her hair was so light, almost blond, that when the sun caught it a brilliant shine emanated, as if she were surrounded by a halo. Pedro found Juana Candelaria de la Cruz to be more than just beautiful; she was sweetness personified. Her kindness and her fragility made her all the more attractive.

At twenty-five, Pedro was a rancher, a true Californio who rarely walked anywhere, completely at one with his horse. He'd been tending the cows and sheep, fields and orchards practically since infancy. As he grew into a man with strong legs and jaw, a swash of thick, black hair, skin darkened by hours in the sun, he began to crave a wife who would be the complete opposite of his mother.

Despite his strength and capabilities, he often felt a hollow in his sternum. A loneliness he described to no one except his beloved sister, Beatriz. She told him she was convinced their upbringing brought that emptiness to him. A mother who was always leaving you, who had little time but for strict lessons and rules and ranching business could leave one longing for comfort and affection. A mother who rode horses like a cowboy and managed an enormous household with a firm fist but who was emotionally unavailable. Who couldn't stand to give birth in her own home, fleeing to her parents every time she was pregnant. Who treated her children like junior vaqueros rather than her own offspring. Who favored her younger sons above all the others. That type of mother could leave a child wanting, Beatriz argued. Pedro saw the logic in her reasoning.

His eight sisters, raised by the fearless Quina and native servants, were tough and ruddy from hard living. They carried water and milked the cows. They rode horses and shucked the stalls. They cheered on the vaqueros' games and sheared the sheep. Really no different than the workers or the three boys in the family. On Quina's Rancho Castro, femininity was a luxury she could not afford.

Pedro wanted a new style of wife who fit the changing times in Las Californias. One who was feminine and well-groomed. A lady. Who was obedient to her husband and focused on comfort, on home-building. Who would be a hostess at his side. A devoted mother to his children and who would support him at every turn. Who would not abandon her family or home, ever.

When Pedro told his father of his desire to marry Candelaria, and someday become the Don of Rancho Castro with her as the ultimate hostess at his side, Diego was skeptical. "I know you're a rancher, not a soldier. I know you want a wife to start a family. But is she strong enough to endure the hardships here? I think she may belong, or be more comfortable, in a Spanish hacienda with fine furniture and dresses, socializing with the important families, putting on great parties, rather than branding cows."

Pedro laughed but neglected to disclose that he had the same concern. "Not everyone can be a pobladora like Mamá," he said. "Alta California's ranchos can expand and one day be like the great

Spanish haciendas. I am a Californio, Papá. I need her at my side to really become one." Beyond the rancho's business, Pedro thought of nothing but having the stunning Candelaria on his arm, forever. Even while on horseback moving the cows from one hillside to another with the vaqueros, he found it impossible to keep her image out of his mind.

Thank goodness her father was the comandante at the presidio in San Diego so he should approve the union of two military families. In her presence, Pedro's breath grew shallow and he lost control of his voice, stumbling over his words when he attempted to court her. Fortunately, speaking to her father did not make him nervous. As the son of Captain Castro, and himself a Californio ranchero outside of Monterrey, he had status.

His future father-in-law was concerned that he'd be taking his darling so far from home, but he was otherwise pleased with the match and allowed the marriage. "She's like a fresh flower, son," Candelaria's father warned. "She's delicate and must be cared for." Pedro had, of course, given his future father-in-law strong assurances to his commitment and worthiness.

On the day of their official betrothal, Candelaria's father permitted them to meet alone, very briefly. Pedro lightly kissed Candelaria's thin hand. As he started to explain that they were now engaged, she shushed him. She placed her arm through his and guided him to sit on the velvety love seat in her father's study. He did as she directed, glad for a moment he could catch his breath and try to get his voice working properly. She seemed more pleased with the arrangement than he expected.

"Pedro, I'm so glad my father said yes. I'm a little nervous to leave my family, but I can't wait to leave San Diego. I'm looking forward to living in the royal capital with you. The natives here attack constantly and the place is little more than a fort. There's no town, no socials. I think my father underestimated how remote this awful place was when we left Spain for this assignment."

Pedro was surprised at the revelation that perhaps the San Diego commander had doubts about his position but quickly pushed that out of his mind, delighted by her enthusiasm. His nerves lessened a little and he was finally able to engage in conversation. He had to promise her something better than San Diego and native attacks. He told her about the rancho, perhaps embellishing a bit. He described his grand plans to build her an adobe of their own, someday. Oh, but soon. He told her more settlers would arrive populating the north and bringing European style and society with them. They would have a social home.

Candelaria appeared delighted at his promises, raised her face for a quick kiss before any family returned. On the lips. Pedro wrapped his arm around her back, holding her firmly yet gently, remembering her father's admonition that she was a delicate flower. She touched his cheek with one hand and wrapped the other around his neck, caressing lightly at his hairline as she pressed her lips into his with enthusiasm. Right there in her father's study. His heart pounded. He was besotted.

Pedro combed his hair again. He adjusted his tunic and fingered the silver buttons, a wedding gift from his mother. His hands trembled as he reached to the bureau for his wax container and swiped his fingers across the stickiness, then shaped his mustache. He took the handkerchief in the salvia perfumed water, wiped his hairline, the back of his neck, his underarms. An old soldier trick from the road his father had passed on. Why was he so nervous? They were already married. He was ecstatic to take the exquisite Candelaria into his bed every night and make love to her in the most tender manner his passion would allow. She was a little quiet during her first weeks in the tiny adobe but she seemed to be relaxing. He noticed she avoided Quina. He was thrilled she and Beatriz seemed to have become friends already.

Today was the celebration of their marriage at the rancho, a grand fandango to which all of Monterrey was invited. Even the priests at the mission were coming for the opening prayers. The vaqueros had spent days cleaning the horses, twisting their tails into braids complete with ribbons, polishing bridles and stirrups. Every saddle glinted in the sun, every reata cracked as the cowboys prepared for the rodéo which would launch the festivities.

Pedro brushed dust off his pants and took a rag to shine his boots once more. There would be more important people from Alta California in one place than had ever assembled in the territory. And it was for his marriage. Sure, his parents would be there as the real hosts, but it was his time to become the patron, the man of the hacienda. He closed his eyes and said a prayer of thanks for his beautiful wife, for his role on the rancho, for his dreams.

He heard a commotion outside. Putting away his grooming supplies, he left his bedroom. It was too early for the guests to arrive.

"Candelaria, what's going on?" he called into the kitchen building as he went out his front door and turned toward the central plaza of the rancho. Flowers and colorful *papel picado* cutouts strung along the newly built second story balconies danced in the breeze. Musicians practiced guitars and sang in the big house courtyard and the music drifted through the adobes. A messenger with two soldier escorts from the Monterrey capital entered the courtyard, a Spanish flag flying behind one of the guards.

"Don Pedro Castro? Is that you, sir?" asked the messenger. "I have an important declaration from the governor and the viceroy."

Diego and Quina, both were still putting on their best clothes, Pedro's siblings in several stages of undress, servants with young children in hand all poured out of the rooms onto the balcony and through the front entry into the plaza.

Diego approached the messenger. "Who sent you, soldado? Oh, Pedro, it must be the governor congratulating you on your marriage. Let's see what we have here," and he reached to take the scrolled paper from the messenger.

"I am to give it to Don Pedro directly, sir. Forgive me, Captain Castro, but I must follow the governor's orders," he said. He blushed a little then cleared his throat and said loudly, "Don Pedro, this is for you directly from the governor. He sends his heartiest congratulations on your excellent marriage." His eyes scanned the buildings likely hoping for a sight of the lovely bride. "He thinks that joining your family with that of Comandante De La Cruz of San Diego was a wise choice and he wishes to congratulate you properly."

"Well, many thanks to the governor," Pedro said. "I do hope he is planning to attend the rodéo and the fandango later this afternoon."

Pedro reached up to take the paper and unrolled it. His brothers and sisters crowded around. Candelaria still preparing her hair for the fiesta, peeked out from her little home with an embroidered shawl covering her head and shoulders.

"Oh my, this is indeed a great wedding present," Pedro said. "The Governor has given me concession to two and a half leagues of land bordering our rancho. Candelaria, come, my darling, look what the governor's given us." He handed the declaration to his father who was embracing him. The littlest of his siblings were hanging on his legs and jumping up and down.

Beatriz came through the crowd to hug him. "Oh, Pedro, it is your dream. Congratulations," she said. Tears welled up in her eyes and he gave her a giant hug and kissed each cheek.

Then he pushed all aside to find his wife still hiding in the shadow of their doorway. He scooped up her tiny frame and swung her around the courtyard, laughing. She shrieked in delight. The black *mantón de Manila* fell to the ground, forgotten in the excitement.

Only Quina stayed back at the grand door to the hacienda main house. Diego watched her witness the celebration without a word, eventually chasing the children and servants back into the house to get ready for the fandango. "No one goes to the rodéo who is not clean and dressed properly," she said. "The governor of Alta California, families from neighboring ranchos and many comandantes will be here tonight. You must make the Rancho Castro proud. Now go on and get ready," she said. She turned and looked back at Pedro, but he had disappeared into the little house with his bride. She shook her head slightly as she passed through the large double door.

Only Diego noticed as he bent down to pick up the mantón. Wonderful news for Pedro but trouble was coming, he could feel it.

~

Sholeta crept past the blacksmith shop, peeking around the workbenches to spy if any of her favorite horses were still in the family herd. Probably not. Fourteen years was a long time for a working horse. As she tiptoed in her deer-hide shoes searching for a hiding place where she'd have a view of the festivities, she was struck by the size and wealth of the hacienda. Clearly Diego and Quina had done well. Maybe Diego had been promoted again and received more silver. They must be selling rancho products. She noticed richly upholstered furniture in the living room and colorful tiles decorating the steps. She hid in an alcove that gave her a view through the open doors to the center of the compound.

Musicians played around the courtyard's fountain. Food and drink covered long tables around the plaza disguising the hitching posts. The ground had been swept clean of all debris and horse manure and the horses were stabled away from the party. The entire front common was alive with children scampering, couples dancing, cowboys joking around fires circling the scene. It was a grand party with more people than Sholeta had ever seen in her life.

What was she was doing here? Was this a mistake? She peered through the twilight for the little ones now grown. She spied tall Beatriz with her hair looped up in a Spanish comb, a spray of magenta bougainvillea artfully entwined in it, and almost cried out. Oh, she was so lovely and elegant. She carried herself with poise as she danced with one handsome sailor and soldier after another.

Sholeta swallowed, patted down her hair, pulled the frayed shawl she had kept from her days at the rancho around her shoulders. She peeked out the doorway again straining to catch a glimpse of Pedro and his new wife. Her heart pumped as she spied Diego, gray salting his dark hair, lines creasing his forehead, escorting a young woman past the musicians to the central dance spot. She was a tiny, beautiful girl in a white dress with flowing hair that glowed and a face so perfect she looked like a white rose. Ahh, that must be the bride. So fragile looking. Would she survive here?

Then suddenly, there he was right in front of her. Striding into the hallway with a sense of purpose, clearly on his way to get something.

"Pedro," she said softly, slipping out from the shadow into the candlelight of the entry hallway. He stopped abruptly, surprised. She continued quickly, before she lost all confidence and fled back to the hills. "Pedro. It's me, Sholeta. Do you remember me? I cared for you and Beatriz and the others when you were little. I was there in the small house before your father built this one. Do you remember?"

Pedro, clearly annoyed at the interruption, looked cautiously at this native woman, hiding in the dark in his father's house. "What are you doing here? You can ask the cook in the kitchen if you need something to eat. There's plenty today."

Sholeta hadn't expected this. "I'm not a beggar. I came to congratulate you on your marriage. Don't you remember me? I raised you from a baby with Beatriz. You two were my little shadows, following me around everywhere, helping me in the garden, with the horses."

"Look, I'm sorry," Pedro said. "I've got a whole party out there to attend to. I do remember you always cooked us really good food. But why are you here? I just need to get something and go back out there. To my new wife. To my guests."

"I came to congratulate you. I have a gift for you."

Hoping to spark a memory of how important she'd been to them, she quickly opened her shawl and pulled an object from a rabbit pelt bag cinched at her waist. She turned it over and it sparkled and glinted beneath the candles mounted on the walls. Pinks, aqua, turquoise and silver flickered from a large abalone shell, perfectly oval with no scratches, not one chip in the alabaster coating.

"I want you to have this. The most perfect one I've ever found. Perhaps your pretty, new wife can store her rings or combs in it." Her voice was soft, tender. She needed him to feel the depth of her love, of her pride in him growing into a man. Not that she was just an annoyance disrupting his big celebration. "I've never forgotten you. You were a good boy. I can see you've grown to be a strong man. Be a good husband to your wife. Be a good father to your children. Take care of yourself, dear Pedro."

She slid out the side entrance, darted to the back of the main house, past the horses and blacksmith tools, and disappeared into the hillside of swaying grass and live oak trees illuminated only by the shine of the full moon. Sholeta stumbled up the hill, crossed a creek, skirted the place with the grove of oaks and then huddled under the pines. She felt like a pile of broken glass, as if she'd been a mirror someone had thrown to the ground in anger. Shards and points digging into her skin, and deeper. Her family dead of disease, her brother executed and his corpse put on display. Babies that poured out of her in rivulets of blood. Babies buried under the pines above the bay. And now she saw her grown son barely remembered the years they had together. How could she keep on?

She ambled down the hill toward the bigger river and eventually the clump of trees surrounding the clearing she now called home. She was so lost in her despair that she didn't see the smoke at first, until she reached her tule hut. And there he was. Asa, now fourteen, stoking the fire for her sister-in-law, Ores' widow. She could see her boy was beginning to grow into a young man. Here was her purpose. She needed to prepare him for the future.

"Ma, you're back," he said and greeted her with arms outspread. She hugged him, then pulled him to sit with her in the grass, where he noticed her tears.

"Ma, what's wrong. Are you okay?" He hugged her fiercely, then said, "I got to go out with my cousins early this morning. They let me take the big bow. Then we followed some elk mamas and babies. We practiced getting really close. They're gonna take me hunting with them next time. Can I go?"

"Listen, Asa. Yes, you can go hunting. Stay with me here for a moment. I've some stories to tell you about your ancestors. It's time I tell you the truth about my past."

And she told him everything. Every story. Every painful detail. Every loss. Except for the truth about his father. And his brother.

❧

Late the next morning with a sleepy hacienda just stirring to life, Pedro emerged from his newlywed bed, heart full with love for his beautiful, sweet wife, mind racing with plans for cultivating his land concession. The fandango had been a success with everyone proclaiming it the best party ever along the El Camino. He sheepishly recalled that in his drunken excitement he'd promised the crowd many more. Well, eventually. First he had to work the land enough to build himself a hacienda even grander than his father's.

"Morning, Mamá," he said as he entered the dining room. It was always awkward between them but Pedro was polite enough to never let on at his discomfort in her presence. He kissed her cheek and thanked her for hosting such a lavish party. They laughed a little at some of the party antics. Quina said nothing about the land concession announcement and Pedro thought better of bringing it up. He could sense that she was not enthusiastic over the news of his land grant. But shouldn't she be happy for him? Then he remembered the strangest part of the day.

"Mamá, do you remember a native maid called Sholeta?"

His mother seemed to stiffen. "That's an odd question. Why?" she asked.

"Oh, it was just so strange. This woman startled me in the hallway last night," he said, pointing to the spot where she'd surprised him. "She said she was one of our maids when we were little. She looked pretty native, like maybe she lives in one of the villages in the hills."

Quina interrupted. "What did she want? Was she trying to steal?"

"Well I thought that too at first," he said. "But she said she wanted to congratulate me. That I was a good man and to be a good husband and she gave me a shell. An abalone shell. It is a beautiful one. And then she ran off. It was so strange."

"Hmmmm, yes, certainly is. I'd take no notice of it. We've had so many maids over the years. Who knows which one it was. And they all loved you children, you know. Don't worry about their strange ramblings. If they aren't Christianized and coming right from the mission, well then they're just lost souls. I'll look around to make sure nothing is missing."

Pedro nodded to his mother and left to cross the plaza toward the little house where his beautiful, new wife should finally be stirring. Why had their native maid from his childhood brought him a wedding gift? She'd left them so long ago. It was indeed an exquisite shell he'd noticed when he gave it to Candelaria after the party last night. Such a simple gift, not like the pistols or the finely carved armoire or trunks of delicate linens or silver candelabras that they'd received from neighboring ranch owners and military officers. He remembered the emotion in the native woman's voice. He'd barely been able to see her in the dark of the hallway, yet he had a vague feeling that perhaps this gift was given with the most love of all. He opened the door to his adobe, enveloped his wife into his arms, pressing his face into that glorious hair and breathed in her jasmine scent. All unusual visitors and unacknowledged land concessions forgotten for some time.

CAPTURED AGAIN

It was so much like the first time. Soldiers raided the village with no warning, no one expecting it, nobody prepared. Yet, it was different in that they should have known. The village had spawned a rebel band making forays at night to the area's missions. Their young warriors stole horses, robbed the food storage rooms, kidnapped children from the nunnery. They broke into the soldiers' barracks and stole pistols and rifles, swords and bullet pellets, leather shields and lances.

Sholeta was asleep in her hut when they arrived. At first, the thundering hooves shook her awake. She thought maybe it was Asa and the warriors returning from their campaign. But she knew that was unlikely. They were far into the big valley this time, recruiting other tribelets to the cause, and would be gone for perhaps a whole moon cycle. No, it was the soldados de cuera looking for her son and the warriors.

They yelled and stamped the horses between the huts. They shot in the air and lit a storage shed on fire. This time she could understand their words. She knew their smells and dress. It was not a mystery at all. She was a captive once again, but this time she knew what to expect.

"Leave us be," she yelled in Spanish. "They're no young men here? Can't you see? We're a peaceful tribelet. *Una rancheria de paz*. We've got no weapons, no warriors here. We just want to live in peace." She hoped her Spanish would convince them of her sincerity and they'd leave the women and elders alone.

"Ah maybe that's so. But where are your young men?" demanded a soldier who appeared to be the leader. "Gone to raid the missions, right? Maybe if we have you as hostages, they'll come looking for you. Now shut up. Let's get going."

Sholeta couldn't help but think of Diego. Is this what he had done all those years? She knew it was. She figured he must have retired by now. It still tormented her at times that she'd betrayed her people for so long and lived with him, like a wife. Had all those babies with him. She hoped Asa was safe wherever he was. She said a little prayer to the Coyote spirit. Keep him tricky and safe. Maybe I betrayed my people but you kept watch over me all those years. Now watch over Asa. After Ores' fate it was frightening to think about what Asa did on his raids with the other rebel natives. But she was proud of the leader he'd become.

Sholeta walked with the others for leagues. They moved into unknown terrain and she realized they were headed north, far from the ocean, far from the hills and valleys she knew well. When they arrived at the church and barracks it looked familiar despite the thirty-seven years since she'd been a captive at the mission by the sea. The adobe structures were more substantial, the church larger and the central courtyard surrounded by more storage rooms. The priests' dormitories, blacksmith shops and stables were larger than she'd ever seen. Several rancherias of tule huts surrounded the grounds. This mission compound looked formidable and that in itself was discouraging. It was a busy place filled with priests, soldiers, native converts, animals. Maybe more native tribes were working in the missions than she had realized. How many of these places had the Spaniards established in their land?

A single widow and still a gentile, never having converted to their religion, the priests would not allow her to stay in the rancheria outside the mission grounds. The lead soldier told her she would be forced into the nunnery with the other girls and unbaptized, unmarried women. He opened the heavy door and pushed her into the dark. A dank, fetid smell hit her nostrils. Every single one of the thin women was covered with red welts. Measles. They lay around moaning in the straw, crying into each other or staring desperately at the large door as she entered the room. It looked like a stable for cows and horses, not an infirmary. One or two tended to the others, bringing water or a cloth for the forehead but mostly this monjerio looked like a place to go to die. Not a jail or a dormitory. Not a clinic. This was a house of death.

Sholeta beat on the door as it was latched, yelling in Spanish to the guards. "They all have measles. Don't leave me here. I'm not sick. Let me out. I can cook. I can translate. Don't leave me here. I'll catch it."

❧

Asa led the warriors through the courtyard, past the cemetery, down the open-air hallway toward the main doors of the mission church. If they could get to the altar, find a priest to hold hostage, gather artworks or one of those damn crosses, then they'd have the missionaries' attention, he figured. He'd assigned one unit to break into the priests' cells and another squadron to shoot any guards in the leg and steal their pistols. Now they had additional firepower. Asa broke the mission door's rusting latch and his rebels swarmed the altar grabbing candlesticks and chalices, a bible and a large cross. As they ransacked the church, Asa's second in command brought in sleepy priests, arrows and guns pointing at their chests.

Asa spoke to his hostages in unaccented Spanish. "You raided our village. You have my mother and many of our elders here. Take me to the prisoners, to all the huts. We're not leaving until they're free to return with us. These women, children and elders live in peace many leagues from here and are no threat to this mission." He pushed a pistol deep into the cloak and chest of the lead priest. "Take me now."

The fathers complied, leading them to the dormitories and the huts at the edge of the plaza. A few villagers exclaimed at seeing their rescuers and quickly joined the warriors. Sholeta was nowhere to be found. "Where do you keep the unbaptized women? I'm looking for my mother," he said. The head priest escorted them to the nunnery,

"The women here are sick with measles. We're trying to stop the spread but some are still suffering." Asa opened the door and looked in but saw no one he recognized.

"I know she was here. Where else?" he demanded. One priest whispered to another.

"We lost several yesterday," the padre said. "We still haven't buried them. They're in the mortuary. You can look there. All the other victims have been buried in the cemetery."

Asa followed the priest to the back of the building where he opened a small dark room. It smelled of lye and disease. He held a candle and peered through the darkness at the bodies lined up on the floor. He gasped and cried out. "Oh Atsia, what have they done to you?"

He noted the spots, the swollen hands and feet. He saw the gentle look on her face and felt that she finally was with their ancestors. With her mother and father, her brothers and sisters, all the tribespeople she had told him about. With her lost babies, his brothers. He called out to his colleagues to come collect Sholeta's body. "Wrap her up. We must take her home and bury her. She cannot rot here with the missionaries or be forgotten in their mass graves."

The Ohlone fighters gingerly wrapped her body, picked her up and carried her outside. They gathered the villagers and set off marching south toward home. Before he left, Asa found the father in charge, grabbed the priest's robe and pushed him up against the wall.

"Your soldiers will be fine. They'll just be numb for a few days. Do not send them looking for us or I'll come back in full force with other tribal soldiers. We're forming militia but we'll stay away from Santa Clara if you leave our villages alone. I wanted to get the innocents back. My mother's death is on your hands, Padre. She was a good person, fluent in Spanish after living with the Español for twenty years. She could have been useful to you, but no, you put her in with the sick. You should be ashamed. If you kidnap other innocent villagers, no mercy next time."

Back home, Asa and the young fighters built a funeral pyre in a tradition reserved for the most revered leaders. As he began the ceremony, he told the villagers, who he assumed were now more loyal than ever after the rescue, "Yes, she was just my mother. She was not a chief or a shaman. But she survived the invaders. For many years, she spied on them for my uncle, the great warrior, Ores. She raised me to be a fighter, like Ores, to defeat the colonizers who poison our land with too many cattle and sheep. Who imprison our people. Who rob us of our beliefs. Who brought us deadly diseases. Who turn our people into workers for their ranches. Who have stolen our home and culture."

Asa looked into the flames and promised his mother, "I'll never stop fighting, Atsia. I'll be stronger and smarter. I'll find others to join us. We won't give up. I'll spend my life honoring your memory, your sacrifices and your love."

The villagers stirred at his words, then mumbled to each other, praising Sholeta. They had heard Ores' stories long ago but had only guessed at Sholeta's pain, as she rarely spoke. Many had questioned her strangeness when she joined them after her more than twenty years living with the enemy. Yet Asa was a great leader, a fearless commander. He was determined to protect them and not give up the fight. Sholeta was a good mother. She had raised that boy all by herself and look how strong, how fierce he was. She had raised a true Ohlone boy they said. She deserved the Ohlone death pyre. She was one of us.

Flames crackled high and soot coated the thatched huts. It rose to meet the gray that had billowed in during the ceremony. Fog and smoke blended, then rolled across the cliffs above the village and over into the next valley. The smoky vapor spiraled down the hill, rustling oak leaves, moistening redwood branches, layering mist over a creek, and finally nestled in among the fluttering yellows and greens of the cottonwoods.

FAMILY TRUST

SANTA CRUZ MOUNTAINS AND SACRAMENTO, CALIFORNIA
2019

Dad *had been relentless. While* Nicole and her great grandmother were hiding out at the winery inn, he'd called and called. She refused to answer, even though the last time she'd ignored his calls it had been about her mother's sudden illness. But she needed some time for Great Gram to get healthier and for her to do the medical evaluations. Then the senior center called. Missy had also tried to reach her, leaving unkind messages. She ignored them all. Then the police called. This time she answered, not recognizing the number.

"Ms. Sinclair?"

"Yes, this is she. Who's this?"

"This is Officer Suarez from the Oakland Police Department. Do you have a Mrs. Irene Sinclair with you? She's a missing person. Her family is real worried about her. They suspect you have her. Do you?" he asked.

"The police. What the—? Yes, she's with me. I am her family. My dad took her and put her into a nursing home against her will."

"Ma'am, you're the one going to be charged with kidnapping if we don't see her back in Oakland in good health in the next twelve hours. Get her to the senior living facility and we'll meet you there.

Oakland PD needs to verify that she's okay. A Mr...uh, let's see, a Mr. Sinclair—you're all a bunch of Sinclairs then, is it? Domestic dispute, I guess? Look, just get her back to the facility. We'll do a welfare check there. Mr. Sinclair and another Ms. Sinclair are going to press charges so I think you better get a move on. Call Oakland PD when you arrive and we'll get patrol over to check on her. Not a bright move, Ms. Sinclair." And he hung up.

The threat of criminal charges got her attention. She didn't think she'd done anything wrong but clearly others didn't agree. Nicole acquiesced and drove Great Gram back to the senior center, never saying anything about the police being involved. She'd invent something when they showed up at the old people's home. In her mind, her first mission had already been accomplished.

The week-long stay at the inn hideaway had been productive and helped Great Gram recover her feistiness and spirit. Two independent doctors had made it to the inn to administer cognitive tests. Great Gram had appeared calm and confident throughout. She had dressed properly each morning and seemed cheerful again. Although they both knew she wouldn't be able to move back in to her home immediately, at least her lawyer seemed to be working on a strategy. Most every afternoon that week Great Gram sat on the inn's patio and had long phone conversations with her lawyer.

Relieved to see Great Gram revive, and feeling somewhat hopeful again, Nicole made her own plans to explore deeper onto the family property, continuing her quest for clues to the past. They couldn't get back into the Victorian attic since Dad and Missy had changed the locks on the flat. So the land trust itself became a target of their search. Old files in the house would have to wait for now.

Each evening, while they sat on the patio to watch the sunset's reflection on the eastern hills, Great Gram tried to recall what she knew of the ancestral land. The rumors from her childhood, the adventurous visits to its special places, the stories of its secrets. But her memories were hazy beyond tramping through the creek and up the dry hills with her cousins eighty years before. She remembered more about the adult responsibility she later gained on the trust board establishing regulations and issuing permits to descendants for hikes and camping.

"Whatever happens next, Nicole, I want you to go out there," Great Gram had directed one evening. "See if you can find anything more up the hill above that mine equipment you found. I know it might not connect to protecting my house but maybe there's something in that cabin. I just know there is one somewhere out there. And keep looking into all those records online. It's okay with me if you start contacting cousins. Who knows what others might find. Keep trying no matter where your dad puts me. We can't hide out at this little inn forever, you know." And they'd looked at each other and the view wistfully, nodding in agreement.

The Sacramento lawyer's office was on the top floor of a gleaming new skyscraper two blocks from the gold-domed state capitol. Nicole adjusted the lapel of her rumpled suit from the days of interviews at the college career center when she'd been looking for "a real job," and clicked her heels together before pushing open the heavy glass door lettered with a long list of names. Great Gram's lawyer's name was on the top row. The Dorothy heel-tapping move gave her a little extra confidence. She wished her great grandmother was with her now so they could encourage each other—no silly superstitions would be needed then.

Nicole presented herself to the receptionist and waited in a soft leather chair in the lobby. An assistant fetched her and escorted her to the lawyer's large corner office with floor-to-ceiling windows, from which she could see the capitol building, the river, the Sacramento sprawl toward the eastern suburbs, and the snow-capped mountains peeking up in the distance. A large bird swooped from above and snatched a smaller bird mid-flight in the middle of the view. Startled, she turned to stare at the attorney.

"Peregrine falcons," the lawyer said. "They have a nesting program on top of our building."

"Oh," she said, giving a stiff smile and sitting in the allotted chair in front of the enormous redwood desk. It looked really old, Nicole noted, still rattled by the falcon catching its prey right before her eyes.

"Nicole, I called you here for some good news and bad news. Thanks for making the drive. I know you are concerned about Mrs. Sinclair's situation. It's a bit tricky."

"Look, I just want to get my great grandmother back into her house. It's not anyone else's to sell, is it? How can they do that?"

"Yes and no. It's complicated. That's why I needed to explain it to you in person. Plus, there are documents..." She stopped and rustled through folders on her desk, clicked through computer files and then turned back to Nicole.

"Mrs. Sinclair has changed her will to give you the deed to her San Francisco house. She's skipping generations."

Nicole's mouth dropped open. Guilt at fooling her great grandmother into meeting that interested buyer when she knew she didn't want to sell flooded in and prickled inside her chest. She had to come clean with Great Gram. What was the lawyer saying now?

"What?" she managed to warble.

But the lawyer continued apparently not noticing Nicole's shock. "There are stringent requirements that you must understand. She's requiring that you sign the stipulations. If you don't agree, she'll figure out something else." She looked up at Nicole finally and must have noticed her surprise. "You following me?" the lawyer asked. Nicole nodded. She forced herself to sit up straighter.

"The tenants must stay as long as they want, leaving only on their own accord. There is a lot of legal language around that, as you can imagine. Around who in the family can stay if the current tenant moves, and so on. She wants an application for the highest status historical landmark completed within one year of her passing. She wants you to move into her old apartment now, well, as soon as she can get back into the house. If you accept this plan, you would be required to find a well-paying job so you have the resources to add to the rent to be able to maintain the building in quality condition. As I said, there are a lot of details. Mrs. Sinclair is quite demanding. She knows what she wants, I must say." She finally stopped talking.

"So what's the bad news?" Nicole asked, trying to quiet the flush in her face and chest as she processed the information.

"Your father and your sister, Missy is it, have gotten a lawyer to declare the intended new will invalid. And they've gotten a judge to issue an injunction while this is all worked out so she has to stay in the senior living complex. They claim Mrs. Sinclair's mental capacity is compromised. That you must have influenced her when you were caring for her. They've also now filed jointly for conservatorship for full control of her assets."

"But you heard her. She never wanted to sell. I was in the room when she told you that on the phone. When that tech guy wanted to buy the house but she wouldn't sell unless he agreed to her terms—that the tenants stay. Remember that?"

"Yes, of course, Nicole. I arranged the visit. He was not happy with what occurred," she said, a little snippily. Weren't lawyers supposed to do what their clients wanted? Great Gram didn't want to sell but had agreed to talk to the guy. Clearly the lawyer was miffed the sale hadn't gone through. The tech guy probably got angry with the attorney for misleading him.

"Look, ma'am. I never changed her mind. I tried to get that tech billionaire to buy the house but he didn't like her conditions. I'm the one who found him. Remember? And I didn't even tell her the truth of that because she didn't want to sell. I still feel horrible I betrayed her trust. But it was all Great Gram, not me, who didn't want to sell."

"Look, as your great grandmother's lawyer, I know that, Nicole. But your father and sister? She's quite persistent. She even showed up here. That's why I've got to be very guarded in who we deal with on this case. I've got the tenants trying to call me too. Right now, I'm doing everything possible to get your dad's lawyer to see sense."

"Can he get conservatorship?" Nicole asked.

"He's trying really hard. Or at least Missy is. The judge is looking into it. We've submitted the doctor evaluations from a few weeks ago. But also, Nicole...look, you have to be sensible here."

Nicole felt as if she were being chastised by a teacher.

"It was not a good move for you to take her out of the care facility for almost a week. No one knew where you were. It came very close to kidnapping, do you understand that? That did not help one bit. Now they can use your actions against us. It lends some credibility to their argument that you have undue influence over her. That maybe her giving you the house in the will was your idea. Don't you see?"

Nicole's frustration bubbled up and the calm veneer she'd been trying to present cracked wide open. Her voice was a little too high and sharp for the formal office. "Kidnapping? Me? My dad is the one who moved her against her will to that horrible old people's home. That seems like kidnapping to me. You can't do that, right? And they can't sell the house legally, right? It isn't theirs. Missy's gone in there flashing her realtor cards, telling the tenants they have to move. She's given them some deadline. That's why they're calling you. They'll start leaving and we need the rent. It's crucial to pay all the expenses."

Her voice trailed off and she scowled at the floor. "Plus, the house to me? That's a real shock. I had no idea. Why would she do that?"

"Nicole. Here. Read through this file. Think over what Mrs. Sinclair is proposing, what she has actually put in her will. You must decide if you agree. Stay away from her and let me work on getting her declared competent and get her back into her home. Don't talk to your dad or your sister. Please, for now. Understand?"

She stood up, signaling the meeting was over. Nicole grabbed her purse and stood too, clumsy in the uncomfortable suit, her skirt sticking to the back of her legs.

"She's not my sister," she said as she took the file. "She's my dad's daughter from his first marriage but I don't know her at all. She's bad news. I think she just wants the money. Can't you tell the judge that? I never even met her until recently. She just showed up asking my dad for money after my mom died. She moved in to my childhood home, my room."

The lawyer nodded, said nothing, and gestured for her to leave. As Nicole walked past the leather sofa seating area with cut glass decanters sparkling on a bar cart, she glanced over her shoulder at the view, looking for the falcon to dive again.

She drove through the Sacramento maze of freeways to Interstate 80 and headed toward Berkeley with the sun blazing into her eyes.

She snapped the visor down and adjusted her sunglasses snug on her nose. She was dying to call Great Gram but thought she'd better heed the attorney's admonition. Giving her the house? Wow. It was a shock. A huge responsibility. Could she handle it? She'd have to get an engineering job to pay for it. Great Gram certainly did want to control as much of the future as possible.

As she drove across the long, flat Yolo Causeway, remembering their little treasure of peace at the inn hideaway, Nicole decided to call the senior care center. She invented a name, saying she was from the pharmacy with a question about a medicine order. The receptionist put her through to Great Gram's apartment. It rang and rang. She finally hung up, then tried again.

"Hello," a weak voice cracked.

"Great Gram, it's Nicole. How are you? I miss you. They told me I can't come visit you for a bit. But everything's going to get worked out. Don't worry. Are you okay?" She stopped, realizing she was speaking too fast. She heard rough breathing on the line.

"Oh, Nicole. So nice to hear your voice," she said. The usual force of her personality sounded faded, as if she were the threadbare upholstery on an antique chair. "I'm okay. I never get out. I don't like it here. Can you get me home? I've got to get there to my tenants. They keep calling me. They're starting to move out. Missy told them the house is on the market and they have one month left before eviction. They can't sell my house, can they, Nicole?"

"I'd love to come talk to you in person but I can't," Nicole said. "I went to see your lawyer today. I'm driving back from Sacramento right now. She's intense but I think she's probably good. She told me I can't come visit you for a while. Cuz of the kidnapping thing, you know, when we went to the winery inn for that week. Anyway, listen. Can you hear me okay? I need to tell you something. It's important."

There was a little cough on the line and then, "Yes, dear. I can hear you. I'm just so glad to talk to you. They told me you couldn't call me. What is it?"

"Oh yeah, that. I pretended to be the pharmacy."

Great Gram laughed at that. "Sounds like you've learned a few tricks from spending so much time with me. Clever girl. Okay, what is it?" Nicole squirmed in the driver's seat, checked that she was far from other cars so she could really concentrate.

"I'm really ashamed to tell you this but I was the one who found Zach Turner, that tech guy who wanted the house, and called his real estate agent. The truth is when I first came to you, I had promised Dad I would prep the house for sale, look for a buyer and get you to move out. I didn't know you at all then. I didn't know you weren't interested in selling. But now I do and I can't imagine you anywhere else. I know you don't like that senior facility. I feel terrible now about what I did behind your back. I'm so sorry."

She held her breath to wait for a reply. She figured that Great Gram might sever the relationship immediately. Now she really regretted she'd run along with someone else's plan and not waited to get to know Great Gram before acting. But she had been trying to patch things up with Dad at the time. She'd made such a mess of things.

"I had a feeling that something like that might have happened. I was just waiting for you to be honest with me," Great Gram said. "Thank you for telling me now, when it really does matter."

"But don't change your will for me. The lawyer told me about that. Why would you do that?" she asked.

"Don't be silly, Nicole. I didn't change it for you," she said. "I did it for me. I just knew I didn't trust my son and grandson. How devious of them. I know you're a bit young to inherit such a big house but your dad and grandpa don't need anything. I trust you even more now that you've been honest with me. You'll respect my wishes after I'm gone. I'm sure of it. You're the family member committed to my house, to the family history. That means a lot to old people. I'll control as much as I possibly can from my grave, darn sure about that. Just like that Joe Brennan did."

LOS CALIFORNIOS

All the rancho was on edge. The vaqueros shined the bridles once more, almost wearing the silver thin with over polishing. The teenagers whispered among themselves and avoided the nervous adults. Beatriz had brought her new baby and toddler over from Rancho Arguëllo to be available. Diego paced, his aching knees and hips causing him to wince at every pivot. The servant girls lined up at the redwood double door, peering over at the neighboring adobe, listening hard for any cry, any sign. Quina sat, stoic, in her usual place, at her desk, the seat of her business.

Pedro and Candelaria were finally to become parents. After years of miscarriages, and the fragile Candelaria often indisposed, the entire compound pulsed with nerves and anticipation. Suddenly, the damp dusk, heavy with mist, was pierced with a cry, shouts. Pedro opened his door and ran into the shared courtyard. He yelled to the estate.

"It's a girl. We have a baby. Everyone's fine. Candelaria's just fine. Thanks to God." His voice cracked and he quickly disappeared back into his house. Beatriz handed her baby to one of the native girls and went running. The servants chattered. Pedro's teenaged siblings shouted and hugged. Diego grabbed his wife from her desk and wrapped her into an embrace.

"Quina, we have another grandchild. Pedro's first. She did it. Candelaria did it. Isn't it wonderful? Our family is growing." His enthusiasm caught Quina by surprise. She stood stiffly as he squeezed her, then patted his back once, quickly extricating herself. She turned to business.

"Excellent. Another girl. The Castro Curse continues." Then under her breath she muttered, "Clearly Francisco will be the heir now. Pedro has no sons." She glared at him as she turned to her account books and ledgers, no interest in the coming celebration.

By 1810 when the ships from Boston, the Sandwich Islands, from Peru and Canton began to slip in to the rounded bay, Quina was ready. They were so distant from México City oversight that trade restrictions in the Californias desperate for any items from civilization were routinely ignored. Her father had taught her the power of the black market in a starved economy. She took up the mantle of trader on her section of the coast, while he still controlled the Santa Bárbara bay. Determined to fulfill the role he suggested and do her duty to God to develop the remote territory, she poured the energy she'd expended in having babies into making the ranch into a profitable trading partner.

At first, the ships would only purchase fresh fruit and vegetables, meats and milk, and sell off anything they could spare to the colonists. She talked the Spanish captains forbidden from trading into making an exception for the desolate settlement of

Monterrey. She knew they carried more hidden in their holds from trips across the Pacific. "No one will know. No records needed," she said. "It's such a long way from Manila, you must be desperate for fresh food. They say scurvy is less likely if you give your sailors lemon juice. Did you hear that Captain Cook gave everyone sauerkraut? We have cabbages for you, Captain, if you're interested. What cloth do you have aboard? Any silk or linen? Silverware? Sugar or tobacco?" She was unrelenting.

Slowly, Alta California was transforming from a land of Spanish priests and soldiers focused on native conversion to a productive trading outpost. Quina was pleased to see the proselytizing priests were finally impacting the natives. Nineteen missions now did God's work along the frontier. Father Serra's zeal at launching mission after mission had led to a cheap workforce, now with years of experience farming, managing cows and horses, working in homes and churches. The fertile soil allowed the industrious padres to replicate the system they'd used for hundreds of years in Central México to produce crops and meats to sell back to more populated Nueva España. Here it was so much faster than on the parched Sinaloan desert or the mountains of Querétaro.

The original pobladores had large families and their first-generation children, called Californios, were doing the same. Presidio Monterrey spawned a pueblo. A tiny settlement developed around Mission San Juan Bautista. The civilian settlements in San Jose up the road and outside Mission Santa Clara were growing. Los Angeles to the south was another new pioneer pueblo, no mission in sight.

Even Mission San Francisco de Asís on the craggy point of Yerba Buena at the great bay's entrance had over ten thousand cows, ten thousand sheep and thousands of horses, mules, goats and pigs. A thousand natives lived at the mission, many of whom worked twenty looms to weave wool into cloth. The padres controlled land for a hundred and twenty five miles in every direction, north across the bay's opening, south down the wide peninsula, east to the hilly coastline and northeast up the tributaries. The north end of the peninsula housed the presidio but was too hilly for much else. Horses grazed the green above Potrero and milking sheds bustled at Mission Dolores. Quina never returned to those foggy hills but she heard of the mission's growth and was proud she'd been in that original group of settlers.

Yes, Quina was a devout pobladora, focused on the religious mission. Her well-used chapel, chaste dress and daily prayers proved her piety. She was beholden to the cause of building and expanding the Catholic civilization into a bustling Spanish paradise. She ensured that the rancho's own natives were devout. Her strict rules kept them from straying to the pueblo saloon, getting pregnant outside of church-sanctioned marriage or running off to their old villages to run about naked and eat squirrels. Her children were all baptized Catholics and well schooled in religious doctrine. The religious zealot in Quina had always done her part. Now it was time to focus on other priorities.

She put her plan in place. As he retired from the military, Diego had received another land concession and the increased size of their property allowed them to raise more cattle. She had a large hacienda to furnish and a new focus. Grow the Rancho Castro into a significant supplier of cattle and produce. At the same time, mold it into an important destination on the El Camino Real. A watering hole for weary soldiers and settlers, for this generation of landed elite— the Californios—and for the newest visitors—foreign sea captains and their crews. Quina aspired for the ranch to be as important in trade as the missions were in religious conversion.

The chaos in Central México over an independence movement working to evict the Spanish meant even less oversight than usual in the northern territories, which allowed trade to flourish. The dons and their families were traveling frequently along the camino to marry off their children to each other, to discuss revolution, to strategize on avoiding native attacks, to watch each other's rodeos and bear and bull fights. They had long been customers for each others' ranch products but now there were new customers and trading partners. Foreigners from all over the world began stopping in at Monterrey and Santa Bárbara, San Diego and San Pedro. Boston merchants hungry for cow hides, Russians seeking fur pelts, English whalers, French explorers and scientists all anchored in the harbors.

Quina made sure a shop boy at the general store in Monterrey knew he could get something to eat or a silver coin if he rode out to the rancho and told the doña immediately when a ship anchored in the bay. She'd quickly saddle up her favorite stallion and head into town to locate the ship's captain. Or she'd stroll through the few empty shelved shops in Monterrey, listening for talk of more ships approaching. Quina was determined to be the first local aboard to survey the merchandise. Once she found the captain and enticed him with her cattle, the crew rowed her out through the rolling surf to do some trading on the ship's deck.

By the time the Boston gentlemen from Bryant, Sturgis and Company arrived, followed soon after by their competitors, she was poised for success. They wanted cow hides? Well, she had plenty of cattle to sell. She always had more cows than they could purchase or process. The Boston merchants set up hide-tanning stations along the beach with giant vats for the tallow, stretching the carcasses out along the dunes to dry. The stench of blood filled the air. Grizzlies circled the sailors' encampments at dusk, forcing a night contingent to stand guard with rifles and pistols. The hide operations quickly dominated the beaches and the tanners and the ships' crews became more customers for the pueblo merchants.

Quina was far from that beach mess, but benefited enormously. In exchange for her cattle, she wanted their wares of silk, wine, sugar, lace, cotton, clothing and hats, tobacco and cutlery, tea and horses. She could find shoes and blacksmithing tools if she were lucky. Some ships carried furniture and tablecloths, candlesticks and china. She furnished her large home and family compound lavishly, then sold off the remaining merchandise to neighboring ranchos and the area's growing pueblos.

Despite flouting the trade laws, she considered herself a loyal Spanish citizen, just as she was devoted to the sacred expedition's religious goals. But always a pragmatist, she expected the rebellion to be successful, as her father had predicted ten years earlier. Whether the Spanish loyalist colonists liked it or not, they would become Mexico. And she saw that as an opportunity. Then the new government would release the traditional Spanish stranglehold on trade and foreign interaction. The black-market traders would move into the open and suddenly the coast of Las Californias would become a desirable stopping point for many more Boston ships, whalers, fur traders and transpacific galleons carrying exotics from the Orient. By the time trade was open and legal she planned to be well established with a head start over her fellow Californios.

Quina always took at least one of her older children with her on every visit to town and the ships so they learned how to negotiate, how to determine an item's value, how to assess fair traders, crooked merchants and faulty merchandise. God's goodness finally sprinkled some prosperity on the Altamiranos, she'd occasionally muse.

She knew that her father said silent prayers for Captain De Anza, just as she did. Thankfully they'd followed him north or they'd still be scratching in the packed dirt of Sinaloa. Quina had been waiting her whole life for this. She would always be a pobladora but now the changes in Alta California allowed her to use her practicality and boundless energy to become a businesswoman.

❧

The night after little Juanita's birth, Quina approached Diego again on the subject of ownership. In the kitchen, the cook and her helpers washed pots and china and silver after the celebration. The last of the musicians was strumming a lullaby outside Pedro's house. Quiet strains of the guitar floated across the jasmine-scented air. Quina leaned out the small window and closed the shutters. She had to get Diego to see sense. All the work she'd devoted to building this Rancho Castro empire, all the children she'd raised, was not going to waste. She needed to fulfill her life's purpose by having a truly Spanish heir continue what she had launched.

"Francisco is almost eighteen. Let's get the governor's blessing to request that the concession continue with him. Pedro has his own concession. He doesn't need ours. He'll be fine," Quina said

"Not tonight, Quina," Diego snapped. "Must you continue with this rant, this refrain? It's inappropriate. Today we are celebrating that our Pedro finally has his own child. It's a blessing, after all they've been through. Where is your compassion? Your joy?"

"Oh, don't be ridiculous. Of course, I'm happy for yet another baby out here. For the darling Candelaria who is nothing but sweetness. She's as good as she is beautiful," she conceded, forcing a smile at him but quickly returned to her businesslike tone. "But don't confuse the issues. I'm not talking about them. I'm talking about Francisco's rightful place in this family."

"I've told you before, I'm telling you one final time. Then I never want to speak of this again," he said. "Pedro is our son. He'll inherit the concession to the rancho and this house and he can join it with his own when you and I are gone."

Quina shook her head. Why was he so resistant? Had his feelings for that native woman years ago confused him over their mission here as Spanish founders of the territory? Another betrayal? Still more loyal to that servant than to his own wife? She wouldn't give up. Just as her father had preached when they were children, they must keep a pure Spanish line on into the future. She'd have to confront him with his infidelity to get him to see sense. Maybe guilt would get him to acquiesce.

Diego did not stop talking, holding his hand up whenever she tried to say something. "And because you've hounded me about this, repeatedly, I went to the governor and had his secretary write it up. Look here. The governor signed the succession as I wish it, as is Spanish law."

He put on his spectacles, pulled out a long scroll from the bottom drawer of his desk and unrolled it, moving closer to the candle-filled wall sconce. She read through the document, silently, keeping her hand away from his, her body as far from him as possible. A slight sigh escaped her lips and she clamped them shut.

Diego looked into her face. "Maria Joaquina, you are my wife, you are always welcome in my home. But we have never been aligned, been truly family. I know you've never loved me. But we are good business partners. We have strong children and a prosperous rancho." He paused, then caressed her cheek.

She flinched and pulled away from him, standing up and walking over to the fireplace, as far as she could get from him without leaving the room. Her back to him. She felt deflated, defeated. He'd outmaneuvered her and that in itself was infuriating. She had pushed right up against the status quo most of her life. But in the end, she remained a wife, a daughter, a mother. Always forced to comply in a man's world. He kept talking. Why was he going on so?

"All our biggest dreams, back when I first came to ask your father for your hand, have come to fruition. We've been true pobladores," he said. She looked back at him surprised at the softness in his voice. Maybe he would relent. A hint of a smile flashed across his lips, then suddenly was gone. She turned back to stare into the fire. Her face hot with more than the fire's heat. Anger and frustration seethed through her. She heard him roll the parchment and tie it with the red ribbon.

Then suddenly he slammed the desk with his hand. She flinched in surprise. "Look at me," he almost shouted. She turned to face him, feeling just as powerless as the time her father had ordered her to marry Diego and move away.

"I've been betraying family my whole life. I won't do it any longer," he said. The implication was clear. He was moving her out of that category. The air between them was ice. She knew Diego's eyes so well and they had grown cold and hard, the crinkling crow's feet smoothed out in solemnity.

"Do not test me," he continued. "Pedro is our son, he inherits per Spanish law, per the governor's declaration. And because it is right. Don't seek to convince me otherwise. I'll never relent." His arms were folded tightly across his chest and as he leaned back into his desk, he reached up to his full height, stretching out the sloping, drooping muscles and shoulders, as if he were trying to recall that proud young man commanding his first group of soldiers.

Quina opened her mouth to speak, not really sure if she would make one more attempt, but it probably wouldn't matter. Clearly he had made up his mind. She'd have to figure out another way to promote Francisco, to leave her legacy intact.

"Oh, and one other issue," he continued. "I've seen and heard you undermine Pedro as he gives orders to the vaqueros, to the stable boys, to the men when they're harvesting. I'll not have that. You contradict his orders publicly and I'll move you out of here so fast you won't know what happened. I'll build a tiny room at the back of the chapel and you'll not be welcome in the main house ever again. You could go beg Beatriz or one of the girls to live with them and their husbands but I don't think that's what either of us want. But you'll no longer be welcome in my house. Understood?"

This was a new threat. Throw her out? She responded immediately, without thinking, "I don't contradict Pedro. True, I've made it no secret that I want Francisco to take over as the don but Pedro and I have learned to work together these past years."

"Bullshit, I've seen you. I've overheard you go behind his back to the lead vaquero. I've heard you put him down to ship captains at our table. How dare you? Once more and you're out of this house. Forever. Understand?"

"My darling," she tried a new tact. "How could we have slipped this far? We're a team. You know we're good parents, good ranchers. Everyone loves stopping at the rancho and dining at our table. The don and doña."

"Don't try it. It's too late. We'll still act as such but I can no longer pretend personally. My loyalty is to my children now and the future of the rancho. I've been a fool these years to not support them more. I was so focused on my own ambitions. Now it seems you're the one doing that."

Quina winced and turned to sit down at her desk. Resigned. Distraught at the loss of a future she could envision but would never materialize, she inadvertently let a sigh escape her lips. What about her sacrifices? He wasn't the one who'd been pregnant and nursing, able to do little else besides raise children, for over twenty years. She noticed Diego seemed to stand taller, to have an energy he'd not shown in a long time. She felt as if she were shrinking just a little, as if the defeat had transferred weight, strength, from her to him.

"One consolation," Diego said. "When Francisco marries, I'll build him his own house, a small one, like Pedro had at first. When we get older, Pedro and Candelaria can move in here and Francisco can have Pedro's adobe. That's plenty for the second son. But that's it. I'll hear no more on this topic. I expect us to conduct rancho business as usual. In the morning, come get your clothes and combs from my room. You can move into the guest suite."

Gripping the parchment tightly, he pushed himself off the desk with the other hand and strode out of the room, boots clacking on the terra cotta tiles. Quina sat, staring at the fire, suddenly exhausted at the interchange and the new state of affairs.

REBELS

CENTRAL VALLEY, ALTA CALIFORNIA

1815—1818

When *Diego finally retired, after* more than forty years in the saddle for the Crown, he had been pleased that his life's work had culminated in a distinguished career. He'd never risen above captain but that suited him. He was fortunate to have been favored by Commander Ortega the entire time. He always knew he was not a commander himself, but a loyal lieutenant to a wise leader. There was enormous upheaval in so remote a territory. But Diego and Ortega's commitment to Alta California, and each other, had never wavered. He proudly reflected that his service had resulted in nineteen missions, and there were rumors that another one or two might be established north of Yerba Buena and the large bay.

Diego himself had profited from land concessions. With a growing population, a thriving ranch and illegal trade occurring unimpeded now, he and his large family had become quite wealthy. Only a kernel of nostalgia remained in the grizzled soldado to remind him that he'd sailed from Spain planning to return a rich man. Well, he did become a wealthy man. Just not in Spain. But he did his duty to God and King. He did settle this land. Spain would continue to benefit. Despite independence rumblings far south in Central New

Spain, Diego, like most of the settlers and Californios, remained a loyal Spaniard. He'd made great sacrifices for his country but it had given him much in return.

Now, after all those years on horseback, he woke every day with aching knees and pain scorching through his hips and lower back. He had a practical wife and good children, most of whom, because they were daughters, had moved to the haciendas of their husbands. But there were still young ones growing who he could teach to black-smith and ride, to raise horses, and plant the garden. He had never been sedentary and he'd never spent much time living with his wife so he was a bit anxious about the future. But he was confident he'd figure it out. And indeed, he did.

When a giant tsunami struck Santa Bárbara flooding the pre-sidio, destroying most of the pueblo and mission, he mounted his horse and rode south to help his comrades and his father-in-law rebuild. When an Argentine pirate ship entered Monterrey Bay and the crew invaded the town, flying their flag over the presidio for six days, many of the townspeople fled inland. Diego and Quina wel-comed several families to take refuge at the rancho. He galloped off to join his soldier colleagues in defeating Bouchard and his pirates and sent him out of the bay. He had to return south again when the pirate tried his tactics next in Santa Bárbara. And when the current presidio commander rode out to the rancho to ask for his help retal-iating against the natives of the Central Valley who were attacking the pueblo of San Jose, he considered riding out again.

By this point, Diego, restless at home, was rarely on speaking terms with Quina. He was tired of continually trying to support Pedro's ranch leadership while she undermined him with the vaque-ros and servants. Or when she left Pedro out of important negoti-ations with customers interested in trading for their products. She was so stealthy and manipulative that he had not caught her in any way that would justify the banishment from the house he'd threatened. They remained business partners and the patriarchs of a brood of eleven children and almost forty grandchildren. But any affection that had once existed between them had turned to cold ashes.

Diego agreed to join the camino campaign. El fantasma wasn't as strong as he used to be, he warned the commanding officer. But the leader reassured him he needed experienced military men. He complained to Diego about the viceroy sending convict-soldiers released from Central Mexican prisons north to supplement his troops. The commander told him he was a knowledgeable resource. So Diego kissed his little granddaughter farewell, nodded to Quina and was back in the saddle. Yes, he ached with every bounce of the trail, but it was familiar. This was who he was. Home life had always confounded him. Horses, soldiers and a military campaign, that he knew.

Within the week, he was out east in the foothills on the way to the large valley leading a small group of soldiers in a search for rebellious natives. Arrows had pounded them that morning from a hillside outpost. He had read the situation and assessed where he would have put a safe camp, where he would have led a retreat after such an attack. He was determined to find the perpetrators as they slept.

He told the lookouts he was off to search for the enemy's camp. After riding some distance, he hobbled his horse deep in the woods away from his platoon's cooking fire. Diego had on his trusty deerskin boots that he preserved safely in a wooden box just for such expeditions. Silently, softly, he slid through the trees and undergrowth searching for the attackers.

Only a tiny sliver of a moon lit up the blackness. His vision was accustomed to night stalking but had dimmed in recent years. He pushed through brush quietly, stepping over downed branches from a recent winter storm. He couldn't afford to trip and make a sound. The scrub brush grew thicker and he had to slow to forge a silent path through the briars. Then he saw it. An orange glow of dying embers radiated ahead. The natives had stopped in a clearing below a cluster of sprawling oak trees. He scanned for guards, identified where the natives slept and determined their perimeter. Suddenly, movement. The leader. He was quite sure from his dress and swagger, from the deference the guards on duty paid him.

Diego waited, not breathing, not moving. The men talked quietly, nodded to each other and moved off to a sleeping area with two left standing night watch. The leader walked toward the woods, alone. Diego followed. He'd take out the leader silently, then he'd bring his colleagues back in the deepest night, or in the morning, to round up the others. El fantasma style. A decapitated rebel group often struggled in the surprised shock of losing their leader.

He grabbed the young man, wrapping his elbow in a lock behind his back and touched a hunting knife to his throat.

"Don't move or I'll slice you open right here," he growled into the native's ear. To his surprise, the man responded in unaccented Spanish.

"Where are your comrades? Are you alone out here? My men will destroy you. I'll cry out so loudly they'll surround you. They'll take you captive or pierce you with poisoned arrows." The fluency of his Spanish took him aback. He almost lost his grip on the knife. Who was this rebel leader?

"How is your Spanish so good? What kind of traitor are you?" He pulled at the native's forearm, twisting the elbow hard. The young man squirmed but swallowed a squawk at the pain. "What do you all want? You've got to stop attacking the missions and settlements. The padres are peaceful. We can all co-exist in this land."

The native laughed bitterly. "Co-exist? Is that really what you Español want? You kill us so quickly. At every possible moment. We're just trying to survive. You're the conquerors. We must defend our people."

Diego pressed on. He'd never spoken with a native who mastered his language so completely. Maybe he could reason with him. "We can all live together here. If you prefer village life, fine. But let your people who want to live in the missions do so." Was it his age and weariness of the trail that led him into such a conversation? He should just slit the man's throat right now.

"Ah yes, so you all say," the captive said. "But my mother lived with the Español for twenty-five years. She returned to natural living, the true Ohlone way, but she still was captured and died of your disease at a mission. They would not listen to her Spanish pleas and imprisoned her with the sick. How's that compassionate? Your God doesn't seem to value natives. So many die, even the baptized."

"Twenty-five years? Then returned to a village? Where was this?" Diego asked, a strange knot forming in his gut.

"South of here, near the bahía they call Monterrey. Since you want to talk so much, put the knife down. I will yell for my men if you don't."

Diego ignored him and persisted with his questions, pushing the knife point into the man's throat. Intuition? Shock? He didn't know what but something propelled him to ask more.

"Near Monterrey? What was her name?"

"Tar, her name was Tar. Moon in our language," the native rebel said. "But they called her Sholeta, our word for daughter. The missionaries named her that."

Diego spun the young man around, removing his knife quickly, counting on surprise to keep him quiet. He kept his grip on the man's shoulder and stuffed a pistol into his chest. Who was this man? Could this be happening?

"Listen to me. Don't yell or I'll shoot you. I knew your mother. She worked in my house. Many years ago. She left suddenly when she was very pregnant." He paused and really looked at his opponent. He could see the rounded jaw line of Sholeta's face, a trace of her in the sweep of his nose to his cheeks. "It must have been with you. Our family missed her but we could never find her. I believe she didn't want to be found. She wanted to raise you as a true Ohlone." He almost dropped his grip on the gun. "Clearly she did that," he mumbled, really to himself, admiration rising in him.

Years of battlefield experience served him well in this unexpected situation. Sensing his enemy about to act, he caught himself and pushed the pistol hard into the man's chest. There was only one thing to do. He quickly continued, "Listen. You have a brother. He's a don of a big rancho of many leagues. You see, we can't attack one another, we're all intertwined now, whether we admit it or not. The Español are not leaving Alta California. Your fight is useless. You must live in peace with the Spanish. Keep your own villages but do not attack ours. Otherwise you natives will die. You've no choice."

The man stared at him. "A brother? I have no brother. I'm an only child."

"No, you have a full blood brother. Sholeta had another son before you. He was raised as a Spaniard but you both have the same parents. Your brother grew up in my house. My wife and I raised him as our own...to help Sholeta out." Diego was drowning in emotions. He had another son. And this one appeared to be a fine soldier. "Look, young man," Diego continued but then faltered.

What now? He had searched for Sholeta, never had any news of the birth. He thought that pain had dulled but he found looking into the eyes of Sholeta's son, his son, tore the scab right off that wound. Sholeta had raised him as a true Ohlone as she had threatened but had taught him Spanish also. Maybe she had mixed feelings as well. Or maybe she was just a brilliant rebel herself.

He could not kill his own son. And yet he couldn't reveal the truth either. He did not see any way either of them could preserve their positions if the truth came out. Diego was a soldier to his core. He would never betray his presidio comrades in arms. He would never purposely fail a mission. But he was a father too. And he had loved Sholeta. She had been his true wife. He saw that now. The mother of two sons, of two more buried in the woods. This son was strong and true, he could feel it.

He couldn't breathe for a moment. He loosened his leather vest, strapped on tight to protect him against the enemy's poisoned arrows. He had been on the camino for so long that the hardships of the trail were burned into his skin, his soul, his identity. Deprivation, a sudden rain of arrows from above, isolation, those were to be expected. But here was an unexpected foe beyond even his most dire of predictions. Now into his retirement, Diego faced an opponent like no other.

He was determined to finally be loyal to family, to not betray the ones he loved, to stand up to avarice, to selfishness, to short-term thinking. He'd finally confronted Quina and defied her wishes, something he'd never before done in their long marriage. Pedro was the don, the heir, the lord of the rancho estate. He'd never relented on that. Now, this son, the blood of his loins, from his dear Sholeta who he still missed, was before him. He had no choice. He had to let him go.

Yet, as a soldier, he had to extract some promise of reduced attacks. Some value to this painful, but revealing, confrontation. Something in exchange for the man's life.

"Listen, young man," he started again, trying to squash some of the rebel's confidence and swagger. He pushed the pistol deep into the young man's sternum. "You must be, what, nineteen? Here's the way it's gonna be. I'll let you go. But you don't say a word to your comrades back at camp. Just pack them up, tell them you saw too big a contingent to fight. Whatever, make it up. Head east, quietly, now. Back to the big valley. At first light, I'll lead my men west. But I'll search your camp near here first so you better be gone. Understand?"

His son nodded with surprise and questioning in his eyes. Diego didn't stop for him to speak. "Send the soldiers back to their triblets and villages. Order them not to raid missions anymore. Then you do the same with your people. No more mission attacks. Understand?" The young man stood perfectly still, glaring. "If you don't do that, I'll do two things," Diego said. "One, I'll come hunt you down in your village. I'll tell your elders you are half Español, speak Spanish and are a traitor. I'll tell them you captured me and then let me go. Proof that you are a traitor.

"Second, I'll come to your village, maybe the same visit, maybe not, and capture everyone and put them all in the presidio jail in Monterrey. Then ship them off to the missions. Every one."

The native soldier squirmed against the pistol. He protested with loud grunts and exclamations in his own language. Diego raised the gun to his son's head. "Don't test me. You know I'll do it. El Fantasma has no mercy. He can strike at any time, just like the grizzly. Now go, get the hell out of here. Do what I said and your village will be safe."

The young man nodded, turned in the direction of the camp, walking slowly. El Fantasma's pistol was still pointed at his skull. Then, suddenly, he turned back.

"Why are you doing this, Fantasma? Why let me go? I know you came to kill me tonight."

That caught Diego unawares. How did he know he'd been struggling with what to do? Why he felt so strongly? But he knew the answer in his gut. In his heart. How to say it to this warrior? "What's your name?"

"What? My name? Why do you care? It's Asatsa, Morning. My mother believed in the possibility for a new beginning each morning."

"That's why. Your mother was a good woman. I do it to honor her memory. Now go."

The native soldier turned and quickly disappeared into the forest.

Diego waited for some time before walking quietly back to his military camp where he replaced the deerskin shoes with his regular trail boots. He stared at the glowing coals of their fire for a few minutes. Then he kicked a pile of dirt onto the embers with his well-worn boot, extinguishing any last coals with the black soil. Never leave any signs of life in the camp area. Old habits. He surveyed the site and his sleeping soldiers, the horses twitching as they dozed. He nodded to the drowsy guards and pulled his blanket off the back of his saddle. He threw it on the ground and lay down to sleep a few hours.

"Did you get 'em, Captain? Did you get the leader?" one of the soldiers whispered in the dark.

"I couldn't find their camp," he said. "We'll look again in the morning. Now sleep. We'll go after them at dawn."

ABUELO'S SECRETS

*J*uanita *was only nine when* her grandfather, *Abuelo* Diego, died so her memories of him were distant, clouded. But she had one clear image that she would conjure up when she needed strength and comfort. It happened on a hot fall day under a cloudless sky so blue all she wanted to do was lie in the grass and stare up. But Grandmother's list of chores stretched long and rarely allowed for idling. She was in the kitchen when he'd called her into his lair.

Abuelo had taken her small hand in his gnarled one, rough with calluses, and escorted her into the library where he and Grandmother spent every evening at their desks or reading in the sitting area. Juanita had only been allowed in the library a few times before. It was cool and damp and the smell of soot from the previous night's candles lingered. She squeezed his hand, nervous.

Abuelo sat her on the chair next to his. It was too big for her and her legs struck straight out. It was just the two of them in the large adobe's grandest room. She felt important, although somewhat bewildered, as a quiet time between two people was rare with so many grown children and young grandchildren constantly swirling through the hacienda's many rooms.

Little Juanita liked the waxy tallow smell of the library with its leather-bound books, framed paintings, velvety furniture, her grandparents' matching redwood desks. Next to Grandfather, holding her doll on her lap, she felt small; he was not only tall but quite formidable. But comforting and safe, at the same time. His deep, sonorous voice calmed her.

"Juanita, things are changing here in Las Californias," he'd said that day. She was so young she wasn't sure what he was talking about but his solemnity got her attention. She understood implicitly that as a girl her job was to sit quietly and listen. She watched his thick gray eyebrows bounce up and down when he spoke. He had long hair, almost to his shoulders, that was a mix of black and gray, as if someone had emptied ground pepper from the mill onto his head. She tried not to giggle when she thought of the pepper grinder and his bushy eyebrows. She squirmed on the scratchy upholstery. She pinched her hand, digging two fingernails into the opposite palm to force herself to sit still.

"Juanita, we are no longer in Spain. This is México now. We must learn to accept that. We would've preferred to stay Spanish." His voice trailed off. She looked at her wooden doll with the long dress that matched her own. "But the world changes, my dear. The only thing for sure is change. You will grow up Mexican, but your Spanish blood will serve you well. It is an advantage. Never forget that."

"Sí, Abuelo," she muttered, instinct telling her it was her turn.

"My little angel," he continued. "I have something for you. I want you to keep it safe for me when I'm gone. But you must keep it secret. Find a hiding place for it. Do you have little treasures you hide? Can you find a special place for it?"

"Where are you going? You'll come back soon, right?" she asked.

"Oh, I'm not going just yet. But my time is coming soon. I know it is. Can you keep my special treasure?"

Juanita nodded solemnly. She hugged the doll to her chest, understanding this was an important moment. "Yes, I can, Abuelo," she whispered.

Diego went to his desk and slipped his hand underneath the bottom set of drawers, fiddled with the wood, then pulled out a small leather-bound book. A red silk ribbon dangled from the top. He knelt in front of her chair and held up the book.

"Juanita, this is my mother's bible. From Spain. That's where I was a little boy. Before I came to Alta California. Before the rancho."

"You lived in Spain before the rancho? That's far. Papá shows us maps in his big books. How did you get here, Abuelo?" She opened her eyes wide, curious. Maybe he was going to tell her a story.

"I sailed on a ship to Veracruz and then walked for many months, and rode on a horse sometimes too. But that is a story for another time. Now listen. Here is the pocket bible that I carried with me on that long journey. Can you keep it safe for me? Look, my mother wrote my name in it when I was baptized." He flipped it open to the front page and pointed. "Your father has a big family bible with your name in it when you were baptized."

"Oh, I know where that is. Papá's shown it to me. He reads to us from another one but he has the family bible in his bookshelf."

"Yes, darling. But this one is different. This one is special. It reminds me of my mother and I want you to keep it safe. And secret. It is my gift to you, to protect you in your Alta California journeys. Just as it has protected me."

"But why do I need a book, a bible? You'll always be here to take care of me, right?"

"Yes, Juanita, I will look after you, of course, and your parents and Grandmother will too. But can you keep this specially for me? Just our secret?"

She understood she was dismissed and struggled to hop down from the chair, then took the bible from his large hands. "Yes, of course, I can. I'm a big girl now. I won't tell anyone. Not even Abuela," she said. He patted her head and nodded. Juanita slipped the bible inside the top of her dress.

As she stepped into the hallway and re-joined the hacienda's commotion she felt very important, carrying a secret from Abuelo. He had seemed quieter and less scary than usual and for a moment she wondered why. Was he all right? But she patted the little bible inside her blouse and it comforted her, as if it were a cloak of protection keeping her safe.

On a cold night a few months later, heavy with the fog's penetrating damp, Diego called his eldest son into the library where he and Quina habitually read. Even though the aches and misunderstandings of the couple's long lives kept them from speaking much, kept them distant and aggrieved, they always spent the evening together in the richly furnished study. Perhaps that habit was their final thread of connection. They were dependent on each other in so many ways. Neither of them could deny that. Unless it was important, no one else dared enter their sanctuary in the evenings.

The fire crackled in its earthen hearth and tallow candles twittered and spit in their sconces, casting long shadows on the walls. Pedro knocked, entered, nodded to his parents and sat in the chair reserved for the audience, the guest. "My son, my wife. I'm not long for this world. We all know that. I have one remaining request, no, demand." Quina looked up from her bible. Pedro adjusted his legs in the chair. They glanced at each other, quickly. His words came out like a hiss. He had their attention.

"When I am gone," he said, "you must put aside your trivial differences. If you don't work together, you'll destroy the rancho we've all built. To tear apart the family with petty jealousies, with suspected slights, is a complete betrayal to me and all I've fought for. My body is scarred with native arrows and knives, bullet wounds and bear claw swipes. If you two cannot manage this great estate and instead descend into squabbles and backstabbing, then we are no better than the natives we Spanish came here to civilize. You two must continue running ranch operations, dividing responsibilities. You two are the real ranchers, the business owners, no disputing that. Look, I've always known that was your strength, not mine. I know I've been the don in name only. I've always been a soldier." He paused. "You understand me? This stops now. You manage the rancho together and share its fruits."

The room was silent save for the crickets thrumming beyond the shuttered window openings. A log dropped from the grate and a spatter of coals glowed on the hearth. Pedro jumped up, grabbed the iron tongs and tossed the largest embers into the fire. Quina moved, as if uncomfortable in her chair, but stared right back at Diego. She did not blink. Gray strands now streaked her hair but the braid past her shoulders she'd always sported was thick, and mostly the same rich earth color as when she'd married him thirty-nine years before.

"But Quina, my dear," Diego said. His voice dropped to a whisper and he leaned forward focusing solely on her. "We did achieve all that was expected of the Sacred Expedition and De Anza's campaign. We did settle and grow this untamed frontier. You will remain the doña always."

Diego turned to his son who was still at the fireplace, gesturing for him to sit. "Pedro, you are now the don of Rancho Castro, with Doña Candelaria at your side, of course. But do not ever leave Doña Maria Joaquina out of any decision making, you understand me? She built this place. She raised all you children. She deserves to be involved in the business until her last breath."

Diego slumped in his chair and rested his elbows on the desk. He was fatigued from the effort and emotion of the speech. He'd long decided on this but to say it out loud, to the two of them together, forced everyone to recognize the upcoming transition.

"Now my dear," Diego said, looking at Quina, "let me speak with Pedro alone for a moment. Then send for the others. I must speak with each one of my children."

Quina stood, bent as if to kiss him, as would have been her habit with anyone else, then straightened suddenly. She stood tall, back erect, stiff and formal. "We will do as you wish," she said, then broke her formality, leaned over and gently put her fingers to his forehead, brushed his graying hair back from his temple and around behind his ear. Diego looked up at her. Surprised. They had not touched each other in years. She swirled her long skirt around abruptly and left the room.

He sat in silence and watched her go, staring at the closed door for some moments. He coughed, pushed himself into the chair's back and looked at Pedro. He cleared his throat. This newfound loyalty to family was complicated. The discovery of another son gnawed at him.

"Son, I want you to know something. You have one more brother. He is far from here and you'll probably never meet him. In fact, I hope you never do. It would be dangerous. But you have a full blood brother that we could not raise. I am so sad about that and that you don't know him. I believe he's a strong, principled man, like you. I'm sorry, I can't tell you more. Now go, bring your brothers to me. Your mother will send messages out to the girls at their ranchos."

"But Papá, what are you talking about? A brother? Full blood? Why wouldn't he be here with us? I don't understand." Diego just shook his head and waved his hand to send him out of the room.

After Pedro left, he stared at the fire wondering. Had he done the right thing? He would never betray Quina completely and reveal Pedro's true parentage, but he had felt compelled to tell a measure of truth to his son. Never a fan of confessing to a priest, Diego wondered if his words, the incomplete information, was yet another cowardly act to relieve some pain now toward the end of his life? Had he just transferred his own burden onto Pedro's shoulders?

THE FAMILY TRADE

"*Hurry up. I want to* be the first on board," Juanita heard her grandmother call from the balcony into the courtyard with the trickling fountain. She pulled on her boots under her long skirt and hurried to the sewing room on the ground floor behind the bougainvillea-adorned arches.

"I'm going to the ship in the harbor with Abuela," Juanita said while kissing her pregnant mother's cheek and sticking her head into the cradle to rub noses with her baby sister. Finally, she was no longer an only child. She rushed out before Candelaria could complain or notice her work boots. She had to be ready before Quina came down from the upstairs suite she had reclaimed after Diego died or her grandmother would leave without her. Juanita jogged past the redwood doors into the plaza where a young vaquero had a horse ready for her.

She was pleased Abuela finally was allowing her to tag along. She had to impress upon her how grown up she was, how ready for adventure and inclusion in the business of the estate. Juanita found indoor pursuits dreadful and dull. "You'll ride your own horse with saddlebags," her grandmother said as she strode into the plaza with her usual quick pace and authority. "Pablo here will come with us with the pack mules. We need as much storage space as possible."

Juanita was thrilled to finally be invited to board one of the sailing vessels now regularly stopping in Bahía de Monterrey to trade European or American goods for local produce and cow hides. Fifty years of settlement on the abundant hinterland had changed it significantly. The Mexican territory welcomed an amalgamation of businessmen from Boston and Liverpool, Pacific Island laborers escaping foreign missionaries, English pirates, Scottish whalers and Russian fur trappers. Tallow harvesters from Lima, seal skin gatherers from Canton and French scientists rounded out the medley. Alta California saw an exciting concoction of the era's explorers and their workers. Juanita was desperate to see ship life up close, now that she was eleven and her grandmother thought she was old enough.

Abuela Quina was the opposite of Doña Candelaria. Juanita adored that. Here was a female role model who vaporized the sense of otherness she felt in the company of her mother. From the moment she could walk, Juanita trailed her grandmother like a puppy. She was relentless with questions, demanding to participate in every physical activity a ranch required.

Quina, who essentially had ignored her own offspring until they were teenagers, did instill business and ranching knowledge in them once they were of age. With Juanita she seemed to make an exception and let her come along even when she could get lost in her skirt. Perhaps out of guilt for the way she treated her own children for so many years, Quina spoiled little Juanita by agreeing to most every request. As soon as she old enough to have any understanding of the conversations, her grandmother sat her on the front of her saddle and took her along to meet sea captains, traders and Mexican officials at the Customs House.

Juanita's early exposure to the messy, noisy frontier with strange languages, travelers and settlers in myriad colors and shapes fascinated her. She wanted to soak it all up as if she were a scientist studying the varied human condition. After she met a Liverpool captain in town, she hounded her father during lessons to teach her more about England, their history and empire and their harsh sounding language. She wanted to learn foreign words, hear the stories of sailors' travels, read about distant lands. She asked questions and more questions pushing her father to acquire more books, atlases and research reports.

With no schools and few tutors on the frontier, Pedro acted as the primary instructor for his daughter and nieces and nephews. For Juanita, he initially focused on religion and literature, music and domestic arts—the realm of the female. But eventually she convinced him to teach her everything he would have taught a son. She read politics and philosophy, history and mathematics, sciences and other languages.

She had been to the pueblo of Monterrey and its government offices quite a few times but she had never been on a sailing vessel. Now riding toward the harbor on her own horse loaded with saddlebags for merchandise, she felt very grown up. Abuela was going on about the visit to the ship. She'd better concentrate.

Attention must be paid to everything or you could make mistakes, her grandmother instructed. One must be careful and serious when trading with the professional merchants sailing into the harbor these days. You could give away more than necessary, have a sailor try to take advantage of you. You could trip on the slippery gunnels or on the rigging ropes. You had to be careful not to leave one precious item behind. Plus, what if you got seasick. Little children just cluttered up the delicate trading balance and were a distraction. Don't mess this up, Quina implied. Juanita was desperate to remember all the rules and make a good impression so she would continue to be invited on forays beyond the rancho's property lines.

The rowboat that picked them up on the beach had puddles of water in its bottom and only rough slats for seats, covered with splinters. Juanita reluctantly took the hand of a sailor as she climbed in. He was skinny and gnarled with age and sea life. He had a bandana tied over his wispy gray hair. He was missing three front teeth that created black holes in his pink mouth when he spoke. He smelled of sweat and saltwater and mildewed cloth. She resisted the urge to cover her nose and mouth with her handkerchief as she sat on the uncomfortable seat. The sailor mumbled a greeting and instructions but Juanita couldn't understand a word.

Another sailor was at the oars and leaned to pull them back once she and her grandmother were aboard. They bounced through the breakers with foamy splashes at each side as the boat bobbed. Juanita was terrified a wave would toss them like crabs poured out of a bucket into the sea. After all, she didn't know how to swim. The sailor kept rowing. They got soaked from the spray but she was relieved to still be in the boat. Her fear calmed as her eyes drank in the strange oarsman, realizing the sailors were one with the boat and water, as every cowboy she knew was when riding horses.

This sailor was enormous, thick, the size of two Papás welded together, with biceps bulging as he rowed. His fleshy cheeks made the slits for his eyes thinner than one would expect for such a big man. His wooly black hair was woven into a long braid that dropped past his shoulders. Juanita had never seen a man with such long hair nor sporting a braid. His leg muscles pushed into his navy pants, appearing to be stressing the seams. And his skin was as dark as the mahogany table in her living room. Juanita tried hard to look away but was finding it difficult. She had never seen anyone who didn't look like her, other than the native servants.

Her grandmother seemed to notice her gawking. Abuela leaned down and whispered, "He's Kanaka—from the Sandwich Islands. Lots of sailors from there. They grow up on the water. Don't stare."

Juanita forced her gaze out to the ship coming into view, to the blue swell dotted with whitecaps. She clenched the boat's rail with one hand and the seat with the other. Grandmother didn't seem nervous, in fact, she was already starting the bargaining, prodding the old sailor about what merchandise was on board.

As Juanita turned to hear his response, she spied the shoreline behind the craggy sailor perched on the gunnel. Her home, from the view on the bay, from the water, startled her. It was sublime. She could see the slope rise up from the wharf leading to the presidio. Flat-topped cypresses spread out along the hills while tall thin conifers punctured the skyline in clumps at an outcropping, a point, another distant rise. She couldn't wait to take it all in from the much higher ship's deck. She grabbed Quina's arm, interrupting her negotiations.

"Oh, it's so beautiful from here, at sea. Monterrey. Where's the mission? I want to see that too." And then she lowered her voice to just above a whisper. "I'm not afraid anymore. He's a good rower to get us out here through the surf."

Quina smiled. "Good girl. Yes he's a good oarsmen and we'll be safe on the boats. Now let's get some trading done." The rowboat touched the side of the sailing vessel and they climbed up a rope ladder to the deck. Juanita was rewarded with a view of the whole coastline while Quina got to work. She reached over and grabbed the girl to come along. "Now you must be careful as everyone is out to rob you blind, my dear. That's the truth of the matter. We must feel the silk and cotton. How fine is it? We must rub the candlesticks and silver to determine if they are real. We know our cow hides are real, right, my girl? Yes. So we expect quality merchandise in return. Oh, look, they've got sugar and molasses. Must have come from the islands. We're getting low so let's stock up."

Juanita scrambled to keep up with her grandmother, who turned every china plate and pair of leather boots over multiple times before asking the price. And then, once she heard it, immediately set to bargain. Not only was seeing her grandmother in action a wonder but the ship itself was something out of a fairytale.

There were ropes and buckets, clasps and canvas sail fabric surrounding them, lying on the deck, dangling from impossibly tall masts. The physical ship was so complex a set of rigging it was impossible to comprehend that anyone could sail it across the Pacific. And then there were the sailors, who were literally from another world. Her father was a tough tutor and pushed her into sophisticated books at a young age. She had studied maps and globes, read stories of other cultures and times. But to see this variety of people up close was a revelation.

There were skinny men with straight black hair like straw and thin slivers of eyes. There were more dark Kanakas but each one a different configuration of largeness and power. She heard languages she did not understand and words in her own language she did not know. One man had reddish hair the color of carrots. Another one was sprinkled with so many dots on his face and arms that she was sure he had measles. There were several men with a skin so light it looked beige and pasty, like dough for dinner rolls. Several had yellowish straw-colored hair, lighter than her mother's. And most surprising were the young boys her age who scaled the masts, washed decks, and carried goods in burlap sacks for Quina to inspect. The sails and lines, the men working them seemed to meld together in a rhythm, as if the ship itself was a body and everything aboard had roles—to pump the blood, digest the food, send messages to the brain. They worked in sync, despite their differences.

Watching the vibrant life of the merchant ship *Hancock*, out of Boston, unfold before her, while also observing her home from a new angle, Juanita experienced that moment of clarity that the adult world held much more in it than her child brain had ever imagined. Her mind opened as if it were one of the giant sails unfurling in a stiff wind. She could see that human experience was diverse, complex and much more varied than her rather predictable life on the ranch. Not unlike her grandmother, so many years before, standing on that hilltop staring at the De Anza party assembled in Tubac, Juanita felt the desire to be a part of something bigger seep into her bones.

As she stood wide-eyed watching the commotion, hearing her grandmother getting agitated with the ship's captain, she felt a hand on her shoulder. She turned and looked into the sharp green eyes of a blond boy with freckles across the bridge of his nose. He was probably not much older than she was, but his scrawny physique, cracked lips and sunburned lines feathering out from his eyelids revealed the hardship of a seafaring life.

"'Ey, lassie. Come wit' me if ya wanna see the treasure chests we got in the hol'." His wide grin revealed several missing teeth. His Spanish was accented and missing the odd word but she understood his meaning. Juanita had jumped at his rough hand on her arm but found his eyes and grin intriguing. She'd never disobeyed her grandmother explicitly before, let alone in her presence, but Abuela was distracted. Juanita was enthralled with the exotic ship and the boy, with the possibility for adventure. And wouldn't Grandmother be pleased if she discovered even better merchandise to trade?

"The really good stuff's still down belo'. Don't know why the cap'n's savin' it for San Pedro. Ya'll got lotta hides here in Monterrey we hear. Come on, lassie. Folla' me." He grabbed her hand with a scratchy, callused one; a blistered sore oozed liquid into her palm. Juanita's heart pulsed in her ears. Her face prickled with blood. Nervous, but curious, she tried to keep up with him while her eyes adjusted to the dark of the ship's belly. Seawater soaked into her boots as she splashed through the leaky hold, ballast rocks and muddy bricks lining the walls. The stench of earth and manure and putrid saltwater was overpowering and her eyes watered. She heard clomping. There must be horses in another hold. He led her up a tight stairwell that opened into a storeroom stacked with wooden crates and leather-bound trunks.

"Looky here," the boy said as he opened one box, then pried off the top slats of a crate with a crowbar. Juanita stooped over and touched the softest white linen and colored silk she'd ever seen. The ship rocked and sank deep to the port side in the bay's swell. She struggled to keep her balance and fell onto an unopened trunk. She pushed herself back up to look at the treasures. The storeroom door swung back and forth, then banged shut. Juanita peered up from the fabrics, then at the boy. She stepped over crates to push open the door but it wouldn't budge.

"You have the key? It's locked. It won't open." The boy stepped on a trunk then jumped down and over to the door.

"Shouldn't need one, don' think," he said. The boy pushed on the door, banged it, then pulled the iron handle up and down, over and over.

"It's stuck," he said. "Can't get it open."

Juanita's interest in the trunks' contents vanished and she jumped in to push the handle with him, throwing all the weight of their two pre-pubescent bodies against the door and its hardware. To no avail. No longer imagining the glory of uncovering spectacular merchandise for her grandmother, she wondered how they she'd get back to the deck and what fury she'd face from Abuela.

"Hey, we're stuck. In the storeroom. Come let us out," she yelled. The boy joined in and they yelled and yelled. He in English while she called out in Spanish, no longer attempting to communicate with each other. He hefted the crowbar over his head and slammed it into the wall, over and over again.

JUANITA

RANCHO CASTRO, ALTA CALIFORNIA

1826–1832

Ever since she'd been trapped in the merchant ship storage room, she'd been both traumatized and enthralled by the experience. It had been claustrophobic being locked in such a small room with a strange boy, unable to keep herself from tossing back and forth atop the crates as the ship rolled. Once they'd gone hoarse from yelling, the ship's boy had tried to comfort her with tales of near shipwrecks and drowning sailors at Cape Horn. Of great sea storms in which giant waves covered the decks with foam and anyone who didn't hang on to the ropes was swept overboard. He regaled her with his land duties such as skinning butchered cows, drying and hauling heavy hides and boiling vats of fat into tallow for candles.

Despite his attempt to distract her, and her fascination at the danger of his work aboard the vessel, confinement and his stories led to weeks of nightmares. She'd been terrified that locked in the storage room she'd be trapped when the craft set sail across the sea, imprisoned on a ship full of coarse men, far from her beloved family and horses. Far from predictable ranch life, even if it was a little dull now and then.

That day, after several hours of confinement, the First Mate unlocked the door releasing Juanita and the boy, revealing the superior commodities. She was saved from Abuela's wrath by the hidden trove of silk, cotton, lace, dinner silver and hats visible as the kids stumbled out, voiceless and seasick. Quina quickly turned her anger at the missing Juanita onto the ship's captain, letting out a torrent of frustration and obscenities as she scooped up her granddaughter and turned to explore the contents of the hidden crates.

Juanita's punishment for insubordination and lack of common sense was reduced participation in ranch affairs for a time. No trips to the pueblos or neighboring ranchos. No allowing her to lie under the table while Abuela and Papá discussed Rancho Castro's sheep and cattle, a Russian captain demanding furs or how many hectares of grapes to plant. Papá ordered her to focus on studies in the library and not on the stables or the orchards. So Juanita took advantage of the restriction and scoured through atlases and globes, travel literature, the reports of scientific exploration and books in unfamiliar languages. Once sufficiently punished, she was allowed to return to her outdoor pursuits.

The daughter of an exquisite woman, indeed one famous for her looks and grace on a remote prairie where there were few women at all, Juanita was fortunate to be quite the opposite of her mother. She was neither bitter or jealous nor obsessed with molding herself into a younger version of the icon. She blazed another path. To her, beauty was not much use on a frontier of thousands of acres of rolling grass dotted with grazing cows and natives shooting arrows from behind sycamores. Her interests occasionally led her to feel superior to her mother, by sewing her mother's beauty into a benign weakness, as if it were a lace, worn and discarded, now used as one small piece of a much larger quilt.

Juanita was a force, a tornado of opinions, a physical specimen more like a boy incased in a girl's body. Indeed, as a child she'd often wished she were a boy. When she was very little she'd even asked her grandfather if he could change her into one. He'd just patted her on the head, then lifted her up onto the horse's saddle before they rode to herd *las vacas* together. She'd live in the barn with the stable boys and horses if her parents would allow it. Naturally, she didn't even ask, as that was clearly not her role as the daughter of a wealthy land baron.

While her mother was pale with light hair and hazel eyes, Juanita was coffee skinned, dark haired, with deep brown eyes and a fleck of gold flashing in one. She looked like her father and seemed to have inherited not only his looks and strong legs, his fearlessness with horses, but also his capacity for managing a large ranch. She'd asked Papá to look at the account books before she could mount a horse without a cowboy launching her up to the stirrups.

As her sisters grew they took another path and sculpted themselves into their mother's image, sitting in quiet corners knitting and darning, reading the bible or the Spanish classics Papá assigned. They chatted about the weather and the El Camino gossip. They collected ribbons to adorn their ginger colored hair and discussed fabrics the ladies were wearing at last month's fandango. As they grew, Candelaria consulted the sisters on what flowers to put in the bouquet at the estate entry or how the gardener should trim the bougainvillea hugging the courtyard walls. What recipes cook should use for the day's almuerzo, usually attended by at least twenty family members.

While openly bored by her mother and sisters frittering away time on silly pastimes, Juanita did not, in any way, despise the other women of the house. Indeed, she was quite protective of them. She loved her mother dearly as she knew that she was not only beautiful but was, in actuality, goodness personified. A pillar of elegance and kindness that the Mexican frontier dearly needed. Juanita just refused to be the one to tame the prairie with niceties.

She recognized that Candelaria was charitable to a fault, overly generous with the native servants she heard her father complain. Her mother learned enough words of two different native dialects to converse in complete sentences with her staff, asking about family members and giving instructions in their language. She was affectionate to her children and husband and considerate of all members of her husband's large family, never complaining about missing her own parents who'd fled San Diego's hardships for a posting in México City.

Juanita was sympathetic that Candelaria was delicate, and arduous ranching life often forced her to take to her bed with headaches and coughs from the dust in dry times or pneumonia during the rainy months. She knew her mother had suffered miscarriages before her and then in the many years until the two much younger sisters arrived. But she noted that her mother did not use her frail constitution as an excuse nor did she appear resigned to her station. She frequently commented to her daughters on the satisfaction she felt in being a dutiful wife and mother. She was the consummate hostess and delighted in sharing her home with travelers visiting the missions, the presidio or the nearby pueblos. She almost never failed, unless exceptionally ill, to be on her husband's arm in the hacienda's plaza, with a smile and a flower in her hair, to greet weary travelers off the El Camino Real.

Throughout Juanita's childhood, so many visitors stopped at the ranch that she overheard that tales of Doña Candelaria and Don Pedro's graciousness always included stories of the doña's legendary beauty and fine features in so rough a locale. She'd even heard it whispered that more than one military man fell in love with the gentle, hazel eyes, soft voice and flowing hair accompanying her mother's impeccable taste and generosity. A few even had the temerity to approach the señora while her husband was entertaining colleagues with glasses of fine port from Portugal and acrid cigars from the islands. Don Pedro took delight in showing his guests into the library each evening, now richly furnished with thick tapestry curtains, fine wood furniture and terra cotta-tiled floor from the kilns of central México. A few brave souls snuck away with an excuse about a horse or stomach ailment in order to corner the comely hostess in the pantry or a dark hallway.

The ever-polite Candelaria, while she might imitate her namesake and flicker and flirt with the admirer just a little, never strayed. She never let even the handsomest comandante or foreign sea captain get more than a twinkle from her bewitching eyes. She was so skilled at offering a word of rejection sweetly that the gentleman barely realized he'd been sent packing empty handed. Naturally, this ability to let a man down without humiliation just added to the stories of her grace. Once seated at the adult table, Juanita heard the gossip directly. How fortunate Don Pedro was to have such a wife, they said. He was a good man, a fine host and prosperous rancher, they said. A true Californio don. Such quality hospitality, just like on the roads of Spain or in Central México. A beautiful and hospitable doña. Three charming daughters, and whoever was the speaker would wink at Juanita at that. The stories swelled and spread and Rancho Castro's lore bloomed like the lavender lupine covering its hillsides every spring.

Juanita respected all of that, she just was determined to be a different type of ranching woman. After observing family dynamics and business up close for years, Juanita remained fascinated by foreign stories and maps but decided her future was on the estate. She told no one but was determined to take over the operation from her father someday. After all her grandmother was a rancher and businesswoman. Why couldn't she be the doña in charge? She also noticed that Quina and Pedro ran the ranch together but in a strange, begrudging way, avoiding each other as much as possible. Her parents served as hosts for rodeos and weddings, fandangos and bear and bull fights. While Quina did most of the trading with the foreign merchants. While they might not like each other, they did run a prosperous business. She sensed a truce at play but the tension hovered over the house and the owners' interactions. She never understood why.

Even by seventeen, Juanita had no interest in marrying and leaving her family anytime soon. She was quite content working the ranch and trailing her grandmother, serving as an associate, almost an assistant rancher. The only men she was interested in were the ones who rode into the plaza to buy their cattle and vegetables or to sell them supplies and luxuries from the U.S., Europe and Asia.

As she matured, somehow Juanita did not acquire the sinewy muscles her grandmother sported from being a cowgirl her whole life. Juanita's puberty left her with curves and a softness that women admired and men found desirable. Perhaps she inherited the femininity from her mother, as her coloring and strength were all her father's doing. Lustrous hair gleaming, cheeks glowing and red lips plumped from daily exertion of the ranch hand work she preferred, Juanita caught the eye of every young soldier, rancher or sailor who stopped off for refreshment and news at the Rancho Castro.

So far she'd successfully avoided being married off to the latest bachelor at nearby ranches. Her parents and grandmother's ambitions for a prosperous marriage were often the only topic they agreed on so the attack on dual fronts required Juanita to resist strongly. The pressure was constant as the adults were anxious to align their interests with a Vallejo or Alvarado, Aceves or Ortega.

She tried to be unavailable by riding most days but also helped her father with his paperwork, books and reading the news from the U.S., Texas, México City and England whenever newspapers arrived from afar. She had to be creative with excuses to her mother especially.

"Father needs me with his account books and legal papers."

"We're short vaqueros after that one was injured during horse training."

"I like it here with you all. My family. I'm not ready to marry and leave. I have plenty of time to be a wife and have babies."

And to her grandmother she said, "Abuela, please. I want to be independent like you. Without a husband telling me what to do." Quina scolded Juanita for her resistance, reminding her she'd been married for thirty-nine years and raised eleven children. She had managed a husband all that time just fine.

In reality, Juanita was terrified she would lose the life she and her grandmother shared, a life of little male oversight and demands. She dreaded becoming like her mother, who organized her days around her husband's needs and activities. Prepare the cook for the governor's visit. Have the maids put clean linens in the guest rooms for the commandant's battalion as they stopped for the night on their ride north to Yerba Buena's presidio. Sew dresses for the three girls to attend a wedding at the Peralta home. Dine with the padres who visited with concerns about the loss of their missions and lands under the Mexican regime.

To Juanita, spending her days on sewing and linens was hell itself. Most men would never understand her interest in riding, in training horses, keeping tabs on health of the cattle or sales of hides and sacks of oranges. She wanted to press the olive oil, not just put it on the table. Juanita stalled and squirmed as she grew past marriage age. She'd be Abuela's assistant and her father's bookkeeper as long as she could convince them to leave her unmarried.

By the time Malachy Brennan strode down the rancho's road to the great house, knocked on the redwood door and offered his services as a barrel maker and furniture builder, Juanita was nineteen, almost an old maid to the Californio elite.

THE FOREIGNER

*M*alachy Brennan, tall with lean muscles and a jaunty air, had fled Ireland's dark hunger as a teenager. Merchant ships and whalers were desperate for young sailors so he had no problem signing on, fleeing the destitute island. He'd rounded Cape Horn chasing rigging and sails. He'd seen the Sandwich Islands and Manila. He'd carried furs for Russian trappers in the cold waters off North America. At San Pedro, he'd joined a Boston merchant ship collecting hides and tallow in exchange for luxuries the Mexican frontier lacked. In Monterrey, he'd negotiated to be let out of his contract to go ashore and try his hand at land-based work—he was a woodworker after all.

Or at least that's how he told it. No one quite knew the truth. He was a swashbuckler with a vague origin story, a mysterious path to wherever he was at that moment. But did anyone really care? Pacific and Atlantic ships and shores were populated with a diverse cast of adventurers in the age of discovery, often abandoning their own cold pasts. Most sailors and whalers were rough, uneducated men and boys who succumbed to a life at sea due to poor circumstances at home. The work was hard, the days long, the nights lonely. So what did every sailor, no matter where they were from, enjoy? Someone who could tell a good story.

Malachy was that born storyteller. He could invent a tale immediately. He loved the funny details, the heartbreakers, the terrifying monsters and heroic conquerors. With a hearty laugh, twinkling blue eyes, gold red hair and a strong cut jaw, he looked the part before he even opened his mouth. Once he got started, it was impossible to look away, to complete a task, to feign boredom. Malachy's tales roped in the listener as he cleverly inserted his audience's present circumstance to enhance the drama.

Had Malachy really been to Manila and Acapulco on the silver run? Had he really rode crow's nest on an English pirate ship at fourteen? Had he witnessed Charleston slave auctions selling newly arrived Africans? Had he really boiled whale blubber on the shore of Nantucket, then used that knowledge to take a narwhal tusk off its owner in the chill of northwest waters? Where was that tusk now, after all? But in the end, did it matter? Malachy brought the heart and laughter of Ireland to every new place he landed with energy and a restlessness. As if he had to keep moving to keep the dingy poverty of his homeland back where it belonged. Far from him.

Malachy arrived at Rancho Castro with nothing but worn boots, an Irish wool sweater, a rucksack, and an ability to speak basic Castellano, acquired on his many travels. He'd heard of the prosperity and hospitality of Rancho Castro, he said. Couldn't they use a woodworker?

Quina, who was the first to meet him as the servants ushered him in to the courtyard, was skeptical. She knew the customs officials and many of the captains that landed on the busy hide and tallow route. Most did not release sailors who had signed on for a year or two. But Malachy produced an official looking letter with a bright red wax stamp. She didn't know any English, but there had been an attempt at a translation at the bottom of the letter and she got the idea.

Quina interviewed him in the entry hallway and concluded that he did indeed know woodwork and they could use his help. They were building more adobes and needed more furniture as her sons were now grown. Not one to be taken in by male charms, she did not notice that he complimented the rancho's furniture and redwood doors with perhaps a bit more enthusiasm than was called for. She had confidence in her hiring ability and so made the decision without consulting Pedro, an oversight she would come to regret.

She explained there was an apprentice period and if after fifteen days he was determined to be slovenly or boorish, uncooperative or a thief, he would be tossed out with no pay and no recommendation letter. They agreed on initial compensation and she led him to a tiny cottage behind the workers' barracks.

"Works for me, ma'am. Can't imagine any of those things will be a problem," he said as he hustled to keep up with her. Someone with as much energy as he had.

"Good day, Mr. Brennan. You can join the vaqueros for supper at their camp tonight as it's late. We'll introduce you to my son, Don Pedro, and our family tomorrow. Why don't you come for our traditional dinner at noon in the big house. Our ranch boy, Pablo, will show you around now. Until tomorrow."

"Thank you so much Doña Quina. I look forward to working in your wood-shop and helping you furnish your new buildings."

As she was closing her shutters that night, Quina leaned out her window and listened. She thought she heard more laughter than usual coming from the cowboys' outdoor kitchen. Perhaps Mr. Brennan was a welcome addition around the campfire as well.

The next day, Quina explained to Pedro just before lunch was laid out that a new woodworker had joined the rancho team. She'd introduce him at the meal. "He's Irish so speaks English but his Spanish is passable. He seems bright and ambitious so I expect he will pick it up quickly."

Pedro was quizzical, wondering aloud how a captain had let a sailor out of his duties. But they could use more help and so he did not argue with his mother. Perhaps Mr. Brennan could teach his brothers, their families and his girls some English. There were so many coming from Boston and England to trade these days.

"Good idea," Quina said with unusual enthusiasm, glad that he was not fighting her on this personnel decision. "You know, I'm not one for languages. No need with the native servants. But now there are so many coming here from other places. Another language besides Latin would be good to add to the young ones' lessons."

They took their places as Pedro's wife and daughters, his brothers and their wives, and their young children, drifted in. At least one of his sisters and her family was usually in attendance as well. They had so many now they had two big tables pushed together to seat everyone. "Perhaps this new woodworker can start with a large redwood table that could seat the whole family," Pedro said to Quina as they sat down.

Juanita walked in with clomping boots under her skirt and waving her wet hands. There hadn't been a towel at the basin so she just made do. Her mother was pestering her about attending a fandango next week up near Mission San Juan Bautista and she was lost in thought on what excuse she could use this time. She sat at her usual place and readied herself for the prayer.

Suddenly, there was a commotion. Squealing and dancing, her little cousins led a big stranger into the room. She tried not to stare but he was the most handsome man she'd ever seen. Her heart thumped. In fact, she had never thought that men could be beautiful. She was stunned and swallowed hard. Forcing her head down as if preparing for the prayer, she peeked up, eyes roaming, drinking all of him in. He was so different from all the men at the fandangos. So much more interesting.

He had a loose shirt open at the collar with his shirtsleeves rolled up. He'd tied a red handkerchief around his neck. His eyes were a piercing blue and his longish, curling hair was yellow and red at the same time, practically pink. It was an almost feminine color. The hairs on his arms were light and sparkled as if he had golden threads attached. His skin was neither white nor brown but a tannish color like light pine that had been briefly toasted in the fireworks. She could see fine muscles in his forearms and tendons straining in his hands as the little ones pulled on him, dragging him to the table.

"Auntie, Abuelo, Papí, this is Señor Brennan. He's so funny. He'll tell us stories at dinner. He's going to live here now. Can he sit by me, Papá?" one asked.

"No, me," another argued.

Francisco was forced to intervene to seat everyone quietly at Pedro and Candelaria's table. Pedro welcomed their guest, said the midday prayer and invited everyone to eat. With so many at one table, the conversation was animated and loud. Everyone talked at once. Save Juanita. She ate silently and stole looks at the foreign woodworker, heart beating in her ears and hands sweating. The need for a fandango excuse long forgotten.

Perhaps it was inevitable that Malachy and Juanita would find each other and become lovers. They were the young and handsome ones on the ranch after all. The unattached. The ones primed for lust, for love. The cousins and her sisters were so little, the aunts all betrothed or married off and the parents getting older. Yet, Juanita did not see it that way, nor expect anything. She was so mortified by her new obsession and so shy in her ability to converse with a stranger, especially in English or limited Spanish, and especially one so handsome and charming, that envisioning a romance did not occur to her. She just wanted to avoid him and get back to the way she used to be.

Juanita kept riding and doing account books and sneaking looks at him whenever she thought she was invisible. She began to lose sleep and dream of Malachy's unique hair and handsome face. After she spied him chopping wood with no shirt on she dreamed of him enveloping her in those strong arms. Repeatedly. What's happened to me, she wondered?

She wasn't even talking to him like the rest of them were. She hadn't experienced the charisma that seemed to have entranced the family. The entire ranch was enthralled with him. Children climbed in his lap and begged for stories. The vaqueros wanted him to ride with them on their long weeks out on the property, but he was committed to the woodshop. Doña Quina consulted him on furniture making. Don Pedro solicited his advice on how to fell a redwood large enough to carve a table to seat the entire family.

Juanita spent so much time in men's work and with the vaqueros that she truly felt as if she were one of them. She was oblivious to any of the cowboys that began to desire her as she matured, never changing how she treated anyone, even as she became a woman. A change she almost didn't notice. Her chaste existence had left Juanita completely unprepared for lust.

She was frustrated at herself that she couldn't concentrate as before, that her father caught her day-dreaming over the books, that she could not invent an excuse to prevent her mother from hounding her about the young men of the nearby ranchos. That she had to spend energy devising ways to avoid being near Mr. Brennan or having to converse with him. She didn't think she'd be able to stop staring and form an intelligible sentence. She kept up her ranch chores and tried to avoid her mother and the new woodworker.

One day, she ran into him at the milking station. She couldn't be rude and so had to offer up some light chatter. "Oh hello, Mr. Brennan, how are you? Are you looking for something? I'm just here to get today's milk for the kitchen." She moved quickly to grab the pails.

"Oh, so nice to finally meet you. Juanita, is it? We haven't really been acquainted. You always seem so busy with the animals and chores. Don't you have vaqueros for all of that?" Even though it was a bit forward, it came out very polite and sweet, Juanita thought.

"Well, I'm not suited for the work of the house, really. I love it out here with the horses, the cows and pigs. The garden and orchard. I should have been born a boy, I guess." Then she blushed furiously, her cheeks heating up with the confession. What was she saying? Oh my, what a fool she was. And to this man she didn't even know.

He laughed and handed her a pail of milk. "Well I'm very glad you weren't born a boy, Señorita Juanita."

She took the pail, grabbed another large one and stomped out of the milking shed. His teeth were very white and his blue eyes crinkled when he smiled. She realized suddenly that most people she knew had sort of gray or brownish teeth or even wooden pieces in place of teeth. Perhaps it was that brilliant smile that made him so irresistible. "Thank you, Mr. Brennan." She hurried toward the house.

"Wait, Juanita. Is it all right if I call you Juanita?" he asked in his rather choppy Spanish. He didn't wait for a reply. "Wait a moment. Tell me why you're not suited for the house but you are for outside work. What is it you like about the barns?"

Good lord he was persistent. He walked beside her and gestured with his hand, offering to take one pail. But not both, she noticed.

"Sorry, am I being too forward?" he continued. "But I'd really like to know. I've never had to sit in soft chairs and sew or learn to sing or decorate rooms, or care for babies. So I don't really know what the work inside is like. What is it that calls you to ranching?"

He was so sincere in his manner that she fell even further under his spell. He wasn't just handsome. He was captivating. She felt as if Malachy Brennan was a deep well with solid earthen walls. It was as if she'd fallen in headfirst and was floundering in the water at the bottom. How would she ever climb out?

"Oh, I love the fresh air, the horses whinnying and galloping. I love the wind in my hair and the scent of the oranges as I harvest them. I like to be exhausted at the end of the day from physical work. But the type of work where you can lead the cows to the new field or birth the lamb or find warm eggs under the chickens." She stopped. Now she'd really embarrassed herself. Speaking about personal things with this stranger. Her face flushed yet again and she juggled the pail, then put it down.

"Do go on," he said softly and reached for the other pail at the same time. She looked up at him with her hand shading her eyes from the setting sun, slipping below the distant hillside. She took in the orange pink sky and breathed deeply.

"Inside, I confess, it is quite boring. And I wilt and shrivel up a bit every day I have to be inside. Please don't tell my mother. Well, actually she knows. That's why they let me do as I please. And because my grandmother is just the same. If it wasn't for her, I'd never have survived this family. Abuela is everything I want to be. Strong, unyielding, smart, and knowledgeable about so much—home and ranch. Animals and people. She spent many years having babies but now she's a businesswoman. And one of the best around the capital. She is respected widely. I admire that." She grabbed the pails from him. He certainly did listen well. "Now Mr. Brennan, I've said too much. Please keep this in your confidence. Best of luck with the table. My father is very excited about it. Good night." She ambled off, pails banging against her thighs as she tried to walk quickly while carrying the heavy jugs.

She did not sleep all night but turned from side to stomach, to other side to back, reliving every morsel of the conversation, every fiber of her torso resonating with a memory she did not want to quit. She re-saw the sunset clouds and thought they were tinged with the same color as his hair. She felt the heat of his hand on the milk pail handle when she retrieved it. She heard the sound of his voice as he asked her personal questions. She pictured that smile and remembered him saying he was glad she was a girl. Over and over again. Dear God, she was lost.

LOVE AND SIN

In the weeks following their first conversation, Juanita feigned indifference but kept an eye open searching for the new woodworker. She listened for the gossip from her siblings and cousins. She discreetly checked in with her father on the quality of his carpentry skills. She no longer ignored the ribbons her sisters left for her hair or clean clothes laid out for dinner. Juanita began to care how presentable she was—something that had never occurred to her before. Her sisters noticed and giggled, quietly agreeing that Juanita looked, and smelled, much better when she cleaned up before coming to the table. The red ribbon in her braid was a delightful nod to their efforts and it complemented her deep black hair and *cafe con leche* skin. She'd gone to a few fandangos before Mr. Brennan had arrived so they figured perhaps a new beau was out on a neighboring rancho. Mother was sending her off to yet another one soon.

After Malachy blended into the rhythm of the ranch, Juanita relaxed her attempts to avoid him. If the whole family had accepted him, then maybe she should speak with him too. She began to walk by the wood shop at the end of the day. He must have noticed as he dropped in on her routines as well, carrying the milk pails for supper, meeting her to check chicken eggs at dawn, taking up a pitchfork and shoveling hay to the milk cows.

One afternoon he asked to ride along to check land boundaries for strays and she wasn't sure how to respond, not in this new paradigm. The sons of a few young dons had asked her to dance at the fandangos or invited her to stroll under the moon. But she'd kept it all very brief, feigning shyness and indifference to get them to stop asking. Not one had sparked any interest in her practical heart. Now, she was dying to shout, "Yes, Yes, so glad you asked. Let's ride on the hills and into the valleys and along the creeks together. I can't think of anything I'd rather do." But clumsily, she just nodded and told him when to meet her at the paddock.

A fog chill greeted them as they rode out toward the land grant's property line looking for wandering cattle and sheep. Juanita had packed a lunch in her satchel and decided to show him her favorite creekside clearing when they got hungry. She was hoping the sun would appear. She pushed her sombrero tight on her head, pulled the poncho close against the damp and galloped up the green slope with the foreigner trying to keep up. She was relieved to see that he did know horses. It would be embarrassing if he were a novice to her advanced horsewoman. More respect oozed into her dreamy-eyed fancying as she'd never seen a foreigner as adept with horses as the Spanish and Mexicans. A lot of the first foreign sailors to Monterrey harbor had basic skills required for carriage or transport, but the passion for reading a horse, the whispering to control him, the skill required to tame a wild stallion—those were the skills her countrymen had almost from birth. It was said that the dons and their Mexican vaqueros were born with a reata in their hand, boots with spurs on their feet. She thought it just might be true.

As they slowed to a trot at the top of the rise and ambled along the ridgeline eyeing the vista, Juanita took a deep breath and spoke. "Mr. Brennan. I think we will have to call you Miguel or Mateo. None of us can pronounce your name."

He laughed and his grin shone in the fog. "Yeah, the woodworkers and cowboys said the same thing. No one could agree on what was closest. They call me Miguel. That's fine. But I can teach you how to pronounce it. *Mal-a-kee*," he said.

She laughed too, mispronounced it, then said, "I'll keep trying. I want to get it right." She dug her heels into the horse and she was off. Malachy rushed to chase her, cheeks flushed from exertion. Juanita showed him the property lines indicated by sycamores and cottonwoods, boulders, crests of hills and a spring. She told him about her grandfather receiving land concessions from the Spanish governors and her father getting one on the day her parents celebrated their wedding at the rancho. "The new Mexican government made them all grants so it is truly our land now. I hope this latest governor, Figueroa, grants my grandmother land. She deserves it."

Malachy asked if they were likely to give it to a woman. She shrugged and he asked more about her growing years, her parents and sisters, her aunts and uncles. It was a big family to get your head around.

After hours of riding, she led him to the stream with a grassy bank. Up the hill, a cluster of redwood trees shaded a perfect picnic spot for a hot day. Her favorite quiet place. She told him so as she spread out the lunch. "And what about your family, Mal-a-kee? Where are your parents? How many siblings do you have? Do you have cousins?"

He looked up sharply. It was as if a cloud appeared over their heads and shaded his face. His eyes dulled. His teeth disappeared.

"They died in Ireland or left. My family had nothing there," he said. "I left on a ship for New York. I had some cousins there. But the tenements were just a different type of starvation. I couldn't breathe in New York. I walked to Boston, found a ship needing help. I went round the Horn. Another kind of hell in that life. But I've seen a lot of the world on board ship. I can tell you stories some time. But right now, Juanita, I'd really like to kiss you. Would that be all right? You look so beautiful and so happy here under the redwoods."

She noticed he looked sheepish. Embarrassed even. He was older and must have more experience with women. She was sure of it but his shy approach betrayed nothing of an experienced past. Juanita felt terror and thrill mixing in her like a cauldron boiling on the kitchen fire. She'd felt sad when he talked about his family, so briefly. But now, she could only nod, not able to concentrate on anything but his blue eyes. His golden hair damp with sweat at the brow. That smile. Those muscular arms. His focus on her. Most men who spent time around the family had really been in love with her mother.

He gently pulled her to him and softly pressed his lips into hers. They were chapped and salty. She moved to her knees, closer to him and engaged in the kiss, surprised that it seemed so natural, that her body responded as if it knew exactly what to do. She figured Malachy's years of travel had provided a great education in the ways of love and suddenly, as if from nowhere, she had a deep interest in learning as much as possible. Her family far away, her responsibilities under control, Juanita gave in to this new heat. Life was complicated and so much more than just ranching, she realized. She was desperate to experience it all and she willingly turned herself over to tutoring from Malachy Brennan.

Juanita felt that with someone so inexperienced he was a sensitive lover. He whispered sweet compliments and gently guided her using that same charm and passion with which he told a story. She was completely entranced. Suddenly she realized what all the fuss was about. She did not want to leave the man's side.

After that first day riding, Juanita and the Irishman spent every possible moment together when they could escape woodshed and stable work. While on chore assignments, they snuck away, into the straw above the milk cow stalls, below the blue sky in the roof-less adobe still under construction, behind the sprawling oak up the hill, in the pantry closet while the cook left her fires to gather garden vegetables. They kept to themselves in the hubbub and appeared separately at family functions so as not to reveal their secret affair. Juanita feared Papá's disapproval of her consorting with a sailor, a foreigner while unmarried. Malachy said he wanted to stay but said he expected Don Pedro had a traditional path in mind for his first born.

Juanita's astonishment at her new obsession dissipated as she suc-cumbed to the pleasures of first love, of physical ardor, of compan-ionship, something she'd never had with anyone close to her own age, let alone a man who shared her adventurous spirit and thirst for the new, the foreign, the unexplained. While making love in every hidden place possible on the compound, they whispered in a mix of Spanish and English, teaching each other their native tongues. Malachy told her stories of his ocean travels, many of them true. She taught him horse control, cattle ranching, sheep shearing, wool spinning and milking. All of it real. They fantasized about a life together living openly on the ranch under the approving gaze of her parents and grandmother.

Several times, lost in romantic daydreams, Juanita even removed Abuelo's secret bible from its hiding place and caressed the thin pages, imagining inscribing an entry for their marriage. She put it back quickly each time, embarrassed at her longing, still mystified at why her grandfather had given her the bible so long ago.

Once they began to reveal secrets to each other, Juanita realized that Malachy was an independent soul with distant obligations and a need for silver. His impoverished upbringing pushed him to obsess over rising up from poverty, making a name for himself, being dependent on no one. He hinted at needing to bring back money from his travels to a cousin or uncle in New York. It was never clear. She didn't ask too much as she focused on demonstrating the type of life they could have together at Rancho Castro. She was thrilled when he told her how much he loved the ranch, how he predicted this Mexican frontier was the future. He promised to figure out a way her father would accept him into the family.

And then one night he disappeared. Leaving only a bouquet of redwood sorrel on her pillow and a short note that read, *Whatever happens, my darling Juanita, please know I will always love you. I must go now to make my own way in the world. Te extrañaré, Malachy*

But nothing else. No encouragement to wait or indication that he'd send letters. No promise to return. No words of regret. Just an empty space where her heart had been so full. Juanita, shocked at the betrayal and loss, pushed herself into ranch tasks, forcing herself to numb and harden her emotions. Once her blood stopped, her breasts grew tender and she tired quickly, she knew he'd left more than the unsatisfying note and ache in her heart.

BANISHED

∝⦿

"*Pedro, Candelaria, I must speak* with you," Quina said bursting in to the library months later. Pedro looked up, perturbed at the interruption. The library was their domain now. No one came in without an invitation, even Quina, who had maintained the same policy with Diego years before.

"What is it, my dear?" Candelaria asked. Pedro shook his head with annoyance. He was reading the Mexican government's secularization declaration, which ordered the missions to disband. A few priests would stay at the churches but the land and wealth were to be distributed, the edict said. Each baptized native on site was supposed to receive some land, tools and animals. The Mexican government also could make land grants to individuals. Interesting. Might be an opportunity for the Rancho Castro to expand as the missions were forced to close and relinquish their land.

"Has Juanita spoken with you?" Quina asked. Her tone was cold. Pedro looked up from the scrolled announcement at his mother, unclear what she was referring to. This secularization order was an important development. He needed to understand its implication for the rancho. He didn't want to talk to anyone right now.

"Didn't you notice anything? She's pregnant."

Pedro looked at his wife. What was his mother saying?

Quina continued. "I've had ten, I mean eleven, kids—so many you lose count—and I know when a woman's pregnant. You should have married her off earlier. You had promising opportunities, for Comandante Ortega's grandson, a Vallejo boy, or even one of the Alvarados. But not now. No one will want her."

Pedro heard the sharp criticism in her voice and was instantly angry. The old fight back again. She had always accused him of poor decisions, some error in his ways. "Mother, what are you talking about?" Pedro said. "How dare you? Juanita wanted to wait on marriage. She didn't like the Vallejo grandson when we were at the San Ysidro fandango. She said he was rude to her. So we've been looking around." Pedro realized he sounded defensive.

"Well maybe she met someone else at the fandango. But she's pregnant. You need to confront her and figure out a plan. I know we agreed to operate our separate areas of the business, Pedro, but this is too important. You'll sacrifice our reputations if you don't take care of it."

"What are you suggesting?" Pedro asked. Candelaria began to cry quietly into her handkerchief. He needed to talk to Juanita immediately. He'd probably have to arrange a quick marriage with whichever don's son was responsible. Damn her. How could she do this to them? That meant she'd be leaving soon. He'd really miss his daughter. She was his positive partner in the ranching business and was quite adept.

"Well, isn't it obvious?" Quina said. "You need to send her away. I don't want my boys' reputations ruined by a niece gone astray.

Something like this can take us all down a notch. Look, maybe it was my fault exposing her to all those foreigners over the years on the ships and in town but it's the parents' responsibility to discipline. What were you thinking letting that woodworker stay around so long? You knew she was fascinated with foreigners, she was determined to learn English. Couldn't you see the potential problem? Maybe it was him. Maybe not. And you know what, it really doesn't matter."

The Irishman? With Juanita? He'd been gone for some months now. Before Pedro could respond, Quina continued. "Send her to the mission in Santa Bárbara. My family's name still carries weight there. Those padres will keep it quiet. They're dismantling the missions so they could use some help—they won't be around forever to solve our moral problems. She can have the baby there and then return. Make up a story about the father dying somewhere."

Pedro was so angry his face flushed and perspiration started to form on his brow. His daughter getting pregnant out of wedlock? His mother threatening and commanding. Sweat dripped from his forehead and chin. In the spots dotting his vision, he wasn't sure if he was more upset at Juanita's sin or his mother's coldhearted suggestion. Easy for her to say, he couldn't help thinking. She always went to Santa Bárbara to have her babies. "Mother, God damn it! This is Juanita you're talking about. Have some respect," he almost shouted. "Let me talk to her and find out what's going on."

"Well, even my favorite granddaughter can get pregnant before marriage. That's sure clear. Candelaria, get ahold of yourself. You've got to toughen up. And I even came up with a solution for you." The scorn in his mother's voice pained Pedro. He'd never gotten used to her dismissive tone with him. He went to comfort Candelaria, who had really started to cry at Quina's proposal.

Quina kept on talking. "Now, I originally wanted to talk to you about my news, but this family emergency got in the way. The good news is that I got a land grant. Governor Figueroa just granted me five leagues adjacent to our southern property line. I'll name it *Rancho de los Pobladores Humildes*. I'll build my own hacienda home there, which Francisco will inherit when I'm gone. This is the culmination of my life's work, you do know that, don't you? Now you two have ruined this moment by besmirching our family name with a loose girl. Take care of it."

She stormed out with as much bluster as when she'd arrived, upsetting the chair and slamming the heavy door. Pedro took Candelaria in his arms to comfort her, whispering reassurances quietly in her ear. At the same time he realized that any truce with his mother had completely collapsed. She sure jumped quickly to suggesting banishing Juanita. And now Francisco was to inherit a grand adobe, probably land too. Would she try to push him out as the don of Rancho Castro?

e͡

Several days later, Juanita paused before pushing the library door open. She breathed in deeply, smoothed her bodice and skirt, hands stopping momentarily on her stomach. As she exhaled, her shoulders dropped and a tingling prickled her skin, heating her cheeks. Nerves. She knew what was coming. She clenched her teeth. Disappointing her parents was already excruciating even though she had yet to face them. That's why she'd been avoiding this confrontation, foolishly trying to wish the pregnancy away.

She walked in, surprised to see they held hands, somewhat uncomfortably, across the wooden scrolled chair arms. Candelaria looked down at her lap as soon as she nodded a greeting. Juanita's nerves then did drop into her gut. Mamá always looked at her, smiling sweetly, or at least sympathetically, even when she'd gotten in trouble as a little girl. The joined hands seemed to indicate unity and no eye contact from Mamá made it clear whatever edict came down she would not argue with Papá. Nausea crept up into her throat like a slithering snake moving toward its prey.

"Juanita, we cannot begin to describe our shock and disappointment with your behavior. You are pregnant, isn't that right? How could this happen? No—" he put his hand up, "don't tell me. I don't want to know. Your actions blackened our family name, our impeccable moral standing. We assume you're some months along and we cannot arrange a quick marriage with the father, correct? Even if we could, the humiliation of going to one of the dons to beg forgiveness and ask for assistance in righting this wrong—well, I don't know if I could do it. We must take care of this ourselves. We are sending you away to have the baby."

Candelaria barely smothered a sob, raising her handkerchief with the hand in her lap. Papá had a firm grip on her other hand squeezing so hard her fingers were white.

Juanita gasped. She moved forward to the chair's edge. "Away? Where? I can have the baby here. With you. At home, with all of—" She stopped, re-thinking her strategy. "Mamá, Papá, I'm so sorry for my sins. Please, please forgive me," she whispered. "It was all a mistake," she said speaking louder. "I thought he loved me. He said he did. I thought he would stay and we would get married. Here in our plaza like you did. We would work the rancho together. He loved this land like I do."

Papá exploded. He shouted and waved the unattached arm, never once letting go of Candelaria's hand. "The Irishman? That's who did this? How could you Juanita? A foreigner? He was never here to stay, surely you knew that. What did he promise you? Oh, how foolish you were, taken in by that man's charms, all those stories."

"Papá, Mamá, please, don't send me away. I know I've made a mistake. I'm heartbroken. I loved him. At first we talked about a life here, with you. He said he loved me. That he would ask your permission to marry. But then he grew restless. He said he didn't want to take your money, that he had to make his own fortune, he had to prove himself without charity. He's a proud man. But he doesn't know. He left before I realized I was pregnant." She hung her head, a tangle of hair falling across her face. "Please forgive me," she whispered to the floor. "I'll take care of the baby. I'll not burden you at all."

"Enough," Pedro bellowed. "It's decided. We've contacted the padres at the Santa Barbara mission. Despite the secularization order, the remaining priests have agreed to take you in. You will get no special treatment, Juanita. They're in the process of disbanding the mission so you will do whatever work they need. No one is to know who you are. Only the father in charge knows. You will have the baby there, remain for the first three critical months of isolation after the birth. Then you can return. Your mother and I will spread a story of a military man who passed away. It's humiliating the position you've put us in. But we will take care of it. Now pack your clothes. You leave day after tomorrow."

Candelaria's sobs grew louder. Pedro consoled her, pulling at her hand. "Hush, my dear. This is the best for everyone, remember"

Juanita gasped. She went to her parents, kneeling before both of them. She grasped their joined hands with her own. "Don't send me away. It's too cruel. I know I made a mistake. I'll work extra hard. Please Mamá, I don't want to have a baby without you there. Please!" Tears slid down her face.

Candelaria took Juanita's cheeks in her hands, bent and kissed each one. "I love you, my darling, but it is decided. Do as your father says and you can come back to us. It will be less than a year. Have this baby and bring us a grandchild. But in a dignified manner. You must go to the mission priests. They'll absolve you of your sins."

The next night Juanita knocked on the library's tall wooden door. She had one last desperate strategy up her sleeve to change her father's mind. She had already asked for her grandmother's help, to no avail. And Candelaria had taken ill from all the stress and retired right after the evening repast. She'd speak with Papá in private. No time to waste, she started in with no preamble.

"Papá, sir, why do you only have one surname? Why was the land given only to Pedro Castro? Why aren't you Pedro Castro Altamirano, Abuela's name, like my aunts and uncles? Who was your mother?" Pedro taken aback by her abrupt entry and accusing questions gasped at her forwardness.

"How dare you talk to me, your father, like that. And after what you've done. Time for you to leave."

She would not relent. "You've always been Pedro Castro only. We've all known that but mostly thought nothing of it. Papá, I know why. Do you?" She reached into her sleeve and pulled out the small bible Abuelo had given her when she was a little girl. His secret. She'd finally figured out why he'd asked her to hide the bible and tell no one. "You're grandpa's secret, aren't you? You're a bastard and now you're sending me away for having a child out of wedlock? You're a hypocrite. The worst kind."

Pedro pushed his desk forward with great force and stepped toward her, trying to grab the bible. "What the hell, Juanita? What are you talking about? Your grandmother is my mother. I was baptized by both my parents. I have the family bible with the date. Bring it over to me, right now." He flipped through the heavy black bible from the shelf and showed her the page.

"Look, here's my name and the date. It does say Pedro Castro. That's true. But I've always been that. There are others who only use one surname."

Juanita noticed his voice rise at that and he seemed to shrug as if he were asking a question. He was the only person she'd ever heard of with only one last name. She knew how important names were to the Spanish. "Flip the page," she said, coldness in her voice. "You only looked for yourself, as most of us do."

He turned the page and ran his finger over the curling script. She pointed to an inscription. "Here's Beatriz," she said, "with both Castro and Altamirano listed. But it's the same date. Why would that be? Everyone's always known you're not twins."

Papá traced the words with his own finger, then turned pages, scrolling his finger down the notations. "Yes, we were raised together but I'm just a bit older. So many babies in those days." He reached for the pocket bible in her hand. "Let me see that. Where'd this come from?" He looked at her before opening the cover.

Juanita was angry and desperate at the same time. She loved her father fiercely. She softened her voice. Maybe if she showed compassion he would not send her away. "Abuelo gave it to me before he died. He said it was a secret and asked me to hide it and tell no one. Not you, not Abuela, no one. He said it was important to him, from his mother in Spain and it had protected him and would protect me."

Pedro looked at her with eyes squinting, color draining from his face. "What?" he mouthed but no sound came out. Juanita continued. "I was little. I didn't understand he expected to die soon. I did what he said. I've kept it secret all this time. I pulled it out of the hiding place recently. You know...for some comfort, thinking about Malachy leaving. I always felt so safe with Abuelo. Maybe his spirit really has protected me all these years. Papá, you're in it. Look, here." She took it gently from his hand and showed him all the inscriptions. At the front were the words:

Diego Castro Cardona baptized in Barcelona, Spain at St. Maria's, 1752.

Then she turned through the pages to one close to the back cover, but not quite. Almost hidden in an unusual place for family bible recordings.

Pedro Castro baptized at Misión San Carlos Borromeo del río Carmelo, to parents Diego Castro Cardona, Capitán of the Dragoons in the Royal Army, and a gentile woman, July 1, 1784. The "gentile woman" had a line through it with *Xolita* written above it.

"Papá, I think your mother was a native woman. Look here, in the big family bible at the entry for your and Tia Beatriz's baptism. The date is months later than the one in Grandpa's little bible."

Pedro peered over her shoulder squinting through his spectacles. "I need to sit down," he mumbled and took the books from her and moved to his desk, laying them out next to each other. He ran his finger back and forth across the inscriptions in each bible. He pulled out a handkerchief and wiped his brow.

Juanita could feel the shock flowing through his veins and despite her enormous love for this man who had tutored her uncomplainingly, who'd created a little university out on the frontier for her thirsty mind, who'd agreed to teach her how to run the family business despite her being born a girl, to whom she owed him her independence and learning, yet, now, he threatened it. Desperation had forced her to act.

"And now, Father, you want to send me away? This is my life, here with you and Mamá, the girls, and my cousins. I'm a Castro and part of this rancho. I know I've sinned terribly. But look, it looks like Grandpa did too. And with all respect, your parents raised you as one of their own and you know, you turned out fine. You're the don."

She felt bad for causing him pain, but she was out of options. Her mother always did what her father said. Abuela wouldn't intervene. She had nothing else.

Pedro's voice broke her reverie. The warble in his usually forceful, clear tone startled her. "If you do what we've arranged, then you can bring your baby back and stay here. But if not, then you are not welcome in our family and will have to leave on your own. You've brought a stain to the Castro name and we must clean it. Now leave me." He waved his hand at her. Juanita knew his voice well and the force in it indicated he would not budge. She felt lost and even more heartbroken than after Malachy had disappeared. Losing her family and home too? That was unimaginable.

$$\mathcal{C}\!\!\sim$$

Juanita rode south in the dim morning light with Pablo, the head vaquero who appeared not to know the journey's purpose. They'd grown up together in the stables and she'd be mortified if he knew of her transgression. Her father explained to her that Pablo carried a letter of instruction detailing Don Pedro's expectations and silver to sweeten the deal in his leather satchel. As she bounced in the saddle, she thought back to a happier trip south.

Years before, she'd been to the Santa Bárbara mission to visit Grandmother's original homestead and meet her grandmother's remaining siblings. Abuela was exceedingly proud that her father, Juanita's great grandfather Don Sebastian, had ushered the pueblo into existence by settling the area even before the mission and presidio were established, before anyone but the natives lived there.

Juanita remembered fondly that the air was warm, with a slight breeze off the ocean sparkling below the town's slope. Purple bougainvillea hugged the solid adobe walls like a cheerful blanket wrapping a spoiled newborn as the mission gleamed with whitewash and terra-cotta roof tiles. She had loved the cool of the church interior in contrast with the heat of sun in the flower garden. The *milpas* nearby burst with corn and barley, wheat and beans. Vegetables flourished in several gardens and vines produced plenty of grapes for the Sunday sacrament wine. Vaqueros busily rode in and out of the stables and corrals, horses dutifully waiting, roped to the rails outside the mission offices, kitchen, dormitories and monjerio.

Grandmother had taken her hand and led into the cemetery to her parents' graves. She'd knelt to pray while young Juanita eyed the gravestones and the bees sucking nectar out of the red hibiscus and tiny pink roses. It had been a special trip, just Abuela and Juanita making a pilgrimage to the gravesite and to introduce Juanita to another growing Alta California pueblo.

Now, as she rode into the pueblo trailing Pablo, she could see that the Santa Bárbara mission had lost its luster. They rode alongside fields with crops past picking time, rotting on their stems. A few natives seemed to live at the compound while others appeared to travel daily between huts outside the walls to work in the kitchens and dormitories, fields and animal stalls. Juanita realized that after generations living at the missions, many suddenly released natives had nowhere to go. Her father had said they'd be given land and animals but she saw no evidence of that as she and Pablo traversed Santa Bárbara.

They entered the central square to find decrepit buildings, crumbling adobe, weeds growing in the once spotless plaza. Only a few priests remained at the church, all of Mexican origin. Mexican officials, fearing Spanish influence, had sent any padres born in Spain back to the land of their birth. Pablo and Juanita tied up their horses and searched through the cold dark rooms looking for the father in charge. Eventually he emerged from the dark sanctuary, squinting in the light of day, and nodded at Pablo as he read through the documents. He stuffed the silver eagerly into the pouch at his waist, shook Pablo's hand, and ushered Juanita into a tiny monk's cell.

With Pablo gone, Juanita listened with despair to the priest read her father's instructions. Her parents told the mission leader to inform no one of her status as the daughter of an important don, nor to give her any special privileges. She was to be treated like a native servant, even as she grew heavy with pregnancy and even when she had a newborn. She was to work in whatever way the padre deemed useful to the mission as it closed down operations. She was to pray for her sins at least twice a day and attend confession weekly and all Masses and services the fathers offered.

As she sat alone in the cell, she realized she'd been quite fortunate in her short life, until Malachy deserted her. But that heartbreak was nothing to what she felt now. She was devastated at being exiled by her parents and sent away from extended family, her home and sisters, the comfort of good food and a warm bed, the loss of the familiar. She arranged her few items in the barren room, knelt to pray at her narrow cot and sobbed quietly, not wanting the priest to hear any sign of weakness. She would get through this so she could return to the good graces of her family.

⁓

For a few months shy of a year, Juanita scrubbed church floors, washed pots, stirred tallow wax and cleaned horse stalls for the head priest and the dwindling mission staff. She prayed and confessed, attended mass and more mass. She never once left the compound, never once saw anyone but the natives and fathers, and soldiers who checked in and made sure the priests were dismantling their empire.

The baby arrived sometime in the weeks after the season's first rain. A midwife from the pueblo attended and provided limited instruction on nursing and infant care. Exhausted after a long labor accompanied by the midwife yelling throughout, Juanita looked into the eyes of her infant, at the tiny limbs and soft cheeks and felt her heart blossom. The hardness she'd needed to survive the past months softened and opened like the petals of a poppy when touched by sunlight. Oh, this was what made the sacrifice worth it, the love she felt for this tiny being, who needed her care to grow. Now, here was the love of her life. A son. She absently noted that she'd broken the Castro Curse by delivering a healthy baby boy at her first go around. She now knew for certain that not even Abuela had done that.

She saw things quite differently now, knees knotted with calluses from scrubbing floors, her hands cracked and reddened from washing and more washing, Malachy's passion long suppressed into nothing more than a distant memory as if it were in one of the novels from her father's library that someone had left out in the sun to fade. Perhaps she had made a mistake in the eyes of the Church, her devout parents and grandmother. But she no longer saw it the same way. The sin had given her a passionate love affair, which she did not actually regret, save for the banishment. Yet much more importantly, it had given her a son, the most perfect creature she'd ever seen. A new reason for living. A reason to thrive. She would raise him at her beloved Rancho Castro as she'd been raised, yet with no further straying off the expected path.

He would be a fine, strong ranch hand. He would be learned and read the great works of the civilized world. He would learn English as the Americans were fast approaching the frontier and were the future's most important trading partners. She would raise this boy to take over from Papá and Abuela. This tiny infant, her little miracle, her son, would grow up to be the don.

Despite praying daily for her parents' forgiveness and for acceptance back into the family as if nothing had happened, she really had no idea how she would be treated. She, a single mother who was only pretending to be a widow for outsiders. Would Papá have the baby baptized? Grandmother was extremely devout and she was sure she would insist on it but she felt unsure if she even wanted this little bundle initiated into the Church. It was their teachings that had sent her away and forced her to live like a servant to the unforgiving padres. But if they would allow it and she acquiesced to keep the peace, they would record the date in the large family bible.

She felt an urgency to mark the lonely birth that had surprised her with such great joy and love. A few days after her son arrived, she reached for Abuelo's pocket bible, which she kept hidden under the thin mattress, and wrote on the page following the one with her father's baptismal notation.

Joaquín Castro, born to Juanita Castro de la Cruz, Misión Santa Bárbara, December, 1834.

She had no idea what the day was but she knew it was the month of the Lord's birth. She said aloud to the empty room, staring into the infant's eyes, "I name you Joaquín, in honor of Abuela."

During the months of exile, she received not one letter from her parents save on Christmas, a short note saying they understood the baby had arrived and would send Pablo to retrieve her in about three months, when the heavy rains slowed. No words of love, endearment, encouragement. Disappointed they had not relaxed their harsh punishment, she felt more alone than ever, but at least they would take her back.

She hoped some forgiveness would welcome her home and she longed to be swallowed up in the bosom of everything she missed. Her mother's sweetness, her sisters' fawning—they would so love the baby—her father's reliance on business advice, the noisy chaos of her aunts and uncles, cousins and more cousins, the vaqueros and her favorite stallions and mares. She missed every brick and shutter of the hacienda. Her parents certainly knew how to make a point, she thought.

She would never stray from their expectations again. She would return home, take her role as the don's daughter and business partner, check in on her beloved grandmother and remain single, a "grieving widow" to outsiders. Perhaps the only silver lining of all that had happened was that she would be independent and free of a

man's demands, save those of her father. Spanish and Catholic traditions what they were, she did not anticipate anyone would ever
want to marry an older woman, one with a child already, even if
her parents did fabricate the story that she was a widow. A celi-
bate, lonely life would be worth it to get back into the warm fold of
her family. She just wanted to finish her sentence and get home to
Rancho Castro.

DISCOVERIES

he went alone, against her better judgment. She didn't think she could explain this pursuit to a friend in any way that made sense. And none of them would be interested in the past or traipsing through the woods looking for, what? It was kind of crazy, she admitted as she adjusted the backpack straps, took a swig from her water bottle and continued climbing up the ravine. Nicole had been so preoccupied with her family's problems lately that she just seemed to bore or mystify her friends. They wondered why she wasn't applying for well-paying engineering positions and taking odd jobs in coffee shops and dog walking. Why wasn't she doing online dating? No boyfriend or dates? Why wasn't she hanging out with people her own age? She really needed to move beyond this Great Gram and history obsession.

She grabbed a boulder with one hand as she stretched her leg up to another and scaled the rocks bordering the waterfall. Great Gram had thought there might be a shack somewhere higher on the land, above the flat part of the creek and the rusting mine equipment. At the top of the cascade, she stopped and sat on a rock, looking down at the forest and where she'd climbed. The creek's *trickle, burble, splash* soothed her.

This was it, just one more exploration around the property. Then, enough. It was time to move on and find a real job. Time to use her engineering degree, as Great Gram had insisted. Time to let go of her interest in the past while she focused on getting Great Gram back home in the present. She pushed off the rock to keep hiking up toward the top of the mountain. As she walked, she repeatedly saw a false summit of light through the trees. There was always another drop down before yet another ridge up.

Once finally at the top, she stretched and surveyed the view, the hills roller-coastering west toward the sea, the valley below with its hum of San Jose. It smelled earthy with buckeye pods littering the ground and decaying maple leaves stretching into a rusted orange carpet beneath her feet. She turned to walk along the ridge line, looking down one side of the mountain, then the other.

What was that? Not another bush but a plank. Cracked boards poked above the line of the hilltop. Was that a roofline where the slope dropped down sharply? She ran ahead and found a shack, or what was left of it, and surveyed the graying, splintered boards, the dirt coating the debris. She stepped in carefully, examining the remnants. A rusted metal cup lay half buried at the back. A wooden table with two broken legs wobbled to one side. The remainder of a metal twin bed frame collapsed into the wall.

Filled with nervous energy, she yanked open a barely covered cupboard, pulled up floorboards, one by one. Nothing. She picked up loose planks with brown, crumbling nails, scouring the rubble. For what she didn't know. Some sign of the past. Of someone who lived here or visited here. It seemed like a hunting blind, too tiny for anyone to live in. She stepped farther into the shack and heard a clink under her foot. She knelt down and tugged at the remaining floorboards. They came loose and in the dirt below lay a blackened, decaying metal box. The lid was rusted shut. Thankfully she'd brought some tools and dug the screwdriver out of her backpack. She pried and twisted the metal until the sides finally crumbled and the cover opened in her hands.

A small, black book was inside, a red thread looped out of the top. Her hands started shaking, her breath dropped. She swallowed hard. She moved to the front door and sat, resting her feet on the ruins of the broken front steps. She gasped. The view across the hills stunned her. The ocean far below was a flat navy blue. The sun, lowering, had colored the sunset clouds purple and pink. No wonder someone built this cabin here, she thought. It was beautiful. Not a hunting blind, but someone's special place.

In the twilight, she set down the box and screwdriver and picked up the book. A black dust coated her fingers. The cover was disintegrating, but she could see that it was a bible Gently, very gently, she opened to the first page.

Diego Castro Cardona baptized in Barcelona, Spain at St. Maria's, 1752.

Oh my God. She read it again. And again. In Spanish, then translated it to English, glad that her intermediate level Spanish was sufficient to understand the text. Then she read it out loud. Out toward the view. To the pines, tall behind her, to the manzanita scrub tangled below the shack's remains.

"Diego Castro Cardona baptized in Barcelona, Spain at St. Maria's, 1752."

Castro. Wasn't that Joe Brennan's other name. Was this from his family? Could this be a puzzle piece for her to fit into the mystery of her ancestry? To connect her and Great Gram's old house and this land all together?

Nicole slowly, carefully turned to the next page. Tiny golden flecks fell, dusting her jeans. She brushed them off and turned the book to its side. The edges of the pages were coated with a gold trim. She turned to another page. And another. She gently shuffled the thin paper with her thumb but didn't see any other inscriptions. She turned to the back cover. Nothing there either. She thumbed the back pages, and loopy script, now a faded sepia, caught her eye. She held her breath and read silently.

Pedro Castro baptized at Misión San Carlos Borromeo del río Carmelo, to parents Diego Castro Cardona, Capitán of the Dragoons in the Royal Army, and a gentile woman, July 1, 1784. The "gentile woman" had a line through it with *Xolita* written above it.

A royal army captain? That must have been in the Spanish Army. So this Diego was born and baptized in Spain according to the entry on the little bible's first page. Then he had a son, Pedro, baptized at a mission. Gentile woman, what did that mean? She'd have to look it up later. No cell service up here. She read it again and again, running her fingertips over the script as if caressing a new baby, tenderly. The old dates took her breath. Awed, she calculated. Over two hundred and fifty years since the first inscription. Who was the Spanish captain? What was he doing here? She stroked the book, then slowly flipped the pages again, finding another entry buried at the back.

Joaquin Castro, born to Juanita Castro de la Cruz, Misión Santa Bárbara, December, 1834.

Joaquin Castro? That's it. That was Joe Brennan's other name in the documents establishing the land trust. Finally. Joe Brennan was here. She just knew it. So was this his bible? And finally, a mention of Juanita Castro de la Cruz, the name Joe Brennan had referenced in the land trust document as his mother. She had existed. This was even better confirmation than she had hoped for. Nicole read the entries over and over. Pedro Castro had also been listed in the land trust signature and dedication page. So how did they all fit together?

She took her notepad out of the backpack and scratched a little family tree. Diego born in Spain, Pedro his son but the mother a bit unclear. Then Joaquin, born fifty years later, was his grandson. Juanita his mother. The names matched the land trust documents but she now had verification of the lineage. And now she had Pedro's parents, it looked like. Big questions remained. Why did both men only have one last name while everyone else had two? She knew something of the Spanish naming tradition with two last names but unclear on how it really worked. She'd look that up later. And what was a gentile and a dragoon? Lots to research.

Nicole sat for a moment, clutching the bible, pressing it into her breastbone. She wanted to imprint its words on her, brand herself with this knowledge. Here was a physical representation of her past, a link to her roots. The Castros. An unlikely name and lineage, an unexpected link so near to the very place she'd grown up. This was way better than finding a new name to add to a *Genetix4You* family tree branch. This felt foundational. She felt as if she had discovered a place in the world and this family belonged to her.

She had to show Dad. Maybe he'd believe her, finally. She wrapped the bible in the sweatshirt and carefully placed it at the top of her backpack. She closed the metal box and put it back where she'd found it, placing the floor planks on top, replacing any other board she'd moved as well. She didn't want it to look like anyone had been rummaging through the cabin remains. Maybe someone else had been there looking for family clues. Well, probably not, but you never know. Best to keep the origin of the bible to herself. Then she strode down the hill and clambered down the rocks next to the waterfall before it got dark.

Once in her car, on impulse, Nicole decided to drive to her father's house on the ranch. She had not been there since she'd discovered Missy had moved in. She had to show him the bible. Prove that she was not crazy. Get him to see some sense and talk to her. With all the drama and conflict over the San Francisco house and the changing wills, Nicole and her dad were estranged. They mostly communicated through lawyers. It was like Missy had replaced her. Was he trying to blot her and Momma out of his memory? She'd get depressed if she allowed herself to wallow in the family dysfunction. It made her so sad.

Dad couldn't accept that his own grandmother had skipped two generations and willed her house to his daughter, freezing him out. And now that she had submitted a counter application for conservatorship, Nicole was persona non grata to both Dad and Missy. They felt it was proof that she was trying to manipulate Great Gram, determined to outmaneuver them. Fortunately, her great grandmother had loved the counter proposal and had her lawyer submit it to the court, but the law moved at a glacial pace it seemed to Nicole.

Great Gram was elderly and getting more frail with each stressful development. Her energy depleted further when two tenants moved out amid the confusion and Missy's threats. She wanted Nicole to get conservatorship, flee the old folks' home and the two of them move back into her top floor flat. But the wait was wearing her down. "I'm not getting any younger. What's taking so long?" she asked Nicole repeatedly.

"The lawyers," Nicole answered during their secret phone conversations.

"Just get me out of here before I die. I want to die in my own home. But goddamn it, I want to live there first."

Nicole hit the accelerator a little harder. She had to get this resolved and find some family peace. The bible would show Dad a link to their past and confirm that she hadn't been crazy searching for their roots. Hopefully Missy wouldn't be there, off at work, selling people's homes out from under them, or whatever the hell she did. This was risky. They were the enemy after all, legally. But she had to get Dad to see straight.

She pulled in next to the house. No sign of Missy's old car. She sighed with relief. "Dad, you here," she called as she went through the front door. The house was still a mess, with dishes in the sink, clothes strewn about, shoes and socks dotting the floor. But again, it did smell good. Maybe a pot roast simmering on the counter this time? Maybe Dad was eating finally with Missy's crockpot cooking. She went out the back door and saw his shadow pitchforking hay into the horse stalls.

"Dad. Hey, it's me. How are you? It's good to see you. Been a long time."

He looked up at her from the pitching, surprised. "Nicole. You shouldn't be here, you know. My lawyer told me you've got some new strategy, to get conservatorship of Great Gram yourself. Too many damn lawyers in all of this. If Missy knew you were here, she'd flip a gasket." He put down the pitchfork and walked toward her, following her into the kitchen.

"Well, maybe it isn't all about Missy...Oh Dad, what have we come to? But look. I came here to show you something." She reached into her backpack and pulled out the bundle. "I found it up on that land trust land, you know, the family land where you can go camping and stuff." She was tempted to ask him why he'd never taken her there but thought better of it. Stick to the subject at hand. She pulled out the bible and opened to the first page.

"Look, Dad, it's over two hundred and fifty years old. Here's an inscription about a guy born in Spain, in 1752. Can you believe that? And then there's more about others born at what I think was the Carmel mission and another one at the Santa Barbara mission in 1834. These are our ancestors. They're that land guy's family."

She stopped, hesitated, then figured she finally had his attention, she'd go for broke. "It wasn't wrong, that DNA test I took. We're descended from the Spanish who came here for the missions. You know with Father Serra and all that? I'm still figuring out the tree, but this is really important evidence. Isn't it amazing that we could see this? Maybe it's not the history you thought but it's really cool to know it and have this artifact, don't you think?" She was so hopeful he'd understand what she'd been searching for all this time. To find their real family tree and embrace it. She decided to tell him all her plans.

"Oh, and one other thing, I'm going to plan a family reunion. Of all the descendants I can find from that side of the family. Your family, Dad. The Brennan Family Trust people. Don't you think they might like to know he was really Joaquin Castro? From right here in California, born in Santa Bárbara, in the early 1800's? I'm not sure about all the details but I'm working on it. I've been connecting with distant cousins online and we pool our information. It's pretty cool. Makes me feel like I have a family." She couldn't help adding that part. She knew it would hurt him, but it was true.

He adjusted his hat, took his glasses from his pocket, held the bible and looked and looked. He read each inscription, turned the bible over, then read them again, all without saying a word. Nicole's heart pounded. Maybe he'd finally believe her, see that she wasn't totally crazy. "It's a fake, Nicole. Where'd you get this? How do I know someone didn't just plant it for you to find? Or you just wrote all that stuff in there. I know it looks old but how do you know it's real? I think you've gotten yourself wishing and hoping and searching for something so bad you're seeing things that aren't real. How you know those people are related to us anyway? Two hundred and fifty years it survived in the dirt on a mountain? Oh, come on. You're more gullible than I ever imagined."

He tossed the small book unceremoniously on the kitchen table where it bounced and almost went over the edge. Nicole lunged to grab for it. "Dad," she screeched.

"Look, Nicole. Drop it," he continued as if nothing had happened. "Why don't you try instead to get in my good graces by getting your great grandmother to sell her house and stop complaining about the senior home? I'm tired of her phone calls. I made sure she's not in one of those crappy places. Can't you stop fighting me on the conservatorship? We're all wasting way too much money on damn lawyers. Missy's coming home for dinner soon. Better get going. You don't wanna be here then."

Nicole felt deflated. Defeated. Her hopes for his acceptance and approval completely dissolved. "But Dad, what are you doing? Why are you so fixated on selling the San Francisco house? It's part of our family history. The descendants of the people in this bible built that house before the earthquake. It's a family treasure. And, by the way, it is Great Gram's home."

"Nope. Don't agree. Your great grandmother's too old for that huge house, you know. We could use the money now when the market's strong. And could anyone really take it on the way she wants? Don't think so. She can't control who lives there from the grave. That's ridiculous. Enough, Nicole. That bible is a goddamned fake. Now, time for you to leave. And call your lawyer's off, would ya?"

❧

A few weeks later, Nicole walked up the granite steps of the Bancroft Library at UC Berkeley and entered the formidable white building with a speck of hope. With lawyers still debating Nicole's conservatorship application, Great Gram fading further, another tenant threatening to move, she put all thoughts of wills and historic houses aside to focus on the little bible. She had an appointment with an archivist familiar with California's Spanish and Mexican eras who would be able to analyze the book's authenticity, as well as the inscriptions. Was it really from the 1750s? She was nervous and excited but mostly just so glad to forget the struggle over the house. It was reassuring to be back on the Berkeley campus. In her mind, she gave a little nod to the Campanile as she walked up the steps into the celebrated library.

Nicole waited on a hard, wooden chair before being ushered into a cool, dim room lined with leather-bound volumes protected behind locked glass doors. The archivist greeted her with a cold handshake and a nod. He was middle-aged, pale-skinned and wore a dark black suit that matched his thick black framed glasses. Donning a pair of gloves, he sat down and began to examine the bible while Nicole stood to his side to watch. It was a laborious process but he was completely focused on the task, never once looking at her or anywhere else in the cavernous room. It was completely silent save for an analog clock ticking on the wall behind some file cabinets. Afraid to disturb him, Nicole pressed her hip into the thick wooden table so she wouldn't move, even slightly.

After he had examined quite a few pages he patted the back casing, on one side, then the other. Then very quickly, before she could cry out to stop him, he took a thin knife and slit around the endpaper. With a set of tweezers, he pulled a piece of browned paper from between the casing and the back cover. He gently unfolded the browned paper with the tweezers and his gloved hands. A corner piece broke off. She could see his pulse, a bluish vein beating in his thin neck. He lay the paper on the table and set worn, rounded river stones on each corner to keep it flat. He stood up and they both leaned over, craning to read the looping handwriting.

Baptismal Record
Misión San Carlos Borromeo de río Carmelo
Año 1784, Julio 1

Parents Diego Castro Cardona, formerly of Barcelona, Spain, a Capitán of the Dragoons in the Royal Army settling Alta California for the King of Spain, and a gentile woman called Xolita, do hereby baptize their son, Pedro. In the eyes of God and our Lord Jesus Christ, the baby Pedro, henceforth to be called Pedro Castro, is baptized and welcomed into the Catholic faith.

Fray Junipero Serra

"Oh, my," she whispered, as she leaned in heavily on the edge of the table. She wanted to sit down but couldn't tear her eyes from the document and the ornate signature. She looked over at the archivist with gratitude. She'd thought she might scream when he slit open the back of the book but look what he'd uncovered. A baptismal record signed by Father Serra himself. "Is it real?" she asked.

"I will do a few more tests on the paper and ink and compare the signature, although I'm quite familiar with Father Serra's signature, you understand. Quite familiar. It matches what we have and the records at the Huntington and the missions. Looks like his, looks like his. He was made a saint recently, you know. Yes, I believe it is real. I do believe so, do believe so." He repeated himself as if he were singing the refrain of a song.

The archivist continued muttering as he worked on the document, looked through the bible again, moved over to a microfiche machine and scanned other documents, then seemed to repeat the whole procedure all over again.

Nicole had to sit as the shock sank in. Here was proof from a primary source document, signed by a famous figure, that her family, her blood line, started with a Spanish soldier and a Native Californian. She asked the historian a few questions and confirmed this was indeed the Carmel Mission and so the father, Diego Castro, had probably been stationed at the presidio in Monterey. The term "gentile" was what the Spanish priests called unbaptized natives.

"Neophytes is what they called the baptized natives, yes they did," the archivist said. "So, since this was in the Carmel and Monterey area, this gentile woman was most likely Ohlone, Costanoan, the Spanish called them. Possibly Rumsen Ohlone—there were several Ohlone triblets. An Ohlone woman who had her baby baptized but was not baptized herself. Interesting, interesting. Father Serra must

have thought he'd get the baby first and then maybe he could convert the mother. Yes, it is all real. All real," he said. "Oh, and note the
date. Father Serra died soon after this. Must have been one of his last
baptisms. Interesting, interesting."

He kept looking back to the baptismal certificate as he talked to
her. "We really like to have such historic documents protected in the
collection, you understand. Important history and all. Important
history. But if you need to keep it for your family records, we can't
restrict that. Just keep it safe. Under museum glass would be best.
With UV protection. Here is your letter of authenticity. The one you
requested. May I take a picture?" Nicole, still stunned, nodded. He
whipped out an iPhone from his pocket and snapped several photos.

Nicole mumbled a thank you, carefully wrapping the book and
document in protective cloth. In shock, she didn't really thank him
properly. Sticking her hand out to shake his at the door at the last
minute before it swung shut.

"Happy to do it, happy to do it. Do consider donating that baptismal record to the Bancroft. If nothing else, maybe in your will.
Yes, you are young for a will, but we all have to protect the past." He
shook her hand and disappeared into the dimly lit library.

THE WARRIOR

Asatsa burned hot. Ever since he'd ordered his mother cremated on the funeral pyre seven years before, it was as if the flames had jumped a fire line to consume his body. He was angry all the time. And he was even more irritated that he couldn't prevent fury from invading his pores, controlling him. Rage motivated his every move now. He became a warrior, always on the move. The peaceful boy who'd loved hunting with his cousins, proudly bringing home rabbits and quail to his mother, had disappeared. Asa couldn't find that boy buried within himself even when he left the trail briefly to return to his village, find a wife, settle her into a hut suitable for a family and get her pregnant. Each new baby deepened his anger.

As a father, Asa finally understood his mother. The sacrifices she'd made for him. He realized that she'd abandoned some type of a home to raise him in the traditional way of their people, even if it had been with the Spaniards. What an innocent he'd been. Now he felt how a parents' love is like no other. In his marrow he knew he would take an arrow for his children. He wanted them to grow up free, natural, away from the changes the Spanish had brought to his homeland, just as she had. Asa also admired that even though his mother encouraged him to be a fighter, she had not raised him to hate. But after her death, the loss and his dreams for his own children filled him with hate for the enemy. He could feel its ugliness destroying him. While Asa had been raiding Spanish ranches and missions since his teen years, he had always returned home. Now, he rarely left the camino for settled village life. The anger drove him to stay constantly in motion, rarely seeing the children he so loved.

Asa also could not quell the disgust he felt for his fellow natives who refused to fight the invader, especially those who moved to the mission prisons willingly. How could they betray their own? Sacrifice their natural living for watery bean stew and liquor squeezed from the grapes that grew in rows alongside the religious compounds? But when some returned, begging to be allowed back into the fold, he was merciless. "There's no going back and forth in our world. You're either with us or against us," he lectured his troops at the training camp he built in the long, wide valley below the snowy mountains.

At first, Asa and his lieutenants taught the recruits to use their hunting skills to defeat the enemy. Sneak up silently, attack swiftly, leave no trace or smell. No needless loss of life. Even in his anger, in those early years, he refused to stoop to what he considered the depravity of his opponents. He would lead his troops to raid, steal, or free imprisoned comrades in the dark of moonless nights or when the target was distracted by a rodeo or a bad storm. They left no sign of the raid beyond what was stolen, save for a large "A" he carved with his *machete* into the pillar of a house, a tree trunk or on the side of a presidio jail. Rumors flew but no one knew who the

A belonged to. Who attacked so ruthlessly and brilliantly at night? Who could steal horses and weapons right under our noses, the Español gossiped in the saloons.

Asa mastered other techniques as well. His ability to speak, read and write Spanish allowed him to disguise himself as a poor native seeking salvation from the priests. He would ingratiate himself with a Californio Don or a priest, reading bible passages at night or offering to pick grapes for a week to do reconnaissance without suspicion. When in disguise, he would invent tales of traveling south searching for a brother who'd been at a mission or for his mother who'd been kidnapped by rogue soldiers. Asa's resentment for the enemy fueled his creativity and his bravado, making his stories all the more believable to the unsuspecting Español and Mexicano.

By the time Asa was thirty-three, he had built up a force of over a thousand trained rebel warriors. He often united with other renowned native leaders like Estaninslao and Yoscolo. By then their raids no longer involved only quiet guerrilla tactics but often were all out battles. San Francisco Presidio soldiers ventured out to the valley to remove bothersome natives near ranchos. Monterrey soldiers left the coast for the inland valley attempting to attack Asa's militia. Finally, that fateful year, the governor sent Mexican Army General Vallejo out to win control over the Laquisimes River area with a large force to defeat Asa and the other native troops.

It was a bloody fight and many of Asa's soldiers were killed or captured. Most fled the bloodshed and chaos after Vallejo's victory. Estanislao himself returned to a mission to beg forgiveness. Yoscolo disappeared west into the coast range above the Pacific. Asa refused to leave his central valley base and returned to his encampment in the foothills. Surprisingly, no Mexican troops had discovered it. The Mexicans, convinced they'd finally defeated the native tribes by claiming the river, returned to their coastal ranches leaving a void in the valley. Asa started all over again.

Once back in his hidden camp, he immediately began recruiting and training any young natives he could convince to join up. Word of his fearlessness in battle and his determination to keep fighting spread. Asa approached village elders and dispirited young men with the same message. Did they know the Mexican government had just ordered the missions to disband? There was new hope. The Spanish priests had promised the natives would get their land back after ten years but that had never happened. Maybe the Mexicans would return the mission lands to those who'd worked them? Asa doubted it but tossed this tempting morsel to potential recruits as if it were bloody elk meat he was throwing for a hungry grizzly.

He told the story of a Mexican soldier who'd been especially brutal in the Vallejo battle and then was convicted by the Mexicans. His punishment was five more years of military service. "There will never be justice for our people. We cannot count on the government. We must take freedom for ourselves," Asa preached.

Once he had fresh-faced young recruits follow him, he pushed them hard. "You know the ferocity Vallejo's troops brought to the fight? We must be steadfast. Out here in the big valley, your tribes are not as poisoned by the mission life like the coast. Many here are strong and free, but we must train and fight to remain so. They are moving east." The ragtag native soldiers and new recruits listened to Asa's determination. He always had big plans. Once they'd recovered imprisoned comrades, had recruited a larger force, stolen more weapons and horses and trained the new troops, they would take over a mission like other natives had done on the south coast.

"Those Santa Bárbara Chumash are our inspiration. But we'll do more. We will not just burn the mission to the ground and hold the land for months. We'll invade the church, imprison the priests and soldiers there, take back our fellow native tribesmen and recolonize the place—I am thinking either at San José or Santa Clara," he said in one of his rousing speeches. "We'll control the land and crop production. We'll breed cows and horses. We'll feed ourselves and trade with other natives. But let them live as before, not imprison them. The reality of this land has changed. Mexicans say we are free now. But after generations of imprisonment many of our people don't know how to live in the old ways. We cannot allow the Mexicans to dictate our values, our culture and language, our beliefs. We need to reclaim our identities and the land of our birthright."

While he worked to rebuild his small army, Asa made a trip west to his home village. He rode for two days to see his wife and children, two sons and a daughter, now growing up. He'd instructed his wife and the village elders that his children were to learn the traditional arts despite the natives' altered reality. They planted now and raised some cows and horses like on the missions and ranchos. As the elk grew scarce, a diminished herd retreating to the mountains away from the invader's guns, there was little hunting. Cattle dominated the grasslands now, leaving nothing but stubby weeds for the surviving elk. However, Asa was determined his sons would learn to hunt.

After greeting his surprised wife and children, checking in on the village leaders, mourning the deaths and congratulating parents on recent births, he took the boys out to the hills. They climbed past manzanita, under a canopy of oak and maples, sycamores and laurel. They practiced shooting at small prey, then scouted for bigger targets. They slept on the ground by a small fire and got up in the morning to do it again. Asa checked his anger at their youth, their inexperience, their fears and told himself he had to do this to pass on his culture, his skills. How would they survive now if they didn't learn to hunt as young boys? He forced himself to be patient, instructive but not cruel.

The father and his boys stalked one elk. They shot and gutted the animal, in the way of his ancestors, with the traditional Ohlone prayers and thanksgiving. Then they took their prize and trudged home to show it to mother and village. The boys seeemed so proud, so happy to have achieved something primal, something of value with their father. Asa stayed one more night to enjoy the feast, taste the elk meat, delicious in the memories of childhood it raised in his hardened soul. Then he kissed them farewell while they lay sleeping and disappeared into the black night. Restless as always, a military mission on his mind. He was his father's son after all.

When Asa returned to the secret training camp in the big valley, his soldiers told him there were new men in the area. French Canadian trappers were visiting nearby ranches. They'd come down from the cold north along the Feather and Sacramento rivers looking for beavers. They were wrapped in heavy furs and skins, far more than was needed in the heat of the central valley spring. They had no interest in capturing natives or in any kind of religious conversion. They just wanted to trade and understand the local landscape. Were there beavers or foxes in the area? Which rivers had the best fish? Did the ranchos or local natives have any medicines? Several trappers were sick so they were looking for doctors who could cure fevers and sweating, shaking and vomiting. But the grizzled trappers kept to themselves. A nomadic crew, they didn't form towns, and many seemed to be respectful trading partners.

Asa had encountered these foreigners before and found them quite useful for tobacco, firearms and food if he and his followers provided information on the small and large fur-covered animals.

These men were completely focused on fur. And they kept moving. Asa liked that.

⌒

By the summer of 1833, Asa was ready to put his plan into action but needed a few more recruits. He knew where to go. He led a small band of his top scouts and lieutenants out of the training hideout. They traveled north, seeking soldiers from the villages lining the Feather River. In previous years, Asa had found the area plentiful with young men willing to join rebel forces among the Miwok, Maidu, Yokut and Wintun settlements bordering the river.

Asa and his most trusted comrade lumbered on their horses at the front of the small regiment, his other lieutenants at the back. They ambled along the river's edge, finding well-worn trails from the villagers who lived next to the clear pools, rippling rapids and wide banks. They should be approaching a village soon, Asa thought.

The horses noticed it first. They began to whinny and shiver, shy and buck. Expert horsemen, Asa and his lieutenants glanced at each other. What was wrong with the horses? Suddenly a dreadful stench hit his nose. The huts they could see around the river bend had no smoke drifting from cooking fires, a standard sign of an active settlement. Giant buzzards with beady black eyes and red throats circled above, croaking and flapping their wings.

"Death," said Asa, reining his stallion to a stop, looking back at his men with a cold, hard stare. "It's the smell of death. On your guard. They must've been attacked."

Men adjusted their riding stance, pulling out pistols. One had a shotgun. Another readied his bow and arrow. Old fashioned, but

Asa allowed the soldiers their weapons of choice. Whatever worked. Once all were ready, he nodded and led them quietly up to the village.

The silence was eerie, threatening, then desperately sad as they spied bodies lining the river under the trees. Decaying corpses swarmed with flies and whitened skulls littered the riverbank. More bodies were decomposing in the huts, beige maggots wriggling out of the flesh. The village was dead. The bodies were so decomposed, or just skeletons, it was impossible to tell what tragedy had befallen here. Asa motioned his men to retreat while he quickly scoured the area. He returned to the men who were pale in their shock, some vomiting off the sides of their horses, others turning away.

"Let's move on," Asa said. He made his voice loud and stern, as commanding as possible. He couldn't lose any of them right now. "There's another village up the way, I remember. Let's head there and see if we can find out what happened."

The men followed without a word, riding in silence alongside the clear pools and frothing rapids. Only the horses' clopping competed with the swirling vultures above to break the tension. As they approached the next village, sweating under their jackets, pistols drawn, Asa and the men noticed the same silence, the same stench, similar black birds circling overhead, squawking at the intrusion. This village was also empty. No smoke. Not a sound. Just skulls and bones strewn along the pathways, bodies that appeared to have been crawling toward the river at their demise. Asa nodded and they continued to ride north. Hour after hour, they found village after village in the same state. No sign of life, bodies and bones everywhere. The devastation consumed the entire Feather River community.

Finally, they approached an outlying hut with a tiny spiral of smoke rising from its roof. Asa raised his right hand to indicate a firm stop to his men. Then he left them and rode alone to the structure, calling out in Miwok, Maidu, Yokut—whatever words he could remember in a peaceful greeting. A woman emerged from the hut, thin and pale, stringy hair hanging along her cheeks, a wild look in her eyes.

"What happened, ma'am?" Asa asked in two different central valley languages. "Are you okay? We are from the south. Warriors fighting the Mexicans. We'll make sure they don't return and harm you." A tiny crease at her lips looked as if she was almost trying to smile.

"Oh, noble warrior, this is not a fight you can win," she said in Maidu, her voice weak with desperation. "There are only ghosts here now. It is not the Spanish or the Mexicans, the army or the rancho vaqueros this time. It is death itself that came to Feather River. The few of us left are not likely to last. You don't want to come near us. If you do, you might catch the shakes, the fevers—a cold one and a hot one, the endless vomiting. Go soldier. Keep fighting the good fight. But Feather River is now awash in death. He came to all the river villages this summer we've heard. None was spared."

She stopped and stumbled as if the speech had drained the last snippet of energy from her body. Asa trotted closer and started to dismount to help her. "Do not come closer, soldier. The evil disease will fly from me to you. It searches for bodies to contaminate. It is hungry for more, for you and your men. Leave now and ride far from this place." Then she turned, spread her shawl over her head and shoulders and retreated into the opening in the tiny hut.

Asa watched her disappear and realized she was probably right. Some new disease, not measles or the pox or ones with which he was familiar had swept into the river settlements. He mounted the horse and returned to his men and repeated the woman's words. The distraught soldiers began to argue among themselves, uncharacteristic for the obedient platoon.

Asa sat atop his horse in silence, allowing them to vent their fears for a few minutes. He knew they were terrified. He had to develop a plan. Some wanted to go farther north to check on their own villages. Others wanted to stop and bury the bones and corpses. Others, not disguising their terror, advocated fleeing the area immediately. Asa listened, then made up his mind.

"Enough. We will head northeast of here to camp and rest. We'll see if there are any survivors to the north and then move inland briefly. Then we must retreat from this death zone and return to the training camp. We'll have to recruit from other native villages farther south. Onward." He galloped off with his soldiers following, some more enthusiastically than others. A few straggled but no one stayed at the hut with the thin gray line rising through the tule to the sky.

After an hour or so, Asa raised his hand and stopped the group. "Look." He pointed ahead to a group of five walking slowly toward them. Once they noticed the horsemen, they stretched out their arms, calling out in Maidu. "Help us, soldiers. Help us. Do you have the drink?"

"Come no closer," Asa ordered. "Do you have the fever? We are from the south. Come to recruit Feather River men for our fight against the Mexicans. We found your villages devastated with disease."

"Just one of us has the chills," said an older man. "We've lost everything. Our families, our villages. We've sworn an oath to stay together. To the end. But there is a cure. This one here"—he pointed to a younger man behind him — "saw the foreign frontiersmen, the ones who wear the heavy furs, give a sick woman and her little daughter a drink. They recovered and walked out of the village. But the foreigner didn't have any more. Everyone else in his village died."

Asa shook his head at the story as some of his men shifted on their horses, hope easing the furrows in their brows. "Are you sure he didn't just dream that? Doesn't sound likely that a drink could cure this fever. The entire river is dead—we've just ridden all day since sunrise and found only one tiny hut with a few survivors." The refugees shook their heads and whispered among themselves. Asa could hear several languages mixing in the conversation.

"We're sorry we can't help you," he said. "We must stay healthy to travel back south and recruit others to fight the rancheros and priests. We've no medicine to give you." He signaled to his men to drop a bag of food for the ragtag group and then get riding. "This is all we can do for you."

He clicked to his horse, waved to his men and rode off. He looked back and noticed his men talk among themselves, then drop more food and extra gourds of water than he had instructed. He was irritated. As a military leader he expected his men to follow his commands. But he understood their compassion at this unprecedented suffering. He'd let it go. The men galloped up alongside him and he said nothing.

They finally stopped an hour later, well after the sun had set, and made camp. Exhausted physically from the long ride and emotionally from the toll, the scope of the loss of so many natives, no one said much, a pall paralyzing their tongues. What horrific new disease had spread along this river? Would it move south and claim more villages? Their own families and homes? Asa attempted a few words of reassurance that night around the dinner fire but he found he could come up with little. The destruction of the river villages was horrifying.

In the morning, four of the men, those from the Feather River area, had disappeared. Asa was not surprised and decided to conceal his disgust and frustration. He might have done the same thing in their situation. He said nothing to the others and got them going quickly, riding them hard, just one more day north, east of the river but still in its vicinity. They found no more survivors and could see no smoke spirals in the distance along the riverbanks. Several more of his troops disappeared in the night.

And then on the third morning, the day they had planned to leave the area, the remaining soldiers awoke with fevers, chills, some ran from the camp clearing to vomit in the forest. Others huddled under their riding blankets, shaking. All of them were sick. Asa tried to hide his symptoms, stirring morning atole for the sickened, forcing them to drink water, muttering words of encouragement as he lifted their heads to sip from the metal ladle he carried from one soldier to another.

After he fed his dwindling band, he propped himself up against a nearby cottonwood, the whitish cracked bark digging into his back. He pressed his spine into the trunk, pushed his buttocks and legs firmly into the dirt, wanting to feel the ground beneath him. He shivered and pulled the trail blanket, stinking of sweat and horse hair, tighter around his shoulders. His teeth chattered and his lips bobbled with each shiver. He was so cold. He couldn't stop the shaking. Suddenly, he was so hot and threw the blanket off, watching as it caught on a bush of wild roses, pink petals floating in the breeze.

The fever took ahold of his mind and as he pressed himself against the tree trunk to try to control the shaking, feeling the earth and bark poking into his flesh through his damp shirt and trousers, he saw his mother again. She was calmly gathering sticks and branches for the evening fire, walking through a field with her bundle headed for their hut. He called her name, laughing and shouting and holding up a rabbit he'd just shot as he ran down the hill, brushing through the tall grasses to reach her.

"Atsia, Atsia," he called but she didn't hear him. He ran faster and called again. He had to show her his prize, and, most importantly, his prowess with the bow and arrow.

DEBTS

The baby on her hip, determined not to cry in front of her parents, Juanita steeled herself for the homecoming she had pined for daily. Pablo led her through the plaza to the formidable front door and helped her dismount without disturbing little Joaquin wrapped in the rebozo. He'd been much gentler on the return journey — stopping frequently, riding at a slower pace, asking how she was feeling — than when he'd deposited her with the padres almost a year before. His sympathy for her diminished status was obvious, no longer the desired daughter of an important man of power, rather a lost soul who must atone for her sins.

No longer soft and curvy, a budding flower waiting to be courted and plucked, Juanita had grown thin and wiry, calloused, as if her youth, her effervescence, had dried and shriveled in her exile. The weight of her failure was lightened only by her baby who now cooed as he grabbed her finger, a hint of a smile at his lips as he recognized his mother's face. She felt she could survive Papá's wrath with Joaquín as her cushion. She hoped the baby would soften her parents and help them forget the circumstances around his arrival. She kissed Pablo gently on the cheek, holding his hand at the same time.

"Thank you, Pablo, for coming to get me and getting us home safely. I so appreciate your protection."

He nodded, eyes soft. He stroked the baby's cheek and whispered, "*Buena suerte* with your father," a surprising boldness as it was not his place to say anything personal to the don's daughter. Juanita nodded with a slight smile, appreciating the kindness and lack of judgment in his tone, took her bag and walked through the redwood door.

Her parents, standing in the entry, greeted her with polite kisses on both cheeks. There were no grand embraces, no staff lined up to greet her, apparently no celebration planned. Her sisters were not even there to welcome her back. She was disappointed and hurt but relieved to finally be home. Papá gestured for her to move to the library. Mamá's eyes were shining as Juanita unwrapped little Joaquin and placed him in his grandmother's arms. Candelaria immediately took the baby toward the bedrooms, probably to introduce him to her sisters.

Papá closed the door and went to his favorite chair. Juanita, feeling uncomfortable, incomplete without Joaquin attached to her for the first time since his birth, sat next to him. What now? More punishment? Couldn't they just welcome her back?

"Juanita, we are glad to have you home. We will have this conversation only once. So you know, your mother agrees with me completely on everything. I wanted to speak to you privately, however." He grunted slightly as he cleared his throat. Juanita settled in her chair. Papá seemed nervous. It was odd, since she was the one coming home in disgrace, hoping for forgiveness. Fear flooded her veins. Had they changed their minds? If they threw her out where would she go? Would Grandmother take pity on her and let her live at Rancho Pobladores Humildes down the road? She wasn't so sure.

"My dear, we will forgive you this once. We expect complete devotion to God and the ranch going forward. We will accept the baby into the family with the Castro name. Your mother and I have spread the word discreetly that you were married to a Spanish colonel who was exiled to Spain by the Mexican government and died in the Carlist civil war. You are a widow, tragically. But do not stray again, do not betray us. We will not forgive you a second time. We expect you to take your place at the rancho as before. I can certainly use your help. Your grandmother is getting older and leaving more to me." He paused. Juanita was relieved it was what she expected but he seemed to have more. Would they impose some other punishment?

"On another matter. This is just between us. Please keep it to yourself. Remember my father's bible you showed me? It has tormented me since you left. The accusations you made. I cannot ask my mother about it—as you know our relationship has never been good. And now I realize perhaps why. My father said something strange to me just before he died. He said that I had a full natural brother who lived far from the ranch and was not raised by him and Mamá. He said he wanted me to know but that he hoped I never met him. That he thought this brother was principled, like me. That was it. I couldn't get anything more out of him. It was so odd but with his passing and difficulties with Mamá, I forgot it."

Juanita's surprise at returning to this topic, and his much gentler tone than when he'd sent her away, caused her to lean in toward him, adopt a sympathetic pose. Was he asking for her help? Would he apologize for what they'd done?

"May I see your bible again? It made no sense but maybe my father and a native woman had another child? But why would that child not be with our family?" He sighed and gazed at her with questioning, a burden on his brow, a darkness in his eyes she had not seen before.

Juanita finally felt just a bit of the warmth and love she'd craved for months. He wanted her advice, to consult on a deeply personal topic. Perhaps she would be able to return to his side to lead the ranch.

"Yes, of course. I have it here in my satchel." She pulled it out and handed it to him. He paged through the first inscriptions and then the later ones. He stopped at her notation for baby Joaquin and looked at her. Was that a shadow of regret passing over his face? she wondered. Perhaps, for a moment, he pictured her having the baby alone in the decrepit mission cell. Determined to not sacrifice this opportunity for reconciliation she remained silent.

"Then one night a few months ago," he continued, "your mother was brushing her hair before bed. I noticed the abalone shell on her nightstand where she keeps her combs, her earrings. And I remembered another strange incident, at our fandango. Your mother and I were married in San Diego but we had a huge party here to celebrate. I know you've heard the story many times. But the one you have not heard is that a native woman approached me in the hallway while everyone was outside. She said she had been a maid in our house and asked if I remembered her. She said I was good man and should be a good father and husband and gave me the abalone shell. Then she ran off. I thought she was there to steal. I only remembered that she was kind to all of us and was a good cook. It was so strange and we were busy with the party, I had some wine. I forgot about it until recently, the bible and all."

He stopped talking and did not say anything for a long time. "We did have a maid we called Sholeta when I was a little boy," he whispered. He looked lost, pained.

"Papá?" she asked.

"Do you think that woman could have been my mother?" he said. "Seems like the only explanation. Maybe she and my father had another child and she left or he kicked her out or my mother did? Who knows but why else would this native woman, a former maid in our house, come see me at my marriage fandango? I cannot ask my mother about it. I don't know what she knows. She raised me as her own, baptizing me with Beatriz. But I think it's possible she doesn't know I was already baptized by my father and this *Xolita*, as it says in your little bible. What do you think?"

He put the bible on his lap, sighed and reached for her hand. "And who do you think would have written in that name? I don't understand it," he said, running his index finger over the entry. "I could not talk about this with anyone else. And we will not speak of it again but I needed to relieve this anguish, this questioning. Thank you my dear."

"Oh, Papá, I'm sorry you've been suffering. I see your logic. What's in the bible seems to match with what Abuelo said and the native woman giving you a gift. Now that I have Joaquin, I cannot imagine ever having to leave my son and not being present when he married. It is too heartbreaking to even contemplate." She squeezed his hand and lowered her voice to almost a whisper. "I think your mother loved you very much, Papá, and gave you this wonderful life on the rancho, knowing she could not do the same as a poor native. You would have been a servant boy, most likely, if she'd raised you as her own. Think of that. I think she sacrificed her love and herself for your future."

He nodded at her, indicating the conversation was over but reached out a hand toward her. She rose, took it and squeezed.

"Thank you, my dear," he said. "It is good to have you home."

⌒

Juanita raised her son exactly as she had grown up, balancing the luxuries of the big house with the daily ranch duties in the fields and corrals. Right from the beginning, Juanita and her father trained the little boy with the expectation he'd take over as the rancho's owner someday. Joaquin paid attention in the absent-minded manner of a boy who mostly loved horses and riding the great swaths of their land, winding through redwood groves and galloping up and down, ridge line to ridge line. He rode horses the minute he could walk and tramped behind the natives who planted and harvested the gardens and orchards. As he got older, he cleaned horse hooves and milked and branded cattle. He scaled the hills with the vaqueros moving the herd to fresh grasses. Joaquin was light-skinned for a Mexican boy, with an auburn tint to his brown hair and dark, yet hazel, eyes. Juanita was happy to let him roam the prairie with the vaqueros, his skin coated with dirt and baked from the sun, his whiteness less obvious to rancho residents and visitors.

Quina welcomed the boy daily before sunset in her somber sitting room for bible study. Papá continued his role as family professor teaching him the classics he had passed on to his daughters and nieces and nephews. Juanita also allowed Joaquin to sit in the corners of the decision-making salon of the rancho, listening as his mother and grandfather managed the complications of a sprawling estate. He even heard his great grandmother's thoughts on the business as she regularly pronounced her opinions after bible study. Since she was no longer at every discussion or negotiation, she seemed to think her great grandson would carry her views back to the main house. And, of course, as an innocent, chatty boy, he often did.

Certain of the growing importance of the United States, Juanita made sure that Joaquín learned English from infancy. She contracted with one of the few priests who'd remained in the area to start English lessons. Once he was older, she took him to a Monterrey Englishman who tutored sons of the elite families. She trotted him out like a circus performer to practice with English-speaking travelers, forcing him to recite passages and poems. Juanita and her grandmother noted the changes afoot. Joaquin would have to be a new kind of don, interacting with foreigners of all nationalities moving in to the territory in an uncertain future.

Politically the place was in chaos. Would the Californios expel the Mexican government and form their own government, as the current Monterrey commander had long advocated? After all, the Texans had done it. México City was far away and, aside from secularizing the missions and distributing mission lands, the government had never been interested in or invested in Alta California. Others remained loyal to the current system but a revolving set of weak governors threatened to divide the territory, with Pío Pico in the south squabbling with the northern commander. Other dons argued Spain and México had never done much for the region, time for a new landlord, maybe England, the United States or France. No one agreed and no one had the power to enforce one option over the others.

Quina, now eighty, grew weary and wary of the increasing numbers of yanqui settlers. They were converting to Catholicism and marrying the daughters of the dons. Even yanquis received land grants from the revolving door of Mexican governors. They were establishing Monterrey stores and building fine houses, several with wooden floors and glass windows. The town now had over one hundred houses spread across its small plain and up the slope. The United States had even appointed a consul to represent it in the territory. He had built a large two-story house, flaunting American wealth at the Californios. Quina fumed. She did not trust one of them, perhaps the memory of Malachy Brennan's promises to her granddaughter still stinging.

"Mark my words," she told Pedro and Juanita as they talked one afternoon about the ambitious settlers bringing wagons over the Sierras, "the United States government is coming this way. That Polk wants our land. I can smell it. I think he's itching for a fight with Mexico. And if there's war, it will not end well for us Spanish, for us Mexicans. You listen to what I'm saying. Watch out for those yanquis. I don't trust them one bit."

Perhaps the only thing Maria Joaquina ever did quietly was to die in her sleep. And she died as she'd entered the territory, a true pobladora. She left a far different frontier than the one she'd helped settle seventy years before. Recognized as a founder of the New California, Quina was much admired by her large family, the neighboring rancheros and Mexican military leaders. With Mission San Carlos abandoned since the breakup of the missions, its roof leaking, its adobe entryway a soupy mud, Pedro ordered Quina's rosary and funeral be performed at the rancho.

Pedro, seated between Candelaria and Juanita, was uneasy as he listened to the padre's sermon. Losing the family matriarch was unsettling. Her unwavering sense of right and wrong, her ability to envision the future, were fixtures in their lives. While it would certainly be easier to conduct business without her criticism, she had been a reliable partner in ranching and trading. She did not let emotions confuse the practicalities required to be successful. Steadfast, she never strayed from her goal. He hoped he could, with Juanita's help, continue to manage the land grant to greater prosperity and that Francisco would agree to his leadership. The priest lauded Quina for her piety and her devotion to the Spanish settlement crusade above all else. She raised honest, devout children and insisted that her native workers be faithful Christians. She was a model for all of the Californios to emulate.

As the family mourned her passing, they told tales of her business acumen, her fierce negotiating skills, her ability to grow anything, to ride horses and brand cows like the men. They laughed at how customs officials feared her. At the time little Juanita had gotten stuck in a ship's hold but had been saved from Quina's wrath by her even greater anger at the captain for hiding merchandise. Her descendants were proud of her land grant, which Francisco now said he would combine with the Rancho Castro, enlarging the property to twelve leagues, forty-eight thousand acres. They praised her foresight that cattle and trade with foreign ships was Alta California's growth opportunity and the way to enrich her family. They joked about Quina's determination that the ranch's adobes have the best furnishings and once a yanqui built a second story with veranda to create the Monterrey Colonial style, she'd added second story patios to her own adobe. And since the wealthy of Monterrey now had glass windows, at eighty years old she had recently insisted on installing glass as well.

As is the way at funerals and wakes, people rarely mention the deceased's sins or slights. The memories no one dares to bring up. No one said a word about her scorn for the natives despite building her wealth on their free labor. Not one grown child mentioned her coldness as a mother, the neglect when she ran south with each baby's arrival. No one described her harsh attitude and eventual separation from Diego when he refused to demote Pedro as the rightful heir. Indeed, perhaps, her frailties had dimmed in the minds of the assembled in the years since Quina returned permanently to the rancho and embraced the mantle of businesswoman.

Juanita, holding ten-year-old Joaquin's hand, felt the weight of time passing and a nervousness at an uncertain future. She expected little to change at the ranch, but knew its growth must be managed. Her grandmother had taught her well. She had to have confidence in the knowledge and skills she'd acquired under her tutelage. As long as the ships, and now overland immigrants, kept pouring in, wherever they were from and whoever was in charge of the Customs House, the Rancho Castro would have a market for its cattle.

Less than a year after Quina passed away, as war fever with the United States was percolating, hundreds of the rancho's cows got sick. The disease spread quickly. Pedro was forced to slaughter sick cattle and quarantine the healthy. The rancho's production of tallow, hides, milk and beef dropped dramatically. He hid the financial devastation from Juanita as much as he could, telling her they would be fine if she focused on production and he worried about the finances. She must have had confidence in his abilities, he realized, as she uncharacteristically did what he asked. She was busy negotiating with merchants, managing the staff and overseeing Francisco's portion of the land, as he had, surprisingly, turned out to be a poor rancher. Pedro made excuses and hid the books from Juanita so she didn't see how drastic the losses were, or his plans to remedy the situation.

Desperate, afraid and too proud to consult anyone, Pedro finally accepted he would have to borrow to keep the ranch operating. Physically distant from established Mexican banks, which were currently absorbed with efforts to fund the army's fight against the

United States, and with no banks yet operating in Alta California, Pedro had to borrow close to home. He had no choice but to humble himself to fellow dons and military leaders, as well as a few yanquis, and ask for loans. Thank goodness Quina was no longer around to see the crisis. What a relief that he didn't have to fight with his mother over how to raise funds to replace the dwindling herd. He wondered what she would have advised. He was pretty sure she would not have wanted to bury her pride and beg their ranching colleagues and likely future enemies for financial assistance. But he had no other choice. War in California? A sick herd? Debts? It felt like the Alta California promise was losing its glow.

Just months after the news that American Captain John Sloat had seized Monterrey for the United States, and was threatening to capture Yerba Buena, reached the rancho, Pedro collapsed on his horse while out riding to inspect new calves. The distressed *peones* brought him in, bouncing on his saddle, but he was dead by the time they returned to the adobe. Juanita, her mother and sisters laid him out on the giant redwood dining table, sent for their favorite priest and prayed. What to do now?

Juanita was the only one who knew anything about the family business. Even though at thirty-three she had a young son and no husband, there was no question she was in charge. Her mother was distraught and her young sisters were useless, picking up their mother's needlepoint skills as their primary talents. Juanita called in an attorney from Monterrey and an accountant from San José to help analyze the will and the land grant financial records. She was shocked to discover there was no money.

Papá had amassed huge debts to finance buying healthy replacement cattle. He had borrowed on much of the land and gotten himself indebted to several dons, captains in the Mexican Army and even a few yanquis. The Mexican officers had offered cash loans just as they were preparing for war with the United States. Expecting to win the war quickly, the Mexicans had started buying up more land in Alta California thinking it would be a good location for trading with the ever-expanding United States next door. But the war was not going well for Mexico. The Americans appeared likely to scoop up an enormous swath of its territory. There was talk of a treaty that would move their land under American governance.

Juanita now suspected that the stress of his debts and the fact that his beloved land would soon belong to the United States had caused her father's heart to quit. She gave her family the bad news. "We are going to have to sell the rancho, Mamá," she told her mother and sisters as they gathered after they had buried Don Pedro in the family cemetery behind the garden. "Papá had huge debts. He borrowed from so many we are facing a new front of enemies if we don't begin paying off his loans. I have gone through everything with our attorney looking for other options. We have no choice."

Juanita was heartbroken at losing both her father and their livelihood but had to be strong for her mother and sisters. There was no time to grieve. She had business to attend to for the family's very survival. Everyone depended on her. Her two uncles and many aunts had their own lives and troubles in the uncertain times. War was not good for rancho business. If only she'd paid more attention to how Papá had raised money to replace the dying cows. Could she have prevented this disaster?

Juanita sent word out through the dons and local mayors, the government leaders, the two militaries and the land-holding networks that her rancho of forty-eight thousand acres was for sale. She steeled herself and her thirteen-year-old son for the inevitable, the unfathomable. The only good fortune was that her grandparents were not alive to see the loss of their greatest pride and joy, their land.

Joaquín was befuddled by the news and didn't understand the changes afoot. When Californio cattlemen and American businessmen came to call, he hid in the heavy drapes at the back of the library to listen in as his mother met the land suitors. Young men in U.S. Army uniforms came through. Older men with swaggers and crusty language, dapper ranchers with fine horses paid their respects to Juanita. But she discovered, and Joaquín heard while spying, that most potential buyers did not have enough to buy the entire land grant. Repeatedly, he heard her refuse to accept small payments for pieces of the property. She had to have significant cash to pay off her father's debts, and the ranch was more valuable as a single parcel. All the land had to go.

RETURN TO THE OLD VICTORIAN

San Francisco, California

2019

You are invited to a combined Brennan Family event—
a 95th Birthday Party for Irene Sinclair and a
Family Reunion for all Brennan Family Descendants

Main Campsite, Brennan Land Trust
New Almaden
Noon, Sunday of Labor Day Weekend
RSVP to Nicole Sinclair via Facebook or Genetix4You message center

"**D**ad, *it's me, Nicole. Can* we talk? Please don't hang up this time." She was hoping to reach a truce with her father. This constant fighting was painful, and expensive.

"What do you want? Gloat in your victory or something?" he said.

"Well, first off, I want to tell you how sorry I am at Grandpa's passing."

Dad didn't answer. It sounded to her like he mumbled thanks or something. But then he jumped right in to their ongoing dispute. "You know Missy is appealing the conservatorship ruling, don't you?"

"Yeah, I heard," Nicole said. "How's she paying all the legal bills? I sure hope she didn't convince you to pay for all of this." Nicole waited in silence for his response, remembering she was trying to not immediately criticize him. But she couldn't stop herself. Missy's constant intervention made it hard. "Geez, did she? Are you covering all the bills? She's still living there? Oh, Dad. What happened to us? I used to be the daughter, remember? What would Momma think?"

Despite her best intentions to remain unemotional, thinking of her mother made her cry. It seemed to take Dad by surprise. "Oh, Nicole, hon. Please don't cry. Look, I'm not unhappy that you're taking care of Great Gram. It's just the whole house thing. I really think the place is a dog and you taking it over when she dies is a huge mistake. It's going to be a weight on you, you know. I was just trying to save you from that."

"Really, is that all this was? Let's be honest here. I think you let Missy get under your skin out of guilt. She guilted you over the years you weren't there when she was a kid. She's manipulating you, Dad. Did you promise her some of the profits from the sale or something?"

"Oh, come on, are you into pop psychology now too, along with that genealogy crap? Both a waste of time. Missy's in this on her own. She just agreed with me that the San Francisco house is too much for the family. Great Gram's elderly. And now my dad's gone. Missy thinks that I should be the one to oversee Great Gram's accounts and bills, with the sale of the house included in that."

"Oh, really? And you aren't in it for the money? You told me to sell when the market was hot, remember? Great Gram never wanted to leave her house. She's lived there for something like fifty years. It was cruel what you guys did. Some people might call it elder abuse."

She couldn't help herself. She was still furious at him for so many things. The betrayals cut deep.

Nicole brushed away her tears and tried to redirect her thoughts to the positive. The judge had assigned her as Great Gram's conservator and given them permission to return to the San Francisco house. They were moving back in next weekend. They'd lost three of the five tenants in the process so they had to find new renters, but it shouldn't be too difficult.

"What the hell's this invitation I got?" Dad asked now. He bellowed into the phone with a spitting sound and Nicole pictured his cell phone covered with saliva. Before she could answer, he continued. "I know you're into this family history shit, but do you really have to plan a reunion? And a ninety-fifth birthday party for Great Gram? Really? Talk about manipulative. Everyone feels they have to come to a ninety-five-year-old's birthday party."

"Good, I hope so. That's the point, Dad. I wanna bring people together. Anything else you want to complain about?"

"I don't know," he said, softening his tone. "I'm getting sick to my stomach with all this fighting. Literally. My doctor says I've got ulcers. He said it's stress that's the cause. All my dad saw when he was dying was all of us fighting. Me and you, his own mother against me and Missy. He wasn't happy about it. He kinda gave me a death bed ultimatum. He told me to mend fences with you, and Great Gram. Well now he's gone, before his mother, amazingly..." His voice drifted off and he didn't finish the sentence. There was silence for some time until Dad cleared his throat.

"Oh, Dad, I'm sorry Grandpa's heart gave him problems for so long. Well, why don't you honor his wishes and listen to him. Stop fighting with me. The judge wanted you to do that too. I'm moving into the house with Great Gram and I'll care for her every day. She'll teach me about the place. It'll be okay. And Dad, I hope you'll be pleased, I'm getting a tech job. I've been interviewing and think I finally found the right company. Using tech to improve water use and distribution. And for Ag too, not just for drinking," she said. "Anyway, I'm excited about the reunion. Please come. I've been working on it for months filling in our family tree and connecting with cousins. It'll be great."

"Hhummph," Dad growled.

"We're going to meet lots of distant relatives we didn't even know," she continued. I've made a huge family tree on a long piece of poster paper and everyone can fill in what they know from their own research. I've made a book of pictures and documents I've found so far. I'm giving everyone a copy."

He still had not interrupted so she figured she'd tell him the works. "Gotta warn you the baptismal certificate is the front cover. I know you think it's a fake but the archivist at Bancroft Library at UC Berkeley says it's real. I included the letter of authenticity in the Shutterfly book. Just, you know, in case anyone else has doubts too."

She just had to get him to the reunion. To make peace. She'd be living with Great Gram soon. If she could reconcile with Dad then maybe she'd finally have her own real family again. "And I know Father Serra isn't popular with lots of folks. I mean including me. The Spanish didn't treat the Native Americans very well, you know, but that's our history. We gotta learn it, deal with it and then figure out how to move forward and make amends, each in our own way."

"Oh, Nicole. I still don't get it. Why's this so important to you? Why so much energy down the history rat hole?" He sounded less angry. Maybe he really wanted to understand her after all. Reconcile even? She sure hoped so.

"What else do I have, Dad?" she asked. "I lost Momma too young. She was amazing, taking care of everyone. But that's not my style. And you, Dad," her voice broke, tears streamed down her cheeks, full on crying now. She couldn't help it. She gulped, hoping he couldn't hear the tears in her voice over the phone. How could she explain to him her need for family connection without alienating him even further? Without blaming him for her loneliness. "You're a farmer," she rallied. "Raising vegetables for America. I mean there is honor in that. I never really appreciated it but maybe it's maturity or whatever you wanna call it, but I'm proud that you grow our food. But, as you know, I'm not a farmer. Since Momma died, I've been lost, unable to find my place in the world. Yeah, I'm an engineer and I can build things. Software tools but that's pretty abstract. But this family history thing and the old house. It makes me feel alive again. Connected. To our past. To others. I was drifting before. Now I have something to really live for, Great Gram, preserving the house, bringing this family together—cousins finding cousins, people learning their own roots."

The silence on the line made her think he wasn't there, but then he mumbled something she couldn't catch.

"Look," she said, "I know you think it's silly, but I feel that we all should know that we're descended from Spaniards and Mexicans, and from Native Americans. We should be proud, not mortified. Knowing our roots grounds us, weaves us together, pushes us to be responsible for those coming after us. We're Californios, whether you like it or not, and we gotta be stewards of this place for future generations. We gotta find common ground, Dad, or we're gonna destroy ourselves." She wiped her tears with the back of her hand as she took some deep breaths. Could he understand her point of view?

"Hummph, hmmmm," he grumbled. "What kinda job you get? How much they gonna pay you? Those goddamned tech companies pay outrageous salaries. Then housing goes up. Gets it all out of alignment. Too much goddamned money around here. But not where you need it the most, you know?"

❦

Nicole and Great Gram sat at the window-front table. It was their first tea since moving back into the flat. Great Gram had shrunk even a little more so she looked like a tiny bird as she scuttled around the familiar apartment, reveling in the homecoming. Her many months in the senior citizen's home had taken their toll and Nicole hoped she could regain her feistiness now that she was back in her apartment and neighborhood.

Nicole had agreed to all of Great Gram's will stipulations. She would inherit the historic house. She was the new landlord, with all the responsibility that entailed. Nerve-wracking, but exciting too. She was determined to keep Great Gram around as long as possible to help her ease into the new role with some grace. They sipped tea and read the paper, Great Gram on newsprint and Nicole on her phone.

"Oh my God. What?" Nicole cried, thumbing vigorously through her phone.

Great Gram lowered one side of the *San Francisco Chronicle* and looked over at her.

"What is it dear? What's the matter?"

"Looks like Dad sold off some farmland for a housing development. Listen to this in the *Central Coast Weekly*. 'County officials announced an agreement with the longtime ranching family of Ray Sinclair to purchase one thousand acres for a housing development. The parcel includes enough land for a school to support the new neighborhoods. Details of the deal are not yet public but those with knowledge of local agricultural real estate say current prices could be in the range of $3,000 to $6,000 per acre. The real estate agent for the transaction was Mr. Sinclair's daughter, Missy Sinclair.' Oh, my God, that traitor. She got Dad to sell off some of the ranch. I mean the city does need room for housing, but from our ranch? Don't you think Grandpa is turning over in his grave right now? That's millions of dollars."

Great Gram looked up sharply.

"Oh, sorry, Great Gram. How rude and insensitive of me. I'm so sorry. It's too soon isn't it? But I'm serious. My grandpa would not have wanted Dad to sell any land for development would he? Wasn't he all about growing food? If you sell, at least sell to another farmer, he used to say. I'm pretty sure I heard that."

"It's all right dear. I know you meant no harm," Great Gram said. "You're right. My son would not be happy with this. But you don't want to go down there and ranch, right? You're staying here managing this property. Maybe your dad can't handle it anymore. What do you think Missy is after? Just the money?"

"I don't know, Great Gram. I really don't. Probably. Hopefully I'll see Dad at the reunion and I can ask him about it."

"Hmmmm, dear. Is that a good idea? You'll be so busy with everything. Maybe a family spat at a big event is not the best idea, you know what I mean?"

JOAQUÍN

*W*here was he? *Joaquín lifted* his knuckle to scrub crusted sleep from his half-opened eyes. Oh right, in the little apartment at the back of the hacienda, he remembered. He took in the unfamiliar garret as anxiety and loss churned in his stomach. Yesterday, Mamá had ordered him to pack his belongings and vacate his childhood rooms, moving them from the master suite into the servants' quarters before the new owner arrived. Disbelieving, he'd gazed past the wooden shutters toward the Coast Range, relishing his favorite view one last time. As far as his eye could see, tilting down the valley covered with green pastures and ancient oak trees and up the gentle slope on the distant side, every hill, field and tree visible had been his grandfather's, and thus, his.

Joaquín and Juanita's new quarters were miniscule. Such a contrast to the luxury of inhabiting an important land grantee's entire rancho. With only one bedroom, a narrow kitchen with an alcove for a table, and a closet, Juanita was forced to convert the storage area into a bedroom for Joaquín. He was too old to sleep with his mother. They had to use the outhouse behind the stables. No silver barreled bathtub in his own suite of rooms anymore. No hot soapy bubbles carried upstairs in buckets by a servant. Now, in order to bathe in the cramped apartment, he had to sponge off in the kitchen with a bucket of water he had hauled up from the well himself.

"But, Mamá, why do we have to move?" he demanded repeatedly, pestering her with teenage indignation. "And in our own home? Abuelo would be furious if he were alive. How did this happen? Why does that horrible, loud family get to take over our house?"

Juanita glared at him with a pained grimace. "You know why, Joaquín," she shrugged. She eventually just stopped answering him. He finally ceased tormenting her and retreated to the stables where he could pretend to be a Mexican prince. An important landowner respected far and wide. At least with the horses he could imagine he'd returned to his former status. But once he had to stuff himself into his new, cramped quarters, he was forced to accept their current reality.

A few months earlier during his mother's search for buyers, a man about ten years her senior came to the front gate on an expensive stallion wearing a stylish hat. He had an Irish lilt to his speech, a cocky grin and a hearty laugh. Captain Malachy Brennan of the U.S. Army, which had recently been victorious in Texas, spoke enough Spanish to charm the few remaining ranch hands to let him meet with the mistress of the house.

"Doña Juanita, I want this land and I have the money to pay for all of it. Though I'm just a humble soldier, I'm fortunate that my cousins benefited from the popularity of dipping snuff. You know I've always loved this property. I heard it was for sale from a fellow soldier from the Texas campaign who ended up in Monterrey. I want you to stay and work here, with your son, sisters and mother. I'll make sure your basic needs are covered. You'll not have to leave.

No one else is offering you such a deal. I know, Juanita. I've checked. Where else will you go? Your son is not old enough yet to be the man of the family. There's a war on."

Joaquín, hidden in the velvet curtains, was surprised at his mother's coldness to this charming man. She did not offer him a cordial or cigar, as she often did with potential buyers. She seemed to want to dismiss him from the library as quickly as possible. He could see the anguish and frustration on her face. Joaquín saw her hesitate but knew she had no other buyers with substantial enough resources to relieve their predicament. Why didn't she leap at his offer? He watched as they shook hands. There was a brief quiet interaction that he could not overhear. Then the captain boomed, "I will be moving Mrs. Brennan and our five children out here immediately from Ohio." Joaquín heard him add softly, rather familiarly, "You've made the right decision, Juanita."

His mother's countenance was somber even though she had found a buyer. Then Joaquín almost fell out of the curtain hideaway as he watched the captain raise his hand, gently caress her cheek and lean gracefully down to give his mother a tender kiss on the lips. His other hand pressed at the back of her shoulder for a moment. Then, just as quickly, the visiting gentleman's bravado returned, he stood his full height, back ramrod straight, swept his hand through his thick mane of tangled auburn and strode confidently out of the room.

Joaquin watched as Captain Brennan was true to his word and within a few months he had moved his family into the land grant's largest adobe. The captain, his wife and their five teenaged children immediately colonized the bedrooms and living space built around the open-air patio. They spilled into the kitchen and dining area, smoking room and library circling the tiled courtyard with the trickling fountain and magenta bougainvillea arbor. Sisters giggled along the upstairs balcony outside their bedrooms. Boys hung on the wrought iron railings, gazing downward to the flowered atrium and eavesdropping on the business of the estate. The large family, rumored to have abandoned a dreary homestead on the plains of Ohio, seemed to revel in the spacious elegance and adapt to their new environment quite easily. They threw clothes on the heavy wooden furniture, dusted food crumbs off the white tablecloths onto the terra cotta tiles and then insisted on cleanliness at every moment.

Joaquín's big eyes took in the changes each morning with astonishment. He watched as his mother started the fire, washed clothes in huge tubs, chopped vegetables and salted meat for the midday feast. His aunts mended ripped blouses, washed linens and tidied bedrooms as they became personal maids to the captain's wife and daughters. His grandmother, always slight and frail, was assigned kitchen duty, scrubbing enormous pots and iron skillets, preparing meals and stoking the kitchen fires. Joaquín's whole family was kept busy attending to the most minute needs of the Brennan children and parents. He worked in the stables and at least got to interact with exquisite horses. But he too was at the constant call of El Capitán's head stableman when an extra horse needed to be saddled up or watered after long rides.

For Juanita, the only thing worse than returning to the nightmare of being a domestic at the Santa Bárbara mission was having her aging mother, sisters and son join her as harshly treated servants. In their own family home of generations. And by someone she thought she'd once known. With the chaos and economic upheaval of war, Juanita had nowhere else to go. Her mother was frail, confused now with who was who and could not travel. In fact, Candelaria had in one surprising moment of clarity told Juanita she refused to leave and would be buried in the family cemetery next to her beloved Pedro. Her relatives were struggling with their businesses and ranches. The grand rancho adobe was the only home the Castros had ever known.

So she did what she could to protect her son, sisters and mother, taking on as many of their tasks as she could despite having her own responsibilities. Captain and Mrs. Brennan had relegated Juanita to the painful position of estate manager over a home and ranch that no longer belonged to her. It was cruel and practical. Understanding the inner workings of the rancho intimately, Juanita was a logical choice. She could curse him all she wanted but she didn't really blame the captain—he was always that in her mind, never Malachy. She would have made the same decision in his position, she reasoned. But would she have? It was too cruel. It seemed he was under the thumb of Mrs. Brennan and would do her every bidding.

So Juanita did the work—shopping for supplies, keeping track of finances, organizing parties and supervising the cowboys and field hands. She hid among the account books in a small office behind the library where she'd spent countless hours with her father. She rarely spoke, except to quietly suggest survival techniques to her family or give orders to key staff members. She took pains to avoid the captain and his wife, presenting them with written instructions or sending a sister on her behalf. They tolerated the arrangement since Juanita was an efficient manager and over time the ranch slowly began to regain its former glory. The military forces colonizing Monterrey and areas north were a new market for beef, milk, tallow and produce, despite war slowing the lucrative cow hide trade.

For her, this new life was about survival. She had no space to contemplate the hell she was in. She had endured banishment and servitude at a dying mission. She would live through the humiliation of being subjugated by her former lover. The man she had believed he was appeared to have evaporated in a swirl of materialism and greed. Dominated by his ambitious wife. Anxious to have the respect and wealth he had observed when Doña Quina and Don Pedro ran the huge estate.

It was too painful to let herself wonder about his path to this point or grieve the past. Her only goal was to protect her family. She made sure everyone was cared for and then had to manage the rancho business back to success. She could not have them thrown out of the house for any reason, any slight, any perceived disloyalty or faltering work ethic. With Joaquín now the fourth generation on Rancho Castro, this had been the family home for so long Juanita could not imagine anywhere else to go. How would they live in the new country that appeared it would soon subsume them? They had not chosen the new American landlord but would have to survive under an unfamiliar flag.

Securing her younger sisters' future a priority, Juanita reached out to area dons with eligible sons, but the dons were distracted with rumors of what the new US government would do with rancho lands. The treaty was supposed to protect them, but most were suspicious. They'd heard of officials sweeping into Monterrey and moving all records to a newly established surveyor's office in Yerba Buena, now called San Francisco. But Juanita's family's reputation, and the tragedy of losing her grandmother, then father, and then the land, forced more than one sympathetic don to grant her an audience. She managed to marry the youngest sister off to the son of a rancher near San José. She matched the other with a Scottish merchant who'd set up a dry goods store in Monterrey where she would help him launch a bakery. Relieved after the matchmaking was complete, she focused on helping her son continue his education and protecting her declining mother.

The captain poured money into the estate, ordering the best from London and New York to please his wife. While Mrs. Brennan stuffed the once elegantly sparse adobe with gaudy furniture, European artwork and garish mirrors, he barked orders at Joaquin and Candelaria and the native servants to assert his authority and impress his wife. Now called the Brennan Seven Hills Ranch, the cattle ranges were a launching pad. From the former Spanish land grant, the Brennans, and their sons and daughters, were staking a claim among the new California elite, landowners in the expanded American territory.

As he matured, Joaquín noted the depth of his mother's pain at their altered status. Juanita's sadness hung over her like a chronic disease. She'd aged so. Her luxuriant black hair grew thin, streaked with gray. The furrows in her forehead became permanent as she worried over their situation and pondered every decision to develop the ranch. She never complained but neither did she smile or laugh anymore.

Joaquín mourned the loss of his mother's dominant personality and vibrancy. Now she was quiet efficiency. She moved like a cat, soft and darting. She seemed smaller. Almost invisible. The intimate moment Joaquín had observed between his mother and El Capitán was so alien to his current reality that it got very fuzzy and confused in his mind. It must not have happened that way.

After living almost two years on the Brennan Seven Hills Ranch, Juanita heard whispers in the kitchen. That Joaquín was getting so tall. And his skin was so light. Didn't he look a bit like El Capitán? Hearing the kitchen gossip, anxiety crept into her bones and flooded her with fear. She had to send Joaquín away or there would be trouble. She couldn't risk them being thrown out on the road with her mother so feeble. El Capitán's wife was a possessive woman focused on the success of her husband and children. She would not tolerate rumors threatening a claim to her new estate. Juanita had to act before the mistress heard the same talk or grew more observant of her servants. Although it broke her heart, she looked for opportunities and then devised a plan.

Late in 1848, when Joaquín was just fifteen and had been serving as a stable boy for two years, Juanita woke him in his closet bed in the middle of the night. He was startled by the tears he saw on her cheeks in the candlelight. "It's time, my son," she whispered, gently caressing the bangs from his forehead. She touched his cheek, just once. Any softness he thought he'd heard in her tone then disappeared. "You have to leave tonight." Joaquín was confused. What was she talking about?

"They've found gold in the foothills by the Sierra. I want you to go up there before the news spreads further. People will pour into Alta California from the East, from México, from Chile and Peru, from Europe even, for this gold. They say there is lots of it, and you can pull nuggets as big as acorns out of the streams. You must go tonight. And Joaquín, you must change."

"But Mamá, what are you talking about?" He didn't want to leave his home, family, the horses he loved. "I want to stay here with you and Abuela. We're here together, still on our land. Don't you think we could get it back some day? A lot of things are changing."

Juanita sighed. "Listen to me. You must become Joe. Speak only English and you'll pass for a yanqui. You've no accent, you're light skinned. There's no future here for Mexicans. We lost the war and the Americans will take over everything. Look at what happened here at our family home. Don't let anyone know you speak Spanish unless absolutely necessary. Go Joaquín, become American, go find gold and make your own fortune. You're a man now."

Joaquín's head began to throb. He felt dizzy. What was his mother saying? He grabbed her hand but she yanked it away. "I'm so sorry you never had a father to teach you how to be a man. And that Abuelo was just getting started when he died. But you're strong and smart. You're good with horses and people. You know how to work. You'll be fine."

"But Mamá, I can't leave you. My job is to take care of you and the family. I don't want to leave. It's still my home here. I'm not going." Why was she kicking him out? Her intensity frightened him. Was she losing sense of reality like Grandma, who didn't recognize him anymore? She was sounding crazy.

"Joaquín, you must. There's no other way." She paused. "I'm sorry to tell you in this manner but, Joaquín, El Capitán is your father."

He let the words sink in. What? The patron? He was related to that horrid family?

"He came here many years ago to work for Abuelo on the rancho. I didn't think I would ever see him again. He always loved the land and apparently had dreamed of living here one day. When we had to sell, he was the only one with enough to buy everything so I could pay off the debts. I realized there could be problems for you but I had no choice. You must leave tonight. Pablo has a horse and bag ready with your warmest coat. Here's all the silver I can spare. Hide it in your clothes."

Joaquín was speechless, breathless with a searing pain in his chest, as if a horse had kicked him in the gut. What did it mean that the patron was his father?

"Joaquín, you're a good boy but you must start your own life. This gold is an opportunity. Go up to Mission San José and head toward the eastern hills until daylight. There'll be trouble for all of us if you stay here."

Joaquín saw the hard line of her jaw and the depth of the blackness in her eyes. Her pupils had disappeared. She was famous for her determination and stubbornness. He had to follow her orders. He always did. They went out to the dark, hushed stables where one of his favorite horses was saddled. There was no sign of anyone. It was very quiet. And very black. No moon to betray his departure. He realized she had picked a moonless night to protect him further.

His mother kissed him quickly and pushed him up onto the horse. It was cold but at least it wasn't raining. "Joaquín, when times get difficult, always remember I did this because I love you more than anything in the world." She handed him something. "This is my grandfather's bible. It protected him on the journey from Spain and he gave it to me. It is our family's talisman to keep God watching over us. Your birth is recorded in it. It will protect you. Now go. Be Joe. Be a yanqui, an American man, and don't look back." She turned and ran into the rear entrance of the servants' quarters.

Joaquín shook his head and sucked in the night air to clear his mind of his mother's mysterious words. He felt dizzy, a nausea rising from his gut but he did as instructed, secured his belongings, clicked the horse into trotting quietly and rode north. As he jounced in the saddle in the dark and drank from his goatskin, trying to calm his stomach, his mind whirled with questions. There was shock and relief at having the mystery of his parentage solved, but what of the captain's behavior? Had he abandoned his mother when she was pregnant? Did the patron even know he was his son? How could he possibly treat his mother so harshly?

The image from the drapery hideout was seared into his memory but he couldn't reconcile the many contradictions. Did the captain have some lingering affection for his mother? But once they moved in he seemed completely controlled by the domineering Mrs.

Brennan. Maybe he really loved her but couldn't be with her because she was Mexican, because she was now poor? But the captain had made Juanita into a servant by taking her land. Clearly there wasn't much love in that. At least two of the annoying teenagers appeared older than him. Mrs. Brennan probably had one or two babies back in Ohio when the captain had worked at the rancho.

He was confused, angry. The very worst was that despite his loyalty to his mother, beneath his rage for the captain, he was furious with her. How could she have kept this secret from him? Why couldn't she have eased him into this understanding of his father? After all, he was part Irish, and now American, and that made things very complicated. He longed for the simpler days of Don Pedro, master of land grant Alta California.

Despite his bewilderment, the loss, the betrayal, Joaquín followed his mother's directions. After several days' ride he arrived at the Coloma gold strike. He settled in an encampment of foreigners and transplants. It was a rough, lawless place. He kept his belongings close and trusted no one. He protected his horse like he was made from pure gold. He spoke only English and told anyone who asked that he was Joe Brennan from Ohio, an orphan. He'd come out to California, like everyone else, to make his fortune. It was easy to go unnoticed.

DEPARTURES

As *Pablo shoveled dirt onto* the coffin, Juanita stepped away from her mother's grave to thank the priest who'd come to the rancho's cemetery for the rite of committal. He was the only priest she could locate in Monterey. It had been a shock to ride into the pueblo where she had not been during the two years since the United States victory in the North American Invasion.

Many storefronts were abandoned with doors blowing open on rusting hinges. The dry goods store was shuttered, the bakery was defunct. Her middle sister also had disappeared, following her husband up to the gold fields, along with most of the town's population. Now spelled Monterey, the pueblo had lost much more than its second R in the transition. The once thriving capital city of Alta California had become a ghost town. The new American masters further decimated the city by establishing the capital of California, as they called it, north in San José. Monterey was once again as quiet as its first days as a frontier outpost anxiously waiting for the twice-yearly supply ships. The long-abandoned mission over the hill lay in disarray with its roof beams fallen in, nothing but a gaping hole to the sky to welcome God.

There were rumors that San Francisco was just the opposite, overflowing with foreigners and Americans who had jumped ship and galloped east to the gold rush in the Sierra foothills. The harbor, it was said, was filled with abandoned ships. Masts protruding from the low tide mud. San Francisco's once-barren hills and empty frontier were flooded with men from all nations and backgrounds, all motivations and abilities, pouring in to gather up the bullet-sized gold nuggets rumored to float down the Sacramento River. Perhaps it was a blessing that her mother would not see the shocking changes afoot.

Juanita deposited the coins into the priest's grimy hand and nodded her appreciation to the servants who'd attended the burial. She had not been able to locate her sister up in gold country; her other sister, who lived on a nearby rancho, had attended the funeral but returned immediately home to her husband. They were busy trying to gather documents to prove his landholdings to the new California state officials. Rumors were flying that the Americans would not be generous in recognizing Spanish or Mexican land grants.

Thank goodness Candelaria had been an angel her entire life. Perhaps, despite the pathetic sendoff with no church funeral, no grand gathering of family and peers, the omission of accepted Catholic practices to shepherd the departed to the afterlife, her generosity would still get her through the pearly gates. Candelaria had been too beautiful and delicate for a pioneering life, but she had borne the task with grace, her sense of duty guiding her to stand by her husband and children, no matter the cost. Juanita figured that in itself ought to be enough to get one into heaven.

After dismissing the priest and servants, Juanita was not quite finished with her own *despedida* to her mother. She picked up her skirt hem and trudged up the hill to the little chapel Quina had built generations before. No one used the place much anymore, but Juanita never allowed it to become completely infested with spiders and lizards. She had a servant clean it each week, lighting candles, polishing candlesticks and sconces and setting out fresh flowers. Juanita figured the devoutly Catholic Mrs. Brennan would not complain about the expense. And she never did.

She stepped into the warmth of the glowing candlelight, closed the wooden door gently behind her and walked slowly to the altar. She knelt, crossed herself, then prayed for her mother to have a peaceful journey to the afterlife, for her sisters struggling with California's changes, for her son, wherever he was, always for her son, and now, for herself. With her mother gone, nothing tied her to the rancho any longer. What would she do now? There was nothing here for her.

At that moment, the door creaked open and Malachy Brennan stepped into the tiny sanctuary. She did not hear him at first, lost in her prayers and thoughts of her changing homeland. He sat in a back pew and cleared his throat. "I'm so sorry, dear Juanita, for your loss," he said softly.

Juanita, startled, stood up and turned. Angry at his intrusion, she also felt just a little grateful for some words of condolence, some sign of compassion. She felt very alone in the house that no longer belonged to her, had no family members left living in it with her. Confused by his comforting voice, the one she remembered from so long ago and had tried desperately to forget, she stepped into the aisle and sat in a pew facing him, leaving several benches between them. She said nothing. Her anger burned but maybe finally here was an opportunity for some closure with him.

"Your mother was a good woman," he said. "I know she was not always strong and the kitchen could be difficult for her. But she never complained and always worked hard." He stopped and looked at her with such kindness in his gaze Juanita was taken aback. Was her old Malachy actually buried within the ranch master he'd become? She'd never seen this side of him save for the time he'd kissed her after they'd agreed he would buy the ranch. Despite her surprise and frustration, and best intentions to maintain a cold demeanor, her heart picked up its pace. She could feel it beating in her chest.

"I remember so well when your mother and father were the don and doña of this great rancho," he continued. "She was a gracious hostess always welcoming strangers, never stingy with her kindness to guests. Even if they were just enthralled with her good looks and wanted to steal her away from your father," he said with a soft laugh. "Doña Candelaria brought a grace to the harshness here on the frontier. Not just with her beauty, but with her charm and taste. She brought the class of old Spain to Alta California. I am so sorry for your loss. You were fortunate to have such a mother."

The intimacy of his words, as if they were friends, or even the lovers of the past, not patron and servant, enraged Juanita. Who was he to talk to her like this? To bring up the past after what he'd done? To speak as if he were a friend to her parents? The gall, the arrogance, the entitlement.

"How dare you, Malachy. How dare you speak of my darling mother like that. What were you to her? Nothing but a traitor, a liar. You killed my fragile mother. She was a princess of Spain and Mexico, a queen of the El Camino, and what did you do but make her the most lowly of servants? Her death is on your hands. You will burn in hell for what you've done to my family." She'd placed her hands on the back of the pew and squeezed the wood so hard her fingers turned white.

Captain Brennan rustled in his seat, leaning toward her, reaching out a hand. "Come now, Juanita, calm down. Isn't that a little harsh? I respected your mother, as I respect you," he said matter-of-factly.

"What? Respect? You have a funny way of showing it. How could you turn us into your servants? And for your god-awful wife and those spoiled children? So you could run your own rancho?"

Malachy winced but responded immediately. "Juanita, I did not push you out even though I bought your land, fair and square. I allowed you to stay in your home."

"As a servant. I stayed out of duty to my mother, my young sisters and my son. It was war time and we had nowhere else to go. But my mother's gone. The war's settled. I'm done. You can take care of the rancho on your own. I've done all the work to get it moving toward profitability. You have no idea how to run a large ranch like this. Now you and your cold, calculating wife can manage it on your own." She started to stand up.

"But I don't love her," he said.

Shocked at the confession, she sat back down. "Well, too bad. That's your problem. You set that up yourself. You could have stayed here. I loved you," she said. There was no reason to hide or hold back anymore. She was free of caring for others. Now she had only herself to take care of. She was starting immediately. Might as well unburden herself with the truth. Juanita bit down hard on her tongue so she wouldn't cry. She would not show this man how much he'd hurt her.

"But Juanita, I couldn't stay. I had nothing—look at me now. I was in the military. I helped get Texas into the United States. I connected with Irish relatives and helped them with their snuff company. I made myself into somebody. I could not live in your father's shadow. Now I'm somebody in the new California."

"Well, clearly I'm not a part of that. You made me your servant. How could you, Malachy?" She'd promised herself never to say that name again but it just came out. She pronounced it with her Spanish accent and his glance deepened. She thought she saw him blush a little. "You betrayed me, my family. I feel nothing for you now but sorrow. What a sad life you have—maybe rich in things but not in goodness, humility, in caring relationships. Your children will turn out like your wife, greedy, materialistic, ambitious only for fame and fortune. You lost your chance. And you lost your son—who I know is a good man, wherever he is."

"My son. What are you talking about? Your son, you mean?" His eyes opened wide. "Why didn't you tell me?" Malachy stood and walked into the pew just behind hers. She did not flinch. She was right, he had never suspected. So absorbed in himself that he didn't even notice Joaquín growing up looking suspiciously like him.

"How could I? You left, abandoned me with no word of where you were going. No way to reach you. Be honest, you didn't want me to contact you."

He was uncharacteristically quiet. She felt him searching her face, trying to see into her heart. She looked away. "I didn't even know I was pregnant until after you left. You know what my parents did? They banished me to be a servant in a decrepit mission in Santa Bárbara during the pregnancy. I had to give birth in a cold cell. I had to stay for three months with a newborn. Alone. To them I'd sinned and had to pay, be punished and learn my lesson. I was there for a year, living like a slave, cleaning and cooking, while I was pregnant and after giving birth. At least it prepared me to work in your household," she spat..

"Oh my God, how horrible. If only I'd known. That must have been terrible for you," he said as he touched her hand still gripping the pew. She flinched and pulled her hand away from his.

"Oh, come on. Would you have come back for me if you'd known? Don't fool yourself. You're ambitious, so focused on getting rich, on becoming the master. The last thing you needed was a little farm girl to clog up your plans. You knew my father would never have agreed to a marriage with a foreigner."

"What do you know of it?" he said, anger filling his voice. "I grew up with nothing. Most of my family died or left Ireland."

"Yes, you told me. I felt so sad and sorry for you at the time. I was rich in family, and land. But now, I have nothing. No land. My family's gone. I have no idea where my son is. I pray and have to have confidence he's doing well in the goldfields or I'll go crazy. At least my sisters are okay for now. And for you, I don't know what the truth is. Did you really make that money in your cousin's snuff business?" It had always seemed strange that he'd become rich. Soldiers didn't get rich; she knew that from her own family history. It was the cattle business that had made them wealthy.

"Well, the really big fortune is my wife's. Her family are the snuff barons. They were distant cousins of mine. That's how we met."

Of course he hadn't told the truth. "You always were free with a story. Bet you told yourself a story about how you weren't to blame for leaving me. Well, make one up now about how it's not your fault you've lost a son. I've lost a son."

"Why did you send him away?"

"Oh, come on. If your wife recognized who he looked like, she would have kicked my whole family out the door, off our family land where my son is the fourth generation. This is the only home, the only business we've ever known. My mother was ill, fading mentally. I had to protect everyone at all costs. But now, with her gone, with nothing left here, I'm leaving. You are just an opportunist, a user."

"Please stay, Juanita," he said. It sounded hollow, half-hearted to her. "I didn't understand you'd sent him away. I thought he'd gone to get a job someplace else. Or had the gold fever."

"Yeah well, you don't pay much attention. The servants were whispering that he looked like you. I had to protect him, and my mother. But that's done. So I'm off. Good luck managing forty-eight thousand across, thousands of cattle and horses, sheep and pigs. Oh and the crops, the orchards, the gardens. The native staff. You have no idea..." She stopped there. What else was there to say? She'd said everything she'd ever wished to tell him. Sadness washed in and began sweeping the anger away. She had to get out of there. She coughed as she found it hard to breathe. She felt she was suffocating.

Malachy didn't seem to notice. "Maybe that's why we were getting letters from the goldfields?" he said, more to himself than to Juanita.

"What did you say? Joaquin wrote me letters? I've never gotten any." Now tears brimmed in her eyes. He wrote her? Oh, what she'd give to have any news.

"My wife threw them out or burned them. She said they had been sent to the ranch by mistake. Oh, maybe she opened one. Maybe she realized who he was? Oh dear," he said with pain on his face. He scratched his scalp and pushed his thick, dark-blond hair back. It was darker now than when Juanita had first fallen for his golden handsomeness but he still had a strong jaw and magnificent hair.

"Looks like your life might be more complicated than you think," she said almost with a hint of humor. But then her black eyes narrowed and she glared at him. "How dare she? My son. Where were they from?" A tear spilled over and rolled down her cheek. To know he had written her and that he had not received a reply—that was excruciating. What must he think? That she didn't care anymore?

"Not sure. She said from the gold mining area. One envelope I saw said something Bar. I think maybe there was one from Placerville."

She was so angry, so destroyed at Mrs. Brennan's cruelty she couldn't see straight. At Malachy's betrayal and oblivion. At the tragedy of it all. Thank God her father and grandparents never knew the extent of the family losing the land and the pain of who owned it now. They would all be heartbroken and the burden for that was too great to bear. This was the final death knell in her life at Rancho Castro. She got up, with no other word and walked out of the chapel. She went to her room and packed up her few threadbare clothes and meager belongings.

As she filled her bag, she pondered the whole exchange. It was so odd. Had he come up to the chapel hoping to seduce her? Or to relieve his guilt? That he would do it just to express a word of kindness seemed unlikely. Well, clearly he got the idea she was not running into his arms. If he had dropped to his knees and begged her to stay, had professed his undying love, would she have been tempted to rekindle that overwhelming passion she'd once had? Probably not. He'd been so cruel. For him it would have been foolish to have an affair with the servant. There was too much risk. Even if he still loved her, his heart would never be in it for fear of what he would lose if Mrs. Brennan discovered them. Her money, the new ranch, the children's loyalty. She was formidable and would undoubtedly kick him out.

No, Juanita thought, Malachy would never do anything to sacrifice what was best for him. She truly accepted that now. Had she really ever hoped otherwise? You fool, she told herself. She tiptoed down the back stairs out to the stables where Pablo gave her the captain's best horse.

"Pablo, thank you for always looking out for me and my family. I am forever grateful. I must go now. Please care for this great place. I know you love it as your own, as I do. I will not see you again."

She mounted the horse while holding his hand, tipped her riding hat at him and rode toward the rancho's large iron entry gate. She reached the property's edge, stopped and took one glance back at the land. Then she trotted out to the main road and paused again. She looked right, looked left. Which way should she go? North or south? She made a decision. She kicked her boots into the horse's flanks, *click clicked* to him, and cantered onto the El Camino Real.

FAMILY REUNION

Finally, it was here. She was ready. The culmination of months of planning, reaching out to cousins on the genealogy website, gathering documents and old photos, consulting experts and interviewing relatives, sending invitations to new connections and trying not to leave anyone out. She stepped out of the clearing into the shadow of the oak trees and surveyed the scene. The Brennan family reunion, on the Brennan Land Trust's shared land, was here at last.

Folding table after folding table was laid out with piles of the Shutterfly Brennan Family books, magic markers, name tags and Sharpies, and an enormous family tree that spanned several pages of butcher paper. A set of instructions at each end of the chart explained this was a living document and asked the gathered to add relatives who were missing. On another set of tables were platters of food and coolers of iced beer and mineral waters, enough to serve the one hundred expected guests. An enormous birthday cake with looping blue icing wished Great Gram a *Happy 95th Birthday*. Nicole was grateful that her new job allowed her to finance everything.

She walked back into the fray and consulted with the photographer and with the attendants who would guide the cars on the packed dirt parking area. She had recruited volunteers, mostly younger cousins, to escort elderly guests to a reserved seating area and bring them food and water. The last thing she needed was an octogenarian to faint in the heat or trip walking in from the parking lot. One set of young volunteers would keep the food trays stocked and prevent napkins from blowing away in the fall breeze. Still others were arranging the kids' play area with corn hole boards, jump ropes, hula hoops, large buckets of bubbles, spray guns, fris-bees and a bocce ball court. She'd rallied the pre-teens to make TikTok videos to keep them interested between refilling sandwich trays. A family reunion had to be fun for everyone, especially the children, she reasoned. The kids were the ones who'd make memo-ries and pester their parents to return each year someone planned another reunion.

Great Gram sat at a round table near the podium, a guest of honor. The seat next to her was empty. No sign of Dad yet, Nicole noted, repeatedly checking the spot as she greeted each guest, point-ing out the family tree and gesturing to the food and drinks. Her heart was heavy at his absence, but what had she expected? Was she hoping this family reunion could lead to one of her own with Dad? It probably wasn't realistic. But the more family members arrived the more she found herself wishing for things to be different. For Dad to really become part of her life.

As more people shuffled in from the parking area, she couldn't help smiling. Maybe she did have some family, besides Great Gram, after all. The Brennan/Castro descendants were showing up.

A cluster crowded around the photo display and giant family tree. Old and young, large family groups and nervous looking cou-ples, sat at the rounded tables with blue-and-white-checked cloths. The picture books littered across the picnic area as children flipped through them and left them lying on a bench or the ground, adults carried them from one family group to another, pointing and nodding. Laughter and greetings, the *pop, shush* of beer and coke cans opening, the low hum of conversation rose above the Brennan Trust main campsite and wafted out beyond the clearing to the trees. Children squealed, running and playing hide and seek among the oaks, bay laurels and maples. The sounds echoed above the crowd as they drank beer and reminisced, laughed at the photo book images or gathered their immediate family members for pictures. She noted it was a racially and ethnically mixed group, reflecting two hundred and fifty years of California's diverse population.

A murmur whispered through the crowd as a minor celebrity arrived, one of those guys who'd sold his startup for a billion dollars to a big tech company. He was so young, they said. He seems pretty down to earth, the gossip ran as people met him and his parents and siblings mingled with other cousins wandering over to the photo booth in the trees. Nicole strolled through the throng, greeting people, hugging those she'd only met online, chuckling over stories, oohing and ahhing over babies and toddlers, or new pictures relatives had brought to show off at the memory table.

Eventually she found the young tech executive waiting in line at the family photo booth. She hadn't seen him since he had tried to buy Great Gram's house. "Hey, Zach Turner. How are you, cousin? Thanks for coming," she said with a quick hug. He pushed his floppy, blond bangs to the side and treated her to his megawatt smile.

"Wow, Nicole, what a great turnout. Amazing you got so many to show up. Hey, it's nice to see you again. Come meet my parents." All seemed to have been forgiven, she was relieved to see.

"I'm glad you could make it. A lot of people want to shake your hand. You know, a Silicon Valley celebrity in the family is pretty exciting to some." The parents were busy chatting with others in line so they stayed put and kept talking.

"Not to you though, right? I remember that. You're not impressed with much, as I recall." He laughed and winked. Was he flirting with her? "Hey, I heard you took a job with one of my competitors. My main one actually. What's up with that?"

"Oh yeah, that," Nicole said, looking down. Now she really was embarrassed. He did have a cool new company but she didn't want to work for him. He'd been kind of a jerk when she'd tried to arrange for him to buy Great Gram's house. He hadn't liked the conditions. Well, to be fair, he'd felt manipulated. And she really hadn't been honest with him or her great grandmother at the time. "Isn't competition a good thing, Zach? You know, for innovation and entrepreneurship to continue? Plus, can't this state use all the help it can get on water issues? Probably never too many of us in that space, right?" She smiled and he smiled back, looking embarrassed himself this time. He pushed the hair back again.

"So, was it just gossip or is it true that your great grandmother ended up getting what she wanted by giving that house to you?"

"Yeah, you heard right. She willed it to me. She and I live together in that top floor flat. We still have tea on weekend afternoons at that window where you sat."

"Wow. Good for you, Nicole. I suppose this protects the tenants and the house. Keeps it in the family like she wanted." She nodded and smiled. "You know a few of the cousins are gossiping that you manipulated all of that to inherit a valuable house. But I don't see it that way. I know Great Gram got what she wanted. Seems like she always gets what she wants." Nicole took a step back, surprised. Her felt her mouth drop open and eyebrows go up in surprise. "Don't worry," he said. "I defended your honor," and he winked at her again. What? She shook her head at him. He just grinned right back at her. She couldn't deal with this now. Nicole gave him a little wave saying she had to go and headed toward the seating area. The cars had slowed, people were settling in and eating lunch. Time to get this event started.

Still no sign of Dad. She reached her table, gave Great Gram a little hug and went to the podium. She welcomed the crowd. She listed off family group offshoots in attendance and each table cheered at their name. She led the entire group in a happy birthday song for Great Gram. Then she outlined the next activity and introduced her special guests.

After everyone finished lunch, Nicole explained, each of these experts would be stationed at a table. For twenty-five-minute blocks, people could gather with the expert to hear a little overview and then ask questions and engage in a dialogue. They would rotate three times. The experts were volunteering their time in the interest of Californians understanding their families and shared history.

"And if you aren't interested in talking to any of our expert guests, then no problem. Over there is the game area," she pointed across to a distant clearing. "There are maps for hikes out on the tables but if you just want to hang out and chat, there is plenty more food and beer. Let's all meet back here at four o'clock for a final farewell and closing."

She then introduced the professionals she'd recruited for the day: an archivist from the Catholic diocese who could answer questions about the missions and Spanish priests; a Native American leader of the Ohlone/Costanoan-Esselen tribe who would talk about recent Monterey County land given to the tribe and efforts to revive the Ohlone language; a Stanford historian who was an expert on Mexican land grants and what happened to the Native Americans and

Mexicans during the transition to American rule after 1850; a history librarian and genealogist who would offer advice on how to use *Genetix4You* to uncover more family history; the Bancroft Library archivist who had verified the authenticity of the Carmel Mission baptismal certificate and could talk about historical documents.

After letting folks finish up lunch, she rang the cowbell she'd brought and sent them off to the stations and activities. She watched as her plan went into motion. Some drifted off with their small children to the games area and others filtered out with a beer or grabbed a map and left on a hike. Some groups did form around the experts, as she had desperately hoped. Not one authority was left with no one at his or her table. What a relief.

Nicole was thrilled. She had been determined to not just put on a party but set up an event where people could learn, could make meaningful connections, maybe think about things they had never thought about before. Was she social engineering as her father had accused her of after reading her reunion emails? Maybe. She preferred to see it as providing an opportunity for learning. No one was forced to participate or engage but she was thrilled to hear dialogue and debate at the tables.

Dad showed up just as the second roundtable was ending. He was purposely late, she realized, but at least he had come. He sat next to Great Gram, who greeted him coldly.

"Hello, Gram," he said to her. "I came to honor my father. I'm sorry we both lost him so young." He held her hand and looked like maybe he'd apologize for everything that had happened, but he said nothing else. "Nicole," he said, nodding at her.

Great Gram did not respond at first, then with ice in her voice she said, "Raymond, how good of you to show up. I appreciate you doing something to bring family together, instead of all the fighting we've been doing this past year. What a waste. So sad. You should know that your daughter has been very good to me. A real comfort in trying times."

Then Great Gram asked him to escort her over to the table where the Ohlone/Costanoan-Esselen tribal elder was presenting. Nicole watched as she held tightly onto Dad's arm and made him stay with her for the presentation. She giggled at Great Gram's pluck. Ninety-five and she was as feisty as ever. Now that they were living together in her old house she seemed to be regaining some of her former strength, her determination to live with purpose. Nicole wandered through the tables and watched Dad squirm as the Ohlone elder described linguists and natives working to rebuild a lost language and culture.

After the round table discussions were complete, Nicole gathered the entire group at the appointed time and made a little speech. She figured she'd earned the right by organizing, and paying for, the whole event—one at which most people seemed to be having a good time. Even if it was just because of the free beer and sandwiches.

"Thank you for coming to the first annual Brennan Family Reunion and thank you to our distinguished guests." The crowd clapped and the experts nodded in response. Nicole cleared her throat. "This has been an amazing coming together for me and I hope for you too. I plan to organize a reunion every other year and I'll keep looking for more relatives in the meantime.

"We may not all like where we've come from or what our ancestors did. You may have been shocked to learn the details of the family tree we've been assembling online. I sure was. But it is our story. I believe it is important to learn it, accept it and deal with it. Junipero Serra baptized a baby boy born to a Spanish soldier and native woman, most certainly an Ohlone woman. That boy, those parents, are all of our common ancestors. Some admire Father Serra and others despise the missions and the Spanish incursion into Alta California. But no matter our points of view, our different backgrounds and family paths over the two hundred and fifty years since, all of us here are descended from those settlers and Native Americans.

"Let's accept who we really are. We're founders, settlers, which also means colonizers, yes, of this land, from Spain, Mexico and then from the U.S. But we are Californios. To me that means that we have a responsibility. The Native Americans thrived here for nine thousand years before Europeans arrived. If we are going to persevere for thousands of years more, we must come together, learn from each other, celebrate our family, and this place. A California of settlers and immigrants, of old families and new, of stories that are known and of those mysteries that remain. We must be stewards of this beautiful land so that we can pass it on to our descendants.

"We don't know yet all the details of the family journey to this moment, of how or why a Mexican boy named Joaquin Castro transformed into Joe Brennan. There are gaps in the family tree. But we must keep learning, to honor our heritage, to do justice to Diego and Xolita, Pedro, Juana Candelaria, Juanita and Joe Brennan, and the many others we still know nothing about. They are us."

The crowd clapped, some more vigorously than others. Some just politely. A few stood up as if to give her a standing ovation. Others, gathering their belongings, prepared to leave. Dad remained focused on Great Gram and did not clap at all. When the clapping waned and the crowd began to stir and talk, Nicole sat down, emotionally exhausted from organizing the huge event and meeting so many relatives. From the clear mix of emotions and views among the cousins at the round table discussions, from the passion she felt toward this family cause. She felt obligated to bring people together in this time of faction and division, distrust and suspicion. She took a few deep breaths. She was still the hostess. She had to collect herself enough to shake hands and say goodbye.

Suddenly, there was a loud voice through the microphone behind her at the raised podium. "Wow, wasn't that a great speech everyone? Very inspirational, Nicole. How about that folks? Let's give a round of applause to my sister, Nicole Sinclair. Didn't she do an amazing job building out those *Genetix4You* trees, finding all of us, gathering info on the family, making these books? Great job, Nicole. Folks, my sister, give her a big hand." The crowd responded and roared with clapping and cheers. Much more loudly than at her own speech, Nicole noted.

Didn't anyone else notice the sarcasm in Missy's voice? God, what was she doing here? She'd never responded to any invites. She'd hoped Missy just wasn't interested. Nicole rose halfway in her seat and waved to the crowd.

"Thanks, Missy," she mouthed toward the podium. As Nicole sat back down, Missy kept on talking into the microphone. "Isn't this cozy? This family love and all? But let me tell you folks, Brennan Family members, I've got a proposition for you before you leave.".

She was almost shouting into the microphone. Most everyone sat back down or froze where they were to listen. Missy's wild mane waved in the breeze and she shoved her sunglasses into her hair to calm it. Her eyes looked feverish as she continued. Nicole moved uncomfortably in her seat, looking over at Dad for an explanation. He would not catch her eye, looking only at Missy at the podium. Great Gram, who'd been trying to move through the crowd back toward Nicole, was standing, leaning against a table as she listened.

"Portions of this land are prime real estate in this boom," Missy said. "There's plenty out here that is buildable. Executives could move here and build on one- or two-acre lots. I've talked to the city of San Jose and Santa Clara County officials about getting this parcel annexed. Might need to do that, but maybe not. They'd want to keep it in pretty big lots but there's two hundred acres here, don't forget." The crowd remained silent; a few shifted in their seats as Missy continued.

"I've got a lawyer looking into the land trust protection for the two hundred acres, to see if we could get that overturned. So we could sell off all of it, or maybe leave a little for a campsite and reunions. Let's get some money for the heirs. The lawyers think it's possible for the board to change the trust specifications and make the land sellable. Seems to me like the best way to honor family. Wouldn't it be great for you all to make some money off that gold rush guy? I've left my cards out at the table by the exit. Give me a call." She stepped away from the podium.

There was a commotion as Great Gram stumbled, seemed to catch herself, then slumped into a nearby chair. Her head resting on her arms, like a child told to take a nap on a school desk. Nicole jumped up and ran to Great Gram's side, knelt down and whispered, "Great Gram, are you okay? Someone bring some water," she yelled over her shoulder to the crowd. "Great Gram, you okay? It's Nicole. Can you hear me?"

"Long-term thinking. Long-term thinking," she repeated in a raspy whisper.

"Yes, I know. Here, have some water. I'll get you home," Nicole said, hugging her tiny frame with one arm and offering a water bottle with the other. She turned to see her father hovering close by as if wanting to help. Had he known about Missy's plan to hijack the reunion?

417

"I got this, Dad. I think you've done enough for one day. I'll take care of her. I'm taking her home. She's my family and that's what we do. Take care of each other," she said. She gave him an icy glare, her meaning clear. "I've got you, Great Gram. Let's go home. The volunteers will clean up. I'll come back tomorrow to finish." They walked slowly toward the parking lot and the crowd parted. Out of the corner of her eye, she spied Missy, gesturing wildly while talking with a few men gathered around her.

Nicole looked away, submerging her anger. She was furious that Missy had exploited all the research she'd done on family history and the family reunion event itself to launch yet another land grab. Another sale of family land to enrich herself? And had Dad known about this and approved? It sure looked like it. What an ass. What a traitor.

No time to lament that now. She had to get Great Gram to the car. As they made their way through the crowd toward the exit, some of the gathered clapped. Others patted Nicole and Great Gram on the shoulder as they passed, everybody talking at once.

"Great job, Nicole. So glad you had a ninety-fifth birthday party, Irene."

"Thanks for the awesome event."

"It was really great to get the family together."

"Maybe we shouldn't wait two years but do it again next year."

"Nicole, we made some cool TikTok videos. We'll post them on the *Genetix4You* site."

"See you online, Nicole, in the public family trees. I found another relative. I want to show you."

Nicole nodded and smiled at everyone as she moved through the crowd, shaking a hand here, giving a high five there. The teenagers were really cute in their excitement over their videos and they had actually been great helpers with the sandwiches and cake. Little ones ran here and there through the crowd shouting and waving goodbye. Everywhere around her people were hugging, exchanging phone numbers, shaking hands, laughing and smiling.

Swarmed by so much warmth and appreciation, she felt a calm happiness come over her. Sure wished Momma could see all this— now she'd have to try to find that side of the family. She realized the ache she'd felt since her mother's death was lessening with all the love, the togetherness right there in the glade. She was a part of something bigger than her own personal pain. She was linked to these people, forever, and these Castro/Brennan descendants seemed to want to become a clan. She had a family after all.

"Look, we did it, Great Gram. Look at the sign-in sheet," she said as they passed the entrance table. "Ninety-six people showed up for your birthday and the reunion. One for every year of your life. How about that?" If she just kept talking and walking then maybe Great Gram would calm down and return to normal. She gave her an extra squeeze around the shoulders. "A first family reunion. And so many came. Don't you think Joe Brennan would've been pleased?"

"Long-term thinking," Great Gram kept whispering, shaking her head back and forth, as they slowly walked to the car. She had to get her there so she could sit and rest. Zach Turner walked up next to them and offered his arm.

"Hey Mrs. Sinclair. I wanted to be sure to say hello. Happy Birthday," he said. "Can I help you to your car? What a wonderful reunion you two put on. People loved it. Look at this huge family we have, everyone coming together, having fun, learning new things too. That was pretty clever including expert discussions at a picnic. That your idea, Nicole?" He grinned and smiled widely at her over Great Gram's gray head. She smiled back at his friendly tone and enthusiasm. Yeah, it had been pretty great, despite Missy's surprise intrusion.

"What was that with your sister?" He whispered to Nicole. She started to shake her head, her lips pursed in a line of displeasure. She shrugged and nodded down to Great Gram indicating she didn't want to talk about it right then.

At that moment, Great Gram stopped them, grasping their arms tighter, "Don't you dare talk over me or whisper. I'm right here—not dead yet. Young man, why don't you go find out for yourself and then tell us later? Go get one of those business cards Missy is handing out and ask about her plans. Maybe you can help us out with some long-term thinking after all." They reached the car and got her settled in the passenger seat. "Go on," she said to Zach. "Now let's get on home, Nicole. I need a nap."

ENDNOTE FOR THE READER

This is a work of fiction. It is not a history textbook or an anthropological study, but a novel. Many of the characters referenced in the book are actual historical figures. However, the primary characters, the family tree and the line through it to present day characters are all figments of my imagination and should not be confused or misconstrued with actual historical figures or events. And where real-life figures appear, the incidents, dialogue and situations concerning those persons are entirely fictional and products of my imagination.

I did research many historical resources to gain a thorough understanding of California's past. The Spanish were great diarists and so there is an endless supply of primary source journals from priests, military leaders and soldiers to examine. In addition, during the Age of Exploration, foreign explorers, scientists and merchants who stopped by the shores of California from France, England, the United States and Russia also wrote observations of life on the remote Spanish frontier. Once the territory moved to U.S. ownership, many American historians and anthropologists researched the area's history, its colonizers and original inhabitants, producing more firsthand accounts and interpretations of the past.

More recently, Native Americans, historians, anthropologists and academics have analyzed California's history from a more contemporary lens to dig into buried events, whitewashed narratives and glamorized images of the past. Many newer works look for previously neglected sources of information to round out the picture in a more inclusive fashion.

Museums are another valuable source of information and inspiration on California history. Small and large museums dot the state with a rich source of images, artifacts, buildings and settings in which history unfolded. Many of even the smallest towns have preserved an old house and staffed it with a dedicated volunteer or two, trying to gain an understanding of what life was like during the over ten thousand years Native Americans inhabited the land and the two hundred and fifty years since the Spanish colonized it.

I found this wide array of primary and secondary sources of great value in helping me to empathize with our ancestors and imagine their lives in those very different times. I have great respect for the librarians, archivists, history buffs, keepers of the culture, docents, Native Americans, academics, historians, educators and researchers who spend time, effort and resources to uncover and preserve the past. Their work is critical for us to learn from our history and push us to move forward with intention and connection to become good ancestors ourselves.

ACKNOWLEDGMENTS

Writing a novel is primarily a solitary activity. Imagining, researching, reading, designing the plot and creating characters and then actually writing it all, revising and editing mostly are done on your own. Fortunately, there are wonderful moments of interaction authors have with a variety of folks while bringing the final product to fruition. Always working toward continuous improvement as a writer and storyteller, I am grateful for all who educated and encouraged me on this journey.

Since writing fiction is a second career for me, and one in which I have little formal training, I have to reach out to find teachers, mentors and guides in the steep learning curve I face. In order to do that I have read books and articles, attended workshops and lectures, taken online courses and participated in the fantastic San Francisco Writers Conference in February, 2019. I am also indebted to the many fine history and writing teachers I've learned from over the years. As a former teacher, I know first-hand the hard work, creativity, persistence and love for the subject and the students that goes into being an effective teacher.

As a result, I dedicate this book to teachers. It is in honor of the truly outstanding English, Social Studies and writing teachers in schools and colleges, blogs and magazines, books and writing workshops across America who toil day after day to ignite their students' passion for writing, reading and learning history.

Those who have particularly helped me learn and grow in these areas are listed in the book's dedication. I am so fortunate to have learned from my high school teachers, Claire Pelton and Leonard Helton; professors at UC Berkeley, Peter Dale Scott, Peter Collier, Stephen Greenblatt; professors at Stanford, Mike Kirst and Larry Cuban; my colleague at San Lorenzo High School, Pam Wilson; and local writers who are also truly gifted teachers, Constance Hale and Susanne Lakin. While all weaknesses in this my book are my own, I am indebted to each of these teachers for outstanding instruction and guidance that made me a better student of history and a stronger writer and storyteller. Susanne Lakin's workshops on the hero's transformational journey and methods of structuring a novel were invaluable to me as a new novelist. I highly recommend her blog and courses to all aspiring fiction writers.

Additional teachers for a writer, I have learned, are editors. I was so fortunate to work with excellent, professional, experienced editors who helped me not only improve this work but also taught me ways to improve my craft for the future.

My critique editor Andrea Robinson was highly skilled at examining the manuscript's overall structure and suggesting ways to frame the contemporary story to work with the historical narrative. She knew immediately what was working and where I needed to revise before handing the manuscript off to the next editor. My developmental/content editor Ronit Wagman's detailed review of every word and line of text was outstanding. She pushed me hard to dig deeper into the characters' motivations, hopes and fears, to strip out repetitive prose and to hone my craft through understanding and structuring point of view properly.

I worked with Larry Habegger as a copy editor on my first book and was thrilled to work with him again in the same role. He is so professional and skilled and his deep experience in writing, editing and publishing was once again invaluable as I moved from final editing into the publishing stage of the process.

As I mentioned in my Endnote for the Reader, writing historical fiction takes a tremendous amount of research. One unexpected, and quite lovely, benefit of undertaking this project was learning more about libraries, librarians, archivists and museum staff. They are wonderful resources whom I knew little about. I am now a great fan of those who match books with readers, maintain historical documents to preserve the past and educate the public on historical events and how they shape a community.

Kathy Nielsen, former California history librarian of the Monterey Public Library is a local treasure. She was a career librarian but, in her retirement, added California History Room Librarian to her list of accomplishments. She is also an expert on genealogy and gives outstanding workshops on conducting historical research and how to tap local and online resources for genealogy buffs. I attended one of her courses, devoured treasures in the California History Room and was treated to a field trip with her to the Monterey County Historical Society's archives. Kathy was enthusiastic about my project from our first meeting and became a regular cheerleader asking for updates on my fictional family tree, suggesting resources at every turn. I am honored to call her a friend and am so grateful for all I learned about libraries and historical research from her.

Eboni Harris, teen librarian at the Monterey Public Library and a fellow novelist, was also an important supporter, always asking about the book and inviting me to participate in local author events.

Many thanks to my fellow writers whose support is unique in

their level of understanding of the writing experience. Tracie White is a lifelong friend since we were college roommates and an accomplished science writer for Stanford Medicine's Communications Department. Tracie secured a significant book deal with a Big Five publisher for a non-fiction book and so we have been writing, revising, working with editors and rewriting yet again throughout the same time frame. Our meet-ups at a coffee shop in Moss Landing where we wrote, chatted, walked on the beach and chatted again, oh, and wrote some more too, were energizing and refreshing encouragement from a fellow writer. Thanks so much, dear friend.

Christine Sleeter, a fellow writer from the Central Coast Writers Club and a professor emeritus of Multicultural Education at Cal State Monterey Bay, was helpful with editor recommendations and also excellent book and article resources on the Ohlone.

I am indebted to the wonderful Laurie Sheehan, long time president extraordinaire of the Central Coast Writers Branch of the California Writers Club. Her leadership led to great monthly speakers and workshop offerings which helped me enormously through these past two and a half years of the novel writing process. Not the least of which was getting out once a month to convene with fellow writers. Central Coast Writers is a prolific and enthusiastic group and I appreciate the welcome and camaraderie.

Many thanks to early readers, my family members David Payne, Sarah Payne, Dwight Payne and my dear friend since second grade, Jane Grossman. Their feedback, questions and suggestions on my draft manuscript were important and useful.

To me, a good book, in addition to being well written, must also be beautiful on the outside and inside. I was fortunate to work with the excellent artists and book designers Alan Hebel and Ian Koviak through their company *the*BookDesigners. Alan and Ian were always responsive, professional and wonderfully creative. Just what an author wants in a book design team.

I had a great time getting feedback on cover artwork and design options from many enthusiastic friends and family. Huge thanks to Carolyn Prowse Fainmel, Allison Bainbridge, Jane Grossman, Noreen Bergin, Dina Lambdany, Dwight Payne, Sarah Payne, David Payne, Alice Olson and Mary Ziegenhagen for giving me their honest opinions on Ian's beautiful cover designs.

Many thanks to the book clubs who have supported my work and keep asking for more. The San Francisco Presidio Book Club listened to me read an early chapter in October, 2018 and encouraged me to keep writing and bring the complete book back to them in a year. Well, I didn't quite make their deadline but I look forward to a lively discussion with them on *In This Land of Plenty*.

My dear friends in the Nosara, Costa Rica Book Club have been a huge source of support, love and many engaging discussions on a variety of books. I am so grateful for the friendship and encouragement from: Beverly Kitson, Angela Phillips, Alice Olson, Susan Loudenslager Smith, Anneke Eggens, Faith Burke, Merry Cavanaugh, Wylly Guterman, Reagan Grant, Pam Lancaster, Angie Cebulske, Barbara Guyton and Linda Wall. Linda's book club in Houston, Texas plans to read *In This Land of Plenty*, as does Beverly's Pelada Heights group. Thanks so much dear friends for your love of reading, books and authors.

I also really appreciate the many family members and friends who showed interest in this project and checked in on my progress when we saw each other or in Zoom calls during Covid quarantine! I feel very fortunate to have too many to name for fear of leaving anyone out.

However, I would like to give a special shout out of gratitude to four family members and friends, all in their mid 80's, who repeatedly asked me about book progress and told me to hurry up and finish so they could read it soon—Peter Grose, Jim Gill and Al and Ardi Breslauer.

Finally, to my husband, David Payne, a toast to yet another adventure in our unbelievable journey together. So glad we survived through two and a half years of me working on my first novel. Thanks for your endless support and your equally never-ending honesty. Both are so important. I am forever grateful.

And one final thank you to all my readers. Thanks to those who read my first book, passed it on to friends, wrote an Amazon or Goodreads review or emailed and called to tell me which story you liked. It is pure joy when the characters and stories that have swirled around an author's head for years come to life in the minds of their readers as well. I sure hope you, dear reader, also fall for the characters and enjoy the family saga of *In This Land of Plenty*.

ABOUT THE AUTHOR

Mary Smathers grew up in Los Altos, California and graduated from UC Berkeley with a degree in Latin American Studies. She earned a Master's degree in Education and another MA in Educational Administration and Policy Analysis from Stanford University. From 1983 to 2013, she worked in public schools throughout California as a high school teacher, administrator, teacher trainer, grant writer and educational entrepreneur, helping to found three education companies and a public charter school.

Since that time, she has focused on writing, reporting for a bilingual, regional Costa Rican newspaper and publishing her first work of fiction, *Fertile Soil: Stories of the California Dream,* in 2016. *In This Land of Plenty* is her debut novel. She divides her time between California's Central Coast and the Pacific Coast of Costa Rica where she is at work chronicling the stories of subsequent generations in the Brennan/Castro family tree.

Made in the USA
Las Vegas, NV
06 August 2022